Spelling MISS

Finalist for the 2002 Pearson Canada Readers' Choice Award

"A smart, sexy, moving jazz riff of a novel." Emma Donoghue

"*Spelling Mississippi* is drenched with an eerie and feminine sensuality from the very start.... There's aggravation, mystery and a strange romance that will haunt you long after the last page is read." *Ottawa Citizen*

"In this bourbon-soaked barnburner of a tale, the Mississippi River becomes the catalyst for one woman's midnight swim and another's plunge into obsession. The setting is a New Orleans stocked with star-crossed lovers, barflies, thwarted dreams and mother-daughter showdowns.... The novel is, at its root, about people overcoming their tangled, traumatic histories to authentically find one another." *Quill and Quire*

"*Spelling Mississippi* is charged with the eccentric energies of its characters and its New Orleans setting. A love story that is tender, but also witty, sexy and highly intoxicating." Timothy Taylor

"[A] richly written, witty and sexy account of two women's unexpected journeys toward self-discovery." *Flare*

"A love letter to New Orleans in all its steamy glory.... Woodrow keeps the sexy story pounding.... Lush [and] satisfying." *NOW*

"With the mighty Mississippi river providing a majestic background of intrigue, and the city of New Orleans the setting for romance and charm, [Marnie Woodrow] delves deeply into the psyche of her exciting and mysterious characters." *Winnipeg Free Press*

"[A] stunning debut . . . full of intelligence, humour and passion [and] executed with shocking grace and considerable skill." *Xtra!*

"An affecting tale of one woman's immersion into the gloriously decadent city of New Orleans." *National Post*

Spelling

A NOVEL

MARNIE WOODROW

MISS ISS IPP I

VINTAGE CANADA

VINTAGE CANADA EDITION, 2003

Published in Canada by Vintage Canada, a division of Random House of Canada Limited, Toronto. Originally published in hardcover in Canada by Alfred A. Knopf Canada, a division of Random House of Canada Limited, Toronto, in 2002. Distributed by Random House of Canada Limited, Toronto.

Vintage Canada and colophon are registered trademarks of Random House of Canada Limited.

National Library of Canada Cataloguing in Publication

Woodrow, Marnie, 1969–
    Spelling Mississippi: a novel / Marnie Woodrow.

ISBN 0-676-97432-5

I. Title. II. Title: Spelling Mississippi

PS8595.O6453S6 2003   C813'.54   C2002-905605-5
PR9199.3.W596S74 2003

www.randomhouse.ca

Printed and bound in the United States of America

2 4 6 8 9 7 5 3 1

Where are you off to, lady? for I see you,
You splash in the water there, yet stay stock still in your room.

—WALT WHITMAN, "Song of Myself"

For you, Mom,
With love and admiration

Spelling MISS ISS IPP I

The Mississippi River belongs to the people. That night, it belonged to just two.

First came the cool, metallic stink of barges moving silently on the river, the ripe scent of things ready to rot and burst from the vines and trees. Magnolia blossoms hung like little yellow corpses, up and down the narrow streets and wider, more American boulevards, their sweet musk a sulky memory. Away from the twenty-four-hour sour of the French Quarter (though still in it, according to any map), she sat alone on the edge of the Governor Nicholls Street Wharf, her feet dangling well above the water. Inhaling the soothing churn of the river, its chilled and unknowable contents, she grew drunk on all these smells—and so didn't catch the scent of someone coming up behind her.

The smog and fog tangoed, twisting her view of the opposite shore, now a strip of ochre fuzz between a moonless sky and the notorious water below. The upriver bridge appeared to be a pretty string of lights along which cars sped. There was scant light on the wharf itself, no more than a pale beam thrown down from a lone standard some distance from where she sat. She didn't see the shadow of a woman racing toward her over the concrete.

The humidity took each individual sound—the thrum of tires on the distant expressway bridge, bass-line thuds from Quarter jukeboxes, horn squeals, a bold crack of what might've been gunfire or the rebellious muffler of a car on a side street—the damp November wind took each of these sounds and perverted them all into one low, seductive moan. A human call rose up here and there, and now and again, a warning blast from a boat. She didn't hear the small thunder of high high heels coming at her from behind.

The woman had come running, dressed in an evening gown and a rhinestone tiara. She hurtled her body over a dark object, not knowing it was a person, and not caring. She made a perfect arc over whatever it was, hitting the water below with gun-crack precision. There was a tidy splash. Touched by the quick wind passing over her shoulder, and startled by a sudden spray of droplets on her bare legs, the seated woman woke from her reverie. All at once the unexpected presence of a stranger collected in her consciousness: the ghost scent of fine perfume, an echo of high heels hurrying, and a shadow, followed by a splash. She would smell and hear and see these things, in and out of sequence, forever.

Leaping to her feet, the young woman stared out at the water for what felt like a very long time. She stood dangerously close to the edge of the wharf, squinting and blinking. The night murmured and twinkled as it had before, as if nothing unusual had taken place. She peered harder at the water, holding her breath. At first it seemed there wasn't anyone out there. But her heart roared to life and she stifled a cry as up bobbed some glittering thing a few yards out, surrounded by the arms and legs of someone who now made a fine, if temporary, show of swimming.

But she knew. The young woman on the wharf knew exactly what she was seeing, for who *but* a suicide would jump into a river so deep-down mean, and in the month of November? And who but a fool would sit there in the dark, courting danger and finding it, too? In that moment she wished she'd been mugged or battered in some other way. An odd thing to wish for, but this woman knew what was happening. Having seen this kind of watery exit from the world before, she did not want to witness a second such act of strange and private violence.

She didn't call out "Stop!" or scream for help to incite a riot of rescue, nor did she leap in after the woman to make a valiant attempt at salvation. No, she didn't do any of the things a person in her position ought to have done. She ran.

The young woman ran until the ground beneath her feet turned from wharf concrete to weeds, to rail track and cobblestones slick with fog. She ran without breathing—or so it seemed to her once she'd stopped. Later on she would realize that the only people who run in the slow city of New Orleans are muggers and dealers and other sorts of criminals, but in those precious moments of flight she didn't care about local pedestrian customs. She had one destination in mind: away from there.

She ran without releasing the scream that coiled inside her. Her conscience pulsed through the blur as she sprinted: *Call the police.* There is still time. *Call the police.* A tourist, she didn't know that the coast guard patrolled the river or that the police station was very near by. Do something, a voice inside her shrieked. And so she did: she ran.

The river looked after the rest.

When she bursts into her room, the first thing Cleo Savoy sees is the red announcement of the hour glowing in the dark. Switching on every available lamp, she keeps one eye on the clock, as if her safety will increase with the forward march of time. When the numbers advance from 1:11 to 1:12 a.m., she exhales. Locks the door and secures the chain with shaking hands, telling herself, Never happened—you imagined the whole thing. Yes, she decides, it was a ghost, the kind of river-apparition one's apt to see after so much bourbon on an empty stomach. A ghost, and nothing more. *If it was 11:11—I'd make a wish. I'll make one anyway: I wish I'd never seen that.*

She remembers sitting comfortably on a stool at the Monks' Bar, where she'd spent the better part of the afternoon and evening drinking up bourbon and local conversation. Recalls the man who sat next to her, telling her about his life, showing her Polaroids nobody should show anybody. Through a tracheal amplifier his voice was a sweet metallic growl. "This is my wife, Annie. I bought her those garters at Saks. This here is Annie right after we made love. Oh, she liked to do it all kinds of ways. That's a rare quality in a woman. Poor thing: we were in a terrible accident. I survived. Look at this one. Isn't she tasty?"

She remembers something urging her down to the river, some deep brown voice that insisted. Doesn't remember excusing herself as the man talked on. With only one day's experience of the city under her belt, she'd simply heeded the call. Walked streets she did not yet know the names of, strolled over and down with a surprising confidence, as if led. Never mind the danger, never mind the dark. In that all-alone place she felt protected by those angels that guard the truly reckless and the drunk, and she was both. For the first time in her careful life she was both, and she'd exulted as she

4

wandered to the wharf, past signs that shouted, Keep Off, Keep Out. The wind had ruffled her hair as she sat with her eyes closed; the smells and sounds had enchanted. And yet the sensation that she'd found heaven at last was to be short-lived, as bliss so often is.

If you tell me it was nothing more than a ghost, I'll never touch bourbon again. She makes this promise to the gods in between gasps for air, pacing in her room at the Pommes Royales Maisonnettes, nicely priced and situated deep, as they like to say, in the heart of the French Quarter. She wills her heart to climb down from the top of her throat, begs her lungs to slow and behave. Wishes hard for the person in the river to have been a phantom, the figment of an imagination unaccustomed to vacationing or the direct result of the six or seven (possibly eight) bourbon sours she'd so lustily consumed. It's quite possible that Cleo has seen, heard and smelled things that weren't really there. People said she often got carried away.

They also said: *Just like your mother, running off when it suits you.*

SHE'S BEEN SWIMMING for just over fifteen minutes, and yet it feels as if an hour has passed. Rolling onto her back to rest, she gazes up at the place where the moon ought to be. A night without a moon is a night of portent—maybe. Tonight the moon is resting, but she can't, not really. The murderous current compels her to keep kicking, to keep drawing her arms back over her head in determined circles. I only meant to go for a walk, she thinks, spitting acrid water from her mouth, rolling onto her belly. She doesn't allow herself to entertain thoughts of speeding barges or the one stray log that could, in a split second, end her crossing. *It's been a long time.* She tries not to think of anything much, which is the whole point of her impulsive decision to commune with the Mississippi, or more accurately, to reunite with it. Romantics envision this river as the wide ribbon of chocolate that carried Huckleberry Finn on his raft, but she knows the truth of the Mississippi: that it stinks, takes lives, sinks boats—all without the slightest belch of remorse.

The water's colder than she remembers. Stronger, too, down here where the Mississippi races to empty its mighty bowels into the Gulf. She curses herself for not starting farther upriver, where she might have made a friend of the current for at least part of the venture. Teeth clenched, she feels every slam and swirl of the current against her spine. *Don't punch the water; cut it as if your hand is a blade.* But that advice was for swimming in pools, not rivers. Keep on, she tells herself, a cramp creeping into her right foot. Eventually her mind will go blank, overcome by pain and sheer exertion, and she looks forward to it. It won't do any good to pause to see where she's heading, nor will it help to look back at where she came from: the Governor Nicholls Street Wharf via Esplanade Avenue via Atchafalaya swamp country via St. Louis.

She points her body and repoints it, though navigation is less important than continuation. Terror licks at the edge of her brain like a flame. She's afraid that she doesn't have what it takes, painfully aware of a mounting fatigue she hadn't reckoned on. She can admit—if only for a fleeting moment—that she is indeed getting what she came for, which is to be away, out here and away from him, and from everything else that troubles her.

She taunts herself: Guess you don't have it in you any

more. Oh, but she does have it in her! She has things on her side now she didn't have back then. The hydroelectric power of anger, for one thing, which is what extended melancholy becomes when combined with a string of decidedly adult disappointments. You have to age to collect those, after all. *Happy birthday.* And then there is sex, or the absence of it, which may be contributing to her present state of mind. *All that one needs is a really good …* If it weren't so deadly, the sucking-down muscle of the river might feel almost sexual, but it doesn't, or at least not yet. As if wiped clear by a terror she denies with increasing success, her mind adopts one pleasing mantra: *swim, you stupid bitch—it's all you're good for.*

CLEO'S FIRST WAKING THOUGHT: She's dead by now. Washed down to wherever bodies go when the Mississippi wins.

Her second thought, which cancels out the first: I need a glass of water. She lifts her head away from the pillow and winces. Her teeth feel like brittle stones surrounding a tongue so swollen and sour she can taste and smell nothing but bourbon and sugared lime. With some confusion she recalls her whereabouts (New Orleans, French Quarter, hotel room, holiday) and yet can't quite explain to herself how every piece of furniture save for the bed has come to be piled up against the door. Someone has even moved the armoire across the room to join the stack of chairs and the side table in a kind of barricade formation. But how? The armoire must surely weigh more than Cleo herself. The well-appointed antiques—of which the hotelier, Mrs. Ryan, is very proud—are no longer so well placed.

Cleo props herself up on her elbows and stares, now recalling the slamming and locking of shutters on the windows of her ground-floor room, a wild animal version of herself piling things against the door. She remembers unplugging the bedside clock with a vicious tug, the sudden need to stop its too-slow measure of the passing night. Sees herself panting, checking and rechecking the locks on the windows, the door. Was it she who snatched three cans of beer from the kitchenette fridge and drank them down in quick succession? Yes. The same one who then dove, boots and all, beneath the feathery armour of the duvet under which she now lies, still fully dressed and sweating profusely? She's amazed by these recollections, and almost amused, until her first thought returns, broken down into simpler terms: Woman, drowning. Me, running. She burrows back under the duvet and closes her eyes tight against the image of the glittering thing in the river and the reality of what she has done, or more importantly, did not do.

Having unplugged the clock, Cleo has no idea what time it is. The *shuck-shuck* of Mrs. Ryan's broom on the courtyard stones outside the door indicates that a new day has been safely delivered. Cleo can almost see the lady hotelier through the wall, carefully coiffed and wearing pearls, and she thinks to herself, rather mournfully, What am I doing in a city where women wear pearls to sweep? The foreign tongues of tourists on the upper balustrade drown out the rhythmic scratch of the broom. It's Saturday. This is a detail Cleo is proud to be able to recollect. She'll take her anchors where she can find them.

Thirst. Cleo swings her legs over the edge of the bed. Notes that her knapsack and all her books, and even her duffel bag, are piled at the end of the bed, as if in preparation for departure. Strange. She's suddenly reminded of her favourite childhood game, the one she called Playing Ship, wherein she took every toy she owned and every book and piled them all on her narrow bed. She would then imagine herself lost at sea for hours. Would refuse to answer her father's call to dinner, insisting that she was trapped in the middle of the ocean and could not risk swimming the shark-infested waters for something as silly as a family meal. In any case, she prepared for those journeys at sea by sneaking apples, cookies and slices of white bread, which she squeezed into delectable balls and stored under her pillow. (For some reason bread tasted more exotic that way, although it disgusted her father when she tried to do it at table.) For whole afternoons Cleo would sit on her bed, surrounded by her worldly possessions, gazing out at imaginary pirate ships and dolphins until she was ordered to join her father on dry land. The game had always made her feel curiously sad, and yet she played it more often than any other game, almost enjoying the acute loneliness it inspired. Something about the game offered comfort, a sense of safety. Just as this room seems safer with the shutters closed and the world locked out.

Cleo's zest for her holiday plans has been overshadowed by her desire for water and more sleep. She decides to forgo sightseeing in favour of remaining in this room until the memory of the woman in the river has faded to a manageable fuzz. In the adult version of Playing Ship, one orders in, watches television, ignores the world and makes lists of ways to adopt a more positive attitude, starting tomorrow.

SHE SLIPS UP OUT of the water at Algiers Point like an alligator, unseen. The Mississippi assists by throwing her roughly against the shore with the other bits of flotsam and jetsam: foam, weeds, garbage, and now women wearing taffeta and rhinestone tiaras. She clings to a log and gasps for breath; the very touch of something solid makes her feel faint. Any triumph she felt during the crossing has been obliterated by absolute physical exhaustion.

At first all she can do is lie trembling in the muck and sludge of the shallows, dreamily convinced that she may in fact die on the shore of her destination. For a moment she believes that she has literally crossed over to the other side. "I'm sorry," she says out loud to an imagined Charon, "I seem to have forgotten my coin." The delusion passes. Realities rush to the forefront: the bracing temperature of the river, its stench, the chill wind fluttering above her face. With a groan she pulls herself upright in the filthy yellow-grey water and falls right back down with an ungraceful *plop*. The possible humiliation of being seen flailing around in the shoreline refuse is too much for her sense of personal dignity. She rises again and this time manages to remain standing, albeit a little clumsily. To her amazement, she's still wearing one of the three-inch heels that did, at the outset, match her gown.

AS SHE MOVES TOWARD THE kitchenette that makes a maisonette what it is, Cleo's sense of dread returns. She cranks the faucets above the tiny sink and waits for the rust-red stream to clear. Is reminded of Mrs. Ryan's instructions regarding the city's tap water—"Oh, it's fine for washing up, maybe just don't drink a glass"—and then bends down to thrust her head under the cloudy stream. She soaks her scalp and splashes her blazing cheeks with handfuls of water, resentful of the fact that she can't drink it. And then she does drink, thinking that if she becomes violently ill as a result, it will still be insufficient punishment for her previous night's excess and the events that followed. She drinks greedily, then returns to the bed, where she intends to remain for the duration of her so-called holiday.

Mrs. Ryan's broom pauses outside Cleo's door and there's a genteel knock. Cleo leaps from the bed and stands on the balls of her feet in order to call "Hello?" over the piled furniture blocking the door. She does a wonderful impersonation of someone who's been awake for hours—just in case Mrs. Ryan is entertaining any suspicious thoughts on the other side of the still-locked door.

Mrs. Ryan doesn't mean to bother Miss Savoy, but she is wondering if and when Miss Savoy will be venturing out. The maid would like to make up the room, is all, and any indication of her potential absence from the room would be appreciated. There's no rush, although the maid does insist on leaving for her other job by two o'clock on Saturdays. Mrs. Ryan realizes this arrangement isn't Miss Savoy's problem, but there is no way around it—good help is so hard to find off-season.

Out? Venturing? Cleo hasn't planned to venture anywhere today but hears herself telling Mrs. Ryan that yes, she'll be going out within the hour. Mortified by her own compliance, she steps back from the piled furniture in defeat. Mrs. Ryan thanks her and the broom moves away again, off toward the front of the hotel. Annoyed with herself, Cleo kicks the armoire, immediately reminded of its original position beside the Degas print Mrs. Ryan had called "local fine art." There'll be no venturing out as long as the monstrous piece of furniture blocks the door. How she will solve this predicament is a small mystery, but she reasons that if she moved it once, she can move it again. While contemplating how this will be achieved, she moves the lighter chairs and side table back to their original positions, her muscles no longer charged with last night's primal fear.

Cleo makes the bed with the skilled hands of a professional. A chambermaid herself until very recently, she is staying for the first time in a hotel other than the one she grew up in. The Little Savoy was—and remains—an establishment far removed from the grander Savoys of London and New York. But it's those years spent as a kind of slave at her father's down-at-the-heel hotel that have reminded her of an old trick. She collects a towel from the bathroom and lifts one end of the hulking dresser, slips the towel under two of its four feet and begins the process of tipping and dragging. One hand lightly rocks the beast, the other tugs the towel. By the time she has dragged it back to its proper position, she is covered in a Wild Turkey sweat but pleasantly distracted by her achievement. There are two long scratches on the dark wood floor where the unprotected legs of the antique behemoth resisted locomotion, but Cleo hopes the Pommes Royales maid won't notice. With any luck she'll be in too much of a rush to get to her other job. Cleo is well aware of the difference between a Saturday morning tidy and a Monday morning scour, and convinces herself that the gouges in the floor are superficial at best.

With just enough time to shower before changing her

clothes, she punishes herself by using ice-cold water. Standing below the freezing stream, Cleo doesn't allow herself to think of anything but the cup of coffee she so desperately covets. She feels wobbly and nervous about re-entering a world in which so many things seem to be conspiring against her plans for a peaceful vacation. Her sensitivity to the needs and feelings of chambermaids everywhere is perhaps a misplaced rush of compassion. Although she would have preferred to feign illness and remain *in camera,* she forgives herself. It will take Cleo some time to forget the trials and tribulations of her former profession. It'll take even longer to shrug off her Canadian tendency to be accommodating at any cost.

The gloomy sky mirrors her mood as she steps out onto Royal Street. She dreads the necessary walk below the infamous balconies that decorate this particular street in the French Quarter. Cleo has already observed that the occupants of the apartments attached to these galleries have a habit of yelling to each other as they water their plants and beat their carpets. This in itself would be a fine, even charming custom if the topics of conversation stayed within the safe limits of the weather and the progress of the Saints against the Bears. But Cleo already knows that within seconds the topics can and will turn from the possibility of rain to who shot whose sister and why, followed by a detailed account of someone's recent liver transplant. Yesterday it had seemed amusing; she had derived great pleasure from slowing her stride and eavesdropping on these intimate tales, had even written some of them down in her notebook. But this morning the balcony gossip doesn't hold the same potential for amusement. Racked with guilt, Cleo now fears that the casual news of a woman who drowned herself in the Mississippi last night may very well sail from one balcony to another with nothing more than a shrug and an "Oh, my" to punctuate it. The natives of what some statisticians call "the murder capital of the United States" are understandably casual about death. One might forgive their seeming apathy regarding the demise of yet another fellow citizen, but Cleo knows that it is never just another death when someone takes her own life. Or is it? she wonders, seized by a pang of rage that propels her forward.

She stumbles along the sidewalk below the balconies, no longer able to appreciate their lush foliage, wrought-iron splendour and the faded curtains of beads from Mardi Gras festivals past. Streams of water splash down from hoses and watering cans; clouds of carpet dust puff out and dissipate. Cleo claps her hands over her ears upon hearing the hoarse call of a woman above her: "Gonna rain!" As if this proclamation is merely a warning bell preceding some more horrific report, Cleo picks up speed until the voices are at last behind her. At St. Philip Street, she turns down toward Decatur, a route she already knows will lead directly to a cup of coffee and a pleasant place to write in her notebook.

Farther down Royal Street is a police precinct where Cleo could still report what she saw by the river last night and thus clear her conscience a little, but she does no such thing. Unaware of the proximity of the police station at this early stage in her visit, she's also convinced that her decision to flee the scene might define her as a kind of criminal. The combination of this fear, a pernicious hangover and an urgent need for caffeine have impaired her judgment, as has the untimely resurgence of some ancient history of her own that Cleo can't quite face on this overcast fourth morning of the month of November.

SHE'S LIKE A BABY learning how to walk for the very first time. Stumbling over submerged rocks and bits of wood with a sudden burst of joie de vivre, she makes her way up the incline of the shore. To her right a departing ferry blasts its horn, and she curses, startled by the noise. The café she plans to visit is a few hundred yards upriver, inland from the ferry dock, and she feels a rush of hope and determination. Do not die, she tells herself, at least not before breakfast.

It's true that this lady could easily have located a decent bowl of turtle soup and a snifter of brandy on her own side of the Mississippi. Or, if she simply had to have the Shore-Do Café's turtle soup, she could've taken the bus over the Mississippi River Bridge that joins the city proper to Algiers and points beyond. (Most people would have at least opted for a taxi, but as you may have guessed, Our Lady of the Mississippi is not most people.) When she reaches the road she sneezes three times, then bends down to remove the remaining waterlogged stiletto from her foot. Souvenir, she muses, limping on toward the restaurant.

The Shore-Do is crowded with early birds when she makes her rather grand entrance. The bells tied to the door jingle gaily and she pauses, hands on her hips, head cocked, dripping water and mud and God knows what else all over the black-and-white tiles of the floor. A sight to see: her tiara caked with weeds, her wet dress plastered to her fine body.

The waitress on duty clucks her tongue, thinking: What's this, a little bit of Mardi Gras come early?

The other patrons in the café grin into their newspapers and coffee cups, wondering what kind of day they've got themselves into. Our Lady sits down at one of the pedestal tables close to the door and waits for the waitress to approach. She studies the menu and rubs her arms to bring the feeling back into them. There will be bruises, she thinks, feeling oddly pleased by the prospect. The sky above the levee is swelling with the promise of a big rain. Let it come, she thinks, the Shore-Do has everything I want for now: turtle soup, brandy, a jukebox. She wouldn't mind a towel, either, but that's probably too much to hope for.

When the waitress finally makes her way over to the table, with her eyes narrowed and a coffee pot held up like a protective shield, the river-swimmer decides to forgo any special requests. She orders turtle soup with extra sherry and a snifter of brandy, ignoring the unabashed disapproval on the waitress's face. It isn't that the *serveuse* minds anybody ordering a drink first thing in the morning. That much is commonplace. It is the state of the new arrival's hair and clothing that trouble her, and the fact that the sign on the café door clearly states No Shirt, No Shoes, No Service! She glares at her new customer's mud-caked bare feet and frowns, then heads for the kitchen.

The eyes of the other diners are pinned to the newcomer. She enjoys the attention but wishes they wouldn't be quite so shameless in what she believes to be their collective admiration. Her private satisfaction is deep. She has reached her desired destination, across the river from the man who calls himself her husband and yet didn't have the decency to remember that it's her birthday. Technically speaking, since a new day begins at the stroke of midnight. When the clock moved on toward one a.m. and he still hadn't shown his face, she'd lost all patience and fled their apartment in a fury, choosing the cool arms of the river over a night spent waiting for the possible embrace of her supposed companion. Passivity will no longer colour her days or nights, or so she vowed last night. *Blind obedience is for the very young,* she decides now, *and I am no longer part of that demographic. Was I ever?*

She's struggling to preserve her good mood when a beefy-faced man saunters by and exclaims, "How'd *you* get here, on a oil tanker?" Her answer to his inquiry is a big, bright smile. She refuses to be wounded by the ripple of snickers his remark inspires among the other patrons. What does she care for the opinions of these do-nothings, these nosy nobodies? Not one of them knows a thing about her or what she's just accomplished. She flashes them another, brighter grin and drops her eyes to the tabletop in a coy pantomime of modesty.

When the steaming bowl of soup arrives, she remembers why she had such a craving for it. The Shore-Do's version is dark red with sherry and thick with the meat of several turtle bellies. She sips daintily at the brandy and marvels at the way her arms and legs are tingling back to life.

Despite her curious personal appearance, no one could say she lacks manners. She is elegant buttering her bread, delicate as she spoons her soup. Graceful as she slips down from her chair and pads to the jukebox to see what the Shore-Do has to offer in the way of music, and equally poised as she realizes she doesn't have a quarter. Back at her table, she holds up her empty snifter, indicating that she'd like another brandy. Her high-heel shoe sits crumpled on the floor, and she regards it with affection. When she gets home she'll mount it on a board like a trophy, and when Johnny V. demands to know why—and he will—she'll refuse to tell him. Then he'll raise his voice in jealous indignation because although he didn't see fit to get himself home at a decent hour, he can't have been pleased to discover her all-night absence from the apartment. He'll imagine the worst, and so he should, because in her mind this swim is only the beginning. She is thirty-nine years old (as of midnight) and she can feel the torpor of her wifely existence dissolving along with the morning fog.

Although she would dearly love to sit out the rest of her days in the Shore-Do Café, her body has other things in mind. Like sleep. Thrilled as she is to have made a successful uninterrupted crossing of the Mississippi River at last, she needs to get home, if only to avoid collapsing in public. Praying her legs will carry her across the room without incident, she slides down from her stool, collects her shoe and approaches the cash register. The waitress is busy refilling hot-sauce bottles behind the bar, a cigarette dangling from her pink lips. Confronted by her unusual customer, she watches with horror as the bedraggled woman digs around in her cleavage and produces a sopping-wet twenty-dollar bill from between her breasts.

"It's on me," the waitress says, refusing the money.

"Why, thank you ever so much," Our Lady says, nodding. "As it happens, today is my birthday. Your kindness will never be forgotten." Tucking the sodden bill back into her décolletage, she winks at the waitress. "You'd make a wonderful husband."

With a snap of hip she turns and makes her way out of the Shore-Do, her shoe held up like a prize. A man sitting at the bar whistles his appreciation and asks the waitress, "How come the pretty ones is always crazy?"

As much as she'd love to swim back the way she came, she's promised herself that there will be no more swimming now that she has achieved this one full crossing. No point in tempting fate, she reminds herself. Last night's crossing wasn't her first attempt to swim the Mississippi. The inaugural leap took place almost thirty years before.

November 4, 1966
St. Louis, Missouri

To turn ten years old might well be the most miserable event of any human life, a mournful occasion that scores high on the cosmic Gloom-O-Meter. Ten marks the beginning of disenchantment; it's when the brain wakes to questions more profound than the dubious validity of Santa Claus. How could a person feel pleased to have passed an entire decade on Earth, a planet where fathers run off without warning, where wars rage and mothers dress their daughters in—of all things—blue suede pinafores and matching tam-o'-shanters? Such thoughts were the cause of Madeline Shockfire's escalating sorrow as she waited with her mother in the dining room of their home. Her philosophical angst was exacerbated by the pinch of her patent-leather shoes, also navy in hue. She looked and felt like a depressed blueberry, and so greeted her mother's questions with deepening sighs. Nothing Mrs. Shockfire said or did seemed to relieve her daughter's melancholy. Frustrated when Madeline did not respond cheerfully to a wake-up call followed by lavish hugs and kisses (and a rare offer of breakfast in bed), Mrs. Shockfire had decided that they would go out, or rather, allow themselves to be taken out.

Burt Oliver was a close friend of Dianne's, a lawyer with an exquisite automobile perfect for tours of the city. They would see a movie in a downtown cinema and have a wonderful restaurant meal, and Madeline would thank heaven that men like Mr. Oliver existed. Or so she was instructed by her mother.

After the promised movie and meal, Madeline was no happier. The adults who'd tried so hard to cheer her decided they had earned a little nightcap. And wouldn't a riverboat cruise be just the thing to please a birthday girl? Mr. Oliver thought it would be, and they boarded the *Magnolia Blossom,* the adults with high hopes for a highball and the briefest smile from Madeline. As soon as they had settled into a plush booth in the riverboat's sheltered cocktail lounge, Madeline announced her need to visit the ladies' room. Dianne thought nothing of it, and clucked her tongue as her daughter plodded out of the lounge as though part of an invisible funeral procession.

It was Mr. Oliver's even higher hope that the boat ride would exhaust Mrs. Shockfire's daughter so that he might have the illusion of being alone with his pretty lady friend. Dianne was a striking woman who knew how to make a man feel good. They tucked into their drinks and were getting to know each other under the cover of the table when the crackle of the riverboat loudspeaker interrupted their ardour.

"CHILD OVERBOARD! CHILD OVERBOARD!"

Several of the lounge patrons scrambled to reach the *Magnolia Blossom*'s upper deck to witness the excitement.

Dianne's mouth fell open with a gasp, and she jumped to her feet, wringing her hands and moaning, "Oh, Lord! Oh my Lord!" Mr. Oliver rose from the table with reluctance and some shame, being aroused as he was. While it simply wouldn't do if he missed a potential lawsuit, he insisted Dianne stay put for Madeline's imminent return from the restroom. Dianne watched him go and then hurried to the ladies' room, where she prayed she'd find Madeline frowning into the mirror. No such luck. There are some things a mother just knows, and what Dianne knew then was that it was Madeline, her baby Madeline, who had fallen overboard. With panicked tears streaming down her face and promises to be a better mother forevermore spilling from her lips, she ran to find Mr. Oliver on the deck of the *Magnolia Blossom*.

There are seldom many children aboard a midnight riverboat cruise, and Burt Oliver stuttered and quaked as he informed Dianne that it was indeed her daughter in the Mississippi River. He pointed into the dark gloom with a sad shake of his head. Dianne clutched Burt's arm as members of the boat crew rowed out to fetch the little girl, with a miniature searchlight trained on the water. It seemed that Madeline was not drowning at all but swimming, and with admirable purpose, in the direction of east St. Louis. Dianne's sudden lack of hysteria made Mr. Oliver nervous. She seemed to be watching the proceedings with open delight, giggling to herself as the men in the lifeboat pulled her daughter from the river. The girl kicked and screamed, her loud profanities heard by the keen observers who waited on the deck.

"I've told her not to use that kind of language," whispered Dianne, feigning disapproval.

Returned to the deck of the riverboat, Madeline was wrapped in a rough blanket and escorted to the captain's office, for the purposes of familial privacy. The Shockfires were left alone, where it was expected that young Madeline would receive the tongue-lashing of her life. But no such thing occurred. She was reminded that cursing wasn't ladylike, and yet her mother grinned at her proudly and pinched her cheeks. When at last they had docked, Mr. Oliver thanked the captain and crew and, with some embarrassment, escorted the two Shockfire ladies back to his Cadillac. In the back seat Dianne absentmindedly rubbed the blanket that contained her daughter, chattering to no one in particular.

"Why, this just tells me a little something about my Madeline," she cooed. "You, my darlin', are a natural-born athlete! Did you see how far across the river this girl got, Burt? My Lord, you're an aquatic wonder, Maddy-girl! Untapped sporting potential right under my nose all this time! Why, you little fish, you—I've never even seen you swim!" She leaned over the front seat and stage-whispered, "I practically have to chase this child into a bathtub. You wouldn't believe the fuss she makes."

Madeline sat silently shivering in her blanket-wrap as her mother loudly proclaimed her obvious talents in the aquatic realm. It hadn't been difficult to jump into the river, as almost everyone on the deck was staggering drunk. She was just tall enough to pop over the railing. The water was so cold it felt like fire, but she wished she hadn't yelled on the way down to it, because then they would never have noticed her in the water. And if she'd planned a little more carefully, she would have waited till the band had burst into song again. That way . . .

"Madeline, are you all right?" Her mother poked her roughly. "I said, I'm going down to the community pool first thing tomorrow to sign you up for lessons, baby doll. Aren't you listening?"

She could hear her mother telling Mr. Oliver to come back another night, that she was exhausted from the upset of Madeline's "near drowning." Madeline hurried upstairs and tucked herself into bed, leaving her wet clothes strewn about the floor. When her mother tiptoed into the room she pretended to be asleep. Madeline did not want to hear about swimming lessons or pools. She wouldn't tell her mother that it was her father who'd taught her how to swim. The thought of him made Madeline want to cry. He was gone and that was that.

Before her daddy had disappeared three years prior, he'd spent one sweet week of afternoons teaching Madeline how to swim. Madeline remembered the lessons with an aching fondness, mostly because, for reasons she still didn't understand, her mother had been away from the house more often than she was in it. Her daddy had smiled and joked and told her that swimming was one of the smartest things man had ever taught himself how to do. "Keeps you young and fresh," he'd said, tousling her hair. And what he said must've been true; some nights he came home from work with wet hair and a leather bag that said YMCA on the side, looking more like a boy than a daddy. After he left, there was no more swimming. Still, it had been their secret that Madeline knew how to swim and, as her daddy pointed out with a wink, her mother didn't.

Now she was a whole decade old and even the swim hadn't helped to make her feel any less despondent about existence. Her mother was proud of her, she knew, but Madeline also knew how her mother's good favour could disappear just as quickly as it came.

Dianne sat down on the edge of the bed, then kicked off her pumps and stretched out next to Madeline with a theatrical yawn. The ice cubes in her nightcap jangled as she sipped, and she whispered suddenly into the dark, "You just wait, honey, till they put that gold medal around your neck. You're gonna thank me, sugar."

Oh, yes, thank you, Mother, thinks Madeline as she waits for the ferry that will take her back to the French Quarter. *Thank you for every little thing.*

THERE'S A LONG LINE OF PEOPLE waiting at the counter of Kaldi's Coffeehouse, an eager crowd anticipating heavy white mugs of coffee infused with chicory, hot milk if you want it. The aroma of roasting coffee beans is overwhelming, whipped through the air by a half-dozen ceiling fans the size of airplane propellers, high above the tables. Cleo feels dizzy as she joins the queue. All around the vast room people are snapping newspapers, smoking cigarettes, gazing out the immense windows with their elbows on the sills, laughing, talking, as in a movie.

Seated at a stool facing onto the street, Cleo opens her notebook. A moist breeze flutters the pages, too many of which are blank. She considers for the first time the possibility of a husband wondering where his wife has gone, of children weeping for a mother now missing, of the myriad ways in which that woman's utterly selfish choice will affect other people's lives for years to come. Cleo hates the woman in the river more than she has ever hated anyone in her twenty-eight years of life.

I want to know why you did it, she scrawls, cutting deep into the page of her notebook with the tip of her pen. She can't manage to write anything more. It's hardly a poem, or even the first line of one, but the act of putting pen to paper calms her. Cleo gazes around the crowded room and decides to record what she sees, instead of what she feels. For future reference. Because she's already decided that just as soon as she has seen everything on her list of must-see things, she'll leave New Orleans. Her room at the Pommes Royales Maisonnettes is hers for a full week. In a burst of naive optimism, Cleo booked it for seven nights without knowing that her trip would be ruined before it even got started. *Woman, drowning. Me, watching, running.* She swats the thought away and watches a group of people in matching orange windbreakers at a distant table, waving their hands and clearly enjoying the fact that their appointed leader is video-taping their every move.

At a table very near her, Cleo spies a man wearing thick glasses and a filthy brown cardigan. The man is cutting things from newspapers plucked from a stack at his elbow. Whoever he is, he takes his work very seriously as he wields a giant pair of scissors with obvious skill. After he snips something from the newspaper in hand, he gives a little nod, then pastes it into a large spiral-bound scrapbook. A grocery cart filled with dozens of other such bulging notebooks is pulled up next to his table, and Cleo watches, fascinated.

She abandons her own slim journal and heads to the counter for a refill.

"Who is that?" Cleo asks the dreadlocked girl behind the coffee-shop counter, gesturing at the man.

"Aloysius," the girl says, pushing Cleo's filled mug back toward her. "Fifty cents." Cleo continues to stare at the man, asks the girl what he's up to. "Cutting up papers. Does it every day." The girl shrugs. "Says he's keeping track of time. People say he's got over two thousand of those scrap-books in his house. He might look poor, but he's rich. Has a big house over on Prytania Street, comes from old money. Fifty cents for the refill." The girl looks impatiently past Cleo, sees a new line forming. "If you give him a dollar, he'll show 'em to you."

Cleo pays for her coffee and returns to her seat. Outside the window the anticipated rain is coming down hard, which gives her a good excuse to stay and watch the man she now thinks of as Mr. Time Machine. She can't help wondering if he has today's obituaries. She's about to approach the man to ask, then it's far too soon for an obituary. Much too soon for that, but perhaps not too soon for a news item. As she sips her coffee and debates whether to ask to see today's paper, the man begins to collect his scrapbooks, scissors and glue. Doesn't he realize it's pouring rain? Cleo glances out the window. When she looks back, he has draped a plastic tarpaulin over the grocery cart and is hurrying out of Kaldi's, easing his wheeled archive down the steps and out into the downpour.

"Maybe tomorrow," Cleo says to herself, "or not." She watches the rain and tells herself that as long as she doesn't know the woman's name or anything about her, she can pretend it never happened. She examines her jotted list of must-see attractions and sips her coffee. Wonders if the Pommes Royales chambermaid has finished her rounds. At this moment Cleo has no desire to see anything but the pillow at the head of her bed. She's drooping in the window of Kaldi's Coffeehouse, in spite of two cups of strong coffee. I'm bad advertising, she thinks. Yawning, she tucks her notebook under her jacket and scurries into the rain.

Reaching the Pommes Royales, she sees its gates festooned with vines and colourful ribbons, the bricks swept immaculate, the soft glow of a lamp in a second-floor window, the fresh-painted gleam of the balcony railings. Cleo stares up at its modest but elegant façade, thinks of its cozy, welcoming interior and sighs. This is what my father dreamt of, she thinks with an unexpected rush of sympathy. This is more like what he had in mind.

April, 1971
Toronto, Ontario

"Oh," said the woman in the red cape. She hung off Cleo's father's arm and stared in disbelief at the sagging three-storey structure before them. Weeds pushed up through the heaps of snow that blocked the walkway. The windows of the house were boarded up with thin sheets of plywood that featured slogans against war and symbols insisting on peace. Rather aptly, someone had scrawled "Welcome to Hell" on the front door in thick red paint.

Cleo looked up at the woman who had attached herself to her father, as if by magic, when they disembarked from the big boat. Her mum wasn't here now; she had refused to come along. Cleo could see why. It wasn't a very nice place. The country was called Canada; the city, Toronto. It was going to be just like England, her father said, only better. Cleo didn't think much of it so far. It was cold and icy and you had to be careful every time you took a step.

"This *is* the right place?" the woman asked. She sounded as if she hoped it wasn't. Her name was Sadie. Cleo's father said she was Cleo's aunt, but that seemed suspicious. An aunt would look like them, wouldn't she? Sadie was stupid and ugly; she wore a lot of blue gunk on her eyes and red grease on her lips. Cleo decided she wanted to leave Toronto with her father and go somewhere warm, someplace where Sadie couldn't find them.

"Roland gave me this address," Cleo's father said, picking up their suitcases. "He did say it needed a bit of work. I told you that."

"I say he was being polite." Sadie pouted as Lyle staggered on through the snow and up the steps of the house. Cleo followed, hoping Sadie wouldn't be able to keep up. Maybe she'd get stuck in the snow and freeze like a statue— one with a very fat bottom. Or maybe she'd go to the place she had talked about the whole way from Montreal. All she ever talked about was New York this and New York that. Cleo hoped Sadie would change her mind about Toronto, but she didn't. Instead she trailed along behind them, slipping and sliding and saying bad words under her breath.

Cleo wanted to ask her father why they had to live in such a horrible place. It seemed to be the sort of building where monsters lived, and looked a lot like the haunted castles in her picture books. How could this be the inn where rich people would stroll in the gardens and sit by fireplaces while Cleo's father made heaps of money? "We'll soon be rich, too," he'd said with a big smile. He wasn't smiling now and Cleo didn't want to be rich any more. She wanted to go home. Or to Italy, where the grown-ups said her mum had gone. Without them. She stood on the top step of the ice-encrusted porch and said in a very loud voice, "I hate it here!" That she had spoken at last should have been cause for celebration. She hadn't spoken for days and had only recently agreed to eat, but Lyle was tired.

"It's your new home, Cleo. Show a little imagination, will you both? Let's have a look inside before we despair." To Sadie he said, "As you well know, looks can be deceiving." When he said this Sadie stuck out her pointy pink tongue, and she and Lyle both laughed. Cleo wanted to disappear into the ground.

The inside of the big, old house was colder than it was outside, which wasn't at all how things were supposed to be. Cleo suddenly missed her gran's house and wondered if the reason they'd been sent away had anything to do with the tablecloth Cleo had ruined when she spilled a cup of tea. It had been an accident, but her gran was very angry about it. She'd said Cleo was "all thumbs and no sense," just like her mum. But no, her dad seemed happy to be here, and Cleo wondered why. There was snow all over the floor, and a bad smell like pee and boiled cabbage. Lyle left Cleo and Sadie in the dark hall and went back out onto the porch. There was a loud snapping sound as he tore away the boards that covered the front windows. Cold winter light spilled in through the broken panes and revealed a front room littered with yellowed newspapers, smashed wine bottles and blankets that

looked as if they'd been nibbled by rats. Cleo covered her
eyes with her gloved hands.

"We can't sleep here!" Sadie cried.

"No, we can't!" Cleo piped in, peeking through her
fingers.

Cleo's father looked around, shrugged and said, "Fine,
we'll get a room for tonight. And then tomorrow we're
going to come back and try to see the bright side of things,
aren't we?"

The bright side of that particular piece of real estate
would have been a good fire, but Lyle wasn't to be swayed
from his dream of opening a small European-style hotel. His
brother, Roland, had insisted that the Toronto neighbourhood was on the upswing and that there was money to be
made in the business of little hotels. It was true that Roland
had purchased the building sight unseen, but as Lyle's
mother so often said, Roland had business instincts that bor-
dered on the supernatural. Faced with the reality of the
place, Lyle felt that the Sherbourne Street house certainly
looked as if it had been possessed by something from the
netherworld. He wouldn't let on, however. By the time
Roland could tear himself away from his dry-cleaning
empire in New Jersey, Lyle felt sure he'd have the hotel
whipped into impressive shape.

While Cleo dozed on a restaurant banquette that
evening, Lyle chattered on about the potential of his new
hotel. Although Roland owned the place on paper, Lyle
thought that it would only be a matter of months before he
could buy his older brother out. Sadie banished the visions
of queen-sized beds and swank velvet curtains she'd imagined when Lyle first told her he was going into the hotel

business. The hotel was disastrous and as far from quaint as anything could possibly be, but Sadie found his blind optimism charming. She listened to him extol the virtues of a neighbourhood he knew nothing about. How he intended to do all the renovations with his own two hands, and how he planned to name the hotel the Little Savoy. "As a kind of joke," he explained, well aware that he was not of *those* Savoys. As she listened, Sadie wondered where he put the pain of what had happened.

Away, obviously. There was no evidence of his grief as he lifted a glass of whiskey and grinned. "Now I ask you, which was worse: finding out the hotel needs a bit of work, or that bloody Canadian immigration queue?" He saw Sadie watching Cleo and patted her hand across the table. "She'll be fine, duck. Probably won't remember any of it when she's older."

Sadie gave Lyle a weak smile and took a long sip of her drink. She quietly vowed to do her best to comfort him and to help get the hotel off the ground. That she might be making a big mistake frightened her a little, but she decided to ignore those kinds of thoughts. She'd only known him for a scant two days when he asked her to move to Canada with them, and yet something had made her accept his invitation. It wasn't just his good looks (he was all clefts and dimples), or his belief that he would soon be rich, or even his brave, clownish humour. Gratitude, maybe. He'd offered to take her away from a life spent singing the same fifteen songs over and over to drunks on ocean liners, to bring her closer to New York City, where she dreamed of singing in posh nightclubs. That was part of it. The other reason made her more uncomfortable. It was pity.

LETHE MIGHT WELL BE the river of forgetfulness, but the Mississippi is the river that brings it all back. Back to that first joyful swim and the subsequent chlorinated hours that followed; to the fad diets meant to reduce her waistline along with her time, marked by the sharp tweets of poolside whistles signalling disapproval from her coach. It all returns with alarming clarity: the suspicious stares of her teammates when she refused to pray before meets; the damp aroma of wadded towels mixed with terrible gusts of girlish perfume; the banging echo of locker doors, as cheery as the sound of a prison cell door slamming. All of it. As she waits for the Canal Street ferry to dock, Madeline shudders, remembering these long-lost sounds and smells and the all-too-vivid emotions they conjure. "Happy birthday," she mutters, rolling her eyes. "You've come so far. Full circle, almost."

But then the thought of Johnny V.'s face as he sees her coming through the door at last makes her giggle out loud. The idea of a good old-fashioned showdown with her husband fills her bones with renewed strength. She can't think of a better way to spend a rainy Saturday than brawling with the man who sometimes loves her enough to lose his temper completely. If there's one thing they do well, it's fight. Or they used to; Madeline can't actually recall the last time they had a real argument. Brief moments of discontent about who forgot to buy milk don't count. This realization takes some of the wind from her muddied mental sails. *What if he isn't even home when I arrive?*

By the time she emerges from the ferry, Madeline is decidedly less cheerful. Passersby will assume (if they notice at all) that it's the rain coming down in cool, staccato drops that causes this morning-after lady to frown with such intensity. She prays for Johnny's presence in the apartment as she slaps along the greasy sidewalk in her bare feet. Up Iberville, where she fits right in with the other half-clad ladies spilling from clubs in similar attire, though without mud-caked crowns. Not even the wolf whistles erupting from under awnings of the so-called gentlemen's clubs can make her smile now. She resents the detour but finds it necessary, since walking along Decatur would put her at risk of running into a neighbour. After she's spent nineteen long years in the French Quarter, virtually the only people Madeline doesn't know are the ones that haven't arrived yet. She avoids Royal Street because its antique stores, galleries and perfume shops would create an unpleasant contrast to a woman in her present state. Refined she is not on this torrential morning, and she doesn't feel like being reminded.

Madeline walks several blocks out of her way in the pouring rain, circumnavigating the core of the Quarter. Her detour takes her along sleepy Dauphine, all the way to Esplanade and down again. For some reason this extended promenade seems more tiring than any swim. When finally she reaches the door of their apartment building and spots the label under their buzzer that reads Valentucci/Shockfire, she feels the first real rush of dread. Dread that he is home, and dread that he isn't. She hadn't thought to bring her keys along for the swim. Staring at their names on the label, she wonders if her refusal to take Johnny's surname (a renegade act in the South, even in 1976) has somehow served to widen the gulf between them over time. Her mother would say, "Yes, it has. What did you expect, Madeline? A man is cuckolded when a woman rejects simple traditions!" She should know...

"Shut up!" Madeline hisses, giving the buzzer a quick jab that may or may not have registered two floors above the street. If he isn't home she'll be forced to take refuge in the Mint Bar and endure the affectionate but razor-sharp quips of Marcus, the daytime bartender and Madeline's very own self-appointed fashion critic. Living above a gay bar has its advantages; Marcus is usually one of them. Right now, however, Madeline isn't in the mood for inquiries and appraisals, at least not from Marcus. Not now, but maybe later. There's no better confidante for man trouble than another man, after all. Madeline's dark opinion of the fair sex has made her a hit with certain men and an object of considerable suspicion among French Quarter females. When Johnny questioned her marked preference for male companions, Madeline stated, with no small amount of venom, "Women are both dull and dangerous. I should know—I am one." Johnny argued that men could be just as dangerous as women, if not more so. "True enough," she concurred, "but there's a difference between aggression—which men invented—and random spitefulness, which is undoubtedly feminine in origin. I find the former easier to bear."

She waits and pokes the buzzer again, eager to escape the downpour. Finally there comes a crackle and a click. He's home, releasing the lock on the downstairs door without a word. Silence, often the precursor to rage, she thinks with a nervous titter. Madeline pushes through the door and on through the courtyard, which should be full of flowers and fountains and stone statues but isn't. She wades through the tall stacks of beer cases stored there by the bar and begins her ascent of the wooden staircase. Upon reaching the top floor, she's momentarily convinced of an impending cardiac arrest and almost wishes it would hurry up, then shakes off this morbid turn of mind. The door is ajar when she approaches, a sight that causes her to inhale quickly and halt.

There's the faint buzz of a radio and the smell of Johnny's Camel Lights, the sound of magazine pages turning. But she doesn't trust these signs of seeming tranquility. She takes another deep breath and sashays into the main room, shoe in hand, ready for him to pounce, accuse and shout. Instead he reclines on the sofa, surrounded by overflowing ashtrays, his long, beautiful feet propped up on the sofa's armrest. He's reading, or pretending to. A man without a care in the world, or so his posture suggests, but Madeline knows Johnny better than that. She clears her throat and swings her shoe by its withered strap.

"Hey, babe," he says with a smile, casually looking up from the magazine that seems to be a source of great fascination. Seeing her, his eyes widen a little. He whistles through his teeth and grins, but says nothing. He reaches for his cigarette pack and the light clank of his Zippo is the only sound in the room. Madeline's heart begins to pound, but not out of fear. Johnny blows out a ring of smoke, raises his eyebrows and asks, "What?" This is all it takes to refresh Madeline's rage. She steps back a little and narrows her eyes as Johnny repeats his question, *"What?"* as if the fact that she has arrived home dishevelled, muddy and carrying one shoe is a common occurrence. As if her all-night absence from their bed is nothing out of the ordinary and thus has no aura of menace, infidelity or scandalous adventure. In short, Madeline is deeply insulted.

She turns on her heel and stomps away from him, toward the bathroom, all the while calling out, in a snide imitation of him, "What? What? Hey, babe! Hey, babe!" He takes the bait and follows behind her at a safe distance.

"What's eating you this morning?" he wonders aloud.

"Or *who?*" she taunts, slamming the door. A framed photo on the wall wobbles and falls to the floor with a light crash.

"Oh, that's nice." Johnny kneels to sweep the broken glass into a pile with his hand. "I never liked that picture anyway," he mutters. "Too bad about the frame, though."

On the other side of the bathroom door Madeline is listening, furious that her bold innuendo has rattled him less than the loss of a picture frame. She waits.

After a brief silence he says through the door, "I'm going to ask you one more time what your problem is."

Madeline flings the bathroom door wide and shouts, "My problem? Buy a fucking calendar, Johnny!" and slams the door again.

"What is this, an episode of *Laugh-In?*" he jokes. *Buy a calendar?* He hears the roar of the bathtub faucets and scowls. "I wasn't the one who stayed out all goddamn night!" Without realizing it, he's given her what she wants. Almost. He scratches his jaw and shrugs and retreats to the living room.

Sequestered in the steam-filled bathroom, Madeline smiles into the clouded mirror with feline satisfaction. She unzips, peels her filthy dress down and steps out of it, kicking it to one side. She sets her shoe in the sink and pours an entire sachet of vetiver bath salts from the Hove Parfumerie into the tub. Watches the clean, hot, foaming water and imagines Johnny pacing around the living room, wild with suspicion now, driven there by her stubborn silence. Madeline slowly and methodically removes her panties and brassiere, contemplating a letter to Victoria's Secret to inform them that their infamous lingerie is perfect, not only for romantic nights *à deux,* but also for solo swims across the Mississippi River. She eases herself into the scalding water and groans with pleasure. While the Mississippi is majestic and impressive in its way, it isn't the most fragrant river in the world, and she's suddenly eager to scrub away the pungent aroma clinging to her skin. *It's enough to know that I've done it,* she thinks, giving the obdurate tiara a few savage tugs to release it from the back of her head. *No matter what he asks, I won't tell him a thing.* She scrubs at herself more furiously, knowing that in forgetting one thing, he has obviously forgotten two, for her birthday is also the anniversary of their marriage. She can't decide which unacknowledged occasion upsets her more. Her skin is scarlet from the rough ministrations of a loofah sponge, and she enjoys the pain. An unpleasant slick of oil and mud appears on the surface of the bath water. Seeing it, Madeline sighs. A shower would have been more effective, but she so hates the sensation of water streaming down on her head. She lifts herself up from the tainted water and steps out of the tub, jittery from the heat of her bath and the anger that's still revving through her. *Not a word about her birthday! Not the slightest idea of what she meant with her jab about his need for a calendar.* She can no longer contain herself.

This time when Johnny looks up from his magazine, Madeline stands before him naked and streaming water and soapsuds, hands planted firmly on her hips. She looks wonderful naked, and his first impulse is to reach out and touch her, but he refrains, recognizing what he calls the Death Stare. Instead he keeps his hands in his lap and prepares for a vicious outpouring of her discontent, for the litany of grievances she hasn't bothered to share with him until this very moment. If things follow their usual course, he'll be invited to touch her, but only after they've brawled. She says nothing, and for a moment Johnny wonders if Madeline has forgotten how to fight, just as she has often wondered if he's forgotten where he lives. In a marriage where anger has been their most reliable aphrodisiac, complacency is a dangerous thing. And yet Johnny can't seem to muster the words that will get things rolling. He stares at his knuckles and chews his moustache, waiting.

"Do you even know what day it is?" she begins, her voice low and deathly quiet. When he nods ever so slightly, she snorts. "I don't think you have the faintest idea what day it is at all, Giovanni. If you did, you might have seen fit to get your skinny ass home at a decent hour last night. But no, that would have been the right thing to do, and as we both know, you're incapable of altering your precious routine for even one night!" She leans forward, right into his face, and hisses, "It's my birthday, you asshole!"

"I know that!" He meets her gaze at last, finally aware of the source of her agitation. "What's that got to do with last night? I came home. *You* were gone." He gives her a triumphant look.

"My birthday officially began at midnight." She folds her arms across her chest, hiding her nipples, which have risen to the occasion along with her ire.

"So you went out," he counters, standing to his full six feet and four inches. "All damned night, I might add. I got home at one-thirty. I had a few drinks. I *always* have a few drinks after work—you know that. I don't see why you're being so unreasonable when *you* were the one who didn't bother to come home."

He reviews her hasty retreat to the bathtub, the state of her appearance when she arrived home. And yet, herein lies the mystery, because she'd come home looking more like someone who'd spent the night in the city sewer than someone who'd been in the arms of another man. Still, who knew what she was capable of lately? "Well, I hope it was good," he says, turning away from her in search of his cigarettes, not believing that she could possibly, after all this time, resort to something as unspectacular as an affair.

"Oh, it was." Her lips curl into a sneer. "It was just what I needed."

She heads for the bedroom but Johnny catches her arm and stares down at her with disgust and hurt flaring in his eyes. He can tell she's trying to cause trouble between them. Not because there's any real trouble, but because she finds it amusing to upset him. The delight in her eyes irritates him, and he drops her arm and swears under his breath. He'd never hit Madeline, although the temptation has been there. For all the violence and infamy of their battles, both public and private, they've never resorted to blows. Well-aimed insults, yes, but never physical blows. She did once throw an ashtray at him early on but thankfully had missed her target.

"Go and get dressed," he commands, lighting a cigarette without looking at her. "I'll take you for breakfast."

"Thank you, I already ate," she sniffs, moving to the bedroom with the air of someone who has finished fighting. He follows and stands in the doorway smoking, watches her rifle through her prodigious collection of dresses. Where did she spend the night? he wonders, though not with the jealous fury she's tried to incite. Irritation, yes, but jealousy? No. The lack of it fills him with a vague sadness.

"Wear the purple one," he suggests, impatient with her dawdling.

"What's the rush?" The day yawns before her with nothing to distinguish it from any other day. She can't decide whether to put on her pyjamas or make a feeble attempt to outfit herself for the larger world. Johnny seems to want the latter, for whatever reason.

"I have a present for you," he announces.

From the inner sanctum of the closet Madeline's voice drips with insincerity. "Oh, Johnny, your very presence alone is enough of a gift." Immediately sorry, she pokes her head out of the closet. "What is it?" Curiosity is her olive branch. She's suddenly too tired to find clever ways to sustain the fight.

"You'll have to wait and see," he says. "Hurry up!"

"Why, is it a bomb?" she quips, pulling the requested purple mini-dress over her head. Slipping into clogs, she fluffs her damp hair, resentful of her genuine interest in the present.

"You're pretty funny." He blows a plume of smoke at her. "You should have your own TV show. Oh, by the way, your mother sent you a letter." He plucks a pale pink envelope from the corner of the bureau mirror. When she holds out her hand to receive it, Johnny lifts it high above his head, well out of reach.

"Well, give it to me, you too-tall sonofabitch!"

"Aww, Madeline," Johnny teases, pretending to be hurt, "I thought you liked it that I'm tall!"

"I like it when you're lying down," she says. "A rather

rare occurrence these days, won't you admit?" Johnny frowns, flings the envelope at her feet and storms toward the living room without another word.

"Good one, Madeline," she curses, putting the envelope in her underwear drawer, which reminds her that she isn't wearing panties. "Fuck it."

There's no need to open the envelope—Madeline already knows what's inside. It's a cheque. At this time of year it is almost always a cheque, sent from way upriver in St. Louis, the enduring residence of her mother, with whom she no longer has any contact other than these pale pink envelopes. In years past, Dianne Shockfire's annual bout of maternal longing had been satisfied by a gift of money and an accompanying letter sweet enough to cause cavities. Not so this year: her mother had added the unwelcome intrusion of a phone call, albeit on the wrong day. The conversation had been brief, and not only because Mrs. Shockfire had erroneously wished her daughter a happy fortieth. Madeline usually tears up these birthday cheques as soon as she receives them. Although this reaction has always piqued Johnny's curiosity, he knows that pressing Madeline for information about the silent feud with her mother is futile. "Where is it written that I have to adore my mother?" she's been known to seethe. "I don't, and never have. When's the last time you called your mother with any feeling other than obligation?"

As she puts on lipstick Madeline adds another resolution to her growing list. *Note to self: try to be more pleasant in the coming year.*

"I'm sorry for that last remark," Madeline says as she enters the living room, where Johnny sits primly on the sofa. "I don't know what came over me." Well, that's a lie. She knows very well what comes over her—and what doesn't. That they haven't made love in months, the exact number of which Madeline doesn't care to tally, is only part of the problem. The bigger problem is simply too big to face, and so she lashes out instead. She hates herself for making such comments, but like her mother before her, she has a sharp tongue that strikes before good sense prevents it. She can see it's too late now. Johnny stands at the door, a smile forced onto his lips.

Madeline's nervous feeling only increases as she follows him along Decatur. All traces of her recent triumph have dissolved. When it becomes clear that they're heading out of the Quarter, she demands to know why.

"We have to go over to Algiers," he explains. His mood lightens as he envisions her excitement when she finally discovers what her birthday present is. He's been beside himself for days with anticipation. And yet she seems deeply distressed when he tells her where they have to go. "Five minutes on the ferry," he says, taking her arm. "Honey, you are gonna die when you see what I have for you!"

I somehow wish I'd died this morning, she thinks, startled by the wave of self-pity. Does he know about the swim? Impossible. She follows him down the ramp to the ferry dock. Of course he doesn't know, she tells herself, though he does look like the cat who swallowed an entire flock of canaries just now. He's all smiles and soft chuckles and winks.

They ride across the water that she conquered only hours before. She keeps her eyes away from the windows as they make the crossing. This sudden trip back to Algiers

Point is creepy. Something about it feels like a trap. By the time they're back on solid ground, Madeline is profoundly shaken and insists that he take her back home.

"Just humour me, Madeline," he pleads. "Please, just this once, humour me."

"They said 'love, honour and obey,' Johnny. I don't recall a word about having to humour each other." They're passing by the Shore-Do and Madeline picks up speed.

"Let's go in there and have a coffee first," he says, pointing at the restaurant. "Build the suspense!"

"NO!" she shouts, grabbing his sleeve and tugging hard.

"But Madeline, I haven't had a single coffee yet!" He doesn't add that some people have already had their breakfast, or so they claim. He can see by the panicked look on her face that she won't give in. Her behaviour of late is nothing short of confusing. But his excitement about what he has waiting for her makes him more agreeable. He keeps walking, all the while wondering what possible reason she could have for wanting to deny him a cup of coffee. Tomorrow, when her birthday is "officially" over, he will demand to know.

"I love it out here," Johnny sighs as they make their way along the quiet streets, past well-kept houses of contrasting architectural styles—French, Spanish, Southern Gothic— most of them featuring compact but lush front-yard gardens and welcome mats. "We should move over here."

"You keep saying," Madeline mutters. "Who do you know over here, anyway?" The only other time Madeline has been to Algiers Point was for lunch with her old friend Rodney, rest his soul. It was Rodney who always said the Shore-Do's turtle soup was the best in the state. And whenever Rodney ate something he approved of, he'd lean back in his chair and shout, "Ooh honey, that's fuck-me fried chicken!" or "Girl, that's do-me-good potato salad!" Poor Rodney, she thinks, slowing down. Johnny turns to see what's holding her up. When she catches up with him she refuses to take his hand and waves away his inquiry about what's wrong. All she says is: "I hate my birthday—you know that."

"Not for much longer, you won't!" Johnny claps his hands together. "Here we are." He takes a ring of keys from his pocket. They're in front of a run-down building that, if it had ever seen better days, saw them long ago. Why Johnny has a key to this dump is incomprehensible. He struggles with the lock and throws the weight of his entire body against the door to force it open.

"All right, very funny, let's go." Madeline is fuming now, arms akimbo. Above their heads a dozen pigeons coo and scrabble around the ornate ledges. But Johnny has disappeared through the door and is waving at her from the shadows. The stench that greets her nose as she follows him is beyond repugnant. She hears someone coughing in what appears to be a hallway, and she begs Johnny to stop fooling around. But he's already making his way up a broken staircase ahead of her, holding up his Zippo like a torch, imploring her to hurry up.

After what feels like an interminable ascent, they reach the top floor, and Madeline again loses her temper as Johnny fumbles with the key to a second door. "I don't know what in hell you think you're doing or what your idea of a surprise is, Giovanni, but let me tell you something: I am too tired to play what's-behind-door-number-one, do you hear me? I mean, really, why can't we just go out for dinner like normal people? Why is my birthday turning into a goddamned treasure hunt?"

Johnny ignores her rant. He pushes the door open and steps aside with a gallant sweep of his arm. Madeline continues complaining about the smell, the dark, the potential for gangrene should one of them step on a rusty nail—the possibility of which is strong, she reasons aloud, pointing at the broken glass and splintered boards on the floor. Johnny watches her and grins. "Go on," he urges, giving her a light push.

"Jesus Christ."

Johnny steps into the room behind her and watches for signs of delight. He can see that she's put her hands over her mouth and that her eyes are definitely on her birthday present. He can't tell if she's crying or laughing; her body shudders slightly and she doesn't say another word. The Steinway baby grand sits gleaming on a platform across the room. It took some serious effort to get the damned thing up here, but he won't explain that just now.

"Pretty, ain't it?" Johnny says, reaching out to massage her shoulders. "Happy birthday, darlin'." She jerks away from his touch and stomps toward the piano. It's suddenly clear to Johnny that ecstasy isn't among her present emotions. He watches open-mouthed as she veers away from the piano and moves to stare out the wall of windows.

"River view," he calls out nervously. "Play something, hon!"

Her voice is flat and cold. "How the fuck did this piano get here, Johnny?"

He knows what she means but instead begins to describe the physical manoeuvres required to get it up to the top floor, no small feat and an operation that called for professional piano movers and, of course, a lengthy and expensive tuning. She listens without looking at him, and he eventually falls silent. In the empty room her footsteps echo as she crosses the freshly polished wood floor. She stops directly in front of him and squints up at his anxious face.

"How?" she asks, her voice barely audible.

"She called and uh ... she asked if I thought you'd want it. I said, of course you would."

Madeline gives a short cough of laughter. "You were both wrong."

Johnny rakes his fingers through his thick hair in frustration and tries to explain. "She said she's selling the house and won't have room for it where she's going. She said no strings, just take it off her hands, so ... I did." He fumbles for his cigarettes and sighs in defeat. The mournful look in his dark eyes keeps Madeline from voicing her full indignation. But her silence is almost more torturous, and after five long minutes, he begs her to say something. Anything at all.

"Thank you for your good intentions," she murmurs. "Let's go home."

"You're not even going to play it? I know the place itself isn't much, but I worked a deal with the landlord, rent to own. Hell, I could even open a restaurant on the ground floor. One day." He searches her face for signs of hope. Madeline stares through him, but Johnny keeps on, desperate to convince her of the greatness of it all. "I thought maybe one day we could even live here. Fix the whole place up. It's got a lot of potential. You can come here any time you like and play. I know you miss playing. You're good, baby! I've heard you with my own ears! I know you need something …"

Madeline moves back toward the piano. It's the very same baby grand that sat for so many years in the living room of the Shockfire household in St. Louis. And now here it is, by way of black magic. How pleased her mother must have been to arrange this little surprise. How delighted she probably was to talk to Johnny after all these years, thrilled to be in cahoots with Madeline's husband at last. No wonder Mother wanted to get rid of this instrument, thinks Madeline, she's always been happier playing the triangle.

When she left St. Louis many years ago, Madeline had vowed never to play piano again, and she hadn't. That is, with the exception of one regrettable night of showboating in a bar after too many cocktails. On that night she'd played for close to an hour, egged on by Johnny. He clearly hasn't forgotten the expression on her face as she hammered the keys, though he's mistaken the look of catharsis for joy. She can't blame Johnny for bringing this particular piano to New Orleans. He doesn't know the story behind it, and so he can't possibly know that it reminds her of her best memory—and of her worst. In his mind he's rescued a happy artifact from Madeline's adolescence. If only he knew.

"If I play it will you take me home?" Johnny watches her from across the room, his brows knitted with worry. He nods.

Madeline seats herself at the piano. Fixing her eyes on the river beyond the windows, she searches her memory for a short piece she can play without much effort. Touching her hands to the keys, she begins to play without allowing herself the luxury of a single clear emotion. The smile on her lips is for Johnny's benefit. When she finishes he claps and shouts, "Brava! Brava!" and assists her climb down from the platform. He's mistaken the song for one of her own compositions instead of recognizing it as the smattering of butchered Bach that it was.

On the ferry back to the Quarter, Johnny is full of hope. The fact that she agreed to play even one song on the piano is to him a promising sign. He chatters on about how she probably ought to practise during the daytime, when the light is more inspirational and the neighbourhood safer and on and on. How with enough practice she could probably record her own CD someday. He's bursting with plans for her musical future, and she listens numbly, realizing that the piano is just another swimming pool in the life of Madeline Elaine Shockfire. She watches Johnny's animated face as he describes the musical glory she might know with what he calls "enough work." Interesting coming from a man who calls in sick at least twice a month. She wonders why it never occurred to her before how much he reminds her of her mother. *People love me for what I do, or for what they think I might become.*

"How about some lunch?" he asks. "Country Flame?"

She shakes her head. "Really, John, I just want to go home."

Exasperated, Johnny says, "Madeline, please. I'm trying to make up for last night. Why won't you let me?"

She takes his hand and pulls him along. "That's precisely what I'm trying to do, Mr. Valentucci. Why else do you think I keep telling you to take me home?" Standing on tiptoe she gives him a kiss on the cheek and whispers, "Happy anniversary, baby."

"Happy what?" he murmurs, nuzzling her neck, thrilled

to have their old pattern back: fight, fuck, eat. What Johnny fails to see is that he's just blown a pleasing return to the good old days. Madeline pulls away and stares up in disbelief, and he realizes he's let go of the kite string of happiness yet again.

"Country Flame, did you say?" She abruptly changes direction and heads back toward Iberville.

"Madeline! I was just kiddin', honey. I know it's our anniversary! Shit, I was just trying to be funny." He tries to catch her but she's fast when she wants to be.

"Which one?" she demands.

"Which one what?" He thinks for a minute, then offers a hopeful guess. "Seventeen." Realizing his error, he changes tack and gives her a long, meaningful look. "I liked the other way we were walking better."

Madeline gives a bitter laugh. "Me too, but as the barroom prophets often say, 'John, you wanna fuck, you gotta eat.'"

Johnny nods, eager as a boy. "You're in charge, Madeline."

"Am I?" she smiles. "Good, then let's just eat and skip the sex. I'm tired."

"Nineteen, I should have said nineteen," Johnny scolds himself. "I meant nineteen, why the hell'd I say seventeen?"

BREAKING HER ORIGINAL VOW, Cleo heads back down to the river. It's daytime—what can happen? Mr. Time Machine wasn't at his usual table at Kaldi's this morning. Disappointed, she'd moved on to Café Du Monde. Now, strolling along the Moon Walk, she keeps her eyes on the swirling brown water to her right. In the distance she can see the Governor Nicholls Street Wharf, its hangar-like buildings looming pale green in the fog. She stops and stares at the sharp bend in the river just past the wharf. A cold, sick feeling swirls up in her stomach. She sits down on a nearby bench. The Mississippi is even more terrifying to contemplate in the daylight, when the lightened sky illuminates the whirlpools and sinkholes and rushing ribbons of current. The word *mesmerizing* thuds in her brain. She's heard it used to describe what happens to people who stare too long at Niagara Falls, though she hadn't understood the concept of aqua-hypnosis until now. She's never been to Niagara Falls and won't, she decides, be going there anytime soon.

Good sense shouts: Go home before you find yourself in there! There is no way on earth she survived. Something deeper than good sense whispers: It's me. I'm the reason bad things happen.

Here in New Orleans, the darker elements of Cleo's conception have never been clearer, her suspicion that she's to blame for unhappy events never quite so pronounced. I am a magnet for trouble, she thinks. I find it, or it finds me. Or, I cause it. If only I'd been conceived on a camping trip, or in the back seat of a car at a drive-in movie. I'd be normal, or at least have a normal life.

Her most recent brush with tragedy only serves to reinforce this lament. She takes one last look at the Mississippi River before hurrying back into the Quarter. You'll be fine, she assures herself. You're probably more like your father.

She hears the plaintive cries of the Lucky Dog salesmen and smells the seductive tang of cheap meat; sees the mustard-and-ketchup-coloured carts shaped like the wares they purvey. There's a sprightly patter of tap shoes on every corner, quite possibly the truest sound of the city. Bottle caps fastened to cheap running shoes, *ta-da-ta, ta-da-da-ta-ta.* Cleo watches as some boys ride up on bicycles, sees them empty the coin-filled shoeboxes at the feet of the young dancers into their own pockets. Doesn't anybody have a mother any more? she wonders, trying to direct her body toward Canal Street, toward the streetcar that would take her down leafy St. Charles, out of here and into something more genteel and old-fashioned, somewhere less malodorous and sad.

At a karaoke bar on Bourbon Street called Gigi's Three-for-One Pussycat, Cleo settles in to drink the first of three bottles of Budweiser that sit in front of her. The bar is morgue cold and hypermodern with its neon-and-chrome decor, but its lack of charm is rather welcome to Cleo. There's a definite shortage of willing songbirds on weekday afternoons. To avoid the remonstrations of the club's lonely host, Cleo hurries off to the bathroom before he can drag her up on stage and force her to sing. As she washes her hands in the grotty little sink, Cleo's eyes fall upon some graffiti that seem to have been placed there by the gods. In red blobs of nail polish the words seem prophetic: BE OBLIVIOUS.

MADELINE *WANTS* TO GO across the river and play the piano, but she can't quite bring herself to do so. Instead she goes downstairs to the Mint, feeds a handful of dollar bills into the jukebox and sits listening to "If I Didn't Care" by the Ink Spots over and over until Marcus begs her to play something else.

"I like it," she says.

"I used to like it, too," Marcus says, making a face. "Hey, how was your birthday? Are you forty yet?"

Madeline glowers. "No, I am not forty yet." She shrugs. "It was fine. Dinner, dancing, the usual breathless excitement."

"Didja get any?" Marcus grins, wiggling his eyebrows. He watches as Madeline frowns and returns to the jukebox, dollar in hand. Uh-oh, he surmises, guess not. He decides to change the subject as soon as Madeline returns to her seat. She's been touchy lately, he thinks. Must be something to do with Johnny V., or maybe the weather.

Madeline punches in her selection and surprises him by heading for the door, leaving him alone with yet another double dose of the Ink Spots.

"Serves me right, I guess," he says out loud, watching her pass by the window.

She stands in front of Aunt Sally's Praline Shop and watches the women inside boxing up candy. Shivers, because she herself used to be one of those women. Before she got fired, that is. Madeline has been fired from each of the half-dozen or so jobs she's held since coming to the city long years ago. Taking orders from other people isn't something Madeline does very easily. For the first few years of her marriage Madeline was the perfect wife, or at least a decent facsimile of one. She was everything her mother wasn't: faithful, selfless, reasonably domestic and content. She poured her excess energies into volunteer work, but even that had required a certain submissiveness she wasn't able to sustain for long. She'd helped out in soup kitchens, hospitals, had even done a stint reading books to the elderly at a home. She was good with people, or so some said. But taking helpful suggestions from sugar-voiced fellow volunteers annoyed her. And then there was the fact that everyone she tried to help reminded her of losses of one kind or another. She's had too much time on her hands for too long and knows it.

While other people are able to anchor themselves in work, Madeline hasn't had that luxury. Johnny supports her and has for quite some time. The cheques her mother sends can hardly be considered income, not once they're torn up into little pieces. The thought of her mother sitting at a little table in the living room writing out those cheques, year after year, sickens her. Guilt money isn't money that interests Madeline, no matter how large the sum. Money can't buy back all the time she spent swimming laps and choking down one grapefruit after another, nor can it purchase the sense of purpose that's been missing from Madeline's life for quite some time. No amount of cash in the world can erase her grudge against her mother, silly as it might seem. The futile years of swim training are only a small part of her resentment. The larger part is the way in which her mother—well intentioned or not—managed to meddle in every aspect of Madeline's life and yet never truly participate. But, had her mother not been as selfish as she was, as eager to preserve her own decadent leisure, Madeline knows she would never have met her first love. The Lord (my Mother) giveth, she thinks, the maxim lingering unfinished in her mind.

September, 1975
St. Louis, Missouri

The demands of Madeline's training schedule made it necessary for Dianne to employ the services of a full-time maid. She would be referred to as a "personal assistant"; Dianne felt the term *maid* only cultivated resentment in hired help. It was a mystery to Madeline why her schedule had any effect on her mother's life, since it wasn't Dianne who rose each morning at four, and certainly not Dianne swimming before and after school, struggling to complete homework in between. And yet her mother insisted that she was simply "exhausted" by Madeline's regimen.

Madeline supposed a person could become weary just talking about a thing. And talk Dianne did, if little else. While her mother seemed to be full of ideas about how Madeline should eat, dress and achieve success, she seldom came out to watch Madeline swim. And yet she could still say—without any apparent shame—that having a talented athlete in the house was running her ragged. Someone, she said, had to look after the little things. That someone was going to arrive any day now.

Warming to the idea, Madeline decided it might be nice to have someone else around, someone more consistently present than Mr. Oliver, who seemed to come and go according to Dianne's mercurial whims. There was a great deal that Madeline didn't understand about her mother's romantic life, and what she did know made her feel a bit ill. If Mr. Oliver thought he was Dianne Shockfire's only beau, he was kidding himself. The others—and there were quite a few—seldom hung around for long. Dianne's idea of sexual discretion involved asking her various paramours to park a few blocks away from the house. Despite Dianne's efforts to conceal her dalliances, Madeline did sometimes bump into her mother's nocturnal visitors. The most surprising of these prowlers was the woman who, tiptoeing out of the bathroom, introduced herself as Dianne's manicurist. Madeline wasn't so naive that she actually believed her mother had broken a nail at three o'clock in the morning or that such an event required urgent attention. When a man emerged from the bathroom a few seconds later, the woman said, "This is my husband, Darl. Darl, this is—" but Madeline had already fled. Yes, it would be a relief to have someone else in the house, Madeline decided, especially if it ensured a reduction in hallway traffic after midnight. She could only hope.

When Madeline came home from the pool one evening, she heard her mother's voice trilling out the family history from the parlour at the back of the house. Dianne loved to explain the absence of Mr. Shockfire in creative ways, and in this particular version he was convalescing up north, the victim of a terrible but undisclosed disease. Disgusted, Madeline crept past the guestroom, now lavishly decorated with fresh-cut flowers in vases she had never seen before. She saw that the "personal assistant" had already placed framed photographs on the bureau, that the bed had been turned down invitingly, and that the bedside lamps were aglow. She longed to sneak a look at the photographs but didn't dare to, for the voice of her mother spiralled up the staircase. Tired from a meet in which the Missouri Muskrats had placed second, Madeline hurried to her own room in order to avoid introductions. Her mother would not be pleased to hear about second-place finishes, and Madeline could not bear the thought of hearing about how the Olympics were just around the corner. In her hysterical conviction that Madeline was destined for glory, Dianne seemed blind to the fact that a person had to have desire as well as talent in order to qualify. Madeline was sorely lacking in the former quality, though she hid it well.

Upon entering the kitchen the next morning, Madeline was surprised to find her mother standing at the counter quartering oranges. It wasn't Dianne's usual habit to rise before the noon hour, and yet, there she was, cheerfully participating in breakfast preparations. The only other time her mother had shown any early-morning enthusiasm was when Madeline first began swimming, an enthusiasm that was to be as short-lived and random as her other gestures of support. In fact, Madeline had been relieved when her mother stopped getting up with her in the mornings after two weeks. Dianne's pre-dawn pep talks always had a counterproductive effect. Now here she was, up early again, making a big show of her role as loving matriarch, albeit one whose open robe gave onlookers a rather traumatic view of her breasts. Madeline had learned to live with her mother's exhibitionist pride in her own feminine bounty. She supposed she should be grateful that her mother was wearing anything at all.

The "personal assistant" seemed not to notice. She peeled potatoes and nodded as Dianne chittered on about the history of the house. Madeline was surprised to discover that the new assistant was very young. She'd expected a matron but instead found a person only slightly older than herself.

"Why, good morning, sleepyhead," her mother cooed, slashing away at the oranges. "This is Carmelle Sanchez-King, honey. Carmelle, this is Madeline Elaine."

Madeline winced and grunted a hello.

"Hello, Madeline," Carmelle said, her voice as smooth and buttery as her name. "Pleased to meet you." Dressed in a snug lemon-yellow skirt and short-sleeved blouse, she wore her hair in a tidy roll like a secretary from the forties. Madeline was instantly ashamed of her own shorn hair and exercise clothes. Her mother insisted on cutting Madeline's hair short and said that there was little point in wearing anything but the sort of clothes that could be pulled on over bathing suits. It struck Madeline as horribly unfair that the maid should be so beautiful when she herself felt plain and ugly.

Over breakfast in the sunroom at the back of the house, Carmelle described her childhood in Memphis and her previous job in St. Louis. Apparently Dianne had been generous enough to tempt Carmelle away from another employer. Madeline found her mother disarmingly conversational, given the early hour. It annoyed her that her mother seemed to hang on Carmelle's every word. Memphis had always been one of Dianne's least favourite cities, and yet now she could be heard offering to drive Carmelle home for visits "whenever it was desired."

"Carmelle isn't just a Negro," Dianne announced, "she's half Mexican. That's why she has such fine skin and wonderful bones."

Madeline blushed scarlet, but Carmelle simply smiled as her striking personal appearance was credited to one specific half of her mixed heritage. Madeline stared at her plate for the duration of the meal, even though she would have liked to look at Carmelle for a long time, without blinking. That her mother stared openly at their new assistant forced Madeline to do the opposite.

"Your mother tells me you'll be heading off to the Olympics one fine day," Carmelle said, and smiled, beginning to clear away the plates. When Madeline jumped up to help, Carmelle frowned and waved her away. Realizing that Carmelle didn't want to seem unnecessary on her first day of employment, she sat back down.

As was her common practice, Dianne refused to let her daughter answer, and launched into a detailed account of Madeline's aquatic prowess and the unusual childhood event that uncovered it. She spoke with vicarious passion about her daughter's gift for swimming, bragged about the private coach she worked with, said to be the best in Missouri, and on, on, on. She finished her speech by hugging Madeline and saying, "Madeline and I aren't just mother and daughter. We're best friends. Always have been, always will be, right, honey?"

Madeline nodded, uncomfortable in her mother's tight embrace.

"Carmelle and I are going to spend the afternoon going over the household accounts," Dianne explained. "You can get your lunch on your own, can't you, baby? Even though Carmelle here is a self-professed mathematical genius, it could take hours. You know what a mess Daddy's books are."

"Oh, yes," Madeline purred back, "a real mess."

As they left the kitchen together Dianne confided to Carmelle, "Madeline's father has left us in a bit of a state where finances are concerned."

"Yes," Madeline whispered to herself, "a state of absolute

wealth." She contemplated writing her father a letter to tell him about the new maid her mother had hired. Perhaps the news would make him angry enough to come back to St. Louis for a visit. She liked to imagine that her father would be against the idea of domestic help. It had been years since Madeline had seen or spoken to him. Eleven, to be exact. Her mother explained her father's seeming disinterest in Madeline's life by lighting a menthol cigarette and saying through a cloud of smoke, "Your daddy is a very selfish man, honey. I know it's hard, but try to think about something else." If Madeline complained about being tired, Dianne would narrow her eyes and say, "Now, Madeline, you have two choices. Do you really want to be a quitter like your father?" The suggestion being that Madeline's other option was to model herself after her mother. By the age of twelve, Madeline had decided to pick another role model. She chose the American swimmer Eleanor Holm, whose fondness for champagne and disregard for curfew got her thrown out of the Berlin Games in 1936.

In those early days, Dianne kept Carmelle busy with such pressing tasks as cleaning out closets—the doorknobs of which hadn't been turned in ten years—and sorting Christmas cards that spanned the same amount of time. At first Mr. Oliver still picked Madeline up early every morning and dropped her at the pool on his way to work. "Justice never sleeps," he'd say to Madeline, "nor does excellence!" His endless supply of corny maxims drove Madeline crazy, though she supposed she preferred Mr. Oliver's pre-dawn philosophizing to her mother's nagging. At least he could be trusted to talk and operate a car simultaneously without endangering the mortality of his passenger and half of St. Louis.

Within a few weeks of Carmelle's arrival, Mr. Oliver was informed that his livery services were no longer required. Carmelle assumed all chauffeur duties involving Madeline and her early-morning practices. By five-thirty each morning Madeline was seated next to Carmelle in the seldom-used Rambler. The car had been just one of the many possessions her father had left behind in his mad rush to leave the city. Although she drove without any seeming concern for the speed limit, Carmelle never shouted, Go, champ! as Mr. Oliver always had when Madeline climbed out of the car. She was likewise grateful that Carmelle refrained from honking the horn as Madeline slunk toward the pool. This happy arrangement helped her endure her strict regimen a little more cheerfully. She began to look forward to the car rides with Carmelle, even if the friendship Madeline had hoped for didn't seem to be developing. All that existed between them was a polite warmth. At first, anyway.

You have two choices, Madeline says to herself today. You can either get yourself a real job—or you can go over to Algiers and play that piano. She frowns at her reflection in the window of Aunt Sally's. I can't even take orders from myself, she thinks miserably, heading back to the apartment to wait for Johnny to come home from work. There's a good wife.

MERE DAYS AGO CLEO had been hell-bent on leaving town. But New Orleans doesn't let go of a person quite that easily, especially not once a visitor has passed more than two days in her loose yet seductive grip. Thus beguiled,

Cleo's assimilation has been swift. She's privately crowned herself Queen of Fun, the reigning monarch of the one-woman parade she calls her new life. At least, that's how she chooses to see it. In truth, she has trouble leaving her room in the mornings and supreme difficulty going back to it once she has emerged. A series of postcards documenting her adventures in the French Quarter fill her bedside table, cards that will never be mailed because she still wishes that her whereabouts remain a secret from her father.

Dear Daddy,
When I first arrived I wasn't sure I liked it here. In fact, I almost left after one day. Now I walk slow and eat heavy, just like the locals, and I LOVE it. I enjoy never knowing what might happen to me. I drink everything I can get my hands on—except bourbon, which doesn't agree with me for some reason. There's football on every television. Nobody here watches soc-cer, thank God. If someone asks for my life story, I ask them to tell theirs first. By the time they finish talking, they seldom remember wanting to know mine, which is good, because I'd rather not tell it, knowing it to be based on lies.

Dear Sadie,
I don't know how anyone could ever bear to leave this place! The air here is like a drug, and the light is unlike anything I've ever seen, so pretty it's almost unbearable. You were right when you said it seems like the kind of place where people come to forget

themselves. I'd sign my name but I can't remember
who I am! (Joke.)

P.S.: May or may not get to New York after this. May
or may not do any number of things: fly a kite, jump
in the river, rewrite Homer's Odyssey *for the sheer fun*
of failing. Who knows?

Sometimes the spatial limitations of postcards force Cleo to
use her notebook.

Darling Notebook,
Everyone who lives in the French Quarter has a
strange nickname: Rock 'n' Roll, Red Wine Linda,
Crazy Bobby Smash, a man called Miss Leon, grown
men who respond to childish names like Little Ray and
Shy Boy and Junior. Like inmates in a madhouse, they
seem to have named each other for the purposes of
easy identification. I sit amazed on the edge of this
menagerie from morning till night, doing my best
to keep my distance, though it isn't always easy.
Americans are so much bolder than Canadians when
it comes to asking questions. I find myself talking to
people here that I would run from at home; I get
drawn in even as I pull back. It hardly seems to matter
that most of what I hear is incredible in the truest
sense of the word. There is an ongoing theme building
all around me, a communal obsession with the one
that got away, the lost chance, the missed crack at the

*big time. The former lives of almost everyone I've met
get poured out by the third round of happy hour....
Speaking of which, will write more later....*

*Darling Notebook,
There are five men for every woman in this town.
Here, even I am considered attractive. Five blind men
for every woman? [illegible] Too drunk to write.
More later....*

In the mornings Cleo heads down to Kaldi's to drink coffee
and study her list of things she means to see. Promises herself she'll do it all tomorrow, or the day after that. The
Audubon Zoo awaits her, as do the streets outside the
French Quarter, the neighbourhoods beyond Canal that
she's read about but hasn't yet managed to get to. The Irish
Channel, Loyola University, Lake Pontchartrain—there's
simply too much to see. And too much to drink. "Sweet nec-
tar," she sighs as she lifts that first beer bottle each day,
"how'd I get this far without you?" The more she drinks, the
more certain bits of unwelcome knowledge begin to fade.

Last week, still unhappily preoccupied, Cleo finally got
up the courage to ask Mr. Time Machine about the obituaries. He'd sneered and said, "Why you wanna bother about
death for? It comes when it feels like it!" He then handed her
a cartoon clipping with a caption that read, *Who is this "me"
that keeps getting in my way?* and held out his hand for pay-
ment. She gave him a dollar and fled. In the days immediately following Cleo's unfortunate sighting, there'd been no
mention of any body found floating in the Mississippi—not

in the paper, not on TV and never among the omniscient Quarterites she encountered in bars. She laughs at herself for having been so uptight, so maudlin. Blocking out unpleasant thoughts merely requires a conscious effort to deny the unconscious: What woman? What river? What ghost of things recent or past?

On this, her second Saturday morning in the city, she emerges from her room at the Pommes Royales to find Mrs. Ryan pouring coffee from a silver service. The hotelier's face lights up when she sees her young guest, and she insists that Cleo join her for a cup of coffee. Cleo happily sits down at the wrought-iron table and picks up a croissant. Who couldn't like Mrs. Ryan? She peppers everything she says with endearments like *heart, chère* and *honey.* She says *leisure* so it rhymes with *seizure.* Two days ago Mrs. Ryan confessed that she, in addition to being the sole proprietor of the Pommes Royales, is also its lone chambermaid. As soon as she heard this surprising bit of news, Cleo had wanted to apologize for the scratches on the floor, but she hadn't been able to find the words. The scratches have since gone, but the guilt hasn't. Cleo makes a mental note to buy Mrs. Ryan a present—or, as locals say, "a prize." Who could leave a city where gifts are prizes, sidewalks are banquettes, where parades flood the streets at the slightest provocation? In Toronto a sidewalk is a sidewalk, and parades elicit nothing but traffic-related scorn and grumbling, as if getting to work on time were the most important thing in life.

"How're you getting on in this crazy town?" Mrs. Ryan asks, pouring Cleo a cup of coffee. "Sugar?"

"Just fine, thank you." *Was that an endearment or an offer of sweetener?*

Mrs. Ryan taps Cleo's notebook. "Off to write more poetry, I see."

Cleo blushes, wishing she hadn't filled out her guest registration card the way she had. In the space where it asked for her occupation, Cleo wrote "poet-chambermaid" in an effort to get her so-called new life off to a good start. As soon as Mrs. Ryan read that, she confessed with great excitement that she, too, is a writer and that she's been working on a novel for the last thirteen years. "It's about love," she said in a shy, breathy voice. When Cleo told her she thought that was a very good topic for a novel, Mrs. Ryan squealed with joy and offered Cleo a free night's stay at the hotel, adding, "We artists have to look out for each other! The world is a miserable place for the gifted, don't you find, Miss Savoy?" Cleo was then forced to confess that she did not yet know if she was gifted or not, having been more chambermaid than poet until very recently. "I've polished more floors than stanzas," she quipped, and then quickly explained that she had yet to complete an entire poem, in the hope of discouraging further literary discussion. Mrs. Ryan was not to be swayed.

"It takes time, Miss Savoy! Oh, I know they say Mr. William Faulkner wrote *As I Lay Dying* in six weeks or so, but let me tell you, it shows. I couldn't understand a word of it!"

This morning Cleo mumbles something about struggling with the question of whether to write rhymed verse, hoping to satisfy Mrs. Ryan's need to give advice on the subject of literature. A copy of the *Times-Picayune* lies folded to the Births and Deaths page. Cleo strains to pay attention to Mrs. Ryan, now making a strong case for rhyming verse.

"I mean, really, the music has all but disappeared from

the English language! Rhyming verse is our last hope. And opera, of course. Italian, now there's a language! Those people know how to string a sentence together. I don't suppose you've been to Italy, have you? I'm dying to go myself. Of course, there's just no way for me to get away, as long as I'm running this place. But if—I mean *when*—I get my novel published"—she gives a nervous whinny of laughter and continues—"*when* I get that first big advance, let me tell you, I am taking myself straight to Italy. Have you been?"

Cleo shakes her head. She wants to say, "I was conceived in Italy," but fears the endless number of questions her confession might inspire. Instead she says, "Do you mind if I take a quick look at the paper?"

"Oh, please do!" exclaims Mrs. Ryan. "Only, I'm afraid I've only got two sections left. The front portion's already in service to my parakeet, Judy, and a guest made off with the financial pages early this morning."

"Any section will do."

"Oh, here!" Mrs. Ryan beams and thrusts the paper at Cleo. "How about Births and Deaths? I read that page every day. I find death so inspiring, don't you? I mean, that's what it's all about, isn't it? We're born, we live, we die. Amazing. That's another thing I love about Italians—they get real excited about two things: babies and funerals. I suppose they like a good wedding, too. Everyone always talks about Italian weddings." Mrs. Ryan has worked herself into such a state of enthusiasm that she begins to fan herself with the Sports section. Cleo drops her eyes to the obituaries and scans the page, her heart troubled by a lingering, irrational fear of finding what she's promised herself she won't look for. Nothing. She exhales.

"My Lord, you looked like you were afraid somebody you knew would be in there!" Mrs. Ryan's face is earnest. "Do you have people here, *chérie?*"

Cleo shakes her head.

"Well, don't let me keep you from your work with all my prattling on. I'd better shake a leg!" She gives her lips a delicate dab with a napkin and pats Cleo's arm. "May the muse be with you, darlin'."

"And you," Cleo murmurs, watching Mrs. Ryan hurry down the corridor, chattering to herself like a manic hen. Who am I to judge? Cleo sulkily observes. I'm the one who thinks she sees women jumping into rivers after I've had a few cocktails. I nearly lost my whole vacation to a hallucination.

I wonder what astrological sign she was, Cleo thinks, turning to the horoscopes. This time she isn't thinking of the woman in the river, but of her mother. Mrs. Ryan's mention of Italy brought Cleo's mother to mind. Any time Cleo asked her father, "Where's Mum?" when she was a little girl, he'd say, "I've told you, she's in Italy, studying Art." Eventually Cleo stopped asking. It's always bothered her that she doesn't even know the date of her own mother's birthday. She reads the forecast for each sign, annoyed that the one for her own, which is Leo, promises nothing terribly exciting. "A pressing family matter," it says. Great, Cleo thinks, now I can feel guilty about leaving my father alone to run the hotel. Well, not alone. He has Sadie. Who does Cleo have? Nobody, and that's the way she likes it. If you don't play the game of love, you can't win—but if you don't play, you won't lose, either. Ladies and gentlemen, welcome to Cleo's Rules of Order. Step right up for pearls of wisdom based on limited personal experience. I need to find a library, she thinks.

I'm obviously suffering from some kind of intellectual deficit, a condition brought on by lack of reading material and too much booze.

Instead of seeking out the local library, Cleo marches straight to Faulkner Books and there spends money she'd planned to use for lunch. For some reason she feels the need to confess this economic truth to the proprietor as the woman rings in Cleo's purchases. The bookseller smiles and offers, "If anyone ever complains about my book fetish—and my husband often does—I just say: It's not a problem, honey—it's a lifestyle. You can eat anytime, but getting smarter's an *emergency*."

Cleo laughs in agreement. "Could I ask you something?" The woman nods, tucking a stray wisp of blond hair behind her ear. Cleo adopts what she hopes is a hypothetical tone. "I'm ... uh ... writing a poem, and I was wondering: if a person swam the Mississippi, what would her—their—chances of survival be?"

The woman regards Cleo with polite suspicion. "About as good as finding a sober citizen during Mardi Gras, I expect. *Not* a good idea."

"Oh, well, that's what I thought," Cleo blusters, tucking her paper bookbag under her arm as she heads for the door. "Thank you!"

"Come again!" the woman calls after Cleo, repeat business the least of her concerns.

VETERANS DAY IS AN OCCASION that Madeline has come to dread. To her relief, Johnny hasn't taken the day off as he has in years past. With luck he'll be too busy at the restaurant to engage in his twice-annual festival of self-flagellation. The other dangerous date is Memorial Day. All week long she's been steeling herself for the announcement that he simply can't go off and cook pasta at his cousin's restaurant on what is for him a painful and ugly reminder that he refused to go to Vietnam.

In fact, any subject connected to that war or any other is enough to send Johnny on a drinking binge that might last anywhere from a day to a week. That New Orleans is home to a large number of Vietnam vets is therefore problematic. Madeline has spent many nights steering Johnny away from fist fights and knife points and a great many more trying to convince him that he isn't the only man who ever declined to fight for his country. She tries to remind him that his choice to remain at home was based on deep convictions he held at the time.

Everyone has an Achilles heel. Johnny's is Vietnam. A youthful passion for peace has turned into a deep, relentless guilt later in life. He pretends not to feel anything when he sees the ravaged creatures who used to be high-school classmates. He avoids contact with anyone who even looks as if he might have participated in the war, which is foolish, because on more than one occasion Johnny has stepped on the equivalent of a conversational landmine after a few drinks and a bellowed opinion in the wrong company. It's Johnny's erroneous belief that all Vietnam vets have long hair and beards, and that the true source of a man's emotional scars is easily detected. She's tried to tell him never to judge a book by its cover, that the way a person looks or behaves isn't necessarily a guarantee of where they've been. Outwardly he seems to have no respect or sympathy for anyone who participated in the war. But on the inside is a heart that breaks every time Johnny encounters a man whose good intentions have left him incapacitated by what he saw or did across an ocean. A part of him is somehow deeply ashamed to be healthy and fine. His own present-day indifference to politics is surprising, considering that at one point he lived his life as if sit-ins and demonstrations and rallies were all that really mattered. That was well before he met Madeline, and before he laid eyes on the first of his friends to come home without the arms to lift a beer bottle. It's been years since Johnny read more than the Sports section of a newspaper, and although it shames him, he can't bring himself to change.

Satisfied that Johnny is by now safely at work in the kitchen of Papa Leone's, Madeline flips restlessly through the day's paper, waiting for her toenail polish to dry. She reads the social page with mounting ennui and flips to the horoscopes. "You will do well to break from routine on this seemingly humdrum Saturday, Scorpio. Family tensions build to the boiling point. Be generous, almost playful. Wear shades of green for an unexpected encounter."

Playful? Madeline thinks. She looks around the apartment she and Johnny have occupied for nineteen years, noting the stacks of unplayed records and piles of unread books. On this Saturday morning, Madeline doesn't feel particularly generous or playful. She feels like screaming. Scream, then, she thinks, but the *clop-clop* of a mule-drawn carriage passing on the street below makes her hesitate. She hears the driver shouting out the historical details of the U.S. Mint, hears his same old speech about the streetcar named Desire, mounted on blocks outside the mint in tribute to Mr. Tennessee Williams, the great bachelor playwright of the

South. She wants to run out onto the balcony and correct the driver by screaming, "Bachelor? Everybody knows he was a ho-mo-sexual!" *That* would wake the tourists up. But she lets the carriage pass by on its happy path of misleading information and removes the cotton batting from between her toes. She pads toward the bedroom, sighing in a way that would make Blanche DuBois proud. And then she gets an idea. *Playful, generous, shades of green*… She nods, devising a plan she feels will be guaranteed to distract Johnny from his Veterans Day funk and help to keep her from throwing herself off the balcony out of sheer boredom. Two birds with one dress, she thinks, pulling a sweater on over her slip. She stuffs some money into her purse and puts on a pair of well-worn pumps. Clatters down the stairs, hell-bent on making sure this particular Saturday will indeed qualify for the adjective *playful*.

She loves Sylvia's Côtérie Méchante more than any other boutique on Decatur Street. While many of the other clothing stores claim to sell vintage clothes, Madeline's trained eye can spot a knock-off or a mock-up at fifty paces. Sylvia deals in the genuine article, swooping in on estate sales like a vulture, before the soul of the deceased has even had time to consider which direction it ought to go. Her specialty is twenties formal wear and casual wear from the forties. Madeline has only ever seen the elusive Sylvia once, but this morning she sincerely hopes the formidable boutique owner will be too busy emptying some well-dressed dead person's closet to make an appearance in her own store.

She's in luck. The girl behind the counter is admiring herself in a mother-of-pearl hand mirror and fails to notice that a potential customer has entered the shop. Madeline moves to a rack at the rear of the cluttered boutique, scanning the other racks from her camouflaged vantage point. "Shades of green, shades of green," she murmurs, flicking through the dresses with a practised eye. She has a passion for clothes and yet no patience for shopping. The girl is still engrossed in her own reflection, and Madeline whispers, "Thank you, Narcissus," as she slips a bottle-green flapper's dress from a hanger and discreetly holds it up to her body. Too short? she wonders. Johnny used to say that her legs were her best feature, next to her face. The dress itself is short, but the diagonal spill of fringes will, she reasons, cover a multitude of flaws. She gazes down at her thighs to see if her recent swim has had any effect on her muscle tone. Playful, indeed. Madeline gives the sales clerk one last look and stuffs the dress into her purse. Be generous, she reminds herself, and moves to the counter and stands right in front of the girl.

"Hi," Madeline purrs. "I need to find a lorgnette. Do you have any I might take a look at?"

The girl blinks, cow-like, and stares at Madeline. "A what?"

Madeline points to her eyes and says, very patiently, "A lorgnette. You know, those eyeglasses on a stick?"

The girl frowns and pretends to study the contents of the display case under her elbows. "I don't think so," she says finally, shaking her head.

Madeline nods forlornly. "Well, thank you very much anyhow. I hope you have yourself a very playful Saturday."

"You . . . too," mutters the girl, thinking, Old people are so strange. . . .

There are still many long hours to go before Madeline

can collect Johnny from work. She's determined to get to him before he slips off to one of his post-work haunts and gets himself into a fight. Combine Johnny's political agitation with the usual hair-trigger vibe of a Saturday night and there'll be trouble. The trouble she has in mind for him is a much healthier sort. It has nothing to do with war and everything to do with desire. She still feels bad about the fact that she refused to go to bed with him over a miscalculation of the length of their marriage. She feels even guiltier for telling him she's been playing the piano every day this week while he's been at work, when she has done no such thing.

But tonight she's going to make up for those things and for anything else she might be guilty of these days. Shoplifting, for example, she thinks with a grin, letting herself back into the apartment. He still doesn't know about her little swim across the river, and that's the way she'd like to keep it. A person has to have some secrets, after all. In a Scorpio, the need for secrets is almost pathological. When he asked about her whereabouts in the early hours of her birthday, she told him she'd gone walking.

"All night?"

"Well, I stopped here and there for a drink." That had been dangerous ground to tread. She worried he might ask who she'd bumped into, and where, and at what time. It was too complicated to start naming names, so she'd taken a more reliable path. "I spent quite a while at La Coquette," she said, naming a gay bar she used to frequent with Rodney. "I was feeling sentimental," she said with a sigh, waiting for the conclusion of his interrogation. Rodney would have applauded her quick thinking.

"Well, at least I know you're safe from pick-ups in there!" he laughed. Bingo.

My God, she thinks now, pulling the dress from her purse and hanging it on the towel rack beside the shower to steam away the wrinkles. Lying, stealing, what next? Cashing my mother's filthy cheques?

CLEO READS THE NOVEL *Frankenstein* as she dines on smothered pork chops in the cozy front room of Fiorella's, a restaurant Mrs. Ryan recommends to all her guests. Cleo can see why: the food is delicious, even to her poorly trained palate. The famous tale of a monster man constructed from the limbs and entrails of corpses is perhaps an unusual choice of dinnertime reading, but Cleo has a strong stomach. She began reading the novel in a bar-laundromat where she washed a few clothes and drank Coke, and hasn't been able to put it down since. It feels good to do something other than listen to people's sob stories and bet on football, a game she still doesn't fully understand. She's promised herself that from now on she will drink alcohol only at night. Having already lost several afternoons to the powerful Dionysian forces of the French Quarter, she knows the jukebox selections in several different bars better than she knows the streets outside them.

In Toronto Cleo did a prodigious amount of reading. She read while eating and while cleaning the rooms at the Little Savoy. She'd perfected the art of reading and vacuuming, of reading and doing just about anything else in tandem. It was a habit that drove her father crazy but she couldn't help herself. Why it bothered him that she enjoyed books was a mysterious source of tension; Cleo didn't know that she had inherited this compulsion from her mother. Sadie's assistance with regard to reading materials was, in Cleo's childhood view, her most redeeming quality. She sneaked books to Cleo until she was old enough to venture to the library on her own. When she wasn't in school or at home, battling the incessant dust that plagued the hotel, Cleo was at the Yorkville public library. There she stocked up on novels, volumes of poetry and any story that featured orphans, with whom she felt a special kinship.

It was no small coincidence that soon after she learned to read, Lyle handed her a mop, the handle of which he sawed in half to make it more manageable. As Cleo's passion for reading increased, so too did the number of chores she was given. By the age of eleven she'd read the complete works of Shakespeare. At sixteen she'd announced that she planned to tackle Proust and so found herself swiftly promoted to the position of full-time chambermaid. Her father hoped her obsession with books would be thwarted by a lack of free time, reasoning that between school and cleaning up after the hotel's guests she'd be too tired to read. But the solution was clear in Cleo's mind; she simply dropped out of high school.

Cleo's raging bibliomania was only ever assuaged by a brief, dissatisfying brush with love. The alarming distractions of *amour fou* (and the sexy feelings that went with it) led Cleo to take up writing poetry in addition to reading it. The only way she was able to process her bewildering emotions—the most predominant being terror and lust—was to record them. The object of Cleo's virginal affections moved on, as involuntary muses often will, leaving Cleo with nothing more than one badly written play and a notebook full of illegible (and rather purple) poetic tributes to the joys and sorrows of love. She burned the notebook and returned to the safer terrain of reading but was mortified to discover that once the libido is awakened (and the heart along with it), it's awfully hard to put back to sleep. She'd thought a good dose of Chekhov would help, but as it turned out, even Chekhov had an unhealthy preoccupation with matters of the heart. The only writer who seemed to be able to take Cleo's mind off sex and romance was Ayn Rand. And now Mary Shelley.

AT HALF PAST NINE Madeline is ready to leave the apartment. She has everything a person could possibly need for a night of thrilling seduction: a bottle of chilled champagne wrapped in silk, smoked oysters and crackers, and a crowbar. She's packed these items in a not-very-fashionable duffel bag, over which she tosses a black lace shawl. Before going out, she picks up her atomizer and sprays herself with the same fragrance and in the same manner in which she has anointed herself for years: throat (left side, right), cleavage, then wrists. She'd be furious if someone pointed out that this is exactly how her mother puts on perfume. But the fragrance Madeline favours is Rocabar, a men's cologne imported from France, once worn by her daddy. The antique atomizer was a gift from Rodney. *How everything informs everything else.* She sighs, rubbing her wrists together. *Don't think about all that right now.* It's time to concentrate on being generous and playful, to focus on the silky swish of her new dress against her bare legs.

When Johnny's cousin tells her Johnny has taken the night off from the restaurant, she's not terribly surprised. Carlo is barely able to conceal his dislike for Madeline, even after all these years. Her apparent refusal to give Johnny a child is unforgivable in Carlo's strict Sicilian view of marriage; he also believes that if a man drinks too much, it is almost always because a woman drives him to it.

"Any idea where he is?" she asks, undaunted.

Carlo tells Madeline he has no idea where Johnny might be, as he glares at her outlandish outfit. She makes a point of wiggling her ass a little harder as she sails out of the restaurant.

It takes her a while, but she finds him at last, slumped over the bar at the All Saints Tavern. When Johnny sees Madeline he raises his beer bottle and flashes her a shit-faced grin. "Madelena! Ciao, bella!"

Funny, that grin used to melt certain parts of me. The rising disgust she feels as she moves toward him is troubling. *Generous, playful.* "Giovanni," she says, trying to muster a genuine sweetness, "how surprising to find you in a bar!" She kisses his sweaty cheek and ignores the bartender, whom she privately (and not so privately) calls Lena the Whore. "Drink up, Johnny. Did you forget all about the party? We're already later than even fashion allows."

"Johnny Valentucci!" says Lena, slapping his hand. "You didn't tell me you had to be somewhere!" Johnny kisses his hand where it stings and drains his bottle of beer.

"He always has to be somewhere." Madeline's smile is icy.

Lena isn't easily spooked. "Belated birthday drink, Madeline?" If the offer is meant to convey to Madeline that

Lena knows something about her life with Johnny, Madeline isn't biting.

"I don't remember no party!" Johnny pats the bar stool next to him. "Come have a drink with me, darlin'." Lena has already set down a snifter of brandy and Benedictine and another bottle of beer.

"Presumption is never very attractive," Madeline tells Lena. She turns to Johnny. "Let's go, John."

"He's had a kind of a rough night," Lena says, raising one knowing eyebrow. "A little chat with some former members of the military."

"So I didn't fight!" Johnny pounds the top of the bar. "I had GOOD REASONS! We had no business—" Reaching recklessly for his beer bottle, he nearly topples to the floor, then rights himself just in time.

Madeline avoids Lena's conspiratorial look and stares at Johnny, silently reconsidering her plan. She wonders if he's ever confided in Lena, if he's told her how he managed to avoid service in Vietnam. The truth is far less glamorous than risked imprisonment and demonstrations. Johnny's uncle was a doctor. He wrote an official medical report that would excuse Johnny from the draft. According to the report, Johnny had chronic asthma—always an interesting medical condition in a chain-smoker. She doubts Johnny has shared the truth of his deferment with anyone but her.

Against her better judgment, Madeline allows him to finish what would appear to be his dozenth beer of the evening. She sips testily at the B&B, enjoying it against her will, watching the coy way Lena fawns over Johnny without ever openly flirting. When her patience reaches its zenith, Madeline stands up and taps Johnny on the shoulder. He staggers to his feet and follows her out of the All Saints, blowing kisses at Lena as he stumbles.

It's crisp and cool outside the bar. A chilly breeze blows in off the Gulf. Madeline shivers and watches as Johnny attempts to tuck his jacket into his pants. Again her plan wavers. Somewhere inside Johnny is the playmate Madeline used to know and love and might want back again. *Generous, Madeline.* He asks what she has in the bag as she rummages through it in search of the blindfold her plan requires.

"Picnic," she says. "Bend down and hold still."

"Ooh, talk dirty to me, Mama!" he slurs, allowing her to cover his eyes and secure the knot. She takes his arm and guides him along the sidewalk in an awkward promenade. She leads him down one street and doubles back along another, hoping to both sober him up and confuse him about the direction they're heading in. When they reach their destination, Madeline tells Johnny to stand still and be patient for one moment more. The crowbar makes a loud squawk and the metal of the door screams against the iron hook. Once she's broken the lock, the door slides open with surprising ease. Madeline glances over her shoulder to make sure no one is watching and then pushes Johnny forward.

"What the hell?" Johnny caws as she guides him up the narrow steps that lead into that famous monument that decorates the lawn of the U.S. Mint, the Desire streetcar. She peers around again to make sure they haven't attracted any unwanted attention and gives him a rougher shove. He lurches forward, protesting all the way, but they are now inside the fabled streetcar, and Madeline is determined to carry her plan to its delectable end.

She pushes him to the floor between the narrow bench seats, and he curses as he bangs one knee on the way down. With some effort she manages to manoeuvre him until he is sitting facing her, the blindfold blocking his view. Madeline slips down between his splayed knees with a carnal giggle.

"Now, baby," she murmurs, tugging his fly in a southerly direction, "my name is Miss Blanche DuBois. *You* are Mr. Stanley Kowalski. And this," she says with a gasp of genuine desire, "is what we should have done in Mr. Williams's wonderful play."

"*Who?*" he says, clawing at the blindfold until it gives way. "I don't think we should be in here, Madeline!"

"Shhh, damn it!" she hisses. "C'mere, Stanley, and give Miss Blanche what she's been wanting all day long." Madeline bends down to kiss Johnny's stomach and he bucks backward. There is the horrible sound a skull makes when it smacks against a wooden seat. In his hysterical refusal to play along, Johnny has knocked himself out cold.

"John?" she asks, giving him a light slap on the leg. When he doesn't respond with anything but a faint murmur, Madeline curses and stands up, nudging him with the toe of her shoe.

"Owww," he moans, and then just as suddenly begins to snore.

This is what we call the straw that broke the camel's wife's back. It's all too much for Madeline's ego. She flees the retired streetcar and all that it implies, leaving Johnny to sleep off his drunk. A capable swimmer, Madeline is also a skilled sprinter and hurdler of objects. She leaps over and races past a variety of obstacles and never once stumbles in her blind trajectory away from the scene of her failed seduction. Blind with two parts shame and one part fury, Madeline exhibits an extraordinary, extrasensory feel for the whereabouts of comfort in the face of rejection.

Wear shades of green for an unexpected dip in the Mississippi.

CLEO WANDERS AWAY from the dining room at Fiorella's in a post-pork-chop haze and embarks on a search for a bar well off the frenzied path of Bourbon Street. She can't bear that stinking street and all its chaos, however festive its reputation may be. Everything about it makes her feel lonely and out of step, from the bleating bars to the girls in hoop skirts posed outside dubious restaurants. She tried to join its sociable mayhem early in her sojourn, but after one stroll up and one down, she still couldn't understand its draw. It's a street better left to the enjoyment of stunned honeymooners and groups of drunken friends.

The hour approaches eleven but she's not in the mood to return to her hotel. What she wants is a cold beer in a grubby, ill-lighted place. She chooses Hank's Bar on Chartres Street because she likes the masculine almost-silence of it and the apparent lack of appeal it holds for tourists. Its windows do not feature posters bragging of Hurricanes or three-for-one happy hours. It sits on the corner of Chartres and Dumaine and waits for the patronage of devoted locals or for thirsty, casual passersby to notice that it's open. Nothing about Hank's begs for business. Cleo found it during one of her afternoon strolls and instantly appreciated its fraternal atmosphere and the low volume at which the jukebox was set. It seems to Cleo to be the best sort of place in which to have a quiet drink and while away the final hours of a French Quarter Saturday night with Frankenstein as her most desired companion.

She takes a seat, orders and listens to some men farther down the bar discussing the sorry state of the NFL in voices charged with despair. She watches the bartender, a round-shouldered man whose unrelenting sense of ritual leads him to point one remote control at the jukebox and another at the television set above the beer fridge. It's as if everyone has received the cue to fall silent. All talk ceases and all eyes turn to the TV with almost religious reverence. Watching the late-night news is clearly an ancient rite here at Hank's. Cleo shows her respect by setting aside her copy of *Frankenstein*. She gives her full attention to the TV screen and wraps her hands around an ice-cold bottle of Miller Draft.

A man slips into the seat next to Cleo and she gives him a quick look. She sees the bartender lean across the bar and over the theme music of the nightly news hears him ask, "Who happened to you?" The man grunts and waves his hand dismissively. Nothing more is said. A beer thunks down in front of the new arrival, and the bartender returns his gaze to the TV, as if to set a good example.

A reluctant member of the congregation, Cleo sits through the day's national highlights, delivered by an anchorwoman with a bullfrog voice and fashion-model hair. Cleo marvels at the way the newsy words are fired out from somewhere deep in the reporter's throat, then volleyed with a surprising musicality, as if all bad news is good news to this woman. She segues from cross-country items to state politics and a recent scandal involving Governor X, Senator So-and-So and some missing funds. The names are meaningless to Cleo, who nevertheless pays polite attention as she absorbs nothing in particular. The current item causes every man at the bar to murmur and *tsk* under his breath. She begins to wonder if there might be a better place to read. The anchorwoman drones on about a reunion of offshore fishermen scheduled to take place the following week, a bit of news that seems to bore the newscaster as much as it does her unseen audience. Cleo gazes longingly at her book and finishes her beer, wondering if it would be sacrilege to leave Hank's before the news has run its course. She glances restlessly at the man beside her. He's got a nasty gash on the side of his head, a wound from which blood is oozing in a dark rivulet down his cheek. He isn't watching the news but seems entranced by the slow revolutions of his beer bottle, as spun by his thumb and forefinger.

"In local news," the anchorwoman says, in her deep and authoritative voice—there's a collective jolt of interest among the patrons—"Coast guard officials have pulled an unnamed woman from the Mississippi River tonight."

Cleo's eyes bulge and her ears ring as she stares at the television in disbelief. Without realizing it, she grabs on to the edge of the bar to steady herself. The film footage shows two uniformed men escorting the woman into a U.S. Coast Guard van, her face obscured by the blanket she's wrapped in. There's a quick blur of cheek and not much else as she tumbles into the waiting vehicle. Cleo's mouth goes dry as she watches and listens.

"A French Quarter resident, the woman was pulled from the midpoint of the river just under an hour ago. According to witnesses aboard the nearby *Natchez* riverboat, she resisted rescue. Authorities are treating the incident as an attempted suicide. The woman's name will not be released. No charges will be laid pending a psychiatric evaluation."

Cleo's heart beats a fierce tattoo: *That's her! That's her!* I've got to find her, she thinks suddenly. *Meet* her. She struggles to maintain control of her jellied limbs, to keep from slipping off her chair, to keep from crying out.

"Hey, Johnny V., ain't that *your* woman?" one man shouts.

"Yeah!" another chimes in. "She the only one around here crazy enough to be doin' that!"

The man next to Cleo stiffens but keeps his eyes on the TV. Over the din she hears him mutter, "Awww, hell."

A third man joins the chorus, pointing straight at her neighbour. "D'y'all see that cut on his head? Bet she did that, too! Whatsa matter, John, she catch you at the peeler bar again?" Every man in the place howls.

Cleo's neighbour sets his beer down hard. The men continue making suggestions directed at him. Johnny V. He flings some money onto the bar and scrapes back his chair. Wincing slightly, his eyes still on the TV, he stands, then turns and walks with exaggerated cool out the door. Some of the men whistle after him and others guffaw. "Poor bastard," someone calls.

The bartender shouts for them all to shut up and points a stern, pudgy finger at the TV, where the news is still in progress. Most of the men quiet down, though a handful continue to whisper and snicker like schoolboys. Cleo doesn't hear another word from the TV. She sits completely still, as if paralyzed, her hands pressed flat against the scarred wood of the bar. *Hey, Johnny V., ain't that* your *woman?* Why would someone even make that suggestion? And what of the inscrutable blame they placed on her for the cut on Johnny V.'s head? Cleo considers waiting around for further gossip, but it doesn't seem right somehow. She feels a curious loyalty to the river-swimmer and to the man the barflies have tormented with their gleeful, accusatory shouts. Cleo tears out of Hank's and peers up and down Chartres Street, but he is long gone. She curses herself for having dawdled, aware of a lost—if possibly misguided—opportunity.

This time when Cleo hurries down to the river she isn't following anything but her heart, which pounds in time with her feet. If there is sorrow in knowing that the woman has made a second attempt to drown herself, there's also something wildly comforting about the news of her existence. Her previous failed attempt is the most beautiful form of failure Cleo can think of. She hurries past the tarot readers who linger late in the shadows of Jackson Square and on past the bright conviviality of Café Du Monde. As she stumbles up the staircase that leads to the Moon Walk promenade, she isn't drunk on anything but hope. The heavy, sleepy feeling she had after dinner has been replaced by a feeling of weightlessness and a new kind of panic.

She stands shivering on the walkway that runs parallel to the mighty river behind Café Du Monde, staring till her eyes ache. One essential question pounds in her head with increasing urgency: *I want to know why you did it—and why you made me watch.*

MUCH TO MADELINE'S RELIEF, the psychiatric ward of Charity Hospital was full when the authorities—such as they were, those two young men whose coast guard uniforms could barely camouflage their inexperience—tried to have her admitted. She calmly explained to the fresh-faced officials that she had merely been trying to alleviate a persistent case of insomnia by getting some exercise in the form of a swim. Yes, she admitted, perhaps the river had been a poor choice of tranquillizer. No, she wasn't without remorse for the trouble she had caused: she would happily write letters of apology to anyone she had inconvenienced. Although they were suspicious of her unnerving calm, the explanation seemed to satisfy the two young men. Their shift was about to end; unable to admit her to the psych ward, they decided to drive her home after extracting a promise from her that she would never do such a thing again. Her promise was genuine, and the ride "home" was pleasantly devoid of further interrogation.

Which is how she's come to find herself stretched out beneath the Steinway baby grand in the studio at Algiers Point. From this curious position she can see a weak spill of moonlight on the floorboards, the Steinway's underbelly, and little else. Released from her wet clothes and shoes, she lies in a state of *au naturel* splendour, shivering only slightly. Well, *splendour* doesn't quite describe her emotional state— she wishes it did, but it doesn't. What she feels is that she has somehow (willingly) been escorted away from her life. The men who rescued her had pitied her, had expected her to feel ashamed somehow. She felt nothing but annoyed by the interruption of her swim but hid that fact to gain her freedom. They had also suggested, as if from a script studied in coast guard school, that she seek professional help. "There are medications for these kinds of problems," the younger one had said with a consoling smile. It had taken everything she had in her to keep from laughing in his face. Instead she had nodded, her smile benign and falsely appreciative. Seeing the dark windows of the warehouse, the men were concerned. "Anyone up there you can talk to?" the consoling one had asked.

"My husband," she lied.

The two officials nodded to each other and the other one said, "Oh, good!" as if the existence of a husband would cure any and all problems, at least until the right pills were prescribed.

Madeline feels the potential for incredible sadness and a lingering sexual frustration, but when she tries to pursue either emotion, they seem to dart away like birds. She sorely wishes that she were the kind of person for whom tears or masturbation provide relief, but she isn't. A barge on the river blasts its horn and she closes her eyes. It isn't death she's wishing for exactly but a long, long sleep from which she might wake to find herself living a completely different life. She doesn't usually indulge herself in lengthy contemplations of the good old days, but lately—and for this sudden onset of persistent nostalgia she blames her recent birthday—certain scenes from what she thinks of as her former life look pretty damned fine.

July, 1976
Atchafalaya Basin, Louisiana

Perhaps the most wonderful thing about cousin Henri was his seeming lack of awareness that the Olympics were taking place. The second most wonderful thing was that he asked no questions. Madeline appreciated anyone whose sense of propriety overshadowed any lurking curiosity. Ask me no questions and I will tell you no lies, etc. To Henri, Madeline was simply the long-lost (or, more accurately, the unknown) cousin, a wayward leaf dropped from the family tree, St. Louis branch.

Blond and tall, with pale eyes eerily reminiscent of Madeline's mother's (Henri's aunt), he welcomed her warmly over the phone and cheerfully agreed to pick her up from the bus stop in Henderson, Louisiana. It had been Madeline's immense good fortune that out of the twenty-eight LeFevres listed in the tattered phone book, she had chosen to call the nicest of them. Henri was also one of the few LeFevres to own a car that actually ran, the wheels of which had not yet been sold out of economic necessity.

As they drove through swamp country, Madeline took in all that she could of her mother's birthplace. She could see why a woman of her mother's social ambition would not have been happy here. Too many trees, too much exotic flora and slumbering fauna, not to mention some of the most peculiar roadkill Madeline had ever seen. Some of the roads they sailed past ended in swampy pools of water; alien-looking birds peered down from half-dead trees or swooped out suddenly from statuesque sugar pines. No, she could not imagine her mother feeling anything but desperate here, and thus Madeline felt an immediate affection for the place. Henri pointed out the house where Dianne Shockfire (née LeFevre) had been born and raised. He then tooted the horn at someone on the road who was, he said, a second or third cousin. Henri had an easy way about him, and although Madeline was unaccustomed to being alone with a man her own age, she felt surprisingly relaxed as they pulled onto a hard-packed dirt road that led to Henri's modest house.

She took a bath while Henri fixed them lunch in the nearby kitchen and felt very much at home as they sat eating on the front porch of the stilted house. Precious little was said at first and yet even the silence felt cordial. Henri seemed to sense that Madeline's sudden arrival in the area was a delicate topic. All he asked was "How long you planning to stay?"

"The remainder of the summer, if I may," Madeline said carefully, giving Henri a bashful look. It was an outrageous request, and she knew it as soon as it escaped her lips. But Henri just shrugged and said that would be fine, that she should make herself right at home.

"If you don't mind me saying so," he said, pouring more coffee into their cups, "you don't look a thing like your mother. I mean, from what I remember of her. Haven't seen her since she left to go up north with your daddy, mind you. How's she doing?"

"Thank you." Madeline beamed without answering his question. She settled back into her chair and gazed out at the yard, where every so often someone would drive up, honk and force Henri to jump up and sell one of the fishing nets he made himself. She'd noticed a sign at the end of the driveway advertising this service, but she hadn't supposed that Henri could really earn his living merely by sitting on his porch drinking coffee.

"I fish and trap and do just about anything to make a dollar," he explained when she marvelled aloud. "I do swamp tours, too," he added. "Twenty-five dollars an hour. A head, of course."

"Oh! Where do I sign up for that?"

Henri pointed in the direction of his truck. "Right over there. Come on, we'd better hurry if you want to see it in daylight."

Deeper into the swamp, Henri cut the motor and the flat-bottomed pirogue glided of its own accord beneath the low-hanging branches. They were far into the backwater now, sheltered from the still-hot afternoon sun and away from everything else on earth, or so it seemed. Here it was cool and quiet, the trees packed with creatures who had thus far escaped being killed and cooked. The water was thick with unseen snakes and fish whose presence could only be detected by the occasional sudden splash or swirl on the surface of the water. Out here Madeline's mother had no clout. Probably why she left, thought Madeline. She couldn't compete with the mute beauty of the place.

"This is the spot," Henri announced, dropping the anchor. He moved to the front of the boat, next to Madeline, who drank in his pleasant aroma of clean sweat and cotton. He rolled onto his belly and leaned far out over the bow, his long, slim thighs holding him in place while his arms reached out. He wet his lips and made a strange sound. Waited and made the sound again.

When the hulking beast smashed through the glassy surface of the water, Madeline's heart wrenched so terribly that she was sure she would never recover. The alligator shot up into Henri's face and pushed its snout within a hair's breadth of his mouth. With a swift forward jerk of his head, Henri kissed the snout and gave a little cheer as the alligator dropped back down below the surface of the water. Henri turned to Madeline wearing the grin of a conqueror, his crooked white teeth flashing joyously.

"That's how you call them," he said, resuming a seated position and recouping his natural modesty.

"Oh," murmured Madeline, who couldn't understand why anyone would want to call such a creature or why on earth they would dare to kiss it thereafter. They must, she reasoned, have a different sense of triumph down here.

"You try now," Henri insisted. It was clear from his expression that his opinion of Madeline rested on her willingness to try. She would have to disappoint him, however, or impress him some other way.

"I'd rather not today, if you don't mind," she whispered.

Henri scowled and shrugged as if to say it made no difference to him if she refused to partake of one of life's greatest pleasures. He had been calling and kissing alligators since he was six years old, but it didn't surprise him if a city girl like Madeline had no concept of the time-honoured tradition. He said as much and moved to fire up the boat motor once again.

"Wait!" Surely he wouldn't ask her to do anything that would endanger her life. More important, Madeline knew that her mother had probably never tried any such thing. She would try. Failure wasn't nearly as life-altering as she had been led to believe. She had failed to qualify for the Olympics by refusing to make the effort. Not trying could have longer-lasting effects, as she knew from recent experience both in and out of the pool. "I'll do it," she said. "Make the sound again?"

When she did it, leaned out over the water and tried it, even the bayou birds stopped to watch. She wet her lips and made a feeble attempt to mimic Henri's call. "A little farther—you got to hang out a little bit farther. Yeah, yeah,"

Henri coached her, putting his hands on the backs of her legs to steady her. Her bare ankles tensed against the cold metal of the boat as her muscles strained. If nothing else, she thought to herself, I have the physical strength to do this. She repeated the sound, letting it come from somewhere deep in her belly.

The alligator smashed through the water again, bringing its cold green jaws toward her. She resisted the urge to scream and reel backwards, closed her eyes and pushed her lips out and kissed. She felt the cold, rough head buss against her lips for a brief few seconds, tasted the slime and mud. The alligator mooed at her slightly before it slipped back into the murk, and Madeline stifled a yelp of amazement. She had done it! The thrill was greater than anything she had known in any damned swimming pool.

Henri patted her leg and hooted suggestively. "She liked you! Oh, she liked you enough to hope you'll come back some other time!"

Madeline reclined on the boat seat and widened her eyes. "How do you know it was a she? Mighta been a he-gator."

"It was a she. Shape of the head, look of the eyes. There's a difference. It's subtle, just like with some people. I mean, look at you with your short hair and baggy clothes. I could tell you were a woman from a long way off, but there's a lot of people might argue with that, from a distance anyway. It takes a trained eye, that's all."

Madeline gave him a faint smile and felt painfully conscious of her short hair, loose shirt and running shoes. She hadn't had the time or opportunity to transform herself from the athletic androgyne her mother had forced her to become into someone more recognizably female. Her mother had insisted she keep her hair short for swimming, had cut it her-self—"I'm a certified beautician in the state of Louisiana!" Dianne said over and over as she raised the scissors. Faced with the results, Madeline doubted that her mother's aes-thetic qualifications had followed her to Missouri. She had packed a few dresses, but they were still in her suitcase. These had been borrowed, or rather stolen, from her mother's trove of gowns. Not one of them seemed suitable for a summer spent wandering in bayou country, and so Madeline had emerged from her bath in her standard shirt-and-jeans ensemble.

"I didn't mean to insult you," Henri apologized, gazing at her from the bow of the boat. She was flushed for some reason, either from excitement or anger; he couldn't tell which.

They were drifting toward the shore and the quiet began to unnerve Madeline. But she was still energized from her brief encounter with the alligator and didn't want that feeling to fade. She gave him a sly smile and said, "Henri, please, I need some noise. All this quiet is making me nervous."

Henri offered Madeline noise. First he gave her the noise of music, amusing her with his attempts to play the banjo. Then came the noise of porch-swing springs, of hot breath escaping throats. He offered her this kind of noise, later that night, without meaning to. It was because she'd offered to trim his hair for him, and then because her hipbones had grazed his back as she manoeuvred the scissors. It was because she smelled so good to him when they were sitting on the dark porch drinking beer and listening to the sounds the night makes and doesn't.

She felt some urgent prowl in her skin and let her hand brush against his. More boldly, she took his hand and squeezed it with what she hoped he'd see as a meaningful degree of pressure. In the pitch black she made the alligator call he had taught her, and he laughed. He kissed her then, which surprised them both because it was such a foolish idea. He'd asked her gruffly, as she pushed her body eagerly against his, if she knew what she was doing. With the breathless voice of someone determined to continue, she said she knew very well. To prove it she pressed her hand against his bare stomach under his shirt, then reached for his cock. Henri made a muffled sobbing sound into Madeline's shoulder, and she felt a rush of sadness. It had been nothing like the first passion she'd known. Still, she refused to let him sleep, convinced that she would grow to like it. Henri told her she was far more dangerous than any alligator he'd ever kissed and she laughed, albeit nervously. When he knelt to drag his mouth down between her hips, she pulled at his hair and made him move back up to kiss her on the mouth. "Not that," she whispered. "Anything but that."

This amazed Henri, who, although he lived out in swamp country and wasn't a man of the world like some other men he knew of, had never met a woman who said no to that. But something about Madeline told him not to ask, and he didn't. As she drifted off to sleep with her back to him, Madeline still refused to believe that the alligator she'd kissed in the swamp had been female.

Madeline didn't stay in the Atchafalaya Basin for the remainder of the summer as she had planned. After a day of uncomfortable silence she asked Henri to drive her to New Orleans. He obliged, telling her she could catch a train back to St. Louis from there if she wanted to. She thanked him, knowing she would do no such thing. She had no idea what she would do. Madeline waved as Henri drove off in his truck, still associating sex with the word "Goodbye!"

Perhaps hoping to eliminate the farewell part of the equation, Madeline married the very next man she had sex with. She told Johnny about her experience with Henri in glowing detail soon after they met. It was one of the few stories of her past she shared with him. Johnny wrongly assumed that the incident with Henri constituted the whole of his wife's sexual experience. She didn't bother to correct this assumption, nor did she tell him that her heart—or what remained of it—actually belonged to someone else. The owner of Madeline's heart wasn't Henri but the person who had taught her to play piano, among other things.

CLEO HASN'T SLEPT since the late news confirmed the river-swimmer survived her first—and now second— attempt to drown herself. That her face had been obscured in the footage made no difference to Cleo; she hadn't seen the swimmer's face the first time. But Cleo was sure the woman shown on the news was the very same woman who'd leapt into the river in front of her. The strange reaction of the man they called Johnny V. only strengthened Cleo's conviction. Something in his body language told her he hadn't needed to see the woman's face to know it was "his woman." Then

again, he might have no connection to the woman whatsoever. It was possible that he was just a man in the throes of an
unhappy night. The teasing, quite possibly well off the mark,
might have annoyed him for any number of reasons.

After the newscast, Cleo had spent a good solid hour in
communion with the Mississippi, after which she retreated
to a table at Café Du Monde. She drank cup after soothing
cup of café au lait. A half-dozen beignets slid down her
throat like warm clouds. At three-thirty in the morning, covered from head to toe in powdered sugar, she returned to her
room at the Pommes Royales Maisonnettes. High from her
banquet of coffee and doughnuts, she wrote in her notebook
till the sun poked through the slats of the blinds. *If at first
you don't succeed, try, try again. Who are you? What makes you
so determined? So sure that life isn't worth living in this beautiful city? Stop, Cleo. Forget it.*

But Cleo doesn't have the luxury of forgetfulness. Not
now. The woman in the river, her identity and whereabouts,
are at the forefront of her mind. She plays what she has seen
and heard over and over in her mind's eye, like a film loop,
until she can't stand it any more.

The Voodoo Museum hasn't yet opened for business. She sits
on the front step, bug-eyed from lack of sleep. The idea of
visiting the strange little museum came to her as she strolled
aimlessly around the Quarter. Her spontaneous decision to
seek occult counsel reminds Cleo of Sadie's reliance on what
she referred to as "the magic arts." In times of despair, of
which there were many, Sadie shuffled tarot cards and studied her own palms. As a child Cleo suspected that Sadie had
special powers of divination that went well beyond a mere

interest in witches and spirits. There was no other explanation for her persistent reminders that there was a future for
Cleo beyond the walls of the Little Savoy, and a life that pre-
dated Sadie's arrival.

October 7, 1975
Toronto, Ontario

The dining room of the Little Savoy was decorated with tinsel, the shredded aluminum kind that Eaton's sold in large
boxes well before Christmas. Sadie loved tinsel; she said it
reminded her of Hollywood or Las Vegas. She'd never been
to either place but she watched a lot of movies and liked to
think of herself as a gambling woman. There was a big cake
in the fridge and a long list of things to do. Cleo grudgingly
began these chores, her dislike for her stepmother deepening
with each task. Her own birthday had never required so
much fussing, that was certain. Cleo wrestled with the
ancient vacuum cleaner and wished it could suck up Sadie
once and for all.

Her remaining duty on the list said: *Tell guests about
Sadie's party.* This one surprised Cleo. Beyond saying hello
and showing them to their rooms, Lyle avoided extraneous
contact with the people who stayed in his hotel. His disdain
for the increasingly motley crew of salesmen and drifters
probably stemmed from the fact that they reminded him
rather sharply of what the hotel was not, which was classy. In
any case, Sadie liked a crowd, a gathering, and so Cleo had
been instructed to invite every single guest at the Little
Savoy to dinner. There were three in total on the register, all

of them red-faced men who claimed to be in sales but seldom left their rooms. Apparently the number of bodies in attendance was more important than the condition of them. Cleo knocked lightly on each of the three doors and was relieved when no one answered. "Birthday party," she mumbled as she made her way from door to door, "please join us in the dining room." Having done her duty, she returned to the kitchen, where her father had left a mess of pots and pans.

Cleo was standing at the sink on her dishwashing stool when Sadie burst through the back door into the kitchen. She had obviously been to the beauty parlour: her hair was blonder than usual and swept into an artful pile on top of her head.

"You look a bit glamorous," Cleo said, trying to be nice. It was Sadie's birthday, after all. She was probably pretty upset about getting old.

Sadie was caught off guard by Cleo's pleasant tone and, as usual, spoiled it by rushing at Cleo to embrace her. Cleo bristled in her clutch and Sadie dropped her arms.

"We're going to have a medium here tonight," she announced, glancing at the Things to Do list on the kitchen table with pleasure.

"A what?" Cleo turned back to the sink.

"A psychic medium. Like a witch. She reads palms. She's going to be the entertainment at the party—isn't that magic?" Sadie nudged in beside Cleo and gazed into the mirror above the sink. She said to the mirror, and to Cleo, who glared back at her in its reflection, "Think up a good question to ask her about your future. It'll be fun!"

Cleo snorted. "I'll ask her when you're leaving, then!" She regretted it immediately, as Sadie's smile dissolved into a frown. Adults had a way of looking hurt that suggested imminent punishment.

"Maybe you shouldn't come to the dinner, after all," Sadie said, flouncing across the linoleum. "It's probably dangerous for a child to be around such powerful spirits anyhow."

I hate you, Cleo thought, scrubbing at the wet flour her father had spilled all over the counter. Still, she was curious. She also knew very well that her father wasn't going to prevent her from having dinner. None of the other guests were going to join them; Cleo's presence would be essential. She renewed her vow to try to be nice to Sadie, at least until tomorrow.

Lyle entered the front door in much the same way as Sadie had entered the back, in a gust of cold air and good cheer. He carried a sack of wine bottles and shouted his customary greeting down the hall: "Where are my duckies? Who's got my kisses?"

He hung up his coat with a flourish, nodding with approval at the tinsel-covered walls and at the presents piled high on the sideboard. Sadie made a dramatic entrance from the kitchen. Cleo rolled her eyes as she watched Sadie curtsy to Lyle.

"There's the birthday girl!" he cried, kissing Sadie noisily. Cleo snickered. Some girl, Cleo thought. She's thirty years old!

"Why hello, madame! You'll join us for dinner, I hope?" her father boomed, ruffling Cleo's hair as he moved past her to the dining room, where more tinsel dangled from the backs of the chairs and from the chandelier above the table.

When the guests in the hotel failed to join them for before-dinner drinks, Lyle shrugged and opened a bottle of red wine. He and Sadie spent the next hour emptying it while

Cleo sat on a footstool, flipping glumly through Sadie's most recent issue of *Chatelaine* magazine. The wine dwindled and Cleo's father leapt up to fetch another bottle. It wasn't a good sign. Cleo knew that the more wine her father drank, the less likely it was that supper would be eaten on time. Sadie pouted and sipped in silence while Cleo's father turned up the volume on the stereo in an effort to creative a festive atmosphere. The only time Sadie spoke was to protest the continuous playing of Neil Sedaka's song "Happy Birthday, Sweet Sixteen," which Lyle seemed to find funnier with each subsequent reprise.

It soon became obvious that no one on the guest register was coming to dinner. Lyle enlisted Cleo's help to carry out the food. There was a short flurry of activity as they carted out the charred roast of beef, boiled vegetables and potatoes. After that, the room fell into an uncomfortable silence, broken only by offerings of beef and carrots and requests to pass the salt, please. Sadie ignored the food on her plate and stared at Cleo from across the table.

"Isn't it funny how it always feels as if someone is missing?" Sadie asked, giving Lyle a meaningful look.

"Oh, well, we asked some friends to join us but they had other plans, didn't they, Clee?" Lyle continued heaping his plate with potatoes. "Just the family tonight!"

"Mmm," replied Sadie, picking at her burnt meat. She set down her fork with a faraway look. Drained her glass of wine and smiled at Cleo.

Hoping to liven things up, Lyle picked up his fork and held it like a microphone, leaning across the table as if to interview Cleo. "Hello, madame! And who would you be?" Cleo giggled and said her name. Lyle then pointed at Sadie and asked, "And who's this lovely lady across from you?"

"She's the woman from the boat," Cleo said. Sadie laughed self-consciously and tried to hide her irritation. That Cleo still referred to her as the woman from the boat troubled Sadie deeply. The atmosphere was far from cele-bratory, and Sadie began to regret her desire for a party.

Lyle frowned and set down his make-believe micro-phone. "Now, Cleo, you know very well who Sadie is. Don't be rude."

Cleo fell silent and stared at the tablecloth. It featured a pale blue map of Florida. Someone had sent it to them as a gift, but Cleo didn't know who. She didn't have aunts and cousins as her classmates at school did. And what was Hollywood doing on a map of Florida, when everyone knew that Hollywood was in California? Cleo scowled.

"Well, why don't we leave pudding for a bit, then?" Lyle lit a cigarette and motioned for Cleo to begin clearing the plates. She went with feigned reluctance to the kitchen, leav-ing her father and Sadie at the table. In truth she was happy to escape the terrible tension between them. She heard the murmur of their voices but couldn't hear what was being said. She puttered about the kitchen for as long as was possible, banging cupboard doors and scraping plates. When Cleo emerged from the kitchen, Sadie wasn't in the living room.

"Where's Sadie?" She joined father on the sofa.

"No idea," Lyle said. Cleo could tell her father was fight-ing off a bad mood, and she gazed longingly at the bookshelf across the room.

There was a tinkling sound at the top of the staircase and Cleo looked up. Lyle fought a smile and shouted, "Who's there?" He jumped to his feet and looked at Cleo with mock surprise. "Are you expecting anyone?" She shook her head and her eyes grew wide as she saw someone descending the staircase wearing a hooded cape and what appeared to be a thousand silver bracelets. When the person reached the doorway to the living room Cleo realized it was only Sadie, done up in spooky make-up with a huge beauty mark painted on her cheek. All Cleo could think was, She watches too many movies.

"Why, it must be the fortune teller, come to tell us of our future riches!" Lyle was enjoying himself again. "Do come in, madame! Cleo, make room for—I'm sorry, what's your name again?" he turned to Sadie.

"Madame Goodluck," Sadie said with a funny accent. She swept into the living room and swirled her cape around. In her hand she carried some kind of weed that smoked and gave off a peculiar aroma. Cleo supposed it was meant to smell good but it didn't. Sadie stuck it in the neck of the empty wine bottle on the coffee table and sat down.

"Well, now," said Sadie with great seriousness, "who's first?"

"Me!" Lyle insisted, settling in next to Sadie on the sofa. She nodded and took his hand. She squeezed it and studied it and turned it over to examine his fingernails, then flipped it back so that his palm was upturned. It took a long time, and Lyle grew restless. Cleo perched on the footstool, fascinated in spite of herself.

"Children," Sadie murmured, tracing her finger along a line on Lyle's palm.

Lyle laughed and shook his head. "Not bloody likely!" Sadie gave him a withering look and he fell silent. Cleo was horrified by the idea that there might be a baby in Sadie's stomach. She didn't like that possibility at all.

"How many?" Lyle asked, playing along.

"One," Sadie said, and continued to study his hand. "The one you have already. Here is interruption in your destiny. A sudden change indicated by break in the line, you see?"

Lyle raised his eyebrows at Sadie.

"But this is not to say you won't have opportunity to fix past mistakes before it is too late," she went on, her fake accent becoming thicker. "I see that good fortune will come if you are honest man, brave and kind, open."

Cleo felt bored. The game no longer seemed funny.

"Now ... sex," Sadie said, giving Lyle a meaningful wink.

Lyle winked back and quickly said to Cleo, "How about doing the dishes, hey?" She got up and sighed. "There's a good girl."

She knew it was Sadie's birthday and not hers, but Cleo didn't want to hear about new babies or the other mumbo-jumbo Sadie had muttered. And now they were going to talk about sex, which was all grown-ups ever seemed to care about, next to winning the lottery. Cleo frowned and climbed up on her stool for what felt like the ten-thousandth time. She filled the sink with hot water that burned her hands when she tried to pluck a dish out. It would be bed-time soon, and it was obvious that "Madame Goodluck" had no interest in telling Cleo *her* fortune. Just as she was about to despair completely, the door between the dining room and kitchen swung open, and Sadie appeared, still wearing her crazy costume.

"Come, Cleo, come sit with me," Sadie said, dropping her accent as she sat wearily on a chair at the kitchen table.

She rummaged in her purse and withdrew a deck of playing cards and a package of cigarettes. Cleo sat across from
her and watched as Sadie lit a cigarette and began to shuf-
fle the cards.

"What're you doing with those?" Cleo asked, prepared
for something related to magic and sorcery.

"Crazy Eights," said Sadie, shuffling them in a fancy sort
of way. "Do you know how?"

"I thought you'd tell me my fortune." Cleo picked up
her cards as soon as Sadie dealt them.

"Soon," Sadie said, lighting the cigarette clenched
between her teeth. "Here we go then, Crazy Eights."

"When did you start smoking?" Cleo asked suspiciously.
"Dad says it's a filthy habit for ladies."

"It is." Sadie puffed. "Never take it up. Let's play."

They played six games of Crazy Eights and two games of
Go Fish and something called Strip the Jack Naked that
made Cleo laugh. The dishwater grew cold and the dinner
mess remained. Cleo was less impressed when Sadie, again
using her accent, said, "Madame Goodluck sees bedtime in
your very near future." She glowered at Sadie and disappeared into her room just off the kitchen. Some fortune, she
thought, remembering that the birthday cake still sat
untouched in the refrigerator. *At least I got out of doing the
dishes.* There was a light tap on her door and Cleo sat up,
hopeful. Sadie asked if she could come in. Cleo shrugged in
response as if to say, Who cares?

"Fortune time," Sadie said, sitting down on the edge of
Cleo's narrow bed. She took Cleo's hand and turned it over,
just as she had done with Lyle's. She traced a line with her
fingertip. "You see this line?" Cleo nodded and tried not to

smile, because Sadie's polished fingernail was tickling her palm. "This is a journey you will take when you get bigger. Until then, you have to read as much as you can. As many books as you can, okay?" Cleo nodded again. Sadie said nothing more for a long time, taking in the small blond girl who eyed her with scorn. Cleo wondered why Sadie looked as if she might cry.

Instead she took Cleo's hand and pressed it against Cleo's chest, saying, "That's where people go when you can't see them any more. Always remember that, okay?" She touched Cleo's cheek and it tingled. It was a gesture that made Cleo forget her animosity toward Sadie for a moment. "It'll make more sense when you get older," Sadie promised, slipping from the tiny room as quickly as possible.

Lyle was working his way through a third bottle of wine when Sadie came to join him in the living room. She removed her cape before sitting down next to him. "Lovely child," she said. "I so wish she didn't hate me. Of course, I can hardly blame her. No one's ever bothered to tell her who I really am. I've half a mind to."

Lyle set his wine glass down roughly on the coffee table. "Don't ever start hinting around like that again. The past is past. That's the only way it's going to be around here, do you understand me?" He snatched up the wine bottle and moved to the doorway. "If you think I'm a bastard because I don't think she needs to know that her mother was a self-ish bitch, that's fine," he said through clenched teeth. "And if keeping your mouth shut is too difficult, then I think you ought to leave."

Sadie sat stunned. Lyle cursed softly and sat back down beside her.

"Please try and understand, Sade. Please. I want to forget. I know it seems strange, but I simply can't imagine telling Cleo about something I can barely understand myself. And besides," he said, taking her hand, "my life is here with you now, with Cleo. I promise you, I know what I'm doing, all right?"

Sadie nodded. *He's right, she may be too young.* After a long interval she said very calmly, "Lyle? In the future, if you're going to suggest that I leave, just be sure you mean it, okay?"

Hearing her father's footsteps, Cleo leapt away from the dining-room door and raced back toward her bed.

"Sadie isn't really my auntie," Cleo said matter-of-factly when he came to tuck her in. He didn't respond with anything but a kiss. She burrowed into her pillow and directed her next announcement to it. "I'm going on a trip one day, when I get big, and you can't stop me."

Lyle stood silently in the doorway with his hand on the light switch, trying to think of something to say. Instead he switched off the light and hurried away.

"I'm going to Italy, too," Cleo murmured. In the dark she felt a pang of sorrow, but she also felt as if she'd been given something very special: a sense of possibility. Because her cheek still tingled where Sadie had touched it, and because of what Sadie had said, Cleo reasoned that she couldn't be all bad. But maybe the stuff about a trip had been a lie, or a way to get rid of Cleo. But no, she decided as she drifted off to sleep, she was pretty sure that this time, for once, a grown-up wasn't lying.

"I wonder if it would be possible to arrange to meet with one of your tarot readers?" Cleo stands at the desk of the Voodoo Museum. The man behind the desk is tar black and handsome, with a friendly face and shiny bald head.

"It would," he says, his voice solemn. Cleo is the first customer of the day at the Voodoo Museum. He's always intrigued by the first person who enters the small, airless room where he has worked for many years selling gris-gris charms to tourists. In his experience, the first person through the door sets the tone for the day. This one is earnest, with eyes the colour of slate, inviting red lips, a nose that suggests French heritage, the forehead of a fiercely intelligent but deeply stubborn creature. Blond and almost boyish, but not without appeal. A natural woman, he decides, one who doesn't hide herself behind a mask of cosmetics.

Cleo, unaware that her physiognomy is being appraised, asks the man who she should talk to about having her cards read.

"Me," he replies, extending his hand. "Father Baby, at your service, miss." When he grins two dimples blossom deep in his cheeks. He presses the tips of his fingers together and rests his chin on them and nods, closes his eyes. "Let me guess," he murmurs. "You are seeking the answer to a question that pertains to romance. A passion." His eyes open wide. "I think love is causing you trouble."

Cleo laughs and shakes her head. "I'd really just like to have my cards read. In general."

"No one," he says confidently, "comes in here without a burning question. It never happens."

The door of the Voodoo Museum opens and two women enter talking at top volume. "Should I come back later?" Cleo asks, annoyed by the women's squeals of delight and disgust over the dried chicken feet displayed on strings by the door.

"Five o'clock?" he suggests. "It's much quieter then."

"Five o'clock," Cleo agrees, though she feels vaguely disappointed. She had hoped that she could get some answers—he'd been right, of course—sooner. The squealing women have moved closer, and Cleo has to squeeze past them in order to exit the museum.

Just as she steps out the door, she hears one of the women ask Father Baby if he can read her *turret* cards. Cleo hears him agree to do it right then and there. No come back later, no delay. She tries to see this disparity as a good omen.

A BUZZER SOUNDS and Johnny opens his eyes, bewildered. Has she finally come back? He sits up on the sofa, rubs his aching head, looks down in confusion at the striped pyjama bottoms he doesn't remember putting on. He looks every inch of the hell he feels as he stumbles toward the intercom. Damn her! He punches the button that releases the lock on the street-level door. The living room is a mess of crumpled cigarette packs, empty Dixie beer bottles and Styrofoam containers of half-eaten food. For a moment he contemplates trying to tidy up, then decides against it. Let her see the suffering she's caused, he thinks. He hasn't been able to show his face in a single Quarter bar in the last two days without being teased about his wife and her comical late-night dip in the Mississippi. It's been hard enough holding his head up while she marches around town wearing bizarre historical costumes that expose half her body, and now this?

Johnny is sure that if it was Madeline they pulled from the river, she wasn't trying to kill herself. Nobody who knows Madeline would believe that. Madeline is many things—crazy, moody, inclined to bouts of melancholy, sure—but suicidal? Her flair for drama would have required her to say something dark and foreboding well in advance. No, she wouldn't do anything that bizarre without a guaranteed audience. People still talk about her long-ago demonstration against the slaughter of alligators. She'd stood in the middle of the French Market wearing nothing but a bikini, a pair of rubber boots and a placard that read STICK TO CHICKENS! (This in reference to the booths that sold gator-on-a-stick to tourists.) That said, it isn't as if Johnny has been completely free of worry these past forty-eight hours. Naturally he's thought of her, wondered how and where she is. And even, in moments, with *whom*. But as for chasing after her, forget it. He knows this much: Madeline wants him to go crazy with worry; she wants him to drink himself sick while he waits. Apparently two days of silence have been deemed punishment enough. Hearing her footsteps on the staircase, Johnny casually lights a cigarette and waits for the showdown to commence.

There's a knock on the door and Johnny shakes his head. "All right, Madeline, I'll play along." He combs his hair with two long fingers, wishing he'd had a shower. "Who is it?" he asks, enjoying the game. Two can play, he thinks, taking a drag of his Camel Light.

"Dianne Shockfire," says the voice on the other side of the door.

Johnny freezes. Madeline's mother? His heart pounds like a Mingus tune as he butts out his cigarette and rushes around the living room trying to scoop up the detritus of his evil ways. He's a human hurricane as he snatches up pizza boxes and beer bottles and throws them into the kitchen sink.

"It is customary to open the door when someone comes to call!" shrieks the voice purporting to belong to Dianne Shockfire.

When Johnny opens the door, he finds a well-dressed woman holding a large parcel wrapped in brown paper, her face pale with indignation. Her resemblance to Madeline is startling. She wears orange gloves that match her shoes, not a good omen in 1995.

"You must be Madeline's husband," she says, giving him a good once-over. She takes him in, head to toe, and the look on her face indicates that she's less than impressed with her findings. Dianne seems to have decided that his physical self doesn't match up to his telephone voice. Under normal conditions, Johnny has a rather beguiling basso-profundo boom to his voice. Not today.

"Yes, ma'am," he croaks like a teenager. "Won't you come in?"

"Is my daughter home?" She tips up on the balls of her feet to peer over his shoulder.

"Not at the moment, ma'am." How right Madeline has been all these years, he thinks, how bang-on her unflattering imitations of her mother. "To be honest, I don't know where she is," he admits.

Dianne's upper lip curls slightly. "Some things never change. Well, Mr.—" She pauses and pretends to search her memory for his surname. He provides it and she smiles. "Valentucci, yes. Italian. Madeline has always loved exotic things."

She seems to reassess him now, and the heat of her gaze causes Johnny fold his arms over his chest like a nervous maiden. "Are you first generation?" she asks coyly.

He nods.

"Well, Mr. Valentucci—Johnny, if I may—it isn't particularly good news that brings me by today. I'm on my way to Florida for the holidays. My husband is waiting in the car." Her green-grey gaze is steady, so reminiscent of Madeline's that Johnny breaks into a fit of coughing.

Recovering, he gestures at the package in the crook of Dianne's arm. "Is there something I can pass on to her?" Judging from look of it, it seems to be some kind of gift, maybe a belated birthday present. Madeline's full name is typed out on a white envelope affixed to the brown paper wrapping.

Handing him the parcel, Dianne says, "How kind of you. I do appreciate it. I wouldn't count on her return, you know. Madeline has been known to cut people out of her life without warning."

"I'm not worried," Johnny lies.

Dianne smiles with what seems like genuine sympathy. Johnny hears Madeline's voice saying, *I wouldn't trust my mother as far as I could throw her—with my teeth.*

Sighing loudly, Dianne holds out a gloved hand. "A pleasure to meet you, Johnny. I wish I could say 'I've heard so much about you,' but of course I've heard nothing. I mean, beyond our brief telephone conversations about the piano. Did she like it?"

"She loved it," he lies again. "Probably over there playing it right now. She has a studio over on Algiers Point."

"Well, good! I should be running along, but I do want

to say one more thing about that *envoi*." She points at the box. "The contents are a little … upsetting. If you could make sure she's calm when you give it to her, it might be better. I'd wait to give it to her myself but—"

"Florida," Johnny says, and nods. "Would you mind if I asked what's in there that could upset her?"

Dianne waves her hand as if swatting at a fly. "Oh, well. Let me just say that death sometimes has a way of stirring up old, unpleasant feelings. Someone who was once very important to Madeline—and to me—has passed on. Someone Madeline was very fond of but fell out with long ago. I'm afraid I might've had something to do with their quarrel, but as far as I'm concerned, it's all water under the bridge. Madeline obviously doesn't share my philosophy of forgiveness. Her bitterness makes her difficult at times. But I'm sure you can attest to that, being married to her." A nervous laugh escapes Dianne's throat. "Anyway, the accompanying letter explains it better than I can. You will make sure she gets it? Sealed?" He nods. With a little waggle of her fingers she backs out of the door. "Goodbye, Johnny. I hope to see you again—soon."

Death? Old, unpleasant feelings? Johnny closes the door. He leans against the cool wood and realizes he's been sweating all through his surprise encounter with Dianne Shockfire. He's tempted to steam the envelope open to see what Madeline's mother has dropped off. He doesn't relish the thought of delivering what could be the equivalent of a grenade. Things are already screwed up enough between the two of them without adding this to the mix. Contrary to what Madeline believes about him, Johnny isn't completely devoid of curiosity. He simply believes in the lost art of privacy, even where his wife is concerned. If she has something to tell him, he reasons, she will.

He sits down on the sofa and smokes. Stares at the large, flat box and groans as he envisions handing it to Madeline. The angry embarrassment he feels over her little river swimming stunt is tempered by the creeping fear that she could very well be that unhappy. Whatever's in the letter Dianne mentioned isn't going to help, he can tell that much. The fact that Madeline's name is typed rather than written by hand seems more than a little strange. He glances at the clock and for the first time in ages is happy to realize he has to go to work. She's fine, he tells himself as he pulls on his jeans and runs a comb through his hair. He feels pretty certain that she is, at this very moment, sulking in the studio on Algiers Point. Sooner or later she'll emerge, ready for a fight and yet sorry to have worried him. If she hasn't come home by tomorrow, Johnny intends to pay a visit to Algiers. Whether he'll take the package with him is still up for debate. He leaves it sitting on the coffee table and promises himself that he'll clean the apartment just as soon as he gets off work.

SHE TAKES A CIRCUITOUS ROUTE along the riverfront, cutting up through the Faubourg Marigny and doubling back. Just in time, she thinks, watching Johnny's departure from across the street. Catching her breath, she waits until he has disappeared from view up Governor Nicholls, late for work as usual. Barefoot and wearing the same dress she's been wearing for two days now, she crosses Esplanade and marches through the door of the Mint, straight to the bar.

Marcus looks up from slicing lemons and limes and grins. "Hey girl, I hear you took a dip in the mighty Mississip'!" After a pregnant pause he asks, "What happened to your hair?"

Madeline has no time for chit-chat. She asks Marcus if he still has the spare key to her apartment. He nods, offended by her brisk all-business attitude. She thanks him and winks. "You didn't see me today."

"I didn't?" he asks. "Oh, I get it. I saw you but I didn't see you." He winks back and whispers, "What're you up to, honey?" but she turns and rushes out of the bar without answering.

The apartment is a pigsty. Madeline smirks at the mess and hurries into the bedroom. The bed is made the way she usually makes it. He hasn't been sleeping in it, she observes, rifling through the closets and drawers like a thief, collecting some clothes and underwear, her perfume. She lifts the cut-glass bottle to her nose and sniffs. Is about to spray herself when she realizes that the cologne might hang in the air and betray her sneaky return. She wraps it in some lingerie and tucks it in a canvas bag along with the waterlogged shoe from her only triumph over the Mississippi. Like a true bandita she scoops up some money that is scattered across the dresser, retrieves her mother's cheque from her panty drawer. *I must've known I'd need this one.* She tiptoes back out to the living room, then on toward the bathroom. Here she takes a quick but thorough bath using Johnny's mild soap and an already damp towel. She hadn't considered the studio's lack of sophisticated plumbing when she so hastily retreated to it. The dehydrated toilet, rusted bath and dysfunctional sink have definitely complicated her recent ablutions. Thus her fugitive's bath in the place she once called home. She doesn't stop to ask herself how and when she'll ever manage to bathe again. Knows only that she can't use the bathroom at Bill's Bar for much longer, at least not without compromising her standards of personal hygiene. In the bathroom mirror she sees exactly why Marcus expressed concern about her hair, but there isn't time for vanity now.

Once she's back in the living room, her eyes fall on a paper-wrapped parcel on the coffee table. She sees her own name typed out in full on the label: Madeline Elaine Shockfire. There's no indication of where the package came from. The envelope looks legal, imposing. Has he been to a lawyer already? she thinks, vaguely impressed by Johnny's uncharacteristic gumption. What grounds could he possibly have for divorce? Contempt begins to swirl through her. Would divorce papers even come in a packet that large? It seems unlikely, but Madeline tucks the package under her arm and gives the room a last look. She slips out the door and smells a faint waft of Estée Lauder Youth-Dew on the landing. I'm going nuts, she decides, spooked by the ghostly aroma of her mother's perfume. She takes the stairs two at a time, rattled by what she believes to be an olfactory hallucination.

"Back again?" Marcus quips as she hands him the key. "I know, I know, I didn't see you. Twice I didn't see you. Well, I hope whoever he is, he's rich!" As she moves away from him Marcus calls out, "It's about that hair, girlfriend! And that swim! We need to have coffee!"

As she hurries down the street in the direction of the ferry dock with her personal effects in hand, it occurs to Madeline that this hasty visit to the apartment might prove to be her last.

A DISSATISFYING FORAY into the kingdom of the occult, with Father Baby as her Virgil, has left Cleo blue. Dark blue.

Examining the spread of tarot cards he'd laid out with impressive care, Father Baby—or Père Bébé, as he sometimes referred to himself, and in the third person, no less—insisted that matters of love and sex informed Cleo's unspoken questions. "Père Bébé sees evidence of a love in vain," he murmured. "But Father Baby is also excited by the delicious presence of a new and intoxicating love in your immediate sphere." Nothing she said would sway him from his conviction that her heart was troubled by some *amour* whose ragged departure from her life had created unfinished karmic business. In some skewed way, he wasn't far off the mark. Unfinished business was indeed part of Cleo's preoccupation, and the fixation definitely involved another human being. But she refused all suggestions of lovers past, present or future as possible fuel for her quest. And now, three long days after her less than illuminating experience at the Voodoo Museum, she's still refusing it.

A more sexually seasoned person might have recognized that Father Baby, with all his talk of healing, catharsis and magical oils, was in fact coming on to Cleo as he examined her very near future. Her refusal to recognize gestures of desire from anyone, male or female, made her blind to the psychic's overtures. And so she is blue, and ashamed of herself for having placed too much hope on one form of divination, or on any form of divination at all. Why, even Sadie might have been wrong about the life-altering possibilities of this trip. Today Cleo sees the distinct difference between optimism and true psychic ability, and thus plunges into a state of despair as soupy and pervasive as the fog outside her window. Still, it's hard to let go of her fantasy: that she will one day meet the woman who jumped over her into the Mississippi River.

The downside of obsession is that it sometimes casts a person into a crippling state of torpor and inactivity. Fixations of this kind aren't good for the tourist trade, since they tend to keep sufferers locked up in their hotel rooms where they may or may not indulge in moping and looking up "key" words in the dictionaries they just happened to bring with them on holiday. Words like *exile, serendipity, catharsis* and *limbo.* The upside is that obsession, as experienced by a poet, almost always stirs the creative juices, especially when combined with the aforementioned study of dictionaries and aided by a large supply of pens. Cleo has written seven villanelles and four sestinas since waking. She'll write several more poems before the day is through, and she will not be the first poet in the history of the trochee and the iamb to flog a dead thematic horse. That she's written eleven poems addressing the same subject (death) with little variation beyond that which defines a sestina or villanelle (its structure) doesn't matter. What's important is that Cleo has started and brought to a state of rough completion a number of poems, her first such efforts since adolescence. She's oblivious to the glory of her return to poesy, caring only for the relief that comes of filling the pages of her notebook. Her only revelation regarding poetry is this: Death is a topic far more fecund than love. She has never written with such abandon.

At two o'clock in the afternoon, she tumbles out of her room and onto the rain-washed cobbles of Royal Street, hungry and disoriented. Like many poets before her, Cleo wears her physical hunger on her face in the form of a stunned frown. Trudging toward Esplanade, she is deaf to everything save for the sound of her own verses as they repeat themselves in her head. Thus, she doesn't hear someone behind her mutter, "S'cuse me," although she does see a body pass through her peripheral vision and enter her immediate view. A man. A tall, dark-haired man with a long back. He seems familiar. Cleo squints, not because her vision is defective, but because this is what she does when she is trying to recall something or someone. Her cognitive powers have been greatly diminished by lack of food and the discombobulated state that comes of hours spent writing poetry, and so she does not recognize Johnny V., the man who fled Hank's Bar.

By the time she realizes who the man is, he has turned down Esplanade Avenue. When Cleo herself reaches the corner of Royal and Esplanade, Johnny V. has disappeared from view. She looks up and down the leafy road, furious with herself for not possessing the mental recall that would have allowed her to— What would it have allowed you to do? she admonishes herself. Say hello? Good afternoon? I don't know if you remember me, but I'd like to meet your wife?

Still, she's spotted him at last, strolling along Royal Street in the afternoon, has seen him turning down Esplanade. The thrill of his proximity lifts Cleo's bleak mood considerably. Where there is Johnny V., there might well be Johnny V.'s woman. And then what? *How will you even know it's her, unless he's with her?*

I won't. It occurs to Cleo that she may well have walked past the river-swimmer ten times in the past few days without knowing it. Bodies pass each other all the time and never meet. "S'cuse me," he'd said, overtaking her on the sidewalk. It was a kind of interaction.

Forgetting that she's vowed to avoid sitting in any one place for too long, Cleo decides that the very thing to do is to sit in Hank's Bar for as many nights as it takes to run into Johnny V. again. Surely he doesn't always go out without her. Or maybe that's the problem, the source of the river-swimmer's despair. He goes out *without her*. Every night. She feels abandoned, desperate. Cleo's sympathy for Johnny V. slips a notch, leans toward the woman whose dangerous swims may have a motive other than the pursuit of death: attention. I'll find him, then her, Cleo vows, completely ignorant of the fact that she is, this very moment, standing right outside the place where Johnny V. lives, at the corner of Esplanade and Decatur. Cleo chews her lip, then heads toward Fiorella's, where an oyster po' boy and a cold root beer will be as ambrosia, a little sustenance for the hunt. Cleo Savoy—poet-chambermaid and now poet-detective.

COMPLETE WITHDRAWAL FROM the human race isn't as easy as it might seem. Because even if you decide to hole up in an abandoned building with nothing but a good piano that you refuse to play and an assortment of your favourite dresses, and even if that building is situated in a neighbourhood where nobody knows you, you'll have to interact with other humans eventually. A pressing and inconvenient need for food arises, as do the myriad other things a person can't—or shouldn't try—to manage without, at least not in a large city with a poor safety record and a bone-chilling autumnal dampness. In his mad rush to provide her with a studio, Johnny seems to have forgotten about little things like heat and light. In her own frenzy to set up house, Madeline has been forced to cash her mother's cheque.

No, Madeline hasn't exactly been without human companionship during the early part of her self-imposed exile. While she isn't averse to the idea of taking all of her meals at a nearby bar, it does expose her to the general population. There are other realities she's had to face, too. For example, that a thirty-nine-year-old person, no matter what good shape she may be in, cannot endure many nights of sleep on a hardwood floor without risking spinal trauma. This revelation forced Madeline to order a bed. Much to her chagrin, the bed couldn't deliver itself, and so she had to interact with the two men who carried it up the three flights of creaking stairs. That their efforts put the men's lives at some risk couldn't go unacknowledged. She'd bantered with them for a few moments, irritated when the younger of the two seemed reluctant to leave. "Total babe," she'd heard him say loudly to his partner as they made their way down the staircase. All Madeline could think was, Away with thee!

Then came the small matter of darkness. Madeline has no tolerance for the dark, at least not indoors and in solitude, and dark is what it gets in her new home shortly after seven o'clock in the evening. There are only so many candles a person can burn and even then there's only so much heat that can be generated by those candles. And so matters of light and heat intrude and force Madeline to tramp down to the public telephone at Bill's Bar to request a visit from NOPSI, the official civic purveyor of light and heat of the electrical variety. Whether or not the decrepit building can be plugged in is a matter currently up for debate.

Madeline stands by as the NOPSI representative taps the walls and inspects the cobwebbed outlets. She chews her nails as he sighs and frowns and shakes his head and mutters cryptic things about the fire marshall. Then, in a complete turnaround, he announces that he will indeed be able to offer Madeline light and heat if she wants it. To herself she can't help thinking, Naw, I didn't really want electricity. What I really wanted—and have wanted all my life—was to meet a real live electrician. She does not say this, however, but thanks him effusively and asks about the possibility of an immediate hookup.

"You got a phone?" He gives a doubtful look around the room. She shakes her head. He shrugs. "Tomorrow morning all right?" She nods. One more night in the dark and damp won't kill me, she reasons. Few things can, it seems, if her recent swims in the river are any indication.

The question of arranging for a telephone isn't a question at all. She doesn't want one and has no intention of making or taking any calls. From anyone. The telephone has never been an instrument of anything but misery in Madeline's view, and she's thrilled to be able to choose, at last, to live without one. Coping—or trying to cope—without a functioning bathtub or running water is a whole other challenge she'll face tomorrow.

After a light lunch at Bill's Bar, where she says nothing more than what's required during such transactions, Madeline returns to the studio to revel in its silence. This lasts about fifteen minutes. A knock on the door startles her. Without thinking, and in defiance of the first rule of solitary living, she opens the door without asking who it is. She shouts at the little balding man who stands before her with a wicker basket in his arms, "How the hell did you get up here?"

The baby-faced man is taken aback but then quickly thrusts the basket at her. "Welcome to the neighbourhood, ma'am! Please accept this basket of non-alcoholic jam and preserves as a welcoming gift from the Algiers Point Neighbourhood Betterment Association." He wipes his forehead with a hanky and gives her a hopeful smile. She glances at the basket in her arms and back at her peculiar visitor. "It's all non-alcoholic," the man repeats with obvious pride.

"Well, I appreciate that," says Madeline, "because I am so tired of getting drunk every time I eat my toast in the morning."

The man gives her a curious look and backs away ever so slightly. The nervous flutter of his hands tells her that his prepared speech hasn't yet ended and she waits, deeply amused. He clears his throat and begins. "We at the association would be more than happy to show you around the neighbourhood. Please also consider joining the association yourself. The APNBA seeks to protect and maintain our community and the Christian values that have made Algiers Point a fine place to live for many years." The man expels a small puff of air, relieved to have concluded his spiel.

"Yes," Madeline says, "I was reading just the other day that Algiers was where the sailors used to come to find whores and cheap liquor and jazz. Tell me, are *those* services still available?" Madeline leans on the doorjamb and rocks the basket of preserves like a baby, fighting a grin.

"Well, uh, welcome to the area, Miss—?" He waits, then

goes on when Madeline does not oblige him with her name. "I hope you find what you're looking for here in Algiers. Good afternoon."

It's all he can do to keep from running, Madeline thinks, watching him hurry down the half-lit hallway. She closes the door and shoves the basket of jam against it for good measure. Wonders again how the man managed to get through the downstairs door, then remembers her downstairs "neighbour," the individual whose nocturnal comings and goings she has noted with mild alarm. She's never seen him (or her? or them?) but decides that whoever it is has a bad habit of leaving the door propped open in order to receive guests.

The stark room unsettles her when she turns to face it. The late afternoon sun bounces off the black piano and spills across the sheetless bed. The sterility of it all is unnerving. She hadn't expected to miss her cluttered existence with Johnny. She had no appreciation for the comfort such domestic disarray could offer. The room is cool and she remembers that she still has to purchase an electric heater, some sheets and blankets for the bed, a few other little odds and ends that she's lacking. And so, although she has wanted nothing more than silence and the opportunity to sit mute for days on end in complete solitude, Madeline decides to take one more trip over to the Quarter. She doesn't possess the energy to explore the commercial offerings of her new neighbourhood just now, and besides, it might be nice to have supper somewhere other than Bill's Bar. And the Shore-Do, even with its delicious turtle soup and fine jukebox selections, simply will not do, at least not at this time.

A WOMAN AT THE OTHER END of the bar has a greasy chicken drumstick in one hand and a Calvin Klein advertisement, obviously torn from a magazine, in the other. From where Cleo sits she can see that the photograph features one of Calvin Klein's signature pretty boys, all hair, eyes, lips and porcelain skin. The woman has affixed the picture to a piece of cardboard and she regards it lovingly as she gnaws on the drumstick. And then, with her mouth full of chicken and her lips dripping grease, she kisses the photograph with tremendous passion, leaving a stain behind when she finally, reluctantly, pulls away. Cleo looks around to see if anyone else in Hank's Bar finds this spectacle as amazing as she does, but the two other patrons are too busy drinking themselves blind to notice. To Cleo's further surprise, the woman retrieves a second drumstick from her purse and repeats her act of passion, this time giving the photo a long, canine lick. For a brief moment Cleo wonders if this woman is *that woman*. It's possible, but instinct and the presence of the bartender soon chase the notion away.

"'Nother one for ya?" the bartender asks. Cleo tears her eyes away from the woman and nods. He delivers a second bottle of beer and gestures toward the woman. "That's Marcy. She's got a new man every week." He leans his elbows wearily on his side of the bar. "Where you from, darlin'?"

"Canada," Cleo says. Marcy barks that both she and her papery escort need another drink, and the bartender sighs and moves off. Cleo hears him tell the woman that she better not get grease all over his bar. The woman flips up her gnarled middle finger and he throws back his head and laughs.

"No wonder she ain't got a real boyfriend," he says as he

resumes his former position. "How about you, darlin', you got a boyfriend back home?"

Cleo shakes her head and wants desperately to ask about Johnny V. but doesn't want to pose such a question right after admitting she's single. The bartender might get ideas. But his erroneous assumption could work in her favour.

After a long pull of beer she makes her inquiry. "Do you know the guy they call Johnny V.?"

"Yup." The bartender looks interested and vaguely surprised. "You know Johnny?"

Cleo shakes her head. "Only to see him."

"All the ladies notice Johnny, that's true. Thing is, he's married, and he even acts like it, most days. Who knows why? Lots of people think he's crazy for putting up with that wife of his for so long." He jerks his thumb at Marcy and winks. "She's just about that crazy, is Johnny V.'s old lady."

Cleo's heart pounds a little faster. How many questions can she safely ask without seeming too interested? "Have they been married a long time?" she ventures.

The bartender smiles slyly. "Yup, that particular civil war's been goin' on a long, long time. Years. I guess they like to fight, else they wouldn't stay together. You know how it is."

"Oh, yeah," Cleo says, knowing nothing of the sort. "I'd like a shot of bourbon, please."

"Well, all right, darlin'. Comin' right up." He takes a bottle of Wild Turkey down from the shelf behind him, and Cleo's stomach gives a frightened lurch. "Don't you worry about bein' alone your whole life through," he says as he sets the glass of bourbon in front of her. "You're a pretty girl, somebody'll come along. Somebody who isn't married."

The somebody Cleo wants to have come along doesn't appear, and she sits in Hank's Bar until long after the late news has aired. The evening bartender is replaced by another man. The first barkeep wishes her a good night and tells his successor to look after her. Cleo has had six bottles of beer and two shots of bourbon. She's played "Free Bird" on the jukebox four times at the request of the new bartender. She's lost all hope of running into Johnny V. tonight, of ever running into him. Even the woman whose greasy kisses fell on paper lips seems to have had the sense to go home.

As she makes her way back to the Pommes Royales, her head spinning and her heart leaden, Cleo curses herself. "It's the bourbon," she says aloud at the door to her room. A banana leaf scuttles across the courtyard stone in reply.

She lies on her bed, hoping the ceiling will soon stop spinning. "M-i-s-s-i-p-p-i," she chants out loud, too drunk to realize that she's spelled it the way some people say it.

HAVING LINGERED OVER A spontaneous dinner with Marcus, she's missed the last ferry back to Algiers Point, and so Madeline heads toward Hank's. She enters the bar carrying a plastic package of bedsheets, a pillow, one bulky duvet and a rather unwieldy electric heater. The overnight bartender furrows his brow. "You get thrown out of a slumber party or something?"

"That's awful funny," Madeline says, her voice dripping with sarcasm. "As it happens, the quality of department-store shopping bags isn't what it used to be." She looks at the clock above the bar and groans. There are still many hours to go before the ferry resumes service. "I'll have a double B&B

straight up. Please." After a few delicate sips, she cocks her head to one side and asks, "Has my husband been by tonight?" The bartender shakes his head. "Good," she nods. She walks over to the jukebox, habitually selecting "If I Didn't Care" by the Ink Spots, as well as a half-dozen other songs. Plunks herself down in the seat previously occupied by Cleo and prepares to wait out the long night. As she nurses her drink, Madeline's ears dine on an aural banquet of musical selections featuring voices guaranteed to arouse complete and total angst: Stevie Nicks, Koko Taylor and Nina Simone.

JOHNNY, NO LONGER ABLE TO SIT upright at the bar where he, too, has been consuming his share of the neighbourhood liquor supply, swerves out the door of the All Saints Tavern and lurches down St. Philip Street. He's been drunk for days now, a binge ignited not by anything war related but by the realization that "someone" has stolen the package Madeline's mother asked him to deliver.

Upon making this alarming discovery some nights ago, Johnny flew out of the apartment, intent on paying a visit to Madeline in Algiers Point. It was 1:00 a.m. when he decided to make his brave pilgrimage, but the cessation of ferry service at midnight posed a small problem. Johnny decided that a better course of action was to have a drink— just one—at the All Saints Tavern, ostensibly to collect his thoughts (or dispense with thoughts altogether). Lena was behind the bar, as usual, and Lena's not the kind of woman who believes in serving anyone just one drink, especially Johnny. Noting his anxiety, she proceeded to do the one thing she knew how to do best, which was to get him stinking drunk on a variety of specialty shots. This in the hopes that he would confess his troubles or declare his undying love, whichever came first. Everybody knows sweet liquors loosen the tongue.

Lena also knew from certain other observant citizens of the Quarter that Madeline and Johnny were "having troubles." This was nothing new, of course, but the fact that Madeline had also been spotted aboard the Canal Street ferry, heading in the direction of Algiers, had given rise to new and exciting theories about a potential and long-anticipated marital break-up. To Lena's disappointment, Johnny would admit no such thing. He did, however, pay a number of subsequent visits to the All Saints, where he pursued a state of serious intoxication each time, a pattern that only served to solidify Lena's theory. Like any hopeful suitor, she's decided to wait and see.

Johnny's anxiety over the missing package is justifiable, but Madeline hasn't actually opened it. It's sealed and sitting on top of the Steinway, gathering dust. All Johnny knows is that Madeline has been to their apartment and removed it. His perpetual drunkenness and inability to confront her might even seem forgivable in light of the fact that he's like a man waiting for a bomb to go off.

CLEO IS SUFFERING FROM that peculiar type of insomnia that only the drunk can understand. Drunk, but not quite drunk enough. Tired, but not quite tired enough. She turns on the bedside lamp and decides to write until she's managed to quiet her manic mind. Slumped over her notebook, she scrawls words she believes to be fine examples of the elasticity of the English language.

So fuking drunk rite now. This place so amazingly spooky I can't believe I'm hear, can you? I may never lea—this pen sucks!—Toronto: cold place were I wasn't born and should never go. . . . [illegible] Where are you, swimmer-lady? [cartoon of drowning woman] "Help! Help!"

"WHAT TIME DO YOU FINISH?" Madeline leans over the bar. She's enjoying what is commonly referred to as a second (or third, considering the hour) wind. Night has at last become morning, but only just.

"You makin' me an offer?" The bartender pushes a coaster toward her and winks.

"Yeah. How about you watch my stuff while I run a little errand?" She winks back in an exaggerated, vaudevillian way.

"Sure, whatever." He reaches out to accept the strange assortment of bedding. Shakes his head as he hoists the electric heater over to his side of the bar. "I'm outta here at ten," he warns. "Don't you dare make me late for breakfast!"

"I owe you." Madeline smiles, all business with a hint of sugar. "Be back soon."

The fog is still riding low in the streets as she hurries up Dumaine to Burgundy and across to Conti Street. Common wisdom generally discourages a lone person from entering the St. Louis cemeteries, Numbers One or Two, even during the day. Her sojourn at Hank's Bar, waiting for the ferry to resume service, gave Madeline plenty of time to think. Among the many items on her food-for-thought menu was the notion that she should be grateful, very grateful, to be alive today.

Under the influence of the spiritual properties of the Benedictine, she can think of no better way to express her thanks than to visit the grave of the renowned voodoo priestess, Marie Laveau. She has no interest in joining a gaggle of wide-eyed tourists, and so the early hour lends itself well to a solo pilgrimage. Having navigated the river twice without losing her life, Madeline feels a little charmed this morning. Some would call it tempting fate, but Madeline sees it as a way to guarantee the continuation of her lucky streak. She has already decided never to swim the river again.

The cemetery is usually inaccessible at this early hour, but someone has smashed the lock. She sails on through the Basin Street gate of St. Louis Cemetery Number One without pausing to cross herself. Blessed be the rebels, she thinks.

What she's doing is crazy, not to mention dangerous, but Madeline has realized that the less sensible she is, the more invigorated she feels. She barely recognizes the woman she's been for the past nineteen years—and she's in no rush to let complacency run her life again as she marches forward. The cemetery is silent and washed with the strange light that is given off by the greys and whites and faded browns of the stone monuments. The grave of Marie Laveau isn't very far. Madeline sees it and yet chooses to walk in a different direction, away from the shrine. She loves the mourning chairs, how they wait invitingly, pale silver or rusted, off-kilter on stones in front of the raised graves. It's an elegant touch not to be found in any northern graveyard. Chrysanthemums wilt on every grave, leftover tokens from All Saints' Day. The wind brings with its cool blast a sudden, faint swirl and hum of harmonica music. Madeline begins to stalk the eerie song, losing it and finding it on the breeze that sails over and through the tight labyrinths of graves. As though commandeered by a mischievous musical poltergeist, the mouth-harp gives a loud blast and then falls mute.

She trips over a piece of tipped slate on the path and imagines she's been pushed from behind. Her heart races but there is no one—at least, no one she can see. She shivers and is about to reconsider this spiritual stroll, when the harmonica bursts into song again from behind a tomb nearest the lakeside wall. She pushes past her fears toward the source of the music. She is surprised enough by what she finds to suck in her breath and hold it—and hold it some more.

By the back wall of the necropolis, a creature dances maniacally between two much-abused tombstones. Its humped back is turned, and even when it spins round—his, her—its head is bowed at such an extreme angle that the facial features are entirely obscured. Whatever it is, male or female, it dances and spins again, playing the harmonica hard, embodying each frantic note with jerks of limb and torso. On the ground surrounding the graves, bouquets of flowers lie trampled and ripped, as though torn apart by a wild animal. When the creature—now discernibly human and female—suddenly stops dancing and playing, Madeline ducks behind a crumbling monument and continues to stare, transfixed.

It seems the woman has finished her *danse macabre* and is preparing to leave. Transformed by a grin, the dark face reveals a breathtaking beauty. Her shaggy head tilts skyward and she mops her sweaty brow with a bright orange rag. As if hearing some silent accolade, she bows deep and curtsies to the graves on either side of her. She gathers the massacred flowers into a heap and kneels, kissing the shredded petals with great ceremony. It's unclear whether she knows her gestures are being admired. Standing to her full height of not more than four and a half feet, she snaps her bright rag at the air in front of her and spits.

"This for the dead *only!*" she says, her eyes fixed on the gravestone Madeline hides behind. She puts her harmonica in her back pocket with the gravity of a gunslinger. A wild laugh erupts from somewhere deep within her; Madeline's skin pebbles with alarm. The woman turns and scales the back wall of the graveyard in three nimble movements that suggest previous experience with the climb. Madeline is unable to move, and she stares at the wall for some long minutes.

There's no need to pay homage to Marie Laveau now. Madeline walks past the famous grave without giving it a glance. If her accidental viewing of the woman's dance for death was meant as a warning, she isn't taking it as such. Although she hadn't come looking for creative inspiration, she's found it. She thanks the musician under her breath and hurries out of the cemetery before Fate and Destiny can introduce her to their ill-tempered sister, Reality.

Now Madeline's only goal is to collect her things from the bar and get back to the studio at Algiers Point as soon as possible. The fog has melted away; the tepid sun pushes through the clouds. She expresses her gratitude to the bartender at Hank's Bar by buying him a drink and says a quick hello to a couple she and Johnny used to socialize with in the early days of their marriage. Back when she still liked spending time with them, Madeline had called them the Two-Headed Calf because they were never apart. She still thinks of them as GusnDeb, all one word instead of two separate names. Johnny said she was just jealous but Madeline had never envied their twinlike unity; in her mind such perpetual togetherness seemed a little unhealthy. Co-dependence wasn't something she and Johnny could brag of, not lately.

"Come over sometime!" Deb cries, and Madeline thinks, I'd rather eat a live snake, as she struggles to squeeze out the door of the bar with her heater and bedclothes. At this rate it'll take her four hours to get to the ferry dock. She goes back inside the bar and asks the morning bartender to call her a cab.

"Where to?" he asks, phone in hand.

"I'd rather not say," says Madeline curtly, glancing at the other patrons who line the bar with their cups of coffee and shots of whiskey.

The bartender scowls. "They're going to ask. I have to tell them something."

Madeline rolls her eyes and says loudly, "All right, if you must know, I'm going to visit my secret lover in Gretna. Happy?" She turns to see GusnDeb looking shocked, gives them a wide smile and waves until they look away, two pairs of eyes with the same basic sentiment glittering in them: *She's no good.*

"Dispatch said you were going to Gretna," the cab driver complains.

"I know. The world is an unpredictable place. People change. Algiers, please."

The river far below the bridge looks pale yellow, almost white from this vantage point. Madeline is relieved to know she will never swim the river again, believing as she does that she has found the perfect substitute. Things are looking up. She can barely wait for the cab to reach the studio, then for night to fall, and not just because she has new sheets.

SOME DETECTIVE, Cleo thinks, glowering. Some poet. A review of the pattern of her days: Kaldi's in the morning; Café Du Monde in the afternoons; Hank's Bar at night. A wander to the river; a meal wolfed down at Fiorella's when her spirits lag; half-hearted trudges through the old French Market, where she gazes at displays of hot sauce and jewellery, vegetables and sunglasses, sighing; the Governor Nicholls Street Wharf looming up beyond the market stalls, increasing her misery; occasional perambulations along any street below Bourbon, squinting into shop windows; a seeming inability to cross over Canal Street to explore the possibility of riding the streetcar along St. Charles Avenue; no more poems since the first burst and no desire whatsoever to climb aboard the *Natchez* steamer for a tour. That people actually line up and buy tickets to ride the boat for fun amazes her. She feels a whisper of envy watching the excited faces of the passengers—serenaded by the blare of Dixieland jazz, drinks in hand—as the *Natchez* eases out into the river. Brave, she thinks, or crazy.

At first Cleo feels tempted to blame New Orleans itself for her increasing loneliness. She walks up and down the streets of the French Quarter, impatient with herself, wondering why she ever left Toronto. And yet she also feels an undeniable affection for the place, a connection she can't explain, even as she mopes and wanders. It's the smell of it, and the light. It's the way it seems utterly female in character, even as it teems with men.

Lethargy creeps in and out of her nervous system like a potion both terrifying and thrilling. The interior tug-of-war between her nervous Northerner's habit of keeping herself busy and her desire to succumb to a deathlike trance of total relaxation begins the moment she opens her eyes. She can't seem to overcome her reluctance to leave the French Quarter. The hope of meeting Johnny V. paralyzes Cleo. She's tired of searching for him in every bar, on every street, but she can't stop herself. Her eyes ache from looking across rooms, over her shoulder, from studying crowds and wondering if any one of the women she sees is *that* woman. She's also afraid to leave the neighbourhood because it feels like a kind of fortress or safer asylum. But even as she relaxes, she tenses and teeters. A feeling of dread washes through her every hour on the hour now, the sick clock of her heart chiming and reminding.

But this senseless hunt for the river-swimmer is good, too. It's a wonderful distraction, after all. Because as long as she obsesses about who the strange woman is and what she felt as she headed for the water and what her husband can and will do about it, where they live and how they spend their happier hours—if they have happier hours—Cleo can forget the more personal, more painful reason for her question: *Why?* Until she saw that woman leap into the Mississippi she had believed—or had at least chosen to think she believed—that her mother really was, as her father said, "In Italy, studying Art."

The range and intensity of her emotions is startling, and Cleo wonders again if she should head for home, climb aboard a bus and return to what is familiar, even if it isn't adventurous or brave. No, not yet, she decides. I'm sick of home, not homesick.

Walking along Royal Street, she feels her throat thicken with a mixture of rage and fear. I'd rather not scream in public, says the Northern voice of reason in her head. Or perhaps it is the new and even more genteel Southern one—*ladies don't scream*—that's crept in to sing a kind of frustrating duet? She can't tell.

Spying a pay phone, she feels a sudden urge to call home. A handful of quarters facilitates the deed. The phone rings and rings at the other end of the line. Cleo holds the receiver with both hands, squeezing till her fingertips turn white. She waits. And waits. Someone picks up the phone at the other end. A gruff and dejected "Little Savoy, hello?" greets her ear, the just-south-of-London accent grating on her nerves.

"Hello, Dad," she says as casually as she can manage. "Is Sadie home?"

"Cleo! Where in God's name are you?" he demands.

"Where am I?" she echoes. After a long pause she says, "Well, I'm not in Italy." She then hangs up the phone with a firm click. In truth, she had really wanted to speak with Sadie. Perhaps her comment had been a bit cruel, but that was also the beauty of it. Silence begets silence, she thinks with satisfaction; mystery begets more mystery.

With her hands in the pockets of her shorts, she strolls along Royal, past her hotel and on to Esplanade Avenue, delighted to be able to wear shorts in November—*take that, Canada!*—and relieved by the absence of concrete thoughts. She doesn't turn down in the direction of the river, but up, in the direction of City Park. It's on her list, you see, her heretofore neglected list of must-see things outside the French Quarter.

IT'S AMAZING HOW MUCH DUST can gather in the course of a few days. The top of the Steinway is now grey-white. "Poor baby grand," Madeline coos, massaging it with a chamois in careful, loving circular motions. She takes her time restoring it to its original gleaming black, tossing the foreboding parcel to the floor next to the piano. Her avoidance of the package is almost diabolical at this point. She steps over it as she moves to polish away the last bit of dust. Steps over it again as she walks back to open the lid and give the keys a cursory tinkle. The notes echo in the vast room. She closes the lid again, then picks up the package and sets it on top of the Steinway. Not yet, she thinks, but soon.

She stretches out on the bed and kicks off her shoes. The wind rattles the panes of the floor-to-ceiling windows beside her. Something skitters in the wall. It's still only late afternoon. The sun hangs stubbornly in the sky, refusing to make way for the moon. The plumber who came this morning hadn't taken up nearly as much time as she had anticipated. She almost misses him. The bathtub sprayed out the most alarming stream of dark red fluid when he first turned on the faucet (after determining that water was indeed available to the building). He replaced some washers and performed a wonderfully loud trick with a copper snake that caused the toilet to cough up all kinds of unsavoury items. That she should find such things fascinating is indicative of her state of mind today. She's putting off taking a bath, just as she is putting off playing the piano. The first thing to do is sleep, but it eludes her.

A swim would tire you, she thinks. No. You said no more swims and you meant it. She stands up on the bed, looks out the window and waves a fist at the river. "I am through with you, do you hear me?" She falls back down on the bed, grinning. She traces the folds in the sheet with her finger and closes her eyes, begging for sleep now. "C'mon," she whispers, "come see old Madeline." But the sandman is obviously busy elsewhere, and she gets up after a few frustrating minutes. "Just like a man," she mutters.

She moves down the dark hallway outside her studio, her shoes crunching over broken glass. At the end of the hall there's another staircase leading down, and this alarms Madeline. She listens at the top of it and hears the muffled sound of male voices. Smells kerosene, and food cooking, hot smells that travel up the stairs. The voices fall silent. She tiptoes back along the hall as noiselessly as possible, walking on the balls of her feet. While she isn't afraid of her neighbours, she isn't exactly in a rush to meet them, either. She has never cared to fraternize and has no plans to start now.

If I was at home, I'd vacuum, she thinks. She remembers reading in a women's magazine that 65 per cent of American housewives prefer vacuuming to sex. At the time she had snorted in disgust. But now, with nothing but time on her hands and celibacy on the horizon, Madeline actually finds herself wishing she could vacuum. This worries her. "Next thing you know, I'll be feeding stray cats and talking to birds!" she says to the piano.

Rodney used to always say, "There's nothing a nice long walk can't cure," when she would complain about her attacks of restlessness. "And if y'all didn't insist on monogamy, most straight people would sleep a whole lot better!" How she misses him, his affectionate, teasing repartee. He was her best friend, the only person she'd allowed herself to get close to in a long time. No point thinking about the past, that old swamp of bad memories and foolish notions. Better to keep moving, as Rodney suggested. Funny how the dead can still give good advice. Not even AIDS could change the fact that Rodney was, and still is, a kind of guru to Madeline. *Walk, Madeline.*

She spots the little house that caught her eye before, the one with over two dozen statuettes and ornaments decorating the tiny front yard. Madeline takes a sly inventory of its offerings as she pretends to admire the garden. Algiers Point is made up of a number of short blocks. Madeline walks up and down several streets, committing to memory the whereabouts of the houses that feature any sort of lawn ornament. She's already decided to avoid taking anything from anybody's porch. Too dangerous, she decides, casing various yards for potential kidnapping victims. It isn't really theft if you plan to bring something back, or so she tells herself as she ambles along. To the onlooker she would seem to be a keen admirer of gardens, pausing in front of certain houses, nodding and murmuring. Anyone would think she's simply identifying plants and flowers under her breath, the way all fetishistic horticulturists tend to do. And it's true that when she sees one of her favourite flowers, a bird of paradise or a cluster of black-eyed Susans, she does sigh and nod in appreciation. But it's the elves and bunnies and plastic geese that have her real interest.

Someone on Pelican Avenue is throwing out furniture. One man's garbage is a resourceful woman's windfall. She rummages through the heap of rejected items, delighted to find a card table and two half-broken chairs. Is only slightly embarrassed when a man emerges from the house shouting, "There's more where that come from!" She follows him, at his invitation, to a shed beside his home, where it seems he's piled a number of similarly decrepit items, not all of which are broken. The man offers to give her the whole lot for twenty-five dollars.

"Deal." Madeline nods, then realizes she didn't bring her purse. She explains her predicament and he shrugs. "If you help me carry a few things, I'll be glad to pay you just as soon as we get to my house."

"Deal." The man grins, tucking a folding table under his arm and grabbing four chairs. Madeline follows him, carrying two more chairs. When they reach the building that houses her studio, the man looks surprised. "I thought only drug addicts lived in there," he says with awe.

"Well, I guess I'm sort of starting over," replies Madeline, unlocking the door. The man trudges up the stairs behind her, but when they reach the studio, he won't accept Madeline's money.

"Shoot, I can't take money from you," he says.

"Please," says Madeline, waving the money, "I really do want all the tables and chairs you showed me. I'm not poor, just … thrifty. I'm having a party tonight and I haven't got anywhere for people to sit."

The man nods. "How about you give me ten and I help you carry the rest? Deal?"

You see, Madeline, all men aren't like your father. Some know how to treat a woman.

"That's kind," Madeline murmurs, feeling somewhat torn. What happened to complete self-sufficiency and exile? What happened to a life without the slightest dependence on a man? She allows this man to help her, this man who tells her his name is Harlan and that he has a wife and three kids. (Why did he tell her that so quickly?) Why shouldn't she accept his assistance? She'll have plenty of opportunity to strain her back this evening, after all.

"That's a real beauty," Harlan says, gazing at the Steinway. "That all you took with you?" His eyes are sad when he turns to Madeline. "I got divorced once. It's awful, way more awful than people realize. People have no idea how sad a person feels after. Even if you fought like cats, it's still awful, isn't it?" He blushes. "Pardon me for being too personal."

Madeline doesn't bother to correct poor Harlan, now red-faced and unable to look her in the eye. They return to his house to collect the rest of the haul. After handing him a ten-dollar bill, Madeline bids him a pleasant afternoon and tells him his wife is a lucky woman. From the window she can see him rushing down the sidewalk. The fewer people you see, the better off you'll be, she tells herself. She gazes at the pile of tables and chairs and then remembers that she still needs to buy liquor. Unlike the French Quarter, Algiers is not an all-night kind of neighbourhood where you can get a bottle at any hour. And so she goes wearily back down the stairs, holding her nose as she passes through the foyer that now reeks of refried beans and candle wax as well as its usual bouquet of rat piss and cigarettes. "Home sweet home," she mutters.

CLEO WALKS THE LENGTH of Esplanade Avenue, from the French Quarter all the way up to City Park. It's a fair hike for the uninitiated, and one that takes a person through some rather alarming stretches of poverty before it regains its elegance. Her feet are blistered and hot inside her Doc Martens by the time she reaches the entrance to the park. She's thirsty and hasn't thought to bring a bottle of water along for the journey. But City Park, an oasis if ever there was one, makes her glad she finally made the effort to leave the French Quarter. Limping slightly, she heads for the art gallery just beyond the Esplanade gate.

Closed Due to Burst Water Main. Apologies, reads the sign taped to the door. Cleo laughs out loud. She can't help herself. She sits down on the steps and removes her boots and socks, rubs her feet and examines the blisters on her heels and toes. City Park has some of the biggest trees Cleo has ever seen, gargantuan oaks whose trunks swoop toward the ground and then curve up again, skyward. There's a lovely aroma of wood and earth curling through the autumnal air, a smell intensified by the warmth of the sun beating through the leaves. Cleo sighs to herself. It *is* glorious. Sadie was right, I'm well-suited to world travel. Destination number one of many, with luck.

She pulls a battered copy of *National Geographic* magazine from her backpack and hugs it to her chest. This particular issue of the magazine—July 1967—holds special meaning for Cleo. It is one of the few things she packed before leaving the Little Savoy. Sadie had given her the magazine on the occasion of her sixteenth birthday. A strange gift, or so it had seemed at first. Cleo didn't know where the magazine had come from, or why it was sealed in plastic. She'd asked. Sadie lowered her voice and said only, "I thought you might like to know where you were conceived. Page one." Cleo had laughed and asked nothing more, surprised by the gift and by Sadie's nervousness as she handed it over. Alone in her room, Cleo opened the magazine, bewildered and yet sensing that something in the article would be a clue to her mother's life before she disappeared from Cleo's. "Florence Rises from the Flood," it said. *She's in Italy, studying Art.* Reading between the lines of text, scrutinizing the shadows in the photographs, Cleo had slowly and dreamily conjured up a mother for herself.

She turns now to the page that shows a young woman carrying a mud-soaked book in her arms, her face turned away from the camera ever so slightly. She wears mud-spattered jeans and a sweatshirt, mud-caked gloves. Her gaze focuses on something beyond the range of the photographer's lens. The photograph is Cleo's favourite of all the photos that accompany the article. She used to imagine that it was her mother in the picture, her mother as a young woman before Cleo came along and ruined everything. No sad thoughts, Cleo warns herself. She knows that the woman in the photograph isn't really her mother, but her heart can't quite let go of the fantasy. The fantasy isn't the whole story, of course. Will she ever know the whole story? It seems unlikely. Her father has always waved off her occasional questions. But the imagined version of events provided tremendous comfort, a romantic explanation for her mother's absence. Until a few days ago, at least.

She balls up her damp socks and stuffs them in her pocket. Wincing as she tugs her boots onto her bare feet, she takes a last disappointed look at the closed gallery. How she would have loved to wander its cool corridors, pretending to rescue paintings from whatever miniature deluge rages inside this very minute.

November–December, 1966
Florence, Italy

The Limonaia was the official shelter for the Pitti Palace lemon trees in winter. After the flood it became a safe haven for rescued works of art. The trees slept on, their high citrus tang obliterated by the reek of human fear and dismay. In the boiler room of the Stazione Centrale, pages of books hung on lines above the boilers, curling slightly after their gentle baths.

Thousands of books were drowned in the flood that ripped through Florence that fourth day of November, 1966. Illuminated manuscripts were reduced to smudged blocks of indeterminate colours. As the pages were rinsed, pressed and worried over, men in masks attended to the rows of lost words, using poles to reach the highest ones. There were tureens of hot, salty soup; carafes of strong, hot coffee. These provided sustenance for the exhausted volunteer workers. Sometimes a voice sang out or a throat coughed in the chemical clouds. Students murmured to one another in a dozen different tongues.

A bakery opened near the Limonaia and sent out its warm, yeasty call of triumph in the face of disaster, and the students clamoured to devour the fresh loaves. Somehow enterprise continued and industry transcended travesty, a testament to the spirit of Florentines. The students were also fed by grateful homeowners whose flooded cellars they had bailed out. The press nicknamed the altruistic youths "*angeli del fango,*" angels of the mud.

Day after day, the students linked arms and formed long human chains leading into the basement of the Uffizi Gallery. The stench of the sewers and of rotted canvas made stomachs turn and necessitated the wearing of masks. It was hard not to faint as the paintings were passed hand over hand to the trucks that waited to whisk them to safety. Protected by sheets of Japanese mulberry paper, the paintings were rushed into humidified rooms at the Limonaia, then sprayed with nystatin, an antibiotic used to retard the growth of mould. There was only so much that could be done in a given day, and it was heartbreaking to see masterpieces reduced to unrecognizable bits of rag and smashed wood, to watch the shopkeepers whose livelihoods had literally been swept away overnight putting on brave faces.

Eventually the rain paused, as if ashamed of what it had done. Water slowly retreated from the piazzas. All night there was the sound of barking dogs and the *skk-skk* of wide brooms pushing more water from the doorways of shops. In the daytime there was the incessant roar and scrape of metal as cars were dragged off. Rotten vegetables collected in the gutters; the carcass of a pig lay on the steps of a church. A small group of people gathered to stare at the sight of a man's arm protruding from beneath an overturned Fiat. Military tanks rolled through the pocked ribbons of streets, past small mountains of cobblestones that had been uprooted by the speeding torrent. Everywhere you went, there was the stink of cold oil and stagnant, sulphuric water. If loss has a smell, it might be that one.

Evacuated from her *pensione* during the flood, Caroline now pillowed down on a cot in a dormitory, along with dozens of other students from all over the world. She felt a guilty happiness in the midst of so much suffering; it was thrilling to feel so essential, so necessary. The good they did now would shape the future. *This* was real life: hands on, mud-covered, back aching, her mind relieved of its usual itchy, racing thoughts. Books, which she had always relied on for comfort, now needed her as much as she needed them. It was an honour to rescue them from the flooded basement of the *biblioteca,* a joy. She learned something each day as she watched the books slowly being resuscitated, hundreds of years of human spirits thanking from beyond, *Grazie! Grazie!* She sometimes couldn't sleep from the excitement of it all, or awoke weeping from dreams wherein the authors of those books—monks and historians—spoke to her vividly. In other dreams she won prizes for her advanced discoveries in the field of art restoration. Those dreams were the ones she had while awake, in between spells of intense nausea.

Her only close friend among the students, an American called Gwendolyn, had heard her throwing up three mornings in a row. "Any chance you might be pregnant?" she'd asked, her thick brows knitted with concern when Caroline emerged from a toilet stall. Gwen was worldly, popular with men in spite of—or because of—her ability to smoke and drink and curse like a sailor. *Me? No, we only did it the one time. Well, the one night.* Caroline said she was merely tired, that the fumes from the sewers upset her stomach.

Lyle Savoy slept one floor above her in the same dormitory, his mind on other things. Caroline's body, her face, her lovely nervous laugh. He had dreams, too: that as soon as it was possible, he'd take her to England and marry her. He wasn't as enchanted by the mess and chaos as Caroline appeared to be. His jeweller's apprenticeship had been shattered along with the shops and studios nestled in the Ponte Vecchio. He was tired of having wet feet, calluses, headaches—tired of missing classes. The only thing that cheered him was the realization that for once his life was finally more exciting than his brother, Roland. This thought, along with the fantasies he had about Caroline, was the only thing that kept him from fleeing the city. She was the most marvellous-looking girl he had ever laid eyes on, a bright white star on his arm when they sloshed through the streets in their coveralls. Many admired Lyle for being able to lure her away from her books. He glowed like an ember whenever the other students looked up from their conversations to watch Caroline enter the room. She was someone you held on to with both hands.

If only you'd been smart enough to recognize that in time, Dad.

Cleo steps down from the Esplanade bus at North Rampart, the river-swimmer far from her thoughts. She'd managed to board and ride the bus with little awareness of her actions. Having disembarked in a similar somnambulistic haze, she walks without thinking where she's heading.

And then she sees him again—Johnny V., disappearing through a doorway on Esplanade, just up from Decatur. Ignoring her blisters, Cleo rushes toward the same door. But she's too late. He has disappeared through a second inner door. She tries the handle. Locked, of course. She turns and sees the row of buzzers, the labels under them, moves her eyes over each one. Vernon? Nope, initial P. Then she sees it: Valentucci/Shockfire. No initials, but it doesn't matter. V for Valentucci. Cleo presses the buzzer.

"Yeah?" comes the voice. Johnny has learned his lesson about unlocking the door without first inquiring about the identity of the caller. "YES?" he bellows. Cleo says nothing, of course. "Get a life!" Johnny shouts from somewhere inside the building. The speaker makes a loud crackling noise and falls silent. She lives here, Cleo thinks. She lives here! She could be upstairs right this very minute—sleeping, cooking, who knows! Cleo takes a last long look at the unremarkable foyer and is then seized by a paranoid fear that the building is equipped with a video surveillance camera. What if he can see you? she thinks frantically, hurrying out onto the street.

Kitty-corner to the building where the Valentucci/Shockfire duo lives is a bar. From her window seat at Charlie's, Cleo has a bird's-eye view of the door Johnny "V-for-Valentucci" went through. She will no longer have to keep up her ridiculous vigil at Hank's Bar. Eventually, she thinks excitedly, he'll emerge. Or *she* will. Will Cleo know the woman to see her? What does a woman named Shockfire look like? Use your imagination, Cleo. If, as the bartender at Hank's suggested, Johnny V.'s wife is crazy, she must at least look like the sort of person who throws herself into rivers.

Cleo pictures someone dark and depressed, the kind of woman who wears long skirts and cardigans even in summer, the type who never smiles, refuses to bathe, who either forgets to put on make-up or wears too much of it. Her mind races with these thoughts and others. Although reluctant to leave her seat, she hurries to the bar and orders a beer. She keeps one eye on the window while she waits to be served. Hurry! she thinks, trying not to frown at the woman behind the bar.

"First one's on me," the bartender says, giving Cleo a slow smile.

"I might only have the one," Cleo says, vaguely irritated by the way the woman stares at her.

"Well, I hope not," the woman flirts. She thrusts her chin in the direction of the window. "People-watching—or waiting on somebody special?"

Cleo shrugs. "Bit of both. Thanks for the drink." She puts a crisp one-dollar bill down on the bar and hurries back to her seat to watch and wait. She can feel the bartender's eyes on her from across the room and tries not to mind. It's a free country, she reminds herself, and Charlie's is, after all, a watcher's paradise.

GIN, BRANDY, VODKA: a bottle of each. Plastic cocktail glasses. One proper glass snifter borrowed from Bill's Bar down the street; the pianist can't be expected to drink from a plastic cup. Two bags of ice melting in the sink. One tray of hors d'oeuvres: Cheese Nips, pretzels and Zapp's famous mesquite-flavoured potato chips. Paper napkins. One dress selected from the limited number of favourite dresses Madeline has with her. Shoes: one of two pairs taken from the apartment during her recent raid. Cologne: good old Rocabar, once worn by her daddy and now ready to be applied with the solemnity of unction. Candles. Check. All that remains: pick up the guests and then bathe. Yes, in that order, strange as it seems. Madness in her method, and vice versa. She can't get on with her evening till the windows are black rectangles throwing her reflection back at her. The guests are waiting in nearby yards, waiting to be taken hostage by Madeline.

She sits on the end of the bed, looks around. Sees the big brown parcel sitting on the floor. Later, she thinks, and not without an adequate number of libations under my belt. No one should have to face any kind of marital legalese sober. While her curiosity is strong, her conviction that Johnny is bluffing is stronger. She's seen the old serving-fake-divorce-papers trick used before by other couples. There's no real need to go through the formal hassle of a divorce, she reasons, unless of course Johnny has decided he wants to marry Lena the Whore. A brief flicker of jealousy, but nothing that can make her rush back to the French Quarter and beg for forgiveness.

She hasn't done anything wrong, after all. A couple of swims, a few tantrums over the years, the occasional silent treatment—yes, she's been known to fall silent for up to three days at a stretch—but hardly grounds for a divorce. In thinking about the possible end of her marriage, Madeline drifts back to the beginning of it.

October, 1976
Aboard the riverboat Natchez

Six and something feet of equine grace; Madeline knew she wanted him. He was classic man: the thick moustache, the dark, laughing eyes under heavy lids, the gigantic hands and sinewy arms roped with veins. He was tall like her daddy, but much darker and more dangerous-looking. Thinner, too. He stood like a cop, his feet spread apart. He smoked like a gangster, pinching his cigarette between his thumb and index finger and drawing it toward his lips as if deep in thought. When he looked up and saw her watching him, she dared to imagine that he would want her, too, and that it would all be very easy. Some red wine, back to his place, their clothes in a heap on the floor.... But when he came and stood next to her at the railing, she realized she was being a bit hasty, that she should attempt coyness, though she had no idea of just how one coyed. She tried to recall how her mother behaved when there was a man in the room. Like a black widow spider or a trained courtesan, Madeline thought rather nastily, hoping there were other ways to attract a man.

"Whatchya doin'?" Those were the first words Johnny ever spoke to Madeline, and as he said them he touched her arm. She had, in truth, been trying to climb over the railing of the riverboat in an effort to leap into the river. This was the part of the story she preferred to leave out when recounting the tale of how they met to interested parties. Yes, in reality, she'd been hoisting herself up and over when he appeared at her elbow, asking, "Whatchya doin'?" He'd touched her arm to keep her from doing something incredibly foolish.

"Just ... trying to get a better look," she said, blushing. Recovering herself a little, she added, "I thought this was a cruise to the Bahamas, but it turns out it's only a river-dragging expedition."

He grinned. "You a student at the university?" He watched her smooth her skirt back down and rearrange her blouse. He liked the way she dressed, thought she looked like a gypsy. She looked young, but her eyes were old. Still, you never could tell, and Johnny didn't need any trouble. In his experience it never hurt to ask a few polite questions regarding the age of a desirable young lady, even if it meant demanding to see ID.

Before Madeline could answer, the Dixieland Disciples burst into song very near where they stood. Instead of talking, they just smiled at each other. She touched his hand where it rested on the railing, a brave half stroke that conveyed her interest. After all, it had worked with Henri. Johnny gave a nervous cough and gazed at her hand as if it had shot down from the sky like a lightning bolt.

"You wanna get some dinner when we dock?" he bellowed over the blaring horns. She nodded ever so slightly, as if to say, Why not?

It was easy somehow. She liked the look of him. She liked that he was shy and that he spilled things at dinner. He had a nervous guffaw of a laugh that charmed her. When he asked her what she did for a living and she told him, "Nothing much, yet," he didn't seem to disapprove. Somehow they managed to hold a lengthy conversation without too many personal questions. During a lull she wondered if his feet were as large as his hands, and if so, did that mean what they always said it meant? Her mother would have been proud of her for wondering such things. Still, she fought off the urge to ask him if he would take her home that very night.

He walked her to the door of where she was living at the time, a horrible little bedsit on Burgundy in a building favoured by massage therapists of dubious certification. He asked if he could call her sometime, and she told him her number, which he wrote on the back of the restaurant cheque. He grinned at the piece of paper as if it was a winning lottery ticket. She stood with her door key in hand and knew right then and there that she wasn't enough like her mother. Her brief experience with Henri had not armed her for further seductions. Johnny leaned down and kissed her, a tickle of a kiss. He then wished her good-night and sweet dreams, and she'd watched him go, hating herself for her cowardice.

When he called fifteen minutes later, Madeline said a quiet "amen." He'd really wanted to invite himself up for a nightcap, he said, but thought he might seem too forward. She needn't think he was expecting anything, he assured her. She replied, very softly, that she couldn't promise him the same.

While she waited for him to return, Madeline had a feeling that she would be with this man for a long, long time. That she would have him and hold him from that night forward.

And of course, she'd been right. But the same nervous guffaw that had charmed her on the first date annoys her now. His clumsiness isn't as cute as it once seemed, nor does his relaxed approach to everything serve to calm her as it had before. They no longer sit smiling at each other in restaurants, and their silence hasn't always been companionable. Too much silence can be as dangerous as too much talk. Madeline prefers the silence of this studio to the hostile quiet that seems to have leaked into the marriage without either of them noticing. If she misses him, she can't quite locate the longing. If he misses her, he has a funny way of showing it.

THE BARTENDER AT CHARLIE'S is somewhat stunned when Cleo, whose acquaintance she has been trying to make, suddenly leaps from her bar stool and runs out. She watches Cleo sprint across Esplanade, then stop in her tracks.

"Darlin'," grunts the bartender, "you are one crazy chick."

And perhaps Cleo *is* a little bit crazy as she follows Johnny V. up Esplanade. She has enough sense not to call out to him, but tails him rather closely. At any moment he could turn around and look right at her, but he doesn't. His long legs challenge her to keep up with him. By the time he turns onto North Rampart Street, Cleo is sweating. She isn't going to give up, however, and she follows for several more blocks. He tosses the cigarette he has been puffing on into the road and goes into a restaurant. Cleo hangs back for a moment and then approaches.

She reads the menu posted in the window of Papa

Leone's. The venetian blinds on the windows are drawn, but the neon sign says OPEN. Is Johnny V. a waiter here? The owner? Cleo checks the prices on the menu. She's on a fixed income—as in *no* income—and so scans the menu to make sure she can afford to eat here. She hasn't counted her money or traveller's cheques in a few days. The money hidden in her room is all the money she has in the world. *Never mind that.* She takes a deep breath and opens the door.

Johnny V. is nowhere to be seen as she sits down at the table closest to the window. She rests her elbows on the green plastic tablecloth and waits for some sign of life in the restaurant. Two male voices holler back and forth in what must be the kitchen. The smell of garlic is strong and Cleo's stomach growls. A man who isn't Johnny emerges from the kitchen and looks surprised to see her there.

"Hello!" He hurries to turn on a stereo behind the bar. "My cook," he says, jerking his thumb over his shoulder. "He's good, but he's late!" The man hands Cleo a menu and smiles, revealing a gold front tooth. "Some wine?" he asks, holding up one finger. "But wait—are you old enough, miss?" Cleo laughs and he grins again. "Red? White?"

"Beer?" she asks hopefully. He gives a half shrug, a nod, waits. "Miller draft?" she suggests, and he nods curtly and hurries off. While he's busy behind the bar, Cleo cranes her neck, hoping for a glimpse of Johnny. When the man returns with her beer and a frosted glass, she asks where the restrooms are.

"This way, this way," he says, motioning for her to follow him. As they walk he puts his hand on her back to guide her. They pass the pick-up window.

"Hey, Carlo! That your girlfriend from Biloxi?" calls a

voice from behind the counter. Johnny peers through the slot, and Cleo ducks her head as Carlo hurries her to the door of the restroom. Her heart thumps as she washes her face and hands, and she hears the man roaring at Johnny in a mixture of Italian and English expletives.

Back at her table, Cleo takes her time selecting something to eat from the extensive menu. She sips her beer and watches as a few other patrons enter the restaurant. One of the new arrivals calls the waiter by name and asks how business is. Again Carlo complains loudly about Johnny with the proviso that he is a talented cook—once he gets started. Johnny emerges from the kitchen, wiping his hands on a towel. Cleo drops her eyes to her placemat, a cartoon map of Italy. Everything conspires! she thinks, averting her gaze slightly, stealing a look at Johnny from the corner of her eye. He's handsome, she decides, even with those dark circles under his eyes. He chats with the customers and tells them that Carlo is a nice guy when he isn't bitching and moaning about his staff. She's trying to guess how old Johnny's wife might be, based on how old he looks. She would guess Johnny to be close to fifty. A youngish fifty.

"How's Madeline these days?" asks one of the recent arrivals, a bleached blond woman in her forties. *Madeline!* Cleo's jaw clenches with excitement. Carlo snorts and Johnny gives him a look. Putting the two names together in her mind like the pieces of a jigsaw puzzle—*Madeline Shockfire*—Cleo murmurs the name to herself, rolling it over her tongue at the lowest possible volume.

"She's good," Johnny says, and shrugs, raising his bony shoulders up to his ears.

Liar, thinks Cleo, still marvelling at the woman's name.

"We saw her at Hank's the other morning," the woman says, nodding her head vigorously. Her earrings swing back and forth with her manic enthusiasm. Cleo curses to herself.

The man beside her nods, too. "She was carrying some kind of—what was it, Deb?"

"A duvet," Deb supplies. "And some sort of appliance. She was having a bit of a time with the door, wasn't she, Gus?" The man nods again.

"That so?" Johnny says, trying hard to maintain a casual demeanour. "Well, gotta get back in the kitchen before I get fired!" He disappears into the back, and Cleo glares at the woman named Deb, even though she has roused Cleo's curiosity to an almost unbearable level. She was at Hank's? In the morning, carrying an appliance? This is all starting to feel like a twisted game of Clue to Cleo, who nevertheless feels torn between wanting Deb to mind her own business and wanting to hear more details about Johnny's wife's comings and goings.

Deb obliges. To Carlo, and in a not-very-discreet whisper, she says, "She said something about a secret lover in Gretna, didn't she, Gus?" This time she shakes her head mournfully.

Gus pipes in, "I think she was kidding, Deb. Don't go causing trouble over hearsay, hon."

Deb gives Gus a pouty look. "Well, Pete called her a cab, didn't he? And she was carrying a duvet, wasn't she? I mean, what should people think with her screaming about a secret lover *and* carrying bedding around town?" Carlo listens to this whole exchange with his lips pursed. He says nothing and then excuses himself, retreating to the kitchen. Deb mutters something to Gus that Cleo can't hear, and they shake their heads in unison.

Cleo half expects Johnny to burst from the kitchen in a jealous rage, but no such thing happens. Instead her plate of penne alla vodka arrives and she picks at it, unable to eat. If it's true that Johnny's wife has a secret lover, why would she shout about it in a bar full of people? Either she wants people to know, Cleo reasons, or she doesn't really have any such person at all. The whole point of a secret lover is that they're just that, a secret. Cleo knows that much about love. And what sort of appliance would a person be carrying around along with a duvet? Cleo wonders. It seems that Johnny's wife's reputation for being crazy is somewhat deserved. And if, as Deb claims, she was waiting for a cab and carrying bedding, then it also seems that she isn't sleeping at home these days. Did they fight? Is that why she jumped into the river? And what of the first attempt? Did she turn back after a change of heart? She must have. But something inspired her to make a second attempt, the one Cleo saw on the news. Does Johnny V. even know about the first time? Cleo doubts it very much.

When Carlo comes by to ask if everything is all right, Cleo asks him to wrap up her uneaten food. He looks disappointed, but does as she asks. The cheque comes on a plastic tray with two candies on it. Cleo finds this odd, as she's dining alone.

"For luck in love." Carlo winks. "You married?"

"No," replies Cleo, tucking the candies in her pocket.

"Smart girl."

It's dark now and Cleo is too nervous to walk along North Rampart Street. The lights glowing white on the gate of Louis Armstrong Park are pretty, but she's heard this can be a dangerous part of town at night. She turns down St. Peter and heads into the Quarter, still shocked and excited by what she's seen and heard at Papa Leone's. She doesn't know who to feel more sorry for: Johnny, his wife, or herself for sitting on the wrong wharf at the wrong time. But still: *Madeline Shockfire.*

"HEY, SNOW WHITE! Your glass is looking a little empty, girl. A woman like you can't walk in here with only four of her seven dwarves *and* go thirsty! Here, let me help you." Madeline slips down from her piano bench and sashays to the bar, or rather, to the kitchen counter. She grabs the gin bottle—it's a little-known fact that Snow White drinks Tanqueray—and turns to face the rest of her clientele, seated in groups of threes and fours at various tables arranged to surround the piano. She tops up the plastic cup that sits before Snow White, or at least the stone replica of her, and bows. "You drink that slow, you'll be a virgin forever," Madeline teases. Her guest of honour doesn't dignify the joke with a response.

Snow White's companions at the table are two plastic geese and a concrete Dopey. Madeline has seated Sleepy, Doc and Grumpy at a separate table. The other three dwarves couldn't make it; they were chained to a commitment on someone's front porch. At another table closer to the window are two cock-eyed elves holding fishing rods, and a stone bunny that may or may not be Thumper. An exhaustive search for Bambi had proved futile. Madeline nods at the various other members of her audience and tops up their glasses, too, continuing her repartee and pausing to take a sip from this and that glass. The gin makes her shiver.

Satisfied that everyone present has what they need in the way of cocktails, Madeline returns to the platform and sits down at the piano. She takes a sip of brandy from the borrowed snifter and wiggles her fingers theatrically. Her wedding band sits on the foreboding package on top of the piano. Soon.

"Ladies and gentlemen, bunnies and elves, Miss White, I sincerely hope you'll enjoy yourselves at this, the grand opening of Café Ornamentia. Let me say that it's a pleasure to play such a finely tuned piano for y'all on this very pleasant night in beautiful downtown Algiers Point. So sit back, relax, enjoy your drinks and allow me to play for you a selection of old favourites." Madeline rests her fingertips on the keys. *Like this. Arch your hands, hold your wrists just so. Like this.* She closes her eyes and takes a deep breath and rips into a rousing version of "Chopsticks" to what she imagines is loud applause. *You've got to be able to touch every key, not just some. Wide.* When Madeline grows weary of "Chopsticks," she pauses and takes another sip of her drink. Glancing at the crowd that stares back at her in inanimate awe, she sees their faces illuminated by candlelight. Macabre, in the fine tradition of graveyard musicians everywhere.

And on it goes. Madeline plays everything she can recall from the primary lesson books right through to the first jazz ballad she ever learned to play, "Stormy Weather." At the close of the first set she feels a bit dizzy. Time to bring the food out, she decides, doing a lightheaded cha-cha across the wooden floor to retrieve the hors d'oeuvres. She prances from table to table, offering her guests something to eat, taking some for herself as she goes. The Zapp's potato chips were an especially good choice, she thinks, licking her lips. Restored by the salt and inspired by the moon, now glowing high above the levee outside her windows, Madeline sits back down at the Steinway.

"Now, my piano teacher told me that if you can learn to play Bach, you can play anything. I don't know if she was right, but I'll give it a whirl," she says, her voice cracking slightly. Within a few bars there is no stopping the memories from flooding in. The woman who taught her how to play piano might as well be there in the room. When Madeline closes her eyes she can see her piano teacher as she remembers her, a young Memphis beauty with skin like overmilked coffee, a garnet ring sparkling on the right index finger of those gorgeous hands, that smile ... Madeline stops playing.

How is it possible to be thirty-nine years old, to be here in a room nothing like that room and yet be transported as if it is that same evening, the night when Madeline's universe had been rearranged? How is it possible to be alone with such a feeling? Is it only ever possible alone—and after the fact? Along came someone and along went someone. That's the name of this song.

November, 1975
St. Louis, Missouri

Dianne had given Carmelle ample warning about Madeline's tendency to brood on her birthday. Carmelle was warned to keep her eye on Madeline because, as Dianne insisted, her daughter had a wild streak that made her do unpredictable things. Carmelle had never personally witnessed that side of Madeline's nature. In fact, the girl she knew had little or no understanding of the concept of rebellion. If anything, she seemed unnaturally obedient, and this was much more troubling than any secret dark side could have been.

For reasons she chose not to explain, Dianne had to go out of town on the weekend of Madeline's birthday. She left behind a sizeable amount of money to facilitate the celebration but offered no suggestions as to how Carmelle should actually fete her. With Dianne's warnings in the back of her mind, Carmelle anticipated a certain resistance when she brought up the subject with Madeline.

Madeline stood in her bedroom completely naked, gazing at herself in a full-length mirror. It was clear she'd presumed household solitude, because her bedroom door was wide open, a rare occurrence. Seeing her, Carmelle turned to creep away down the hall, but it was too late. Madeline saw her in the doorway and addressed her. Years spent in crowded change rooms had erased all traces of modesty. Madeline knew that even if she had a boyish haircut and what she believed was an unremarkable face, she did at least, as a result of her swimming, have a fairly stunning physique.

"Hello," Madeline said, moving to sit on the edge of her bed. She could see by the flush in Carmelle's cheeks that the young woman was uncomfortable. This delighted Madeline. She'd seen her mother do it to many men, many times. "What is it?" she asked, eyes wide and innocent.

Carmelle was impressed by Madeline's unexpected calm. She entered the room to make her offer regarding the birthday celebration.

"I wondered what you plan to do about your birthday," Carmelle began, and then stopped. Her eyes travelled to the walls, decorated with posters of swimmers and medallions collected from national meets. There were several photographs of one particular swimmer adorning the wall above Madeline's bed, and Carmelle wondered aloud who the woman was.

"Eleanor Holm," said Madeline, eager to dismiss the depressing subject of her birthday to pursue idle chatter.

"She your favourite?" Carmelle stared fixedly at the photographs to avoid looking at Madeline.

"Mmmm," Madeline responded, turning to join Carmelle in viewing the photographs. "She was disqualified from the Berlin Games for drinking champagne and missing her curfew on the ship over to Germany in 1936. Isn't that wonderful?"

"I guess you like the rebel swimmers, huh?" Carmelle smiled. Out of the corner of her eye she saw Madeline's breasts.

"Eleanor Holm was amazing. She didn't take any shit," Madeline sighed, turning her back on the photographs. She could see that Carmelle was nervous, and decided to allow the poor thing a chance to get on with her spiel about what a wonderful time they would have together. She sprawled out on the bed with her hands clasped behind her head and reminded Carmelle of the reason for her visit.

"Well"—Carmelle wet her lips and sat cautiously on the end of Madeline's bed—"I wondered what you planned to do about turning nineteen." She kept her amber-coloured eyes on the pictures of Eleanor Holm and the brittle, yellowed pieces of tape that held them to the wall.

"I think what I plan to do is turn nineteen." Madeline could see now that her mother had obviously insisted that Carmelle make a big deal of it, even if she herself couldn't be bothered to.

Carmelle's eyes dropped from the wall to the bedspread. When she looked up, her gold-flecked eyes loped over the stunning length of Madeline's legs, over the flat of her stomach and the muscular curve of her arms, over the shameless sprawl of her employer's daughter's body. It was a body too fit, too well trained and almost unbearably perfect. Carmelle felt a sudden, almost diabolical desire to make it less healthy, less pure.

"Have you ever been drunk, Miss Madeline?" she asked, her eyes travelling back up to Madeline's face. Eye to eye again, Madeline suddenly felt nervous and pulled the bedspread over herself. She had never been looked at in that way before.

"No." Madeline continued tugging at the bedspread. "Why?"

Carmelle stood up, aware that she had made Madeline uncomfortable. She pretended to look out the window, saying, "I wonder if you'd like to spend your birthday like Miss Holm over there. Since you admire her so...."

Madeline was amused by the idea and impressed by Carmelle's quick recovery. But Carmelle's eyes were on the door she seemed to long to bolt toward. Yes, Madeline thought, there is something strange happening here. It was a good strangeness, but terrifying, too.

"I thought maybe we could have dinner together and drink a few drinks. You know, celebrate you getting closer to adulthood and all that."

"And you liken my drinking with you to Eleanor Holm getting kicked out of the Olympic Games?" Madeline laughed. She decided to behave as her mother would, just to see if her bravado would fool Carmelle.

"It might be seen that way by your mother." Carmelle held a finger to her lips as if to emphasize the need for secrecy.

"Then of course I'd like to," Madeline said. "Do you think you can get me kicked off my swim team, too?"

Madeline passed the time between Carmelle's invitation and dinner itself by praying to her photographs of Eleanor Holm. She had never considered herself a religious person, or a supporter of mystical interventions, but she was willing to try anything to soothe her nerves. She'd always refused to join in team prayers before meets. The mumbled words of hope to dear Lord Jesus and whining requests for God's help in obtaining an out-of-state victory had always seemed pathetic to Madeline. After all, Madeline knew that it was her mother, not God, who was in charge of her life, both at the pool and away from it. Amazed by the possibility of an entire evening alone with Carmelle, Madeline knelt down and gave thanks to Ms. Holm without hesitation.

"Happy birthday to me," she sang to herself, winking at her favourite photo of the notorious swimmer, posed like a peacock in her Aquacade costume. After a manic search of her mother's closets, Madeline located a long black satin skirt and a shimmery silver top. If such a get-up was a touch *de trop* for the dining room of the Shockfire household, Madeline didn't care. Thinking again of the way Carmelle had stared at her, Madeline swallowed nervously. She couldn't imagine being drunk, especially with someone who stared like that. But then she thought about Eleanor Holm laughing and drinking, thumbing her nose at her unfair disqualification from the 1936 Games, and Madeline decided to be brave. It was probably nothing to get excited about. Girls on her swim team often regarded each other's body in the change room, though not with that intensity. If you stared too long you'd be branded a "lezzy," but everyone still looked at each other, if only to see whose ass was fatter than your own.

At seven o'clock sharp Madeline strolled into the kitchen, where she found Carmelle sitting at the table in semi-darkness. She didn't smell any food cooking and felt disappointed. Were they were going out for their meal? She half considered running upstairs to change into something less audacious, but Carmelle waved her into the room. Carmelle had already partaken of a quick, solitary whiskey. A bottle sat on the table next to her with its top off, an empty glass next to it.

Madeline moved to sit down, but Carmelle shook her head and jumped up from her chair. She grabbed another bottle from the counter and headed for the door that led to the Shockfire living room. This was all very confusing to Madeline, who now assumed they were going out for dinner. She mumbled that she was hungry as Carmelle pushed ahead of her with great purpose.

The forbidden terrain of the living room had been turned into a salon. Candles flickered on every available surface, casting a cozy glow over a room that was usually rather austere, even cold. Dianne had redone it in mint green and white at the suggestion of her interior decorator, and the results were positively arctic. That was during what Madeline called the Harry Says period, when every opinion expressed by her mother was prefaced with the words, "Harry says …". At the tender age of twenty, Harry was an apparent expert on everything pertaining to fashion, cooking and decor. If mint wasn't in style now, Harry had told them in his strangely squeaky voice, it soon would be. Madeline hadn't been at all surprised when the furnishings outlasted Harry. Dianne's affection for the much younger man faded around the time that the last fey cushion was artfully arranged.

Now Carmelle had penetrated the peppermint sanctum with her candles and made it her own. She set the bottle of liquor down on the coffee table and moved to the record player. Music such as Madeline had never heard before tumbled from the speakers, and she remained standing, dumbfounded. When she did sit, as instructed by Carmelle, she sat on the very edge of the sofa, bewildered by the soft lights and romantic music.

"This," said Carmelle, "is how a birthday ought to be spent." She handed Madeline a glass of neat liquor and plopped down next to her, her body exuding spicy perfume and surprising heat. The music was some kind of jazz, and Madeline liked the female voice that soared out over the piano and bass very much. She decided that the record was too wonderful to be part of her mother's collection. The liquor bit into Madeline's tongue and made her lips burn. It was a delightful sensation. Eleanor Holm was even smarter than Madeline had suspected. Carmelle said very little, drank very quickly and refilled her own glass several times.

"You've been drunk before?"

Carmelle nodded and laughed. She didn't seem drunk, whereas Madeline felt odd after only a few sips. She asked what they were listening to and what they were drinking, in that order.

"Nina Simone for your ears," Carmelle said, "and B&B for your belly." She produced a package of cigarettes and lit one, waving away the smoke before she handed it to Madeline, who took it awkwardly in her free hand. There was a smudge of Carmelle's dark lipstick on the filter. Carmelle lit one for herself and said as she exhaled a puff of smoke, "Now, I wouldn't recommend getting drunk all the time, but once in a while it feels good to just *relax*. You need that, I think. Doesn't seem to me you get to have much fun, what with all that swimming you do."

The bottle of B&B dwindled away and the candles shrank down to stumps, and they both seemed to have forgotten that dinner had ever been part of the plan. Carmelle put on one record after another and danced, and made Madeline dance, and the more sweet, warm liquor she drank, the more Carmelle laughed. The alcohol made Madeline brave, and she asked Carmelle a million questions about herself. But Carmelle's response to each of Madeline's inquiries was a throaty, uninformative chuckle.

By midnight Carmelle was shouting drunk. "Let's eat!" she roared, disappearing into the kitchen in her stocking feet. Her high-heeled shoes lay on the floor beside the sofa; Madeline regarded them as if they were mysterious objects. The smell of hot oil and batter wafted out from the kitchen, and Madeline's stomach clenched with anticipation. When Carmelle reappeared a seeming eternity later, she carried a platter piled high with hot fried chicken and napkins, and under her arm, a second bottle of liquor. Madeline wasn't sure that eating fried chicken on her mother's white velvet sofa was a wise idea and said so.

"Madeline, can I tell you something about yourself?" Carmelle's face was gravely serious as she set down the platter. She sat down with her kneecap pressed against Madeline's leg. "*You* are in serious danger. You're more of a servant than I'll ever be. Eat your chicken. This is your birthday, a night when you can do whatever you damned well please. Get drunk, eat up and stop worrying, all right?" She challenged Madeline with wide amber eyes and poured them each a generous shot. "Tell me, have you ever had any fun in your life?"

"No," Madeline admitted. It was true, she couldn't think of a single time when gaiety had been the prevailing mood.

"I didn't think so." Carmelle sighed. She lifted up a piece of fried chicken, plump and dripping grease, cupped her other hand under it to prevent disaster and pushed it toward Madeline's mouth. Madeline leaned in and closed her eyes and took a big fat bite, and was startled when Carmelle bit into the opposite side at the very same time. Madeline pulled back, her heart wild and her hands suddenly damp. The record on the player began to skip, and Carmelle continued to sit with the chicken breast hanging from her mouth. She sat there like that and she started to giggle, and Madeline did too, sobered only when Carmelle tossed the hunk of chicken onto the carpet.

Madeline was horrified by this last gesture, but Carmelle seemed nonplussed. She walked over to the piano, lifted the lid and began playing one of the songs Madeline had heard coming from the record player. Madeline moved to join Carmelle on the piano bench, sitting as close as possible. Carmelle kept playing and turned to look at Madeline. She smiled a slow and knowing smile, and Madeline's breath caught in her lungs. Carmelle leaned over and kissed Madeline right on the mouth, and for a long time. The music stopped flowing from the Steinway, but the kiss went on and on, igniting every cell in Madeline's body. At last Carmelle pulled back, and Madeline was both sorry and relieved. Carmelle resumed playing the piano as if nothing unusual had happened.

"Will you teach me how to play?" Madeline asked, her voice cracking ever so slightly.

Carmelle laughed and vamped on the keys. "When're we gonna find time to do that, midnights?"

Madeline nodded, insisting they could find the time. "My mother's never home anyway," she said matter-of-factly. It wasn't really piano lessons she was interested in, but more time alone with Carmelle. More times like this.

"All right, then," Carmelle whispered. "But I sure hope your mother doesn't find out."

"I won't be telling her. Will you?" Madeline laughed. She grew bold again, barely recognizing the certainty in her own voice. "Kiss me again? I hear practice makes perfect."

JOHNNY IS WEEPING BECAUSE, after six double shots of Kentucky bourbon, he's convinced himself that Madeline is having an affair. Carlo didn't tell him any of what Deb had said. For all Carlo's faults, he isn't a cruel man, nor is he foolish enough to believe French Quarter gossip. But when Lena—a seasoned devil's advocate with her own agenda—suggested to Johnny that perhaps Madeline had a passion for something other than swimming the river, or, more important, for someone other than him, he'd snapped. His mind filled with all sorts of unpleasant images of Madeline in the arms of another man, and so he turned to the man he trusted most in times of despair, Mr. Jack Daniel.

Cleo is weeping because she has somehow managed to lock herself out of her room at the Pommes Royales Maisonnettes and is too embarrassed—or too Canadian—to bother Mrs. Ryan at this late hour. She sits miserably on the low curb outside the hotel, cursing herself for her foolish decision to stop by Hank's for what was supposed to be a tranquilizing end-of-the-night drink. Somewhere between the first bourbon sour and the third, she lost her keys. Upon making this unhappy discovery, she elected to sit crying on the curb instead of returning to Hank's Bar. If and when she manages to regain her composure, she'll go to Café Du Monde and console herself with doughnuts and coffee, and wait out the remainder of this unlucky night.

Madeline is weeping because she has allowed herself to think about Carmelle—and feel about her—after years of successfully avoiding certain memories and the feelings of rage and sorrow said recollections inspire. Well, most of the time. She won't be any happier when she opens the white envelope, because its contents are not, as she believes, connected to her marriage. The unhappy combination of booze and nostalgia has led Madeline to realize that when she gave her heart away the first time, she never quite got it back. In the world of lovers there may be nothing quite as powerful as the ongoing ache of four simple words: what might have been.

A trio of weepers, each one drowning in a flood of self-pity. Somebody in this trio should do something. By morning, each somebody will.

THE MISSISSIPPI RIVER IS FULL of *things*. People use that body of water as a symbolic depository for what they no longer need or want. In this sense it is both Lethe, the river of forgetfulness, and Mnemosyne, spring of eternal memory.

If the entire river were dragged at any given time, a multitude of personal items would be extracted—some recognizable, others not so. Poems and manuscripts thrown mournfully from any and all bridges crossing over; wedding and engagement rings by the hundreds, maybe even toe-rings and thumb-rings, too; a guitar someone vowed they would never play again because the pursuit of art turned out to be nothing but a foolish dream; knitting needles; love letters torn into tiny squares; incriminating photographs; and who knows what else. All that matters is that these things mattered to somebody, or maybe to more than one somebody.

The river—with its speeding current and deadly under-tow—surely washes most of these things right down to the Gulf of Mexico eventually. Like bodies swept away unfound (and the Mississippi has known quite a few of those in its own long life), these discarded and yet meaningful objects won't remain anywhere near the places they were cast from. And yet for so many people these gestures are incredibly empowering. The river offers a welcome end to some imagined futility or even the beginning of an intended recovery. Half the magic of the Mississippi may well be stored in the objects it contains, its true energy gathered from all those determined tosses. In a sense, the river is one long wishing well of muddy water streaming by, a body of water full of dreams lost and some found, of pain carried out to sea or caught way down near the bottom, where it becomes as good as invisible, as good as gone, for whomever did the throwing.

Madeline imagines being able to carry the Steinway up to the midpoint of the Mississippi River Bridge, can see herself possessed of the superhuman strength required to throw the piano into the river from that great height. What a thrill it would be to watch it sail down, turning and shifting according to the dictates of physics, to see it finally hit the water below with a great splash, disappearing once and for all from her life, taking certain memories with it.

But it's not the piano's fault the letter contained what it did: a tumble of words, poured out in her mother's girlish hand. That these words have had the opposite effect than intended is unfortunate, but typical of the strained relations between Madeline and her mother. The unexpected missive touched on many things. Madeline had sat for a long time with the pages in front of her, the accompanying parcel cast to one side. At first she hadn't been at all moved by what she read. But then the tears came, fast and furious, followed by an overwhelming urge to throttle her mother. Instead, she'd pounded the top of the Steinway until her fingers were numb and all the rage she felt toward her mother was turned in against herself.

She's punching the water; she is not cutting it as if her hand is a blade. She shows no strength, no endurance, no flexibility—none of the three principles of a good competitive swim, principles she'd once abided by. She makes no effort to regulate her breathing or to synchronize it with her furious strokes. Her legs thrash out of rhythm with her arms. This time when she swims she isn't camouflaged by darkness, and this time she isn't wearing any clothes. Somewhere on the shore behind her is the midnight-blue sheath she was wearing during her all-night "concert." Somewhere along the levee are her shoes. When she had run toward the river, tearing at her clothes and at the strand of fake pearls around her neck, she hadn't been thinking about the differences between this swim and all the others. That it's daytime, that she's naked and has also consumed a tremendous quantity of liquor. This time, as she'd thrown herself hard against the cold body of the Mississippi, she'd cried. And so instead of donating her piano to the Mississippi River's lost and found, her contribution for today is her own body and a deluge of angry tears.

Stop, a gentler voice seems to say, *just ... stop*—swimming, breathing, hating, feeling sad ... but she can't. For whatever reason, she can't keep her arms from making windmills, her legs from kicking, her lungs from drawing whatever ragged breaths they can in between mouthfuls of water. Not even when the boat approaches does she stop, or when they throw a kind of lasso around her and drag her toward that boat, and not when they haul her up onto the deck, where she continues making swimming motions with her arms, crying. The men are yelling something at her, and now someone's warm lips are on her mouth. She goes in and out of consciousness and sees the world tip over on its side, the floor of the boat and a tidal wave of vomit. Then she sees the sky, grey-white and pleasant above her head, and she relaxes. Someone is stroking her forehead and everything is all right.

The letter from her mother is on its way to the Gulf of Mexico. Perhaps if she had been willing to read between its lines, this particular swim wouldn't have been necessary.

At 8:00 a.m. Cleo stands sheepishly at the intercom outside the Pommes Royales and explains her predicament to Mrs. Ryan, who buzzes her into the hotel. The only admonishment Mrs. Ryan offers is, "Now, heart, if that ever happens again—"

"It won't, I promise."

"Well, just in case it does, I want you to call me. At any hour. What if something happened to you? I'd just be sick over it, wouldn't I? Now, do you want some hot coffee or would you rather go to bed?"

Although she's already had quite a bit of coffee, Cleo says yes to Mrs. Ryan's offer. She's reached that euphoric state that a lack of sleep can bring on. She's also tired of being alone with her thoughts.

"Come, we'll take it in my sitting room. It's gonna rain any minute," Mrs. Ryan says, opening a door off the foyer that Cleo has never noticed before. There's a loveseat covered with chintz cushions and a rolltop desk where Mrs. Ryan works on her novel of love. The room, tiny but serene, faces out onto a narrow walkway and a wall covered in lush vines.

Mrs. Ryan tells Cleo to make herself comfortable and hurries off to get the coffee. Cleo stares at an empty birdcage in the corner, wondering where its resident parakeet is. Among her various manageable phobias is a genuine fear of birds, especially those found flapping around indoors. When Mrs. Ryan returns, Cleo decides not to inquire after Judy's health in case the bird's possible demise has gone unmentioned for a reason. Why haven't I ever heard it chirping? she wonders, accepting a cup of coffee.

They've only just taken their first tentative sips when the rain begins to fall outside the window.

"What'd I tell you?" Mrs. Ryan nods. "My tailbone started throbbing about an hour ago, and voilà, rain. I've always thought the Fox Network oughta hire me and my psychic tailbone to do their weather!" She sets her cup and saucer down on the coffee table and yawns. "I've been up since four-thirty. I just could not sleep."

Cleo stifles her own yawn and asks how Mrs. Ryan passes the time when she can't sleep. Cleo balances her cup and saucer carefully on her knee and listens as Mrs. Ryan describes her coping methods.

"And then this morning, out of sheer desperation, I turned on the TV. I thought maybe I could bore myself back to sleep. Well, no. Can you believe that some woman actually tried to swim the Mississippi River this morning? And naked! I mean, really, we all know what that means, don't we?"

"What woman? When did this happen?" Cleo nearly spills her coffee.

Mrs. Ryan looks at her with surprise. "A woman," she says, shrugging. "Just some sad lady, I guess. Why? They said she was trying to commit suicide. No kidding! It's so sad, isn't it? And she'll be sadder today because it didn't quite work out the way she planned. Apparently it wasn't her first try, either. They grabbed her early this morning and took her to the police station, as they should have. She obviously needs help, swimming naked in November! Why are you looking at me like that, Miss Cleopatra?"

"I have to go." Cleo sets her cup and saucer down on the table with exaggerated care. She stands up, confused, and reaches for the doorknob, which seems to be a hundred miles away from her hand.

"What's the matter, sugar?" Mrs. Ryan jumps up. She watches in utter amazement as Cleo flings the door open, looks wildly at the empty birdcage and runs out of the room. She runs right out of the hotel, not back to the room she has waited all night to be let into.

"Huh," says Mrs. Ryan. "You just can never know what will set some people off."

Sighing, Mrs. Ryan moves toward her private quarters, calling, "Judy? JUDY! This is no time to be fooling, do you hear me?" Under her breath she mutters in a not-very-belle-like manner, "Stupid-ass bird! I never liked you anyway. Wish he'd taken you along."

Dear Madeline,
This isn't quite the way I'd hoped to re-establish con-
tact with you, but our brief telephone conversation on
your birthday tells me you still do not wish to see or
even talk to me. I'm writing this letter because I know
that even if I do manage to see you when I come to

town, you'll refuse to talk. Still and all, I will never lose my hope of reuniting with you. You may be a grown woman, but you're still my only daughter, my only child. . . .

My darling, there is no easy way to tell you this, but Carmelle has passed on. I spoke with her sister in Memphis, who said she died of natural causes. I ask how it can ever be considered "natural" when anyone dies at such a young age. She wasn't much older than you, after all! Cancer. . . . It was very quick, her sister said. It seems Carmelle had a daughter, though her sister made no mention of a husband. Perhaps he came and went, as husbands do, or perhaps she never married. . . . I sent along some money for the little girl and enclose the family's address in this letter. Carmelle's sister called me to ask for your current address. As you will see from the contents of the parcel, Carmelle had set aside some record albums that she wished for you to have. When her sister, Amy, referred to you as "your daughter who used to swim," I knew Carmelle must have mentioned you with great fondness. So you see, Madeline, Carmelle did not forget you, as I am sure you've never forgotten her. Out of sight isn't out of mind, no matter what you may tell yourself. You seem to have a very good memory—but only for the bad things. Why not forgive and forget?

You will also find enclosed my telephone number in Florida, which I hope you'll use. Mr. Oliver and I have a lovely home in Port Charlotte now, which you and your husband are welcome to visit anytime. . . . I'd love to get to know him and, of course, to see you and

*hear all about your life in wicked old New Orleans
these past years. I can just imagine how beautiful
you've become. You have the LeFevre bones—and the
Shockfire temperament.*

*I know this will be very sad news for you. I know
how much you adored Carmelle. I adored her, too,
even if she did cause lasting strife between you and me.
I'm sure she didn't mean any real harm. Why must you
continue to punish me for something that happened so
long ago? You seem to want me to pay eternally. I had
your best interests in mind, you know, or believed I did
at the time. I hope you'll explain the real reasons for
your behaviour one fine day. Maybe now that you're a
married woman you realize that people aren't perfect.
That everyone does the best they can. What seems like
a simple choice can turn out to be a terrible mistake;
and sometimes what seemed so terrible in the moment
isn't really anything but a choice made once upon a
time. Or maybe you no longer think about any of this.
I just want you to know that I am here for you, and
like it or not, I will remain,*

Your loving mother.

THE PHONE AND THE downstairs buzzer sound in
unison. Johnny looks at the ringing telephone and then at
the wall where the intercom continues to squawk. He reso-
lutely ignores them both. The phone falls silent first; the
buzzer is a little more insistent. He pulls a sofa cushion over
his head and groans. That Madeline may have opened the

package from her mother and might be trying to call him dawns too late. He snatches the phone from the cradle and listens helplessly to the dial tone. The doorbell is likewise mute. Johnny curses as he struggles into his jeans and flies down the staircase, bare-chested and barefooted. Someone is standing in the foyer and it isn't Madeline. Some kid, probably selling chocolate bars door to door. Johnny sighs and is about to turn when the boy pounds fiercely on the glass door separating them. Then he realizes it isn't a boy at all but a young woman, and one that seems hell-bent on getting his attention. Johnny opens the door a crack.

"Who're you lookin' for?" He keeps one hand on the doorknob.

"You," she says, so softly he can barely hear her. "You have to get down to the police station right away." When he stares at her she becomes more insistent. "Please! Your wife ..."

Johnny feels a jolt of panic and slams the door. He races up the stairs without asking any more questions, leaving the young woman in the foyer. His mind is a carousel of obscenities and self-recriminations as he hunts for his wallet and pulls on a shirt. Shoes, he remembers as he steps barefoot out into the hallway. *Jesus! What has she done now?* He searches frantically for his cowboy boots. *And who the hell was that in the downstairs hall?*

The young woman is still there when he bursts through the door. As he pushes past her, she thrusts something into his hand, an envelope of some kind. It's a phone bill, addressed to him, with something scrawled on the back. Rushing along Decatur Street, he glances at it. "I need to talk to you. Please call me as soon as possible," it says.

There's a name and a telephone number. He snorts and stuffs the bill in his back pocket as he hurries on to the police station. Who the hell was that, and why does she want to talk to him? And why would he call some chick he doesn't even know when his whole life is falling to pieces?

Cleo could follow Johnny to the police station and wait outside for a glimpse, but she doesn't. Instead she hurries back to the Pommes Royales Maisonnettes to wait for his call. Had she followed him she would have seen Johnny emerge from the police station alone, chewing his moustache in consternation. When he arrives at the Conti Street precinct he's told that his wife has already been released. He asks how this could be possible. The clerk shrugs and says she called someone, and they came to get her and that's that. He demands to know who came to get her. The clerk says, "Some man who swore he would assume full responsibility for her, being her next of kin. That's all we ask in these situations, sir. May I ask who *you* are?"

"I'm her goddamned husband, that's who!"

"I'll have to ask you to lower your voice, sir," says the clerk, enjoying her power. "Your wife has gone home. Maybe you ought to try looking for her there?" She gives Johnny an omniscient little smile as she folds her hands in front of her to indicate that their conversation has come to its end. But he isn't satisfied with this at all.

"I demand to know what happened!" Two cops look over and frown. One approaches and asks what the problem seems to be. Johnny tells him.

The cop nods. "She was pulled from the river this morning. Seems she's pretty upset about some things." He puts his hand on Johnny's shoulder and drops his voice. "You two having some difficulties, sir? Maybe we could talk about it over a cup of coffee, you and me?"

Johnny shrugs off the cop's hand. "Thanks anyway. I guess I'd better be getting home."

"I guess so," the cop says, with more than a hint of accusation in his voice.

Johnny resists the urge to punch the cop, but just barely. The only thing stopping him is the realization that he has enough problems already. Walking back to his apartment, Johnny is cross-eyed with green fury. Who picked Madeline up, and where did the smug bastard take her? Certainly not home! He stops short and then heads in the opposite direction, away from his apartment and back toward the ferry dock. Maybe she and her mysterious knight in shining armour are curled up in the studio right this minute. Maybe not. It's worth a try, he reasons, feeling his blood begin to boil anew. Under the swirling lava of his jealousy is a genuine concern for Madeline and a deepening guilt. He hasn't heard from her since before that package disappeared. If only he'd been on time for her birthday, none of this would have happened.

MARCUS DIDN'T FEEL GOOD about leaving her alone, but Madeline had insisted she was fine. She thanked him for his help and sent him on his way with promises to call if she needed anything. He was visibly disappointed when she refused to invite him in to see the so-called studio, which he was dying to get a look at. To his credit, Marcus didn't make a single quip about her police-issue outfit beyond, "You look good in grey!" Of her gnarled hair and bloodshot eyes he said nothing. He thought she looked like someone who'd been crying or drinking (or both) for about ten hours straight. As a bartender and confidante to several drag queens, Marcus knew that particular look all too well.

She was wearing a plain cotton shift and handcuffs when the police officer led Marcus to where Madeline was waiting. Marcus rose to the occasion beautifully, making a big show of his brotherly affection for her. Convinced that he was an able and appropriate handler, the police released her into his custody after what seemed like an awful lot of paperwork. The charge of public mischief was dropped when Madeline agreed to seek psychiatric help.

Marcus was only mildly surprised when Madeline informed him that "home" was no longer the apartment above the Mint Bar, but across the river in Algiers. He paid for a cab so they wouldn't have to endure the ferry, and she was grateful for that. She had had enough river travel for a lifetime, she said, and wanted only to change her clothes and sleep off her monumental headache. She sent him home in the same cab and waited until it disappeared down Patterson before making her weary climb to the top floor.

In the back seat of the cab, Marcus is inclined to believe that Madeline's attempt to swim the Mississippi was nothing more serious than a spell of drunken foolishness. And yet something about the episode will prove troubling enough to keep even Marcus, who loves tidbits and gossip as much as the next person, from making light of it at the bar. When the story of her second swim makes its way around the Quarter, and it will, Marcus will keep his knowledge to himself. The story of her first swim remains a secret. At least, that's what Madeline thinks.

Something has happened to Madeline in the last two hours. She feels downright serene as she removes her police-issue dress and climbs into the bathtub. It's a sort of *well-that's-that* sensation. Not even when she emerges from the bath and sees the piano surrounded by the garish lawn ornaments does she feel a fresh rush of grief. It's as if the river has performed the kind of heart surgery jilted lovers dream of: complete removal of the body's most symbolic and troublesome organ. The sensation is pleasurable when compared with the vengeful fantasies that have tortured her all these years. The piece of paper on which her mother had written both her own and Carmelle's sister's phone numbers lies on the floor. She kneels and picks it up, regards the numbers for a moment and drops the page into the space between the mattress and the window. The unwrapped parcel is tucked here, too. Its contents already revealed in her mother's letter, there's no real need to open it. Later, she thinks, or maybe never.

She hears a far-off rumble of thunder and thinks what a nice lullaby a big storm would make right now, not realizing that the thundering sound is being made by Johnny's fists on the downstairs door. For once, Madeline's negligent neighbours on the lower floor haven't propped the street door wide open. They aren't receiving callers today due to their own recent troubles with the police. This is fortunate for Madeline, but unlucky for Johnny, who stands ratlike in the downpour, gazing up at her window. He contemplates screaming her name until she comes to the window but can't seem to set aside his pride in order to do so. He gives the door a final, violent pounding and then gives up.

Surely there's some less degrading way to get your wife back,

Valentucci. He remembers the strange young woman who rang the doorbell earlier and wonders if he should call her. By the time he reaches the shore of the French Quarter, he has talked himself into and out of the idea six or seven times. *Why should I humiliate myself any more than I already have?* He plods toward Papa Leone's, where he knows he'll have to face Carlo's speeches about the superiority of the Italian female as wife yet again. Just thinking of the Sicilian version of "I told you so" is too much for Johnny to bear. He goes home instead.

Still wearing his rain-soaked clothes, he unplugs the phone and, with the aid of a hammer, takes out what is left of his jealous fury on the intercom. There. Now nobody can reach anybody. This is the Italianate version of what's good for the goose, only Johnny doesn't share his wife's sense of tranquility. He grabs a bottle of brandy and Benedictine he finds stashed under the sink. Sits on the sofa, contemplates the bottle, then swigs. Gags and curses with his mouth full of something awful. Windex. He runs to the sink and rinses his mouth, cursing Madeline's sudden penchant for reusing and recycling.

"IF ANYONE CALLS FOR ME, can you put them on hold?" Cleo asks, pausing at the front desk of the Pommes Royales. Mrs. Ryan says of course. "I'm just going to run down to the Verti Mart for a minute. Do you need anything?" Cleo has been trying to think of ways to make amends for storming out on Mrs. Ryan the other day without thanking her for the coffee.

"I'd love a Mars bar," Mrs. Ryan says.

"Done. So, if anyone calls, I'll be right back."

"Gotcha." Mrs. Ryan struggles to hide her curiosity. "Someone important, I gather?" Cleo nods. "Well, scoot then!"

"And then my pancreas started actin' up, so the doctor brought me back in for another look, and that's the only reason I'm not number one on the football pool at McGibberty's no more," laments the man ahead of Cleo. She's in line at the Verti Mart and has been for several minutes. She shifts her weight from foot to foot, hoping the monologue will end soon. It took her two short minutes to gather her groceries, but it looks as if it might take an entire lifetime to pay for them. "How's things with you these days, heart?" the man asks the cashier, a young girl who then launches into her own account of her troubles. Cleo tries hard to control her temper. After a seeming eternity, she edges toward the cash register and manages to set down her loaf of bread, a jar of peanut butter, a six-pack of beer and a carton of Verti Mart's famous potato salad.

The man wheezes and launches into a new monologue, this one about the hunting camp he and his cousin are planning to open next fall. Cleo is sure she'll go mad. An irritated sigh escapes her lips and the man turns and narrows his eyes at her; she has just betrayed herself as a non-native.

"Some folks just oughta move to New York and be done with it," the man says to the cashier, and she nods, giving Cleo a disapproving look. The man finally moves aside but continues to chat to the cashier as she rings in Cleo's purchases. The stopwatch in Cleo's brain ticks maniacally, and she practically snatches her change from the girl's hand. As she's leaving the store she hears the man say, "That one's gonna rush right to her grave!"

It isn't until Cleo is at the gate of the Pommes Royales that she realizes she's forgotten Mrs. Ryan's Mars bar. "Shit!" she cries, turning back toward the Verti Mart. She re-enters the shop, ignores the same heavy-set, wheezing man when he says, "Forget somethin'? No wonder!" and hurries to buy the chocolate bar, cursing herself silently as she races back to the hotel.

The look on Mrs. Ryan's face tells her everything she needs to know. Someone called. Cleo sets down her grocery bag and listens as Mrs. Ryan sheepishly explains that the man—yes, it was a man—said he would call back later. "He wouldn't let me put him on hold for even five seconds," Mrs. Ryan sighs. "Everyone's in such a rush these days!" Cleo nods sadly and excuses herself from the lobby.

She's eating her potato salad with great sorrow when the phone rings. To her further disappointment it's Mrs. Ryan, just calling to say how much she enjoyed her Mars bar. "I also meant to ask you, Miss Cleo, if you're planning to be with us through the Thanksgiving holiday?" Mrs. Ryan always says "us," even though she's the sole operator of the little hotel. Cleo supposes it's a habit left over from the days when there was a Mr. Ryan. "I'm offering a holiday special," she continues, "six nights for the price of four."

Cleo sits mute, wondering if she ought to give up and leave town. He called once, she reminds herself; he might call back. She tells Mrs. Ryan that she'll take the holiday special but that she might not stay for the full six nights.

"Well, you just let me know, all right?"

"OK," Cleo promises, opening the refrigerator to retrieve a beer.

"Whoops, gotta go. Phone's ringing!" sings Mrs. Ryan, and Cleo quickly hangs up, crossing her fingers that she won't need to finish the beer she's just opened. She waits. The phone in her room doesn't ring. She takes a sip of beer and feels her hopes droop further.

By the last swallow of the sixth can, Cleo's spirits are at an all-time low. She resists the temptation to go out for more beer and opens her notebook.

I need to meet you, she writes, her handwriting slightly crabbed after she's consumed the six-pack. She writes *Madeline Shockfire* over and over until she's filled two full pages with the woman's name.

What Cleo doesn't know—can never know—is that her mother once felt exactly as she feels now: crazy with longing and completely dependent on another human being's good will.

February 14, 1973
Reigate, England

The chocolate in England was quite good, much better than anything Caroline had ever had in Canada. On this day it came in a heart-shaped box covered in shiny foil and was handed to her over the breakfast table. Lyle gave her a quick peck on the cheek and winked at his father, who sat opposite him, next to Mrs. Savoy senior, whose box of candy was significantly larger. Later that night they would all sit down to a proper meal with wine. There'd be red food colouring in the mashed potatoes, a whimsical touch Mr. Savoy insisted on every year. Lyle was off to his classes at business college in

London, and as Caroline watched him go, she felt a blanket of despair drop over her. She couldn't bear the thought of another long day alone with her mother-in-law and the baby. Lyle's father would be off to the pub where he worked as a maintenance man, and the day would grind on, with chores divided by pots of tea and inane chatter about where Lyle and Caroline should look for property. Too innocent to understand the tension between her mother and her gran, Cleo sat playing with the teddy bear her granddad had given her for Valentine's Day.

Agnes got up from the table and went to the kitchen to wash the breakfast dishes. When she returned to clear the table, she was amazed to find Caroline stabbing her fingernail into each of the chocolates in her Valentine's box with what seemed like vicious glee.

"Tsk! What're you doing?" cried Agnes, horrified.

"I'm just trying to find where the orange creams are lurking." Caroline's voice was flat. "These mixed boxes are full of them." She continued stabbing at the chocolates until Agnes snatched them away. Caroline stood up from the table and went to Cleo, who she picked up from the floor and murmured to in Italian.

"I wish you'd speak English. The poor child won't have much use for Latin in this world, will she?" Agnes clutched the box of chocolates to her bosom, her eyes wide. Her daughter-in-law seemed normal till the men left for the day, and then who knew what she would do? Agnes had tried to let Lyle know there was something odd about his wife, but he had refused to listen. It was normal for a woman to be a little moody after the birth of a child. "Milk mad," they'd called it in Agnes's day. But this! Cleo was three years old, for goodness' sake! Caroline's unusual behaviour could no longer be explained away by saying it was female trouble. She was mad, and it had nothing to do with milk at this late stage. All she ever did was moon around the house, looking like the world had ended. She was usually good with Cleo but insisted on speaking to the child in gibberish, some odd combination of Italian and English. Other times she seemed not to notice that the child was even there. Unbeknownst to her husband, Caroline often spent several hours a day in bed, staring at the wall and leaving Agnes to look after the house and Cleo. Agnes had given up trying to coerce Caroline into helping out, because when she did lend a hand she made a mess of everything she touched.

"Why don't you lie down for a bit?" Agnes suggested, moving her own box of chocolates out of reach.

Caroline smiled, and yet it wasn't a sane smile, in Agnes's estimation. Her eyes seemed to look right through her mother-in-law. "We're going to the Tate," she said dreamily, kissing the top of Cleo's white-blond head.

In that moment Agnes looked at her daughter-in-law and saw someone capable of climbing onto the London tube without ever returning. Small blessing if she did, she thought, but not with my son's child in her arms. Agnes moved with authority and put her hands on Cleo's shoulders, hissing, "If you have to be an oddie, do it by yourself!" She anticipated a struggle, but Caroline released the child immediately. Agnes watched as Caroline put on her coat, picked up her handbag and drifted out the front door.

"Poor cow," Agnes whispered to Cleo, who had begun to whimper. "I hope you're a bit more right in the head than your mum."

He'd said they were going to live in London. Reigate was not London. Caroline walked in a daze, relieved to be out of the house. She did intend to go to the Tate Gallery in London and so walked until she came to the train station. There she purchased a ticket and waited on the platform for what seemed like hours. She didn't have a book and wouldn't have been able to read one anyway. Her desire to read had disappeared. Nothing appealed. Try as she might, she couldn't make herself concentrate, and it had only got worse after the baby was born.

When she boarded the train she knew something was very wrong, and yet she couldn't pinpoint what it was. A blanket of numbness had swept in to cover the blanket of despair, and she wandered up and down the train wondering how to shake it. She was glad not to have Cleo with her now; she didn't trust herself to keep track of her own child. It took all she had to remember where she was and where she was going. By the time she reached the Tate Gallery she felt a bit better.

"Two, please," she said to the gallery's ticket seller, who looked over the edge of the counter and back at Caroline with some puzzlement. The man's look of concern amused her. "One's for my doppelgänger," she whispered. The man nodded gravely. "I used to be pretty," she explained, gesturing to her face. The man frowned ever so slightly as she took the tickets and moved into the gallery. It was cool and quiet. She disliked the way her heels clicked on the polished floor as she moved past the paintings. The echo was disturbing, so she slipped off her shoes and padded around in her stockings. A guard asked her to please put her shoes on, and she frowned but obeyed. She stood before Frederic Lord Leighton's painting *The Bath of Psyche*. It showed a nude Psyche gazing serenely at her reflection, delighting in her own sensuality. Cupid was nowhere to be seen. Hence her happiness, Caroline decided, hurrying away in search of the Rossetti painting that had inspired her trip to the gallery in the first place.

"There she is!" she cried out, spotting *Beata Beatrix*. She went to the painting as if running to meet an old friend and sat on the floor in front of it. Another guard asked her to please refrain from sitting on the floor. She got to her feet and tried to admire the foreground of the picture but the background kept leaping out at her. The intense expression on Beatrice's face couldn't compete with the Ponte Vecchio shimmering behind her, and Caroline squinted to try to make it recede. The figure of Dante on the right side of the canvas made her feel uneasy. The Angel of Love shown on the left suddenly seemed to Caroline to be siphoning up all of the oxygen in the gallery. "Stop it!" she shouted, and the guard rushed over to see what she was yelling about. She didn't answer his question but rushed off, convinced that she could now hear the portraits on the walls breathing in and out. She broke into a full run and didn't stop until she reached the front steps of the Tate. Then ran again without looking through the traffic that whizzed by. It was a miracle she wasn't killed in her mad dash to get to the river.

The Thames sneered at her. Gazing across the water, she missed Florence with an unbearable intensity. It was the same regretful longing that swept through her at meals when Agnes put down all the food at once, in bowls, the meat and potatoes and vegetables all served together with an offensive and overwhelming thud. Caroline preferred the more civilized Italian approach to eating: in stages, with wine and with bread that didn't taste like old sponge. She leaned on the wall overlooking the river, rested her chin on her arms and thought, If he would just take me back to Italy, everything would be all right again.

She had never in her wildest dreams imagined getting stuck in England. They were supposed to marry here to appease Lyle's parents, then return to Florence. Her own parents had no idea where she was. She hadn't been able to bring herself to call them when she'd first arrived in England, having convinced herself that not telling her parents would charm her chances for a quicker return to Italy. It was then decided that she would have the baby in England, too, and that made some sense. She was violently sick to her stomach every day and so couldn't have taken a job in any of the galleries or museums in Florence anyway. As soon as the baby was born, they were definitely going back to Italy. Lyle promised, had sworn up and down on his own mother's life. She should have realized that Lyle's fear of his mother and worship of his father rendered such promises empty. But she'd believed him when he said he hated England and couldn't wait to leave.

However, as soon as the baby was born, Caroline lost interest in most things. A bleakness swooped in, accompanied by a terrifying array of emotions, none of them pleasant. She would hold the baby and become panic-stricken, then panic if anyone else held the child for too long. Cleo refused to breastfeed, perhaps sensing her mother's nervousness, and only cried instead. Agnes stepped in and assumed full care of the baby, whose ridiculous name, Cleopatra, riled her every time she heard it used. For a time she'd insisted on calling the baby Elizabeth, after the queen.

Caroline's only show of spirit came when she realized that her habit of speaking to the baby in Italian drove her mother-in-law nuts. In all other areas she bent to Agnes's will, which had a curious effect on Caroline's perception of time. She imagined that her life had been reduced to one long day that had begun at Heathrow airport and still seemed to be unfolding one agonizing moment at a time. Conversely, in given moments, her whole life seemed to be speeding ahead without her permission.

She wanted to say: I'm not well. I don't feel right. I'm frightened, but the words never reached her mouth. How could she possibly explain the strange blend of lethargy and overexcitement that coursed through her to a man who'd been raised by Agnes, she who believed all genuine suffering had ended with World War II? According to Lyle's mother all subsequent generations were spoiled, ungrateful, incapable of weathering basic challenges. One could hardly complain of a racing heart and dark, irrational thoughts to a woman like that.

Now Cleo was three. Three Christmases had gone by, three years of birthdays and letters from friends still living and working in Florence. The city itself had been put back together with remarkable speed, but the damaged art and manuscripts would require years of attention. At first the letters made Caroline feel desperate to return. After the baby was born she read the missives from Italy as if receiving news from another planet. Eventually the letters stopped arriving, mostly because she didn't—couldn't—answer them. The innocent questions asked by her former fellow students— Had she been to Carnaby Street? Had they ever spotted a Beatle? Was the fashion scene in London as far out as people said it was?—only reinforced Caroline's belief that she had made a terrible mistake.

She inhaled deeply. London did not smell like Florence. Florence smelled of stone and bread and the fields surrounding it; it was bus fumes mixed with leather and vegetables. Poppies. London was not that. It was boiled potatoes, wet wool and cold grey; it was blackened fingernails and nostrils. London smelled like a newspaper, Florence like soup. London was the Industrial Revolution, Florence the Renaissance. Machines versus flowers, factories versus love. Comedies of manners against comedies divine. She hated London because it wasn't Florence, and yet even her hatred was bland now. The malaise she felt frightened her more than the nervousness.

No, peace of mind wouldn't come until she was safe and sound in Florence. She'd got herself into a bad spot was all; she'd allowed too much time to pass. It would be all right. She would beg Lyle to take her back to Italy, or to send her back with Cleo if he wouldn't go himself. There were ways, she told herself, ways to feel better and make up for her mistakes. He was passionate underneath; she'd experienced a side of him his mother didn't know existed. He'd understand how heartsick she felt if she could only find the right words to convey her unhappiness. If she could get him away from his mother for just a few hours, she felt certain he'd listen the way he used to. She wanted nothing more than to get back to the place where she felt most at home. Not Canada, where she was from, but Florence, where she had felt alive, needed. Yes, she realized that there was a simple solution. He would simply have to help her. She straightened up and decided to walk for a few blocks before taking the train back to face Agnes.

Her return to the Savoy household resembled an errant dog slinking in with its tail between its legs. Agnes nodded and handed her the cutlery, and Caroline dutifully laid it out. Cleo hadn't even seemed to notice that her mother had gone, though she did chirp when Caroline knelt to chuck her under the chin. Agnes said nothing. There were some benefits to the English habit of perpetual politeness. Everything got swept under the carpet, everything unpleasant was kept under the tongue.

No mention was made of Caroline's quixotic trip to London. If the male members of the Savoy family noticed her increasingly erratic behaviour, they didn't discuss it. There were more important things on the horizon. Namely, Lyle's sudden decision to immigrate to Canada, a journey he didn't mention to his wife until he'd booked the tickets. It would be the second time he'd taken it upon himself to arrange a voyage without her consent. It would also be the last.

CURIOUS, HE'D CALLED HER ONCE. She wasn't there. Johnny was in no mood for jokes or pranks or for waiting around. Whoever she is, she isn't worth the trouble. It's been a long time since a woman just gave him her phone number out of the blue like that. Especially a younger woman. Sure, she looked like a boy when he first saw her, but she was pretty, from what he remembered. Blond, too. Maybe that's what made him call. He'd refused to give the front-desk clerk at her hotel his name and then refused to be put on hold. Embarrassed, he refuses to call again. He'll have to figure out a way to convince Carlo to give him his job back without having to beg. And then Johnny thinks to himself, Why not beg? Good practice for when I see Madeline again.

"Look who it is! Johnny No-Show!" Carlo bellows as Johnny walks through the door of Papa Leone's, invisible hat in hand. Carlo cracks an unexpected smile. "I was worried about you. Everything okay?"

Johnny shakes his head. "Carlo," he begins, his voice preparing to beg, "I ... can you—"

Carlo waves his hand. "Forget it. Get your ass into the kitchen and make me something to eat." He pats Johnny's shoulder. With surprising benevolence, he asks, "She okay?"

It's Johnny's turn to wave away the question. He disappears into the kitchen and sees the mess. "You guys have a hurricane while I was gone?" he calls out.

"Hurricane Carlo," replies his cousin.

"Cara mia!" Cleo blushes at Carlo's warm greeting and sits down at the same table by the window. "You bring your appetite with you today?" He sets a menu down.

"I'd like to speak with Johnny V., please," she says, attempting a firm nod.

"Oh," says Carlo, taken aback. "Let me see if he's in today," he lies, retreating to the kitchen. "You dog!" he hisses at Johnny. Johnny looks at him without comprehension. Carlo is excited. "She's here!"

"Who?" Johnny asks, suddenly terrified that Madeline has shown up at the restaurant, but hopeful, too.

"Your girlfriend," Carlo insists. "Out front, the little blonde!" He folds his arms across his chest and nods knowingly. "Didn't I tell ya? Didn't I say a little action on the side would help? How old is she, you pig?" He follows Johnny to the door of the kitchen and giggles to himself as he watches Johnny wipe his hands nervously on his apron.

"She's not my girlfriend," Johnny whispers. "I don't know who she is. She gave me her number the other day. She was waiting in the lobby of my building when I came down." He peers into the dining room and sees Cleo sitting by the window.

"Go," Carlo says, giving Johnny a shove.

"Hey." Johnny stands at Cleo's table. Her mouth goes dry and she can only nod up at him. "You wanted to see me?"

Cleo glances over at Carlo, who grins widely at them from behind the bar. She lowers her voice so that only Johnny can hear. "I need to talk to you as soon as possible," she says, her eyes on Carlo.

Johnny shrugs. "Talk to me now. I gotta get back to work in a minute."

Do it, Cleo, she thinks, taking a deep breath. "I was wondering if you could ... introduce me to your wife?" Before he can interject she hurries on, speaking off the top of her head. "I'm a reporter for a newspaper in Canada. I'm doing a piece on local heroes and ... I'd like to talk to your wife about her swims across the Mississippi."

Johnny frowns. "I don't think so." He glances at Carlo and turns back to Cleo. His voice is low and fierce. "My wife isn't a 'local hero,' as you call it. She's nothing of the kind. Enjoy your dinner."

Cleo grabs Johnny by the sleeve, a gesture that surprises them both. "Please," she begs. "Please think about it and call me. Do you still have my number?" Reluctantly, Johnny nods. "I've wanted to talk to her ever since I saw her ... on the news."

Me too, thinks Johnny. He wonders how this odd little chick has figured out that he knows Madeline. "How did you know Madeline is my wife?" He nibbles his moustache.

Madeline. Again the name flares across Cleo's brain like a meteor shower. Recovering, she explains that she simply put two and two together. "I was in a bar one night. Someone mentioned it. I've seen you around the Quarter."

"Have you?" Johnny says, with a sly grin. "Well, maybe we can have dinner sometime and talk about how you saw me." He stands with his feet farther apart and leans forward a little, aware that Carlo is watching.

"Well, I'm only in town for a few more days and I really want ... this story," Cleo begins to falter in her lie, thrown by Johnny's flirtatious manner. He's making her uncomfortable and it shows. "I'd like to talk to ... Madeline ... as soon as possible."

Johnny straightens up and gives a little shrug of macho indifference. "I'll think about it," he grunts, walking away from the table and past Carlo, who looks at him like he's lost his mind. Cleo pushes her chair back and hurries out of Papa Leone's, now determined to wait more patiently for Johnny's help.

Carlo pokes his head through the pick-up window and says to Johnny, "I don't know, maybe I wasn't wrong. Maybe you *are* bad for business."

MADELINE'S NEW ROUTINE is almost as strict as the one she lived by in her childhood and adolescence. She wakes early with the help of the bright light streaming in through the wall of windows beside her bed. As soon as she's dressed she heads down to Bill's Bar and orders a Barq's root beer, which she sips from the bottle while reading the *Times-Picayune* social pages. She then strolls up and down the leafy streets of Algiers Point, pausing to watch the children at Holy Name of Mary playing in the schoolyard. She avoids the houses she so recently plundered for lawn ornaments and shies away from the river entirely. Short on money, she subsists on a diet of white toast with lots of butter and her morning soda. She's neither gaining nor losing weight on this unusual diet. Its effect on her complexion is a surprisingly positive one, giving her a radiance she hasn't had in years. And it sure beats the hell out of her mother's long-ago idea that eating grapefruit morning, noon and night is the path to physical perfection. Adult life does have its charms, after all.

The lawn ornaments remain at their tables surrounding the piano, and Madeline plays for them each afternoon for an hour or two. She avoids Bach and sticks to a repertoire of jazzy nonsense songs she makes up as she goes, singing along in a cracked yet cheerful voice. If her behaviour seems odd, she doesn't recognize it as such. What Madeline feels is something that bears a striking resemblance to happiness, and that's enough for her. Complete solitude feels good, even natural. Aside from her daily check-in with Marcus from the pay phone at Bill's Bar, she's had no other contact with the world across the river.

The hardest part of her new lifestyle—if this hermit's life

can be so called—is nightfall. During the long hours of darkness, Madeline has to work to keep from submitting to fear of the future and nostalgic wallowing with equal effort. She eschews the easy oblivion of alcohol in favour of eavesdropping. Crouched at the top of the back staircase, Madeline can hear bits and pieces of the conversations conducted by her addle-brained downstairs neighbours. The disembodied voices offer up a kind of hallucinogenic soap opera. The plot lines aren't always easy to follow, but there's certainly plenty of drama. Instead of fearing the owners of these voices, Madeline has realized that much like her, they simply want to be left alone to enjoy themselves. They've shown no interest whatsoever in her activities. And if it's a lack of ambition that's kept them from climbing either staircase leading up to her studio, hooray for lost ambition! Her only lingering fear is that they may—accidentally, of course—set the building on fire some night.

Tonight, instead of eavesdropping, Madeline is writing a love song for Eleanor Holm. She allows herself the small pleasure of a glass of brandy but barely touches it. The electric heater hums pleasantly at her feet, its bright orange coils throwing impressive warmth. Playing and replaying certain chords, Madeline smiles. Good old clear-eyed hindsight: she's amused to realize that her feelings for Eleanor Holm were one hundred per cent romantic in nature. She's never had much tolerance for blurry feelings. Madeline either loves or hates, wants or does not want. It's when things threaten to blur that she becomes frightened and shuts down completely.

Which is why it suits her not to think too much about Johnny, whose role in her life is less and less clear with each passing day. If her mind so much as heads in his direction, Madeline quickly returns her focus to the lawn ornaments or the floorboards or to the business of her neighbours. Or, as in the case of this evening, to Eleanor Holm. Now *there* was a woman who knew how to handle her talents. When the Olympics were no longer an option, she simply moved on to the next logical arena: the movies. If there is any one item Madeline feels sorry to have left behind in St. Louis, it's her Eleanor Holm scrapbook. She's seized by a sudden desire to know whether the scrapbook still exists, which then reminds her of the records Carmelle supposedly left her. For a brief moment she considers calling her mother in Florida to ask about the scrapbook, then laughs at the ridiculousness of the idea. Calling Memphis holds even less appeal. Besides, she thinks, I don't have a phone. Madeline climbs down from the piano and retrieves the piece of paper. Is about to plunge it into the flame of a nearby candle when she decides against it.

"It's your job to keep me from getting stupid," she tells Snow White. She then returns to the piano to work on her ballad of love for the great Eleanor Holm. Freud himself would have applauded Madeline's talent for sublimation.

January, 1976
St. Louis, Missouri

Madeline was a quick study in all senses. She sailed through the primary songbooks, tackling simple ballads on the Steinway with relative ease. When the lessons became more challenging, Madeline practised on those rare occasions when both Carmelle and her mother were away from the house. Knowing this, Carmelle took Dianne to a beauty salon halfway across the city every Saturday morning, smartly sensing that her employer couldn't resist an opportunity to enhance her looks. During these scheduled moments of solitude, Madeline played the piano until she heard the car pull up in the driveway.

Dianne's social life was humming as always, which meant that Madeline and Carmelle also had a fair amount of time alone together. As soon as Dianne had issued her customary warning—"Early to bed, do you hear me?"—and slipped out the door, Madeline and Carmelle would rush to the living room to squeeze in a piano lesson. As a reward, or so Madeline believed at first, Carmelle would kiss her. Sometimes the kisses were friendly, other times they were passionate. Madeline practised all the harder in an effort to please Carmelle and reap the rewards of her teacher's approval.

Nothing compared to the elation Madeline felt when Carmelle, after a particularly unsuccessful piano lesson late one Friday night, led her upstairs. "Where are we going?" Madeline protested, sorry that she hadn't played very well. She'd been distracted, had suggested they play records and drink brandy again instead of practising arpeggios. But then she realized that Carmelle's sudden decision to go upstairs wasn't signalling the end of the evening.

"You're tired," Carmelle said, gently pushing Madeline into her room. At the piano Carmelle was a strict but encouraging teacher. Upstairs in Madeline's bedroom, under the watchful eyes of Eleanor Holm, Carmelle was demanding in a different sort of way. "Lie down," she said, though her voice wasn't quite as authoritative as it had been during the piano lesson. She was trembling as she stretched out on the bed next to Madeline.

"I love you," Madeline whispered, kissing Carmelle's neck.

"No, you don't," Carmelle replied. "You just think you love me." She took Madeline's face in her hands, kissing her with unprecedented aggression. Madeline didn't have time to question Carmelle's strange refusal to believe that Madeline loved her. They were soon undressing each other with clumsy fingers, working buttons and zippers until their bare bodies were pressed together. It's like clouds, Madeline thought, her breasts wedged against Carmelle's.

"I don't know what to do," Madeline murmured. "Tell me."

"Shhh," Carmelle said, and she began kissing Madeline's neck, her breasts and then her stomach, moving her mouth down and down until Madeline was breathless with fear and desire. Above her head Madeline saw her collage of pictures of Eleanor Holm. She closed her eyes and gasped as Carmelle made her forget swimming pools, piano lessons and everything else Madeline believed she'd known about life thus far. Who knew what a mouth and hands could do? Who'd ever guess at what one woman could do for another? If this was feminism (which her mother decried at every opportunity), well, bring on the picket signs!

Soon it wasn't clear whether they were eager for Dianne to leave the house because they wanted to play piano or because they wanted to go upstairs. Madeline adored either option, if only because the piano lessons often ended in her bedroom anyway. Sometimes Madeline grew reckless and crept along the hallway in the middle of the night, even when her mother was home. "Go back to bed!" Carmelle would hiss, terrified of discovery. Sometimes Madeline would obey; other times not. If Carmelle protested too vehemently, Madeline would crawl into bed next to her giggling, "You're the one always telling me I'm too obedient. Here I am, refusing to take orders." Arguing was pointless. Like all lovers who think they've discovered some new and improved form of sex, they found it difficult to be sensible.

As she moved through the lessons and became more and more skilled at piano, Madeline also mastered certain skills in the boudoir. She loved the feeling that she and Carmelle were getting away with something. But more than that, she loved the idea that one fine day they were going to escape to a place where they could be alone together *all the time*. They'd already decided to run away to New Orleans and become famous lounge singers: Carmelle had promised. Together, alone, away from here. Madeline was ready to flee the house immediately, but Carmelle insisted they had to bide their time and be patient. "Freedom costs money, you know," she'd say whenever Madeline would insist that they ought to just go. "Don't be foolish," Carmelle scolded her one night. "If it's meant to happen, it'll happen. Come on, now, you still can't play that Bach the way I showed you."

"I'm good at other things." Madeline grinned.

"That's true," Carmelle agreed, "no doubt about that. Now play that adagio one time without making me cringe. Like this. Hold your wrists like this. Uh-huh."

Madeline's hands shift from the love song for Eleanor Holm to the once-challenging adagio. Having navigated it at last, she slams down the lid of the piano and curses. She folds her arms across her chest and says to the lawn ornaments, "If it's meant to happen, my ass."

Though it's a far cry from Alcatraz, Cleo is starting to feel imprisoned by the four walls of her room at the Pommes Royales Maisonnettes. She stares at the blades of the ceiling fan above her bed and tries not to notice the silent telephone on the night table. As prisons go, the Pommes Royales is rather pleasant, but Cleo didn't have incarceration in mind when she came south for what was supposed to be a vacation.

What did she have in mind? What drew her to New Orleans in the first place, when a trip to Italy would have made more sense? She supposes it might have something to do with the way the city looked in movies—*King Creole, The Big Easy, JFK* and so many others—or with Sadie's insistence that it seemed like a place where people went to forget their troubles. "After all," she'd said, "they call it 'The City That Care Forgot.'" For whatever reason, Cleo had become obsessed, seemingly overnight, with the notion of coming here. So obsessed that she'd taken the bus all the way from Toronto, an escape assisted by Sadie, who unbeknownst to Lyle had scooped Cleo's stockpiled wages from the office safe.

As the bus sped across Causeway bridge, her certainty had swelled. Her eyes had fallen in love even before the bus pulled into the Greyhound station. This is where I'm meant to be, she'd thought with tremendous excitement. Not in Italy, but *here,* in the land of Walker Percy, Tennessee

Williams, Kate Chopin and countless other scribblers of distinction. Thus, to find herself lying miserably on a too-soft mattress next to a silent telephone—writing nothing—is more than a little enraging. Care forgot the city—and Johnny has obviously forgotten about her.

Cleo is beginning to buckle under the strain of her obsession with Madeline Shockfire, whose name she has written on several more pages of her notebook where poems ought to be. And she is quite frankly sick to death of wondering who this Madeline person is and what she feels and the dozens of other questions that have been teeming through her mind with the intensity of a Louisiana downpour. It would be one thing if her preoccupation with Madeline Shockfire had obliterated Cleo's other obsession, which involves dismissing—or trying to dismiss—the stories she's invented about her mother's life. But the one preoccupation only serves to remind her of the other; the two have become maddeningly entangled.

Even Mrs. Ryan has stopped asking after the progress of Cleo's poetry. She seems to have intuited that her young guest is in the throes of something, and like the clairvoyant Father Baby, Mrs. Ryan has put it down to a matter of the heart. Why can't anyone accept that Cleo is immune to love? Just because she happens to be a poet doesn't mean she has to be interested in sex, does it? These angry thoughts remind Cleo that she hasn't written a single poem in days, which may be adding to her mental strain and overall frustration. She takes out her notebook and opens it, leafs through the lunatic repetitions of Madeline Shockfire's name, past the jotted dates and names and other details Cleo has collected like clues. But none of these so-called clues have brought her any closer to an answer. In fact, they've only helped to imprison her.

Some of the world's finest literature has floated out of prison cells, smoke signals that say: "I am still here!" Faced with the blank page, Cleo must admit that in order to send such signals out into the world, you have to believe that someone will care enough to see them. Care, then, she tells herself, picking up her pen.

Sitting on the wharf with my legs dangling over the cool yellow water, I smell river-bottom mud and the fuel of passing barges. It's quiet and dark down here, not loud and frantic like Bourbon Street. I hear someone, someone running up behind me, the clatter of high-heeled shoes on concrete. I turn to see a woman, but her face is obscured by shadows. She stops when she sees me. Is about to turn and run away when I call out, "Beautiful night, isn't it?"

The woman is as still as a doe. She steps back a little and murmurs, "Yes, beautiful night, thank you."

She runs off, her high heels clacking down the wharf. Goes home to her husband, who asks her why she looks so nervous and sad. She takes off her coat and sits down next to him on the sofa and starts to cry, "I don't know. I don't know.... I think someone just saved my life."

The woman's husband puts his arms around her and kisses away her tears. Nothing bad happens. I get back on the bus and heads for the desert, where there are no rivers to tempt anyone, including me. And nothing bad happens. A bell starts to ring; it could be the bell of a church, announcing the arrival of morning.

"Miss Cleo, you have a gentleman caller!"

Cleo puts down her pen. "Pardon?"

Mrs. Ryan's voice is soft and excited. "He's handsome, too! A Mr. Valentucci. You want me to tell him to come back later?"

"NO!" Cleo shouts into the phone, cognizant of her surroundings at last. She tells Mrs. Ryan she'll be right out. She takes a quick look at herself in the mirror, gives her unruly hair a few ineffectual swipes with a comb, is soon flying through the corridor that connects the courtyard to the miniature front lobby of the Pommes Royales.

"Hey," says Johnny. He's settled in a wingback chair, with a cup of coffee balanced uncertainly in his large hands.

Mrs. Ryan gives Cleo a look that says she wishes Cleo had taken more time with her toilette. She surveys Cleo's untied shoelaces and wild hair with a disapproving shake of her head.

"You ready to go?" Johnny asks, looking around for somewhere to set his cup and saucer. Cleo takes it from him and sets it on the front desk next to a tiny silver bell.

"Go?" Cleo wonders aloud, confused and rattled by her abrupt awakening. Mrs. Ryan pretends not to listen; she hums and makes a point of rustling a handful of papers.

"You said you wanted to interview my wife," Johnny says, spreading his hands wide. "It's now or never."

"Uh, sure, let's go," Cleo stammers, moving toward the door.

"Don't you have to get a tape recorder or something?" he asks, his eyebrows raised.

Cleo should get her notebook but she doesn't want to leave Johnny in the lobby with Mrs. Ryan, afraid that she might blow Cleo's already precarious cover. "I work from memory," she says with as firm a grip on professional nonchalance as she can manage. Do reporters ever work from memory? Surely they must, or why else would so much of the news we read turn out to be inaccurate? And anyway, it isn't really a lie: Cleo has been working from memory all her life.

Johnny seems to believe that Cleo is a real reporter. He waves goodbye to Mrs. Ryan, thanking her for the coffee and wishing her a pleasant day. Nice manners, thinks Mrs. Ryan, though he does seem a little old for Cleo. She makes a quick note on her memo pad to explore the idea of May–December romances in her next novel of love. She sighs heavily and stares after what she thinks is a newly minted romantic pairing.

"What paper did you say you write for up in Canada?" Johnny pauses on the sidewalk to light a cigarette. He holds the pack out to Cleo, who shakes her head and struggles to think up an answer.

"*The Cabbagetown News,*" she says at last, bending to lace her boots so she can avoid looking Johnny in the eye. "It's a Toronto paper."

"I see," he says, smoking and walking ahead of Cleo. He says nothing more for a time and they amble along in silence. His long strides make it hard for her to stay beside him. She's confused when he pushes on along Royal in the direction of Canal Street, but follows anyway. Perhaps they're going to see Madeline in some secret location for reasons that will become clearer in due course?

"Where are we going?" Cleo finally asks. She's alarmed when they turn down Canal. It occurs to her that Johnny may be leading her somewhere else with Madeline as a ruse. She begins to question the safety of this enterprise.

Johnny turns and gives her an impatient look as he puffs furiously on his cigarette. "Do you want to meet my wife or not?" Cleo nods. "Well then, let's go. I've got things to do, so let's step on it, all right? We just have to get down to the ferry dock."

"The ferry?" Cleo asks, stopping in mid-step. "Why do we have to take the ferry?" A cold sweat breaks out along her spine.

Johnny flicks his cigarette butt into traffic. "You got a car?" She shakes her head. "Then the ferry it is. Madeline's over in Algiers right now. It's only a five-minute ride by boat." He looks at Cleo closely, sees that she's pale and sweaty, and asks if there's a problem. *What is it with you women and the goddamned ferry?*

"No problem," Cleo mutters, squinting up at him. "Can we take a cab there?"

"Sure we can take a cab." He shrugs. "As long as you're paying."

"Good." They walk to a nearby hotel and poach a taxi from the stand. Cleo feels so thrown by her near-miss boat ride that it takes her several minutes to realize she's finally going to meet Madeline Shockfire. The cab is halfway over the bridge when the surreality of it all finally hits her.

Johnny studies Cleo's profile, thinking she looks a bit too artsy to be a journalist. Cute, though. Might have a real nice body under all those clothes; it's hard to tell. She's got nice lips, real nice eyes when she manages to look at something other than her feet. "You been a reporter long?" he asks.

Cleo keeps her eyes on the river passing below them on

the bridge. "Not long. A couple of years." She wishes she'd taken the time to grab her notebook, knowing she'd feel a lot more convincing if she could at least hold a pen and pretend to take notes. When the cab stops abruptly outside a restaurant on the other side of the river, Johnny holds out his hand for the money. Cleo hands him a twenty.

"Keep the change, mac," he says to the driver. He swings his long legs out of the car and Cleo follows, cursing herself for not bringing more money along. Johnny's sudden arrival at her hotel means that she isn't prepared—emotionally *or* financially—for this surprise introduction to the infamous wife of Johnny V.

"Hang on a sec," Johnny says, lighting another cigarette. Cleo notices that his hands are shaking and she wonders why. And one could describe his gait as downright reluctant as they make their way along the quiet residential streets of Algiers Point. Snails have been known to move faster than Johnny right now.

"Does she live out here?" Cleo asks, trying to make conversation.

"She doesn't *live* out here, she *works* out here." Johnny chews his moustache in between drags of his cigarette. He seems nervous for some reason, and his nervousness makes Cleo feel even more panicky.

"What does she work at?" Algiers Point seems to be short on shops and restaurants compared with the French Quarter, but then, most places would by that measure. Johnny doesn't answer Cleo's question. He seems hell-bent on devouring his own facial hair, and Cleo finds this tic more than a little disturbing. She supposes it must be the male equivalent to non-stop hair twirling, an annoying but harmless compulsion that large numbers of women seem unable to shake. Male expressions of anxiety are quite different from those of females, Cleo thinks, pleasantly distracted by her own mental tangent. Jaw rubbing, beard stroking, the non-stop hitching up of pants despite the presence of a belt, shameless ass scratching. Yes, she thinks, men have their fair share of strange habits. She's willing to bet that huge numbers of them are in fact undiagnosed neurotics despite the ancient belief that women are the more hysterical sex.

"Here we are," Johnny says brightly, still chewing his moustache. Cleo feels sorry for him until he adds, "I sure hope she's in."

"She doesn't know we're coming?" Cleo gasps upon hearing that Madeline has no knowledge of their impending arrival. Her excitement is greatly diminished by a deeply Torontonian conviction that dropping by unannounced is never a good idea. The building they now stand in front of doesn't look as if it plays host to anything other than the pigeons moaning lustily above their heads in the ornate brickwork.

"C'mon," says Johnny, tugging on the heavy steel door that is, to his quiet delight, ajar. They crunch through a fetid foyer and up a flight of stairs. Johnny pauses on the landing and listens, his breath rattling in his chest. The staircase is dark and smelly, and Cleo's only reason for not fleeing the scene is that she's afraid to go back down on her own. She sticks close to Johnny in the dark, grateful when they reach the top of the staircase. A window at the end of the hallway lets in a small amount of light. Johnny listens again, this time with his ear pressed against another door.

"She's in there," he whispers. "I can smell her perfume." While Cleo thinks it's sweet of Johnny to have such a keen nose for his wife's fragrance, her own mounting anxiety blots out any further appreciation she might have for his sentimental side. He raises his hand to knock on the door and Cleo's heart leaps into her mouth. She hides herself behind him, suddenly wishing she hadn't come here at all.

I want to know ...

Cleo fights to breathe normally. Johnny sighs and knocks again, this time with a little more force. He seems to be having trouble breathing too, and Cleo wonders why they don't give up and come back another time. Maybe she's asleep. Maybe she isn't home. Or maybe she just doesn't feel like answering. The sound of approaching footsteps on the stairs behind them causes Cleo's heart to sink another league. No longer shielded by Johnny, she's afraid to turn around.

"Looking for someone?" The voice is husky sweet.

Johnny whirls around and looks over Cleo's head. "Baby!" It's awkward to keep facing Johnny's chest, but even so, Cleo would rather not look. Not yet.

"Hello, Johnny," Madeline says without emotion. She displays no surprise, no anger and certainly no delight. She nods at Cleo's back. "Who's this?"

Johnny spins Cleo around to face Madeline. Cleo braces herself and looks up as Johnny says, "This is Cleo, honey. She's a journalist from Toronto. She wants to interview you." Madeline stares back at Cleo, a faint smile twitching at the corners of her mouth. In the dim light Madeline's bright eyes flicker like lamps. She moves past Cleo, around Johnny and puts a key in the door he has been pounding on. A gentle trail of perfume hovers discreetly in the air. No wonder

Johnny knows the fragrance so well, Cleo thinks, allowing herself to be ushered through the door.

The room they follow Madeline into is big and bright—and sparsely furnished, to say the least. Cleo sees a piano at the other end of the room and a strange assortment of statuettes seated at little tables. Lawn ornaments. She lingers by the door, too nervous to move forward, whereas Johnny marches right into the centre of the room where he, too, is staring at the odd collection of ornaments.

"What's this?" he asks, fighting a snicker.

Madeline ignores his question and turns to Cleo, whose eyes are still focused on the stony menagerie across the room. She looks up to find Madeline staring at her with an inscrutable look on her face. It could be curiosity or annoyance, Cleo can't tell. Madeline's eyes are a disarming green, with flecks of silver-grey. Training these eyes on Cleo, she takes her in from head to toe. Smiles, or almost does, then raises a perfectly arched eyebrow. Cleo's stomach flips over like a record in a jukebox.

Johnny clops around the room as if he feels right at home, again demanding to know what the tables and statuettes are all about. Madeline folds her arms across her chest and watches him, her back to Cleo. She says nothing as she moves toward him. Cleo's mental portrait of the kind of lady desperate enough to jump into the Mississippi was way off the mark. Madeline isn't wearing a long skirt and dowdy cardigan but a tight dark purple dress made of something shiny, the cut of which looks vaguely Oriental. When she moves the fabric shimmers, and when she walks her high-heeled black suede pumps click ever so slightly on the floorboards. She isn't tall or short, either, but something in between. Her body is muscular yet curvaceous. It's a physique that could indeed swim rivers—or do anything else it wanted to, for that matter. Madeline's attention is entirely focused on Johnny, who picks up one of the plastic geese, guffaws and asks, "Seriously, what is this?"

"It's a goose," Madeline says, adding, "a member of the bird family." She turns and smirks at Cleo. Cleo averts her eyes, ashamed to be caught staring and afraid to share in Madeline's mirth at Johnny's expense. Without Johnny's help, Cleo wouldn't be here right now.

"So how are ya, babe?" Johnny moves toward Madeline with his arms open, the plastic goose dangling from one hand. Madeline doesn't move into his embrace but instead snatches the goose away from him and puts it back on its rightful chair.

"I'm fine," she says, turning back to Cleo. "Please come in, Miss—"

"Savoy," Cleo says, moving reluctantly into the room.

Johnny starts to light a cigarette, and Madeline barks at him, "Please, not in here." He looks at her with amazement and puts the cigarette back in his pack, whistling through his teeth.

"So, you're a reporter," Madeline says, busily setting some of the statues on the floor to make room for her human guests.

Johnny plunks himself down on a chair and brushes a lock of dark hair out of his eyes. "She wants to interview you for a paper up in Canada, honey."

Madeline motions for Cleo to take a seat. "Yes, Montreal, didn't Johnny say?" She now behaves as if Johnny isn't even in the room.

"It's Toronto, actually, but yes, I thought it would be ... great ... to interview you." Cleo stammers, proud to have relocated the power of speech. Madeline sits down across from her and seems to be waiting. Johnny stares at Cleo expectantly, too, tapping his cigarette package on the table. It's Cleo who feels as if she's about to be interviewed.

"What did you want to interview me about?" Madeline studies her fingernails with a frown. When she looks up at Cleo her eyes are clouded with mistrust. "Because I don't really have anything worth telling." She glances at Johnny and her frown intensifies. "May I ask what this is really all about?"

Cleo's throat constricts. Finally she stammers, "I'm interested in your swimming." Johnny seems to be enjoying Cleo's lack of poise. He tilts back on his chair and watches.

"My *swimming?*" Madeline asks, incredulous. "I swim. Or rather, I swam. Not a very interesting story, is it?" Madeline waves her hand in the air. "Woman swims. So what? I mean, I could see if I had done something truly interesting, that might be—"

Johnny interrupts her. "Madeline, be nice. She's only interested in your—"

Madeline sneers. "I know what she's interested in. She's interested in helping you gain access to me. This is some sort of joke, I guess? Some little scheme you cooked up so you could march in here to make sure I haven't taken up with another man? Rest assured, Giovanni, that'll never happen." She glares at Johnny and says nothing more.

The inhospitable current in the room makes Cleo sweat. She eases her chair back. "I'm sorry to have bothered you, Miss Shockfire." When Madeline doesn't respond Cleo gets up, her legs wobbly. This isn't quite how she'd hoped things would go, but when she considers the fact that Madeline wasn't given any sort of warning, Cleo can understand her irritability. And with all Madeline is probably going through mentally and emotionally, she can't really be expected to be happy to give an interview. Cleo wishes she hadn't lied her way into this mess and looks helplessly at Johnny, who is no longer enjoying the tension in the room.

"I'll see you out," he offers, standing up.

"Why don't *you* leave and let *her* stay?" Madeline jerks her head in Cleo's direction. "That way I'll know this isn't a load of bullshit."

Johnny looks from Madeline to Cleo and back at Madeline again. "All right," he says. "Can I come back later, take you out for supper?"

"Don't you have to get to work, Giovanni?" she asks, her voice suddenly sweet. Cleo stands helplessly in the middle of the room. He nods. "Come back some other time, then." The storm clouds retreat from her eyes as quickly as they moved in.

He walks stiffly toward the door. He leans and whispers to Cleo as he passes, "Watch yourself."

Johnny gives the door a light slam as he exits. Madeline stares at the door and then looks at Cleo, who hasn't moved in several minutes. Cleo isn't sure if she should stay or go. The silence is agonizing. She wishes she could break it by confessing her real reason for seeking Madeline out, but something makes her choose the lie.

"Well, then." Madeline points at the chair Cleo so recently evacuated. She leans on her elbows and waits for Cleo to sit. "So," she says, smiling a little more warmly. She holds out her hand. "I'm Madeline. Please don't call me Miss Shockfire—it makes me feel like a spinster."

Cleo shakes Madeline's hand, holding on to her fingers for a few seconds longer than she means to. Madeline's frown returns and Cleo quickly withdraws her hand, blushing furiously, wishing she could drop through the floor. Madeline smiles to herself and looks away, suddenly very interested in the windows across the room. *What am I doing? Hermits don't entertain strangers, no matter how kind they may seem.*

Say something, you dolt! Cleo scolds herself. She clears her throat and is about to speak when Madeline stands up and stretches. She asks Cleo if she'd like something to drink.

"Some water would be lovely," Cleo says.

Madeline looks embarrassed. "Oh. I don't think I can subject you to the tap water in this place—the pipes are ancient. And I don't have any bottled water just now." She glances over at the kitchen counter and Cleo sees the row of half-finished bottles of liquor. "We could go out someplace. Why don't we go out someplace?" Without waiting for Cleo's response she grabs her purse and marches toward the door, keys in hand.

"Sure." Cleo follows Madeline out of the studio, noting the scent of vetiver in her perfumed wake. Cleo wonders what it's called. It has a clean, almost masculine aroma, both light and sultry. She decides to ask what it is, hoping to make casual conversation. The tension between them is peculiar, though not altogether unpleasant.

"Rocabar," Madeline says, rolling the *r*. "My daddy used to wear it. I wouldn't be caught dead without it."

"It's nice," Cleo murmurs, noting the words *caught dead.* Cleo surmises that Madeline must be very close to her father, although she did say "used to," past tense. Uh-oh, thinks Cleo, I *will* have to watch myself.

Madeline looks down Verret Street and decides to take Cleo to the Shore-Do Café. *It's about time I stopped avoiding the place anyway.* It's close to the ferry dock, too; if things go poorly, she can simply put Miss Cleo on the ferry and head home, nice and tidy. The wind is damp and she wishes she'd worn a coat. *Do I even have a coat?* She shivers.

"Would you like to wear my sweatshirt?" Cleo can see that Madeline is freezing in her short sleeves.

"Oh, I couldn't," Madeline says, surprised by the offer.

Cleo pulls her sweatshirt over her head. "I'm Canadian. We're tough when it comes to the cold." She grins and adds, "Not like you people."

Madeline smiles. "I know a thing or two about Canada, don't you worry."

"Have you been?"

"No, no I haven't. But I've always thought it might be sort of fun to go up there and see you-all, huddled in your igloos and such, but ..."

"Very funny."

"I thought so."

They stand awkwardly on the street for a minute. Finally Madeline suggests that they move along. "It's not far, where I'm taking you," she promises, picking up speed so that Cleo won't catch a chill. She can see the girl's cold but putting on a show of not minding. Out of the corner of her eye Madeline studies Cleo's profile. Striking, she thinks, what they call *sui generis*. When Madeline had come up the studio stairs and seen Johnny and his then-mysterious friend, she'd been tempted to make a joke. Something along the lines of: "Ooo, Johnny, how thoughtful of you, bringing me such a beautiful young boy!" As soon as Madeline saw Cleo in the proper light of the studio, she knew that Cleo was unequivocally female. And more than a little attractive. Oh well, she thinks now, we'll do our interview and that'll be that, and I'll never see her again. Perfect, the way life should be, a series of quick, fifteen-minute interviews. Conversation without commitment—a rare thing between women.

The waitress at the Shore-Do is the very same one who served Madeline her breakfast of champions after the first of her three recent swims. She doesn't appear to recognize Madeline, or if she does, may hope that Madeline doesn't recognize her. "Morning, ladies," she says. "Coffee?"

"Oh God, yes!" Cleo cries, all shyness dissolved. She's never waded so deeply into a morning without a coffee before.

"Just water for me," Madeline says, staring hard at the menu.

"Oh, for me, too," Cleo adds. When the waitress moves off, Cleo quotes, "'Thousands have lived without love, not one without water.'" She pauses and then says, almost shyly, "Auden."

"That's beautiful," Madeline remarks. "And also true."

Please don't let this day end, Cleo thinks, addressing whoever's in charge of fortuitous turns. She hadn't expected to find such enigmatic beauty when she came chasing after death. The invalid she expected to find is nowhere to be seen. The trouble is, Madeline's beauty makes her hard to look at for too long. Cleo has never experienced this particular predicament before. She forces herself to look directly at Madeline, telling herself that reporters never get nervous.

All Madeline can think is: What the hell am I doing? What she says is: "I'd like to know a little more about you before we continue with the interview. If you don't mind."

"Sure, of course. What would you like to know?" Cleo begins formulating a mental list of false credentials, cursing herself all the while.

"Tell me why I should talk to you. I mean, why should I tell *you* anything about my life? For all I know, you might just be playing some kind of game, to protect Johnny." Madeline folds her hands on the tabletop. No rings, not even a wedding band. "How did you happen to meet my husband, by the way?"

Cleo is taken aback by Madeline's challenging tone. "In a bar," she admits.

"How surprising." Madeline appears to be waiting for more details.

Something tells Cleo that she's going to have to impress Madeline quickly or lose this hard-won opportunity. *Should I explain that I don't really know Johnny, that I saw her on the news and he was there watching, too—or lie again?*

"What do you come from?" Madeline asks before Cleo can prove herself.

"'What do I come from?'" Cleo repeats. "I'm sorry, I don't think I understand. Do you mean where am I from?"

Madeline smiles mysteriously. "No, I mean *what* do you come from. For example, I come from a long line of bisexuals on my mother's side. I come from money, from generations of disappointed entrepreneurs, from saint-fearing Acadians and English boors, from a house on a corner with too many unused rooms. *Comprends?* What do *you* come from?"

A long line of bisexuals? Cleo thinks, surprised by the first admission. Whose *mother* is bisexual? Tell her! she urges herself. Just tell her why you're really here.

"I come from a flood," Cleo says instead, leaping into the story of her conception with the gusto of someone 100 per cent certain that what she's saying is true.

November 4, 1966
Florence, Italy

The Italian rainy season usually waited for November. That year it jump-started itself in September. A beautiful young woman—her name was Caroline—sat in the window of her room on the third floor of her *pensione,* watching the rain fall in great cold sheets of silver and grey. She'd left her native city of Montreal in August with an inexplicable fever in her veins, convinced that Italy offered an answer, an escape. In the university brochure Caroline had seen more than just an opportunity to study David's muscles up close; she'd seen freedom. More incredibly than she ever dreamt it would, Florence offered this young woman the chance to explore the possibility of becoming something more than a daughter who always did what was expected of her. She'd promised herself in advance of her departure that she would never return to Canada.

The sense of freedom Florence gave her also made her feel lonely, and loneliness drove her back to caution and prudence, the very things she had wished to dispense with. She reached for and held on to the one anchor she always relied on—reading. Not merely avid reading, but compulsive. Anywhere, anytime. She felt about books as a devoted drunk might feel about flagons of wine: I *need* them. Books were both a comfort and a problem, albeit one that caused no physical harm, except perhaps to her eyes, red-rimmed from the strain of trying to keep up with the appetites of her brain. Later she would break down and wear eyeglasses. For now, she told herself that this return to her old habit was a temporary lapse caused by the doldrums of the approaching winter.

She'd begun her time in Italy with a grand flourish, riding alone (and without so much as a newspaper to distract her) on a crowded train. She spoke without reservation to strange men, looking them in the eye, laughing at their jokes, nodding at their wedding rings. Men were an experiment, and Italy was a very good lab. She then spent the remainder of the month of August writing passionate (unmailed) letters to a man she'd met on the train from Florence to Rome. A painter who restored churches in summer and did portraits in winter, Vollo Principere had charmed her with photographs of his work. While her preoccupation with him continued, the sense of recklessness he awakened in her was set aside once the school year commenced. Old habits die hard. Instead of seeing her life as an erotically charged vista, she dropped her eyes to books and seldom looked up, except, as on this night, to examine the weather.

In the downstairs kitchen, the *padrona* of the *pensione* busily sacrificed some three hundred *pomodori* for a sauce. Enough sauce for the Italian army, but Caroline would not be invited to taste even a spoonful of it. Signora Bianchi was suspicious of her foreign boarder, a girl who had been permitted to come alone to Florence. Yes, to study, but the signora was not convinced that Caroline spent all of her time with books. She was too beautiful to be a real scholar—anyone so blond and pale was surely of suspect character, or so she quickly decided when she met Caroline. For one thing, Signora Bianchi knew that Catholics were seldom blond—not the good ones, anyway. And she did not wish to have her son mingling with any lone North American girls. In fact, it was this son's absence that drove Signora Bianchi to such prolific sauce making. Her son, Paolo, was late returning from his position at the bank. Usually a good boy, a responsible son, he had not called to explain his delay. He had also begun of late to argue with his mother about everything, and even refused to attend Mass. Too like his father for her comfort.

The smell of the sauce nudged, red and robust, at Caroline's door, slipping beneath it to remind her of her foolish haste in returning to the *pensione* to study. She had left her fellow students behind at a trattoria they all liked, only to find herself gazing at the rain with a growling belly and zero concentration. They had only just begun to enjoy a bottle of wine when Caroline's desperate need to read something drove her off. The restaurant menu was delivered verbally, and there was no delicate way for her to sneak in a few lines of her copy of Boccaccio's *Decameron*; everyone would have teased her. As it was, they expressed great disappointment when she announced her intention to leave without eating. But now, for whatever reason—barometric pressure or physical hunger—she couldn't concentrate with her usual mad focus. She pressed her forehead to the cool glass pane of the *pensione* window and willed herself to return to the Boccaccio. Caroline found some comfort in the realization that the following day was a national holiday, celebrating the armistice, an occasion that offered an opportunity to study for an entire day without the interruption of formal classes. Within minutes of this realization, she fell asleep in the window, oblivious to the increasing violence of the rain.

Signora Bianchi angrily bottled her sauce, slamming it onto the pantry shelves. The hour was late, the sauce unhurried even by Italian standards, and still Paolo had not returned. With deepening suspicion and increasing vehemence, the signora snapped off the lamps in the front rooms, leaving the ground floor black and foreboding. Yet she could not bear to bolt the door against her only son. He would come home wet and hungry, probably ill, and expect his mother's sympathy. The *puttana* who led him astray would not have to make him soup or put a cold cloth to his forehead, no! Signora Bianchi retreated to her bedroom on the second floor of the *pensione,* clutching her rosary and shaking her head. It was her firm belief that men disappeared in the season of heavy rain. First her husband, curse his soul, and now her beloved Paolo. No explanations, only the guarantee that it had something to do with an immoral woman, too much wine and the easy excuse of poor weather.

Across the city, several pairs of feverish hands filled boxes with jewellery and silver. These were not the hands of thieves but the terrified hands of jewellers whose shops occupied the Ponte Vecchio. A night watchman beamed his flashlight down upon the Arno, saw the foaming river and quickly alerted the silversmiths and craftsmen of the bridge. Now they scrambled to gather their precious tools and gems, praying to God, shouting to one another to "hurry up!" They thought of their wives, of their automobiles parked on the *lungarno,* and in rushing, some treasure or other was invariably forgotten. There was no time to linger as the rain threatened to reach biblical proportions.

The owner of the trattoria sent the noisy students packing, though later than usual. On this night he was somehow in the mood for their loud Americano songs, and they'd drunk a great deal of wine in anticipation of the next day's holiday. He felt generous toward them for this reason alone. He bade them farewell at the door, warning them to hurry out of the rain, and amiably slipped one of the boys an extra bottle of wine to take away. This young man wore the look of a hopeful *amante* and had spent much of the evening glancing nervously out the window. *How can an Englishman be afraid of the rain?* the owner had teased his young customer. The other students laughed at their glum friend and made lewd smacking sounds with their mouths. *La buona fortuna!* he shouted after the students, locking his door against the miserable night.

There was a loud, explosive cracking sound in the street, and it startled Caroline from her deep slumber. Even more startling was the knocking at her door, inexplicable at this late hour. The sky was milky, indicating morning. Thinking it must be the signora, she unwound herself from the shawl of curtain she'd gathered around herself in sleep and stumbled across the carpet. The room was dark, which was odd, because she did not remember turning off the lamp, and cold, too. She struggled to locate the door handle. It wasn't the signora at all, but some other thing that glowed yellow in the dim hall. Caroline gasped and stepped back, for a terrible, rancid odour accompanied the form—that of burnt things, or fuel. When her eyes adjusted to the dim light, she let out a little cry. It was a man, his yellow raincoat and face smeared with black, his hair and eyes wild with water and something too dark to be mud.

"Caroline?" he rasped, sputtering the muck away from his lips. "It's Lyle Savoy. We met at the Biblioteca Nazionale this afternoon, and you ran off from the restaurant tonight before I could...." He faltered here and wiped his mouth with the back of his hand. "Your friend Gwen told me where to find you. She said she thought you wouldn't mind a visitor." She now remembered him, if vaguely, and wished he would be quiet, because the signora had a strict rule against visitors venturing past a certain point on the tiles in the front hall. He shifted his weight impatiently from one foot to the other and asked if he could come in.

Insisting she did not know him, but fearing the signora more, Caroline stepped aside so that he could enter the room, dripping as he walked. The smell of him made her dizzy, and she wondered which circle of hell he had erupted from. Begging him to watch his greasy coat as he stumbled, Caroline backed up toward the window, unsure what she should do about this sudden and strange visitor. He joined her at the window and parted the curtains wide so that some of the pre-dawn light could fall on his face. Another larger explosion in the streets caused him to jump, and he looked at Caroline with even wilder eyes. The rain continued to beat against the window, and Lyle Savoy began to pace.

What do you want? she wondered, watching him make oily circles on the carpet as his raincoat dripped incessantly. Instead she asked him what it was that covered him.

"Furnace oil," he gasped, clutching his stomach in a most bizarre fashion. "They're blowing all over the city. Bad business. They say a flood, they say—"

"*L'inondazione! L'inondazione!*" came the scream of the signora from two floors below. Lyle dug beneath the clasps of his raincoat and produced a bottle of wine, its label ragged and wet. He struggled to open it, his blackened hands slippery against the glass, and all the while he was gasping and looking at her, pleading, as though she should know his thoughts. After a few wild wrenches of his army knife, he pulled the greasy cork from the bottle and thrust the wine at her. When she refused it, he shook the bottle at her, then brought it to his own mouth, chugging greedily.

"We're going to die!" he shouted, insisting that she take a drink. She obliged, if only to keep him quiet, and tasted the faint flavour of fuel as she swallowed. He peeled off his coat and placed it in the small sink in the room, travelling in odd animal strides around the carpet. He forced her to face the window, to accept the rain for what it obviously was, as supported by the screams of the landlady. Standing close behind her, he whispered, "November 4, 1333, the same disaster!" He turned her gently to face him and suddenly blurted out, "May I kiss you?" Although he begged, he did not wait for permission, and pressed his mouth hungrily to Caroline's. She shocked herself by responding, and was only pulled from the kiss by the insistent screams of Signora Bianchi from the floor below.

"We're not going to die," Caroline said, but her voice sounded feeble and unsure even to herself, and she glanced out the window and then back at Lyle. He was nothing like Vollo Principere, whose heavy eyelids and almost feminine manner had made her giddy with sexual desire. The man who stood before her calling himself Lyle was fair-haired and nervous, a little boy in a big English body, but his desperation was somehow touching. As the signora loudly lamented the probable death of her son, the demise of the city of Firenze, her *pensione,* and all things good, her list of grievances gained operatic volume. Caroline was suddenly aware that she had missed a great deal in life, now that she felt certain it was about to end. And so, if death was indeed approaching, she didn't want to meet it as a virgin. She had failed, during the long trip from Florence to Rome, to convince Vollo Principere that he desired her, and so she now transferred that thwarted lust to Lyle, who did appear to want her, very much.

She pulled him nervously toward the small bed, a young woman unsure of how one presented herself for what romance novels called "ravishment." Should she lie still and let him do what he wished, or act on her own impulses? In her fantasies starring Vollo Principere, she most definitely did not lie still. But that was fantasy, and Caroline had a sneaking suspicion that real sex was nothing like the artful ballet described in books. In any case she was about to find out, and that was all that mattered. A siren in the street wailed, though it might have been a car horn stuck on one note; she couldn't tell, nor did she care. Sounds blended, and soon she was no longer aware of the stink of fuel on Lyle Savoy as they tugged at each other's clothes: his wet and hers dry, a tangle of fabrics that fell to the floor.

As he rolled on top of her, naked and convinced of death's watery approach, Caroline was sure that she'd been formally introduced to him by *someone* but what difference did formalities make in this final hour? She closed her eyes, half-enjoying herself, though she wished he'd stop panting so that she could hear the rain that was going to take their lives. She now knew why it had been so important for her to come to Florence: she was meant to die there, young and beautiful and delivered from the glumness of Canada, like a sort of scholarly Marilyn Monroe.

At precisely 7:26 a.m. on November 4, 1966, the electrical clocks in Florence stopped. The following August, welcomed into the world by two parents who were, as it happened, very much alive, Cleopatra Firenze Savoy was born under the drama-loving sign of Leo. She landed on the fifth day of the month at 12:28 p.m., London time. "Just in time for lunch," as her father would later tease her. The fact that Cleo's father could even recall the date and time of her birth constituted a minor miracle. Where all other aspects of the past were concerned, Lyle Savoy seemed to suffer from a convenient case of amnesia.

"Wow," Madeline whispers. "That's quite a story. You tell it well."

Cleo nods, dropping her eyes to the table. It's true what people say, then; she does get carried away. She knows that the reason she tells it well is because it's a story she has told herself a million times since Sadie gave her the copy of *National Geographic*.

"But how do you know all those.... Were you really conceived in a flood?" Madeline asks, leaning forward. "In Italy?"

"Yes. That part's true. I sort of embellished here and there." She glances nervously at Madeline. "I'm sorry, I didn't mean to go on so much. I'm supposed to be interviewing you, after all."

"Are you kidding me? It's an amazing story! Where's your mother now?"

"She's in Italy," Cleo says, her voice high and reflexive. "Listen, I didn't mean to take up your whole day with my life story. I'd like to talk about you. I'm sorry for talking about myself so much."

"Are all Canadians as apologetic as you?" Madeline teases, hoping her smile will reassure Cleo that she hasn't minded, that she has in fact loved hearing Cleo's tale. "But that can't be the whole story."

"Well, no," Cleo admits, smiling self-consciously. She picks up the cheque the waitress has dropped on the table, then realizes she has five dollars left after the cab ride from the French Quarter. She regrets having ordered a sandwich somewhere in the middle of her elaborate tale. What was she thinking?

"Gimme that!" Madeline says, snatching the cheque from Cleo's hand. "After a story that good, I think I should be the one to pay." She tucks some money into the plastic sleeve and says, "C'mon, I'll walk you to the ferry."

Cleo shakes her head. "You don't have to do that. How about I walk you back to your place? That way you won't get cold." She gestures to her sweatshirt, which Madeline is still wearing. *Quick thinking, Cleo, but what will you do after? And what about the interview? You've blown it, that's what.*

"Well, all right," Madeline agrees. "But you can't have your sweater back till tomorrow. I want some insurance."

"Insurance?" Cleo laughs.

"That you'll come back tomorrow."

"Sure," Cleo says. "As long as you let me ask all the questions."

When they reach the door of her studio, Madeline feels a strange reluctance to say goodbye. It scares her. It annoys her, too, because she's been doing so well in her self-imposed quarantine from the human race. She takes off Cleo's sweatshirt and hands it back. "Here," she says. "I'm a nice person, despite what you may have heard. I don't want you to be cold on the ferry." She wraps her arms around herself and tries to smile. "Where are you staying, if you don't mind me asking?" In her head she's thinking, It would be good to know where to call when I have to cancel.

"The Pommes Royales Maisonnettes. Cheap and cheerful. It's on Royal Street."

"Yes, I think I know the place. Well, it's been lovely talking to you, Cleopatra. I look forward to seeing you tomorrow." *Too bad it isn't going to happen.* Can't *happen.*

Cleo sees the return of Madeline's frown, but tries to remain upbeat. "Me too. What time is good for you?"

No time. "Ten?" Madeline suggests, rubbing her bare arms.

"See you at ten, then." Cleo nods, backing away. She gives a little wave. Madeline gives a little wave back. Cleo watches Madeline go into her building.

"Oh boy," Cleo mutters, walking away. Triumph and dread course through her simultaneously. With five dollars and a crippling fear of boats, Cleo realizes she can't get back to the French Quarter. That the Canal Street ferry is free for pedestrians makes no difference, because Cleo won't be going anywhere near the ferry dock. Five dollars and no courage: this is what we call a quandary.

Standing at the kitchen counter, Madeline pours herself a brandy. "All right, I give up. What're you trying to tell me?" she wonders aloud. The lawn ornaments stare back at her, as if unsure about what they might say. Madeline repeats the question. "Well?" The ornaments still don't respond. She throws back the brandy and pours herself another, this one for sipping.

"Might as well have a bath," she says to her silent companions. Cleo Savoy's story about her conception lingers in Madeline's mind, refusing to float off. She props her feet on the bathtub faucet and sips her brandy. "Yup," she says, closing her eyes, "I am definitely going to have to call and cancel. I don't want any new friends, especially not interesting ones."

If Mrs. Ryan was worried about Cleo before, she has even more cause for concern now. It's eleven o'clock at night, and the man Cleo went off with this morning has called twice. If she were Cleo's mother, she'd feel she had the right to ask the man why Cleo isn't with him, but in her profession nosiness of that sort isn't acceptable. She's a hotelier, not a babysitter. Well aware of the comings and goings of her guests, Mrs. Ryan can't help noticing that Cleo hasn't returned to her room. She's probably just out having fun like any other young woman, but Mrs. Ryan feels a certain motherly concern tonight.

In fact, almost as soon as she laid eyes on Cleo Savoy, she couldn't help thinking, Something about that girl needs looking after. She isn't sure what it is about Cleo that makes her feel this way. Maybe it's the fact that Cleo, with her waif-like looks, ill-fitting clothes and that positively angelic smile, seems lost. Her pale grey eyes, combined with a tendency to look worried in between rare smiles, make her seem both old beyond her years and much younger than she is. And then there was the odd way Cleo had reacted when Mrs. Ryan told her what she'd seen on the news, the bit about the woman who tried to swim the Mississippi. Cleo had run right out of the hotel after that. Strange. It was almost as if she knew the woman, the way she flew off.

Mrs. Ryan decides that when Cleo returns she'll have a gentle word with her about taking care in New Orleans. The French Quarter is full of ill-intentioned people who would happily prey on the innocence (or ignorance) of an outsider. Mrs. Ryan ought to know—she was once foolish enough to fall in love with that very sort of scoundrel. Surely there is some effective but casual way to warn Cleo away from making the same mistake.

When Johnny calls a third time at five minutes past midnight, Mrs. Ryan informs him that she would appreciate it very much if he'd leave off calling until a more reasonable hour. "Some of us would like to get some sleep," she says sternly.

But Mrs. Ryan can already tell as she bangs down the phone that no amount of hot milk, yoga or extra-strength NyQuil is going to send her off to the Land of Nod tonight. A terrifying thought occurs to her as she puts her hair up in rollers: What if he's murdered Cleo and the real reason he keeps calling is to create an alibi for himself? What if he's sitting right there with the poor girl's body, laughing to himself each time he calls the hotel? People do such things, she thinks in a panic. People do all kinds of crazy things! And say them. And think them, too.

There's only so much a non-resident can do to keep herself busy in Algiers Point. Cleo might have a better knowledge of the neighbourhood than Madeline does. Not only has Cleo taken an extensive tour *à pied* of most of the neighbourhood streets, but she's also attended a meeting of the Algiers Point Neighbourhood Betterment Association. She read about it on the bulletin board at the public library where she managed to kill several hours. The librarian was pleased to locate a copy of *Frankenstein* for Cleo, who sat down at a table and proceeded to read the second half of the novel in one sitting. But libraries close and the Algiers Point library closes earlier than most, which is how Cleo came to attend the APNBA meeting.

Although most of what was discussed at the meeting held little meaning for an outsider, Cleo was happy to have somewhere to be for two more hours. She sat through a protracted discussion about the increasing problem of vandalism in the quaint little neighbourhood, watching and listening as if she found it all very interesting. The only awkward moment came when a woman who introduced herself as Mary-Louise demanded to know what street Cleo lived on in Algiers. Cleo lied and said she was looking at Algiers as a possible place of residence, which then inspired Mary-Louise to hold Cleo hostage for a half-hour as she extolled the virtues of Algiers.

"It sounds wonderful," Cleo consented. "I wonder if you could tell me where a person can get herself a drink after nine o'clock at night? It's pretty quiet over here, isn't it?"

Mary-Louise was clearly displeased by this remark. She frowned and turned on her heel and left Cleo standing outside the community hall.

Cleo has metamorphosed from being a prisoner in her room at the Pommes Royales into a prisoner of the elements. She's awfully glad Madeline decided to give her sweatshirt back. There are two reasons she's grateful, one of which is the cold night air. The other is that Madeline's perfume, or rather, her cologne, still clings to the sweatshirt. It's this gorgeous aroma that keeps Cleo's spirits from bottoming out completely as she tramps around Algiers in the dark and damp, a captive of her own fear of boats. Fear of water is called aquaphobia, she thinks, but what's the clinical name for boat-fear—ferryphobia? No—she shakes her head—that's something else entirely.

The inexperienced solo traveller isn't always the most rational creature in the world. In addition to her naïveté, Cleo's problem-solving skills have taken a back seat to her preoccupation with Madeline Shockfire. She hasn't yet figured out that there are city buses that cross the same bridge she crossed in the taxi, buses that will eventually transport a person back to the French Quarter. She also fails to imagine that another cab could and would happily take her to her hotel and wait while she retrieved the money for the fare. None of these sensible solutions occur to her as she wanders up and down the somnolent streets of Algiers. While her hotel room may have felt like a kind of cell, it was definitely a much warmer alternative to this endless nocturnal wandering.

Cleo pauses outside Madeline's building. Rectangles of light spill down from the top-floor windows that face out onto Verret Street. *Watch yourself.* The last thing Cleo wants is to be caught lurking around Madeline's door. She skulks around to the front of the building that faces onto Patterson and sits in the dark on the cold stone steps. An occasional car zooms by, but other than that, there doesn't seem to be much late-night activity in Algiers. Mary-Louise may have been insulted by Cleo's remark about the sleepy quality of the place, but it wasn't inaccurate.

She wonders what Madeline is doing right this minute. It's obvious to Cleo that Madeline has set up house in the decrepit old building. While Johnny may want to believe his wife is merely hiding out for a time—working—it's pretty clear to Cleo that Madeline has begun to build herself a nest. It isn't just the fact that Madeline has a bed up there, but the curious presence of the statuettes that gives pause. Something about the arrangement of them around the piano had seemed important, almost symbolic. Having heard at the Neighbourhood Betterment Association meeting about the recent theft of several lawn ornaments from local yards, Cleo knows exactly where those little statuettes came from. She hopes some of the stolen ornaments belonged to Mary-Louise.

Ten a.m. seems awfully far off. If she perches here too long she may fall asleep, probably not a smart move in such a desolate area. She pulls her sweatshirt up over her nose, sniffing the cotton as she walks along Patterson, away from the building and toward a neon sign that glows a few short blocks away.

High above the street on the top floor of her building, Madeline begins to play her piano. Cleo couldn't know this even if she'd stayed on the steps, but the song Madeline is composing is all about a flood, a shock of blond hair and the most peculiar blue-grey eyes Madeline has ever seen. The song is called, very simply, "Amnesia."

"Pommes Royales Maisonnettes," Mrs. Ryan says wearily. Commerce doesn't stop just because a person suffers from insomnia. This morning commerce is starting rather early. She cradles the phone between her chin and shoulder and glances at the clock behind her. Seven! Lord ...

"Cleopatra Savoy, please," says the female voice at the other end of the line.

"I'm afraid I'll have to take a message for Miss Savoy." Mrs. Ryan does her best to contain her curiosity by adopting an extra-professional telephone manner.

The woman sighs. "Please tell her that Madeline called and that something's come up."

Something's come up? It sounds vague enough to be exciting. "Madeline?" Mrs. Ryan repeats, hoping the woman will supply her surname.

"Yes. Please make sure Miss Savoy gets the message. We were supposed to meet this morning, but I have to cancel."

"All righty, I'll make sure she gets the message." Mrs. Ryan carefully writes the words *something came up* on her pink message pad under the name *Madeline*. "Bye now," she adds, realizing that she's left the other woman sitting on the line in silence. Almost as soon as she hangs up, the phone rings again. She groans. "Pommes Royales Maisonnettes," she chimes, sneaking a surreptitious sip of her coffee. A person can't even get properly caffeinated these days before the world starts pushing in.

"Cleo Savoy," grunts a male voice. It's Mr. Valentucci, calling for the fourth time.

"I'm sorry, I'll have to take a message." Mrs. Ryan's pen is poised above her message pad, but Mr. Valentucci elects to slam the phone down in her ear instead. His obvious

annoyance erodes Mrs. Ryan's fear that he's murdered Cleo.
Anyone that angry must be a scorned amour, she reasons,
gulping at her coffee before the phone can intrude again.
She's hoping Cleo herself will call from wherever she is, perhaps to check for messages or to let her know if she'll be back
anytime soon. The phone remains quiet, but for how long?
For reasons too morbid for Mrs. Ryan to ever admit, she
hurries into her study and turns on the TV. To her immense
relief, none of the murders reported involves a Canadian
tourist. Just the usual domestic homicides and drug-related
shootouts today, thank God. Mrs. Ryan busies herself in the
courtyard, chattering to her geraniums while she waits for
the complimentary coffee to brew for those guests who
deign to appear.

BILL'S BAR DOESN'T OPEN until 8:00 a.m., so
Madeline had to walk to the pay phone at the ferry dock to
call Cleo and cancel their meeting. For this reason she didn't
see Cleo sound asleep on the ground in the Larkin Parkette,
situated along the route to Bill's. The little park, named in
honour of Father Thomas Larkin and decorated with a
plaque celebrating Father Larkin's "great love of little children," has given Cleo a benevolent if damp place to lay her
head. Few would advise anyone to spend an entire night out
of doors in this sleepy part of New Orleans where muggers
do lurk in the shadows. But it may well be the gentle influence of Father Larkin's ghost that's kept Cleo from falling
prey to any such attack. She began her chilled slumber on
one of the narrow benches, but now wakes to find herself on
the wet, leafy ground, unharmed.

Picking herself up off the grass, Cleo limps out of the parkette, her bones stiff with cold. She has no idea what time it is, but can tell from the fog still drifting along the levee that it isn't anywhere near 10:00 a.m. To her relief the door of Bill's Bar is propped open. "Morning," says the bartender with a bob of his head. "Coffee's just about ready."

In the restroom Cleo splashes cool water on her face and uses the toilet with unprecedented gratitude. As she studies herself in the mirror, she hopes that Madeline won't notice that she's wearing the same clothes, now rumpled from her long night alfresco. She brushes some pine needles from her sleeves and runs her fingers through her hair but despairs of making any further improvements. For a brief second she sees her father—or a feminized version at least—staring back at her in the mirror. No doubt about paternity here, she thinks, frowning, recalling her adolescent dream that someone else had been her real father.

The bartender has set out a mug of coffee. Cleo produces a crumpled dollar bill. "Coffee first, money later," says the bartender, waving her away. She sits with her back to the window and wraps her fingers around the mug to warm them. The TV above the bar is on, but mute. Cleo watches the news without hearing what is said. She's so busy drinking her coffee and gazing up at the overtanned anchorman on the screen that she doesn't see Madeline walk in.

"Cleo!" Madeline exclaims. "Didn't you get my message?"

Cleo swallows her mouthful of hot coffee and shakes her head, aware of how odd it must seem to Madeline that Cleo's sitting in a bar down the street from her studio, two full hours before their scheduled meeting. How to explain? "What was the message?" she asks instead.

Madeline gives her a perplexed smile. "Never mind." She moves toward the bar and orders, then returns to the table with a brown bottle of Barq's root beer, her variation on the morning coffee ritual. "Mind if I join you?" She takes a long swig, sits down and says, "You're early." She isn't unfriendly, just tentative.

"I came over early to get some ideas. For atmosphere. For the story." *Shut up, Cleo.*

"Still ... I wonder why you didn't get my message," Madeline says, more to herself than to Cleo. "You got back to the Quarter all right, I hope?" She's now noticed that Cleo hasn't changed her clothes.

"Yes. I didn't end up taking the ferry, though," Cleo explains. "I—didn't have my wallet with me yesterday. So I had to walk back, over the bridge. Kind of embarrassing, huh? I'm usually much more prepared...."

"Mmmm." Madeline nods. She reaches over and plucks a dried leaf from Cleo's hair. "Cleopatra?"

"Yes?"

"The ferry is free," she plucks another dried leaf from Cleo's sleeve, "and you can't actually walk over that bridge." She sets the leaves on the table between them and looks up.

"You can't?" Cleo croaks. Madeline shakes her head.

"More coffee?" The bartender stands over them, steaming carafe in hand. Cleo nods ever so slightly and he refills her mug. Please don't leave, she thinks, watching him return to his post behind the bar.

"Where'd you sleep?"

"The Larkin Parkette," Cleo confesses. The bartender turns up the volume on the television set and a talk-show theme song blares from the speaker. "I'm not good with boats," Cleo admits, staring into her coffee cup. "I mean, I'm *really* not good with boats."

"Sleeping in a park is much more dangerous than riding the Canal Street ferry," Madeline says. "There's a bus, too. Although I have to admit that I don't know where a person would catch it, so how could you? I guess you were right about being tough when it comes to the weather! It was freezing last night—I'm impressed. Are you hungry?"

"No," Cleo lies.

"Want to split an order of toast?" Madeline prods. "Doyle, can we please have an order of toast over here?" she calls out over the roar of the TV set. "We'll eat and then go; it's too noisy in here this morning."

"But I'm here too early," Cleo reminds her. "You probably have things to do, things you planned before you knew I'd be here."

"Actually, I left a message at your hotel saying I couldn't meet you, if you want to know the truth. The whole truth is, I was going to cancel because I was nervous about continuing our interview. How about that?" The bartender delivers two orders of toast and two napkins. "I said one order," Madeline points out.

"Two-for-one toast day at Bill's," he says with a wink.

"You can still cancel," Cleo offers, nibbling her toast, trying to hide the fact that she's ravenous.

"Oh no," Madeline says. "Not after you were brave enough to sleep outside. Wouldn't I look like a real coward then! Uh-uh." She takes a giant bite of her toast and smiles with her mouth full.

"Let's talk about who the real coward is," Cleo says, scowling.

"I am not getting into the Who's-a-Chicken Olympics with you, Miss Cleo. I'd win, hands down, I can promise you that." She makes a face in the direction of the noisy TV and gobbles up her remaining toast. "Ready?" she asks, wiping her lips on her napkin.

"Sure." Cleo pops a last crust in her mouth.

"You gals be good!" calls Doyle, waving.

Madeline rolls her eyes at Cleo and holds the door open. "I'll settle with you tomorrow morning, Doyle!" she says over her shoulder. "I go there every morning for toast and root beer," she explains, walking closely alongside Cleo. "Root beer: an unsung but very important part of any balanced breakfast." She stops and gives Cleo a grave look. "You do like root beer, I hope?"

"Love it." Cleo nods with solemnity.

"I'm very relieved to hear that, Miss Savoy. Because you know, I would never grant an interview to someone who didn't." Madeline cackles and resumes walking. "I thought we could go back up to the studio and talk. How long is this story you're writing supposed to be?"

Cleo shrugs. "Couple thousand pages."

"What?" Madeline sees that Cleo is kidding and gives her a light slap on the arm. "I can tell you right now it's going to be a very short story. And not very juicy, I'm afraid." She takes out her key and struggles to open the street door. Cleo breathes in the soft cloud of Madeline's perfume. How could this person ever dream of killing herself? she thinks mournfully.

"Well, hello there, ladies." Johnny approaches, hands in his jacket pockets. He nods at Cleo and then says to Madeline, "I wonder if I could have a word with you?" He looks tired, has big black circles under his pouchy eyes. He doesn't look like a young fifty to Cleo this morning. She notices the silver threaded through his dark hair for the first time.

Madeline pauses in her battle with the door. "What's got you up so early this morning?"

"Things," he says. "Cleo, would you mind?"

"She would. And so would I." Madeline yanks on the door. "We're conducting an interview, or trying to. What's on your mind?"

"I brought your mail," Johnny says in a low voice. "Want it?" Madeline holds out her hand and waits. Johnny laughs and says, "Uh-uh. I want to talk to you first. Alone." He jerks his chin in Cleo's direction. "What's she doing here again?"

"I might ask you the same question."

"Yesterday you said, 'Come back some other time.' Here I am. I had an invitation." He folds his arms across his chest and grins down at Madeline.

"So did she," Madeline parries, shaking her extended palm impatiently. "I'm quite popular these days, it seems." Cleo busies herself by gazing across the road at the levee, a steep swell of grass that blocks the view of the river from where they stand.

"All right, here." He grudgingly places a pale pink envelope in her hand. "But we need to talk, Madeline. This is crazy. Why don't I come up for a minute? She can wait down here for two minutes, can't she?"

Madeline tucks the envelope in the pocket of her dress and turns her attention back to the door lock. This time the door gives way, and Madeline taps Cleo on the shoulder. "Miss Savoy, would you mind waiting inside a minute?" She ushers Cleo through the doorway but holds the door ajar. She says nothing and waits with one foot on the doorstep.

"What's the matter with you?" Johnny asks in a whisper.

"Nothing," she replies. "Nothing at all. Why?"

His laugh comes out as an exasperated wheeze. "*Why?* Well, shit, where should I begin? I could start with the fact that you didn't come home all night on the night before your birthday! Or how about that streetcar stunt, followed by a ridiculous decision to jump into the Mississippi? And then another! Where should I start?"

"Stunt?" She narrows her eyes, making her lips a hard line. "Goodbye, Johnny." She moves to open the door but he puts his hand up to prevent her.

"What? What'd I say? Jesus, girl, I'm not the one who's acting crazy!"

"Thank you, Johnny, that'll be all for today," she says, giving the door a vicious yank. He drops his hand away and his eyes are on the door as she slams it in his face.

"That'll be all for today?" he parrots. And suddenly he knows, or thinks he does, what this is all about. Cleo Savoy is here very early, and she wasn't at her hotel last night when he called three times and again early this morning. From this Johnny deduces that the girl reporter never even left Madeline's place. And why is that? Because Madeline probably fed her some bullshit poor-me tale about her mean old husband, that's why. How he stays out late—boo hoo—and how he isn't in the mood for sex every goddamned minute. They probably sat up all night complaining over cocktails, making nasty jokes and plans for revenge. Oh yes, they've bonded as women always will whenever the topic is how awful men are.

Johnny pounds on the door in outrage. She'll talk to a complete stranger and not to him? He pounds and hammers until he's red in the face. Pauses to catch his breath and is about to start hammering again when a woman comes along with a tiny white dog in her arms and glares at Johnny.

"Morning," he says, tugging his jacket down. The woman gives him a filthy look and walks on.

Madeline may think she has him beat, but she's wrong. He'll let her think she's won by leaving her be for a few days. Johnny starts walking around the curved road that leads to the ferry dock. Sure, he'll let her sit up there crying on the shoulder of the strange girl with the even stranger hair. Because Johnny sees Cleo's hair for what it is now. He's seen it before on other young women, and even on some older ones. It's what he calls "feminist hair." And with a name like Cleopatra, what else could she be but a man-hater? Wasn't Cleopatra the one who turned men to stone with one look? Or maybe that was some other man-hater—Johnny can't keep track of them all. Why, Madeline doesn't even like women, he reasons. She won't even talk to her own mother! It won't be long before she gets tired of Cleo and her man-hating agenda; of this Johnny is certain.

"SORRY ABOUT THAT," Madeline apologizes, locking the door from inside. She leans against the wall and gives Cleo a weak smile. "So, where would you like to do the interview?"

Cleo's gaze is trained on the piano across the room. Madeline has dismantled her arrangement of tables and chairs and statuettes. The chairs and tables are shoved against a wall; the lawn ornaments are tucked under the piano. She turns and gives Madeline a questioning look.

"The clutter was getting on my nerves," Madeline explains, crossing the room to the chairs. She picks up two and carries them over to the windows. "How about over here?"

In the bright morning light Cleo can see the tiny lines around Madeline's eyes, a faint white scar at the edge of her upper lip. *I wonder where that came from?* Cleo thinks, wishing she could see photographs of Madeline as a child. Madeline looks uneasily out the window, her hands folded in her lap. Cleo wishes she could think of some clever way to bring up the subject of Madeline's so-called attempts to swim the river, but there seems to be no subtle entrée. She glances at Madeline staring intently out the fogged window. Finds herself wishing that Madeline was ugly and pale and unhappy-looking. All she sees is the profile of a breathtakingly beautiful woman with the posture of a dancer, a face serene in repose. If Madeline is consumed by an inner darkness, she hides it awfully well. But such people do, Cleo reminds herself, still unable to find the right words.

A few moments pass. Madeline sighs. Without turning to look at Cleo she says, "This has to be the quietest interview I have ever given." Her smile is devilish. "Of the hundreds of interviews I've given, that is."

Cleo blushes. "All right, here goes. Let's start with the basics. Where were you born?"

"St. Louis," Madeline states. "As in 'St. Louis Blues.'"

Cleo pretends to write this on the palm of her hand with an imaginary pen. "OK. What's your birth date?"

"November fourth." When Cleo doesn't say anything

Madeline frowns. "I am *not* telling you which year, if that's what you're waiting for!"

"No. It's just that's the date of the flood I told you about. It's weird, don't you think?" Cleo feels too thrown by the coincidence to play at note taking. Madeline stares back without comprehension. "You swam the river on your birthday."

Madeline snorts, "When I was ten!"

Cleo pinches her hands between her knees to keep them from shaking. "You swam the Mississippi River when you were ten?"

Madeline nods ever so slightly. "Yes." Her frown returns. "In 1966." After a pause she says, "You needn't do the math."

"You swam the Mississippi River on November fourth, 1966?"

"Yes," Madeline repeats, impatient.

"Was that the first time?" Cleo asks.

Madeline doesn't answer.

They sit in silence, regarding each other with confusion and curiosity. A barge on the river blasts its horn. Madeline's heart thuds under her blouse. She wants to ask Cleo to leave but can't speak over the cotton in her throat. Instead she turns to look out the window again, though she can't see much through the steamed pane. *Why is she making such a big deal out of a swim?*

"I like to swim," Madeline says in a faraway voice.

"You swam to celebrate your birthday this year, too." Cleo holds her breath as soon as the words have tumbled out.

Madeline gives her a quick look. "No, I didn't." She

laces her fingers together and tries to think of a polite but effective way to get this young woman out of her studio. Something about this whole thing is suddenly very alarming, very weird. Up until now she'd been enjoying the snap in the air between them. She wishes she hadn't sent Johnny away, even if he is the last person she'd choose to be with right now. This young woman may be beautiful, she may even be charming in a shy sort of way, but there's an agenda in the air that Madeline doesn't care for.

Cleo sees that she's edging along a dangerous precipice, that she'll have to move carefully in order to get the conversation back to a more comfortable place. Tiny muscles in Madeline's jaw are twitching, and Cleo wants to say something perfect.

"I'd love to hear more about your first swim. You must have been a remarkable child."

"Topic change." Madeline's expression dares Cleo to defy her request.

Clearing her throat, Cleo attempts a courageous smile. "OK. How long have you been playing the piano?"

"Two and a half weeks." Madeline relaxes ever so slightly.

"Really?"

"Sometimes a lie is just as pretty as the truth," Madeline says. "Why don't you tell me about your fear of boats?"

"I just don't like them. Topic change."

"Touché," Madeline says, and laughs without reserve. "But you'll have to figure out *some* way to get back to your hotel. I'd be happy to loan you the money for a cab." She pats the envelope sticking out of her pocket. "In a manner of speaking, it's payday. We could go to the bank and I could cash my cheque." She can't stop thinking about what Cleo said: *You swam on your birthday this year, too.* How does Cleo know about that night? How could she possibly know a thing about it? She realizes Cleo has said something and is waiting for an answer. "I'm sorry, I didn't catch that."

"I asked if you'd like me to leave," Cleo repeats.

Madeline nibbles her bottom lip. "I don't know." She extracts the envelope and tears it open. There's a cheque with a note paperclipped to it: *Cash it. I know you need it, you proud fool.* There's no time to wonder why her mother has sent a second cheque. "Let's go to the bank. You can pay me back, all right?" She stands up and fans herself with the torn envelope, embarrassed by her indecisive behaviour. *I like this, but I don't.*

"I didn't mean to upset you," Cleo apologizes. "I really didn't."

"I'm fine." Madeline shrugs. "I think I'm just feeling a little ... unsettled. You see, I did swim across the river on my birthday. I did. But that time, nobody caught me. Or saw me. So I'm a little unnerved by the fact that you mentioned it. Why did you?" She stops playing with the envelope and waits.

"I was there. On the wharf, when you dove. I thought whoever it was must have died. And then you didn't. So here I am."

Madeline wraps her arms around herself. "I see." She licks her lips, stares hard at Cleo. "And you're not really a reporter." Cleo shakes her head, sure that she's just kissed goodbye her chance to talk to Madeline about why she does what she does. Instead, Madeline laughs with obvious delight. It's a gorgeous, generous sound. When she recovers, her eyes are dancing, but Cleo doesn't understand. "Just don't tell Johnny that, OK?"

"About the swim?"

Madeline hoots, says nothing more and gets up. She crosses the floor to the kitchen counter. Fills a snifter with gin and pours the rest into a plastic cup and waves Cleo over. Handing her the snifter she asks, "Is your name really Cleopatra?" Cleo nods. "To Cleopatra," she says, downing the gin, "the one interesting woman in all of history." She shudders and picks up her purse. "C'mon. I just love going to a bank with liquor on my breath and a big cheque in my pocket!" She holds the door open for Cleo and laughs to herself as they head down the stairs.

"I'll pay you back." Cleo tucks the twenty-dollar bill in her jeans pocket. They stand outside the Shore-Do Café, which cashed Madeline's cheque after the bank refused. They were also kind enough to call a cab for Cleo.

"No rush," Madeline says with a smile. The cab pulls up in front of the Shore-Do. "Bon voyage, then. I'm sorry our interview didn't work out."

"That's okay," Cleo says, fighting to conceal her disappointment. "Really though, how will I pay you back? I hate owing people money."

"I can see that," Madeline jokes. "Don't worry about it, it's only money." The driver revs the engine impatiently, and Madeline pats the side of the taxi as if it were a horse. "Maybe I'll see you around the Quarter, or you can mail it to me from Toronto."

"Sure," Cleo mumbles.

"Or maybe we could have lunch before you leave. When

are you leaving?" The driver sighs and drums his thumbs on the steering wheel.

"I'm not sure. Pretty soon, I think. That's why I was sort of anxious to talk to you."

"I am sorry," Madeline says. "I don't mean to be difficult. Well, usually I do, but in this case, I'm really not trying to be. It's just ... right now my life is kind of—"

"Are you ladies going to yak through the window all day long?" the cabbie barks. Madeline gives him the finger and he shakes his head.

"I just remembered, I have an errand to run across the river," Madeline announces suddenly. "Shove over." She slides into the back seat next to Cleo and tells the driver to take them to Royal and Esplanade. Opening her compact, she sees herself. "Sweet Jesus!" she cries, slamming it shut again.

Cleo feels a fluttery lightness in her chest, or rather, she notices it for the first time. Her throat aches and her hands and feet feel jumpy. Great, she thinks, I'm getting a cold. That's what I get for sleeping in a parkette. Madeline crosses her legs and uncrosses them, restless. Her cologne fills the back seat of the cab and makes the feathery feeling in Cleo's chest drop down into her belly. Great, Cleo thinks, I'm not getting a cold. I'm just losing my mind, one brain cell at a time.

Out of the blue Madeline says, "Tell me about the signora's son. Where'd he get to?"

"The signora's son? Oh. Uhmm." Cleo stammers, because the story in her head isn't based on anything factual.

Madeline nods eagerly. "I wondered about him all last night. Was he killed in the flood?"

"Nooo." Cleo stalls for time, the cab lurching and rocking as they speed down the exit ramp away from the bridge. Madeline's thigh bumps against Cleo's. Say you don't know where the signora's son got to, she thinks. Say you have no idea. That'd be the truth, after all. "I can't remember," she says finally.

"You're an interesting creature, Miss Cleopatra." Madeline sighs. She makes no effort to mask her irritation, then realizes that she hasn't exactly been forthcoming in the department of yarns and recollections herself. They're approaching Esplanade Avenue; she wonders what to do.

"If you've got a few minutes, I'll tell you what I think happened to the signora's son," Cleo offers as the cab pulls up at the corner of Esplanade and Royal. The cabbie sighs and fiddles with the radio, then turns around to glare at them again. Cleo hurriedly hands him her borrowed twenty and glances at Madeline. "It's not a long story," she adds, climbing out of the taxi.

"All right. But only if you agree to tell it over lunch. As I said, I have something I need to do first, but I'll come meet you at your hotel in about half an hour, OK?"

"Great." Cleo watches Madeline hurry off. Is suddenly overcome by the irrational fear that she'll never see her again, that whatever curious force threw them together might just as easily pull them apart in the same way, without warning.

In truth, Madeline has no errand to run, no something she needs to do. She's simply overwhelmed by the ambivalence of her emotions this morning. As she passes by the street-level door to the apartment she used to call home until recently, she thinks of the big brown parcel of doom, of all the other envelopes that have floated down from St. Louis over the years. The one Johnny delivered this morning was postmarked Florida; the other bore no stamps at all. She must have walked right up to my door and knocked, Madeline thinks as she passes the building, as if she had every right. That's the whole trouble right there; my mother never imagines that anything isn't her right. How she must have enjoyed handing that envelope to Johnny while she rated him on her unspoken tall-dark-and-handsome scale. How quietly pleased she must have been to get a good look at him at last.

Madeline marches into the Mint, clacking across the pretty tile floor to the bar. Marcus's back is turned as he counts beer bottles in the refrigerator. "Gimme a Separator!" she roars.

He whirls around. "Jesus, Madeline, spare what's left of my heart, would you please?" Marcus pats his chest and shakes his head. "How are you?"

Madeline smiles slyly. "All better now. I wasn't kidding about the Separator, though. I have a few minutes to kill before a lunch date."

Marcus clucks his tongue and busies himself making the drink. The Mint's trademark frozen Kahlua cocktail is Madeline's second favourite libation—when given a choice. When the blender falls silent he says, over his shoulder, "Meeting Johnny?" When Madeline says "Nope," Marcus grins. "I see! So it's true what they've been saying! You did get yourself a lover, after all." He sets the Separator down on a napkin.

"I did not get myself a lover after all." Madeline takes a long, leisurely sip. "What I have is a reporter from Canada who's writing my life story for a paper in Toronto. She's going to interview me over lunch."

"That's exciting. I had a man from Toronto once. He was amazing, as I recall. A surprisingly hot-blooded people, the Canadians." Marcus cocks his head and flashes her a wicked smile. "Is she attractive?"

"I didn't notice." Marcus scoffs, slaps the bar top and rolls his eyes all in one fluid motion. Madeline scoffs back, "Please. I've had enough trouble for one lifetime. The last thing I need is to get tangled up with some pretty little Canadian girl!"

"Aha! Then she *is* attractive and you *did* notice. And you said *girl,* indicating that she's younger than you. Madeline!" She frowns and he pats her hand. "I'm just kidding, hon. I know y'all women don't think like that. You're pure of thought and action every minute, right?" He laughs and then whispers with mock horror, "Are you sure she isn't a rabid lesbian? Maybe she's stalking you!"

"Oh, for God's sake!" Madeline pushes her drink away. "How the hell would I know? It hasn't come up. And she isn't stalking me, as you put it. She's a reporter. That's what they do." Madeline looks around for a clock. "What time is it, anyhow? Why don't the male members of the species ever see the need for a clock?"

"I could say something rude, but I won't," Marcus teases. He holds out his wrist so she can look at his watch. "You know, Madeline," he says slowly, "as the object of desire, you're allowed—practically required, in fact—to show up late for lunch dates. Especially lunch dates with lusty practitioners of the literary arts."

Madeline glowers, drawing her drink back toward her mouth.

Marcus rolls his eyes again, then becomes gentle. "By

the way, sweetie, have you called the psychiatrist they rec-ommended when we were at the police station?"

"No, I have not."

"Well, all right. I'm just asking. No more thoughts, I hope?"

Madeline smiles. "Not a single one. Thanks for the drink. Come over and see us sometime," she says, slipping down off the cushy bar stool. She gives Marcus a jaunty salute and heads out the door.

"Us?" Marcus repeats to himself.

"PLEASE, HAVE A SEAT. I didn't realize Miss Cleo had friends in the city," says Mrs. Ryan, taking Madeline in with unabashed curiosity.

Madeline, perched on the edge of the cushion of the wingbacked chair in the tiny lobby of the Pommes Royales, pretends not to notice she's being studied. She crosses her legs, smoothes her skirt and decides to forgo an explanation of how she and Cleo have come to know each other.

"She ever let you read any of her poetry?" Mrs. Ryan asks, fussing with a potted plant on the front desk.

"No, she hasn't." Madeline pauses. "Not yet." *Poetry?*

"I'm dying to read some of her work, personally. I can tell just by looking at a person if they have talent. She's mod-est. Are you an actress, by chance?"

Madeline says no, but thinks to herself, Sometimes. All my life, to varying degrees. She picks lint from her blouse and wonders what's keeping Cleo. Mrs. Ryan has already called Cleo's room once but there was no answer. Madeline had asked if there was any chance that Cleo wasn't actually in her room.

"Oh, she's in there, probably in the shower. I don't like to go knocking unless it's absolutely necessary," Mrs. Ryan explained. She seems content to wait before she calls again, and Madeline feels impatient, eager to get going. She watches Mrs. Ryan with her plants and wonders if Cleo was ever going to mention that she's a poet. Probably not.

"I don't mean to seem impatient," Madeline says at last, "but would you mind trying her room again?"

Mrs. Ryan claps her hand over her mouth. "My Lord! I guess I was off in a daydream. What's the matter with me?" She picks up the phone and dials Cleo's room, smiling at Madeline as she waits for Cleo to pick up. After a moment she says very brightly, "Miss Cleo, your friend is here." When Johnny enters the lobby, Mrs. Ryan gives a little gasp. "Pardon me—both your friends are here. Mr. Valentucci just walked in, too." She listens. "All right." To Madeline and Johnny she says, "She'll be right out." Mr. Valentucci and Miss Madeline seem to know each other. They greet each other stiffly. Miss Madeline is decidedly less happy to see Mr. Valentucci than he is to see her.

"What are you doing here?" Madeline hisses.

"Just thought I'd come by, see how the interview was going," Johnny says. He gives Mrs. Ryan a polite smile, then spots Cleo. "Cleopatra!"

Cleo is understandably anxious about the tandem arrival of Madeline and Johnny, mostly because she fears that some kind of showdown is about to take place in Mrs. Ryan's tiny lobby. Madeline gazes at her intently but says nothing.

"Y'all know each other, then?" chirps Mrs. Ryan, glancing from Johnny to Madeline to Cleo.

Johnny is about to explain that Madeline is his wife and that he introduced Cleo to her for the purposes of a newspaper interview, but Cleo cuts him off at the pass. "Ready to go?" she asks them both, making a beeline for the door. "Have a good day, Mrs. Ryan!" she calls, holding the door wide, hoping Johnny and Madeline will follow her outside. They do.

"Why aren't you ever at work any more?" Madeline plants her hands on her hips to indicate the degree of her displeasure. Johnny lights a cigarette and blows a plume of smoke high in the air. "We're still doing the interview," she insists, glancing at Cleo, hoping she'll jump in and corroborate the story.

Johnny turns to Cleo and raises his thick eyebrows. "How's it coming along? She giving you anything interesting?"

"Yes," Cleo says. "We're not quite finished talking, though."

Johnny looks steadily at Madeline. "Why don't you two come up to Papa Leone's for some lunch? You can talk there."

"No thanks," Madeline says. "I know the chef." After a long pause she gazes up at him with unfettered disgust. "Why are you following me around? Don't you have anything better to do with your time?"

Cleo shifts her knapsack and watches a plump cockroach amble across the brick walkway. *Gregor Samsa,* she mouths.

"Madeline." Johnny's tone is halfway between pleading and scolding. "Please don't make a fool of me."

"You don't need me to help you with that."

"Uhmm, Johnny," Cleo interrupts, hoping to diffuse the tension that is filling the flowery walkway like a poisonous gas. "If I can have just one more hour with Madeline, I'll have my story all wrapped up."

Johnny stares at Madeline for a long minute and then turns to Cleo, who seems to be the only female in the trio with any manners. "All right," he says, "she's all yours." He reaches out to open the gate. "You might want to ask her why she doesn't talk to her mother," he suggests darkly. "I wouldn't mind reading about that myself. Do send us a copy."

"Or two," Madeline mutters. Watching Johnny beat his slow retreat down the sidewalk, Madeline leans out of the gate and yells after him, "Cleo might only need an hour, Johnny, but I'll need a hell of a lot more time away from you than that!" She then turns back to face Cleo and asks very sweetly, "Lunch?"

November 3, 1966
Florence, Italy

It would have begun with Paolo Bianchi's limited command of English and Richard Thomas's even more impoverished Italian. As he watched the man, obviously an American, approach his wicket at the counter of the Banco del Firenze, Paolo found it more and more difficult to breathe. The man's impossibly green eyes, wavy hair and sheepish smile all served to impair Paolo's hearing as Richard Thomas announced his desire to deposit funds when what he really meant to do was transfer them. Paolo had to ask Richard to repeat his request three times, and not only because Richard's grammar was atrocious. No matter, they soon spoke another more intelligible language, one of glances and flushed cheeks and suppressed smiles. As the transaction progressed Paolo's stomach churned with fear: the fear that he might never see this face again, or that he would. It was a foolish fear on both counts, because there was every possibility they'd meet again. A bank was, after all, a place people returned to of necessity—but still, a sense of electricity snapped in the air that November afternoon, a sense of urgency and caution to the wind.

"Meet me," Richard Thomas whispered, hopeful and yet forceful, too, "in front of the Pitti Palace, seven o'clock?"

Paolo, kept his eyes on the official paperwork before him. "Five o'clock?" He stole a glance sideways to make sure the nosy teller next to him wasn't listening to their exchange. Loudly, but with what he imagined was bureaucratic restraint, Paolo said, "*Buona sera, signore, e buona fortuna con il matrimonio.*"

Richard tipped an imaginary hat and tapped his watch as if to say, Five o'clock.

They both arrived at four-thirty, the rain falling as it had for days on end. It soaked the paper bag of bread and meat and oranges that Richard held. Paulo carried a sack full of bottles of Heineken, sure that beer would please his American friend. No mention of a picnic had been made aloud by either of them when they agreed to meet. The grounds of the Pitti Palace, already half-submerged by the heavy rain, offered no suitable place for a picnic anyway; the weather forced them to go elsewhere, indoors. They sloshed through deep puddles and made their way along the several blocks to Richard's room, which Paolo discovered was situated in a strippers' hotel, and a filthy one at that. Like a child he marvelled at the garbage in the vestibule, at the odour of cigarettes and fried meat and eggs that stung their nostrils. Was it possible that this was the same Florence inhabited by his fastidious mother? It was. He rejoiced, then relaxed, and the latter sensation frightened him. His spine seemed to melt as they sat on the cold stone floor of Richard's tiny *camera,* eating meat sandwiches and draining bottles of Heineken. Paolo's happiness alarmed him; it felt as if death itself was sweeping through his veins. There had been other men, of course, furtive meetings near the Ponte Vecchio. Older men, married men, their zippers pulled down and their faces turned away to hide their shameful want. Nothing like this: the desire to kiss a mouth and to hear it talk, too. Those other interludes were never relaxed; they were guilty and satisfying in some brief but stolen way. In alleys and even behind churches, those encounters were almost blasphemous and definitely quick. They weren't even worthy of confession, and so were omitted from Paolo's memory as soon as they ended.

The rain pounded harder against the half-open window. Paolo and Richard watched it make a puddle on the sloping floor. Richard suggested that they call it Lake Placido and Paolo fell in love, vowing to never leave this room, not as long as a man with eyes that green and teeth that perfect lived in Florence. He would hold himself hostage, if such a thing could be done. His silent hope was that Richard would prove to be a willing kidnapper.

"Do you want to call home?" Richard's voice interrupted Paolo's thoughts as he gazed forlornly out the window. Richard had interpreted Paolo's silence as worry—perhaps it had occurred to him that his family might be in danger. Richard's room was located just beyond where the deluge would eventually rip the city in half. Though the streets were slowly but steadily filling with water, there was no indication of how bad things would get. The civic drains were slow, even though there was always a great deal of rain at this time of year. No one seemed particularly worried. The strippers cackled two floors below, playing Frank Sinatra records at full volume and shouting over the din. Corks were liberated from bottles of champagne on the half-hour, marking the sweet hours of oblivion.

"No." Paolo shook his head. "My mother could survive ten earthquakes. This is nothing. A little rain, so what?" He turned and gave Richard a brave smile, motioned for him to come to the window and look. He pointed, "Look: *niente*. This is nothing."

Richard's voice was low as he placed his hand on the back of Paolo's neck. "Funny, it doesn't feel like nothing to me."

Cleo nods to indicate that the story of the signora's son and his possible whereabouts during the flood is finished. Madeline hasn't even touched her chef's salad, though her fork hovers a few inches above the bowl as if she intends to eat. She sits in stunned silence, looking at Cleo and thinking, Where did you come from? What she finally says is, "That's it? But what happened after that?" Madeline wonders.

"No idea. To be honest, I haven't really thought about what happened after." Cleo points at two men across the room. "Maybe that's them over there, celebrating their anniversary." Madeline turns to look at the two men Cleo has indicated: a chubby man in a baseball cap and a darker, smaller companion in a Saints sweatshirt.

"Maybe," Madeline murmurs.

Cleo hoists her oyster po'boy and takes a bite. Some lettuce tumbles out and a piece of tomato threatens to follow. She wipes mayonnaise from the corners of her lips with the tip of her finger and smiles self-consciously. "I guess you call a sandwich *dressed* because you end up wearing half of it?" After swallowing another bite she says, "Your turn."

"Oh no," Madeline groans. "I knew there'd be a catch."

"No catch. But I am supposed to be interviewing you, and we do only have an hour."

"Who says?" Madeline scowls. "I have all the time in the world. I answer to no one. Ask me something—it's easier if you ask me questions. I'm not a writer—I can't come up with things off the top of my head like you can." She takes a bite of her salad, chews, and continues, "Mrs. Ryan asked me if you'd shown me any of your poetry. I said, 'No, not yet.' Any other secrets you'd like to confess?"

"I ask the questions." Cleo tries to sound firm while inwardly cursing poor Mrs. Ryan. "OK. How long have you been married to Johnny?"

"A long time. What's it like up there in Toronto?"

"Very pleasant for about three months of the year. How did you meet?"

"It was an arranged marriage." Cleo's face registers her surprise. "Arranged by me and my blind determination to be married at any cost." Madeline begins sorting her salad ingredients into piles. "How about you, are you married?" She's thinking about what Marcus said. He was wrong, of course, but his words hang stubbornly in the back of Madeline's mind. Object of desire indeed.

"I am not now—nor have I ever been—married. Nor will I ever get married in the future," Cleo says with absolute confidence. She takes another large bite of her sandwich as if to finalize this pact with herself.

"Any particular reason why not?" Madeline tries to sound casual, the furthest thing from what she feels just now.

"Because I don't plan to fall in love," Cleo explains. "Ever."

"Not with man or beast?" Madeline quips. "Well, that's a vow that doesn't necessarily negate the possibility of marriage."

"You're right. Next question. Let me think." *I want to know why you jumped into the Mississippi when you were ten, and why you did it again so recently. I want to know if you were—are—trying to kill yourself, and if so, why? I want to know why I'm so afraid to ask the questions I want to ask, and why I forget in moments what the questions even are.*

"So, you've never been in love?" It's Madeline's turn to press for answers. "I don't see how you could make up a story like the one you just told me if you'd never, ever, been in love. Besides, you must have all kinds of people chasing after you. Surely you've had the odd *occasional—*"

"Nope." Cleo shakes her head. "Never been chased."

"Uh-huh. All right, then. You've never loved, never been pursued. Ever." Madeline sets her fork down. "Maybe sometime I'll tell you about the time I fell in love."

"How about now?"

Madeline rests her chin on one hand and looks sideways at Cleo. "Why were you on that wharf, the one I jumped from?"

"I'd had a few drinks," Cleo says slowly, "and I got it into my head that I wanted to go down and sit by the river. One hears so much about the Mississippi. I was curious."

"Maybe. But, I mean, it was kind of dangerous, don't you think? At that hour? You may not know it, but that's a real good place to get mugged." She closes her eyes and, remembering her own swift flight toward the river that night, wonders why she didn't see anyone sitting there.

"Why did you decide to swim it, then, all those times?" Cleo asks. All around them the lunch crowd at Fiorella's shifts and clatters. Cleo feels as if she could happily wait for Madeline's answer for days if necessary. Years, even. But Madeline just sits there, chin in hand, eyes closed, rocking slightly, thinking whatever she's thinking. Watching her, Cleo thinks, I wish you weren't beautiful.

Madeline opens her eyes. She looks at Cleo with such intensity that Cleo almost looks away. *Talk, Madeline. Say something dismissive and unpleasant. Get up and walk out of the restaurant. Tell me I'm nosy, rude, anything.* But Madeline keeps on staring and Cleo begins to feel very nervous.

"I didn't decide to swim, I just did it," Madeline says at last. "What did you do when you saw me? Did you call the police?"

I ran.

"I figured it wasn't any of my business." Cleo toys with the paper wrapper from her straw. "It's a free country, after all."

"That it is," Madeline nods. No, no, no, she thinks angrily, do not remind me of that part of me. Do not sit there looking at me with those too-kind eyes and smiling with that perfect mouth of yours, sharing my view of personal liberty till freedom's the last thing I want. And you, what do you want from me? Panicked, Madeline contemplates terminating this mock interview right here and now, before things can get even close to foolish. Cleo looks as if she'd welcome an end to the conversation, too. Would she? Madeline wonders. She straightens up on her wooden stool and flings her arms out in a wide stretch. Regards each of her hands with a sort of amazement, as if she's just realized that she has two of them. "The way I see it, Miss Savoy, we have two options here."

Cleo waits, her heart tight, convinced that Madeline has grown weary of her questions, of her company.

Madeline bounces her left hand and stares at it. "We can get drunk," she says, then looks at her right hand and bounces it, too. "Or we can get *very* drunk." She folds her hands in her lap and smiles. "Which would you prefer?"

Relieved, Cleo grins and points at Madeline's right hand.

"So it is," Madeline says with a nod, "very drunk we soon shall be."

THERE ARE SEVERAL HUNDRED BARS in the city of New Orleans. A great number of them are concentrated in the French Quarter. In addition to the regular bars and live-music clubs, there are also dozens of take-out windows proffering booze, and brightly lit daiquiri shops that have spread along Bourbon Street like neon spores. Which came first, the booze or the reputation? It's hard to say. In any case, getting very drunk in the French Quarter isn't something that requires much effort, even on a blustery afternoon prior to Thanksgiving Day.

It's been a long time since Madeline actively hopped from bar to bar. The only tricky aspect is trying to find places where the likelihood of running into old acquaintances is lessened. When she does see someone she knows, Madeline gives a quick wave and then hurries Cleo along. There's a civilized way to drink your way to drunkenness, and only the tourists ignore this approach in favour of instant, constant inebriation. What Madeline is seeking is the kind of slow, almost elegant state of intoxication that leads people to reveal things about themselves. She isn't 100 per cent sure whether she wishes to reveal herself or to have Cleo drop her guard. Probably a little bit of both.

They begin their quest at an infamous Irish bar known for its tourist appeal. Although Madeline herself has no stomach for Hurricanes, she encourages Cleo to order one of the sickly sweet, bright rum punches. They sit in the courtyard by a fountain that spews flames along with water. When Cleo tries to say something, Madeline holds up her hand and says, "Shh, no talking until you've drunk up that whole glass!"

Madeline sips at her own cocktail, a brandy Alexander, refusing to speak until they've both finished their drinks. What this vow of silence means is that Cleo drinks more quickly than she normally would, which is precisely the point. But Madeline herself isn't in any hurry. In addition, she isn't particularly eager to reach the unavoidable end of the afternoon (or evening). At some point Cleo will probably want to go back to her hotel and pass out. While Madeline is subtly encouraging Cleo to gulp the first of what she hopes will be many libations, it's only this first one that needs to be downed with haste.

"That was so good." Cleo licks her lips. She looks around the courtyard at the other tables. The patronage here has a decidedly ark-like feel to it, with everyone paired off in romantic twosomes and jovial foursomes. Madeline watches from behind the rim of her glass, amused. Cleo catches her watching and leans on her elbows. "I wonder if I should have another?"

"I don't recommend two of those," Madeline warns. "They sneak up." She drains her own glass and looks around. "A little domestic out here, isn't it? Let's go some-where else."

The Blacksmith is dark, even in daytime. When tourists do stop by to check it out, they seldom stay, put off by the roaches meandering across the tabletops. But it's a nice place to sit when it rains, and it is most definitely about to rain. Hoping the cockroaches are otherwise engaged, Madeline chooses a table by a window.

"What would you like to drink, Miss Cleo?"

"A gin martini, please." Cleo has only ever had one mar-tini in her life but seems to remember that it did something nice to her nervous system, made her feel more stoned than drunk. She watches Madeline lean on the bar as she orders their drinks and can't quite believe that after all that won-dering and worrying, she's simply out for drinks with some-one who may or may not have tried—more than once—to take her own life. Madeline seems to be the embodiment of pleasure for pleasure's sake.

"I forgot to ask if you wanted olives or a twist," Madeline apologizes, setting the glass down on the scarred wooden table. "I got you both."

"Yum." Cleo feels excited, ridiculous and slightly

hysterical from all the sugar in the Hurricane. Madeline has a martini, too, with olives and a twist. She raises her brim-full glass without spilling a drop and makes a toast. "To Signora Bianchi's son."

"Oh God." Cleo blushes. "I'm so embarrassed about that." She takes a long sip from her glass and tries not to slosh it all over herself. A beer bottle would have been much easier to manage, but not nearly as elegant. Cleo suddenly wishes that she smoked. The idea seems like a good one and she asks Madeline if she smokes.

"I guess I always thought Johnny smoked enough for both of us." Madeline pops an olive into her mouth. "But we can get some cigarettes if you'd like."

Cleo waves her hand lazily. "Naw. I don't smoke. I'm just nervous." She blanches at her own confession. Out of habit, or maybe to keep herself from guzzling her entire drink all at once, she sits on her hands. Madeline takes a long sip of her martini to camouflage her smile. Cleo stares at Madeline's lips as they curve over the rim of her glass. She drinks and drinks, her eyes never leaving Cleo's face. Now that, thinks Cleo fuzzily, would make a great poem....

"... someone as beautiful as yourself could claim to have never been in love," Madeline is saying, shaking her russet-coloured curls in wonder.

To Cleo's mildly stoned surprise, she catches herself thinking, I could die, right now, and feel completely happy.

"Cleo, are you okay?"

"I'm fine." She sits up straight in her chair and takes another sip of her martini. "You were going to tell me about the time you fell in love."

"Which time?" Madeline pretends not to remember having said any such thing.

"There was more than one time?"

Madeline laughs. "Who knows?" She nibbles lemon rind and wonders if she could really manage to talk about it after all these years. Just tell it, already, she thinks, looking at Cleo. "Your eyes are the most unusual colour," she says instead.

"Good try," Cleo chuckles.

"I mean it. They're really something. Did you get them from your mother or your father?"

"My father, I guess." Cleo cranes around to look at the bar. "Would you like another martini? I would."

Is it just my imagination, or does she become skittish whenever I ask her anything about her family? Madeline wonders, silently acknowledging that the topic of her own family isn't a source of joyful repartee either. *I like you because you're broken and bright at the very same time. Someday I might even tell you that.*

When Cleo returns to the table carrying two more martinis, Madeline makes a silent promise to tell Cleo something personal, something revealing. Why? Why not? Although she isn't quite as drunk as she planned to be, Madeline proceeds bravely, hoping that her story will inspire Cleo to tell another one of hers.

"All right." Madeline takes a deep breath followed by a greedy gulp of gin. "There was this one person." Cleo gives an encouraging nod. "Who worked for my family, for my mother, really. Lived with us, took care of things around the house. I was on a competitive swim team at the time. And so I was busy going to meets and trying to manage my schoolwork, and my mother was busy with whatever she was busy with, who knows?"

"Her bisexuality?" Cleo suggests.

Madeline laughs—"Maybe"—then blushes ever so slightly. "Anyway, it might sound silly, but I became involved with this individual. We were left alone together in the house quite a bit, so it sort of just happened, by degrees. Oh, Jesus." Madeline takes a tiny sip of her drink and begins to lose her nerve. It's not too late to turn back, she thinks, avoiding Cleo's gaze. "Anyhow, it's not a very exciting story, now that I think about it."

Anything about you is exciting to me, Cleo thinks, but she doesn't speak for fear of derailing Madeline's train of thought.

"And then, you know, it didn't last, of course. I was young . . . younger. Why would it have lasted? But the memory of it endured, unfortunately."

Cleo remembers Madeline's strange announcement—*I come from a long line of bisexuals on my mother's side*—aware that it might have been a joke, something intended to test Cleo's shockability. Or not. "Was the person older than you?" Cleo asks, aware that she's adopted Madeline's avoidance of pronouns.

"Not much older, no. Oh, look, it's raining!" Madeline taps on the windowpane beside the table, where rain smears down in long rivulets. "We should walk in it. Unless of course you don't care for rain."

"I like rain," Cleo says.

"I suppose you would, having originated with so much of it! Shall we?" Madeline stands up. Cleo follows her out into the rainy street. They stroll along Bourbon. The heart of it is decidedly less chaotic in poor weather. Everything looks a little sad: the windows full of cheap coloured beads and T-shirts, the racks of postcards tugged just inside the doorways, the blare of neon reflected on the greasy cobblestones and sidewalks.

"Where should we go?" Madeline asks with a frown. "I don't think I feel like being very drunk any more, do you?" The rain streams down Madeline's cheeks, runs along her bare arms, soaks her clothes. "How about I walk you back to your hotel?"

"Or maybe we could go back to your place?" Cleo suggests, emboldened by the martinis. "You can tell me the rest of your story on the ride over. I'd like to hear it." She blinks raindrops out of her eyes, feeling reckless as she says, "We can take the ferry."

"But you don't like boats," Madeline reminds her. "You told me, remember?"

"I'll close my eyes—it'll be fine. Really. You can tell me your story on the way over—that'll help me stay calm." Cleo nods, mostly to convince herself.

But not me, Madeline thinks. "All right, I suppose that's a fair trade. Are you sure you'll be OK? It seems like a pretty serious phobia you've got...." She's thinking of the fact that Cleo chose to sleep outside, in November, merely to avoid a short boat ride.

Cleo's voice: "I'll be fine, I promise."

Cleo's gut: What the hell are you doing?

When Madeline takes Cleo's hand as they walk toward Canal Street and down to the Plaza d'España, Cleo faces a respiratory challenge unlike any she's ever known before. It isn't just her terror of boats and the warm buzz of gin in her blood that makes it hard to breathe, but the easy way Madeline's hand fits itself into hers. It's impossible to distinguish the cool sweat running down her back from the rain that does the same. Her stomach sends signals of terror to her brain, but even those are impossible to separate from the involuntary jolts of excitement emanating from the same source. Cleo climbs the stairs leading up to the ferry dock, pushes herself along and down the ramp toward the gate where she's determined to board the ferry. *Who did I imagine was the invalid?* She glances at Madeline, whose hair is curling darkly all around her face, making her eyes seem greener than ever. It's either fortune or misfortune that the ferry is nudging into the dock this very moment. There'll be no agonizing wait, which is good, or awful, depending.

"You OK?" Madeline asks, squeezing Cleo's fingers. While she hasn't held many hands in her lifetime, Cleo's fairly certain that this is how it ought to feel, as if the two hands in question were meant for each other. Her life thus far has been relatively short on touch. Nothing beyond a hug here and a pat there, the odd awkward kiss. In spite of her first (and last) brush with almost-love, there hasn't been any handholding at all. Feeling the warm strength of Madeline's fingers entwined in her own, Cleo has one thought that obliterates all others: Somebody please shoot me now.

"I'm fine," Cleo insists. Stepping across the threshold from dock to ferry, they let go of each other's hand. *"Molto bene,"* she mumbles, heading toward a row of bright orange plastic seats. To her great relief it seems that they won't have to stand on deck with the wind whipping their hair and a full view of the waves. That's what she'd imagined the ride would involve, and it hadn't thrilled her. She wishes she could tell Madeline why she's so afraid of boats. She feels she could, then decides against it. Don't talk, she tells herself, just get through it.

Madeline sits down next to Cleo, smelling of rain and perfume and gin. Realizing that Cleo isn't at all *fine,* she leans over and whispers in Cleo's ear, "The person I mentioned?" Cleo nods almost imperceptibly. "Her name was Carmelle." Cleo smiles inwardly, even as the ferry eases out into the water, and instead of closing her eyes, she focuses them on the cabinets of lifejackets across from her.

March, 1976
St. Louis, Missouri

If Madeline thought Carmelle was beautiful when she first came into the Shockfire household, she now found her unbearably so. But it was the best form of suffering. Now Madeline went off to the pool, where she swam with a vigour that surprised her coach and teammates. While her swimming skills had always been strong enough to make her a valued member of the Muskrats, everyone knew that Madeline was only swimming because her mother insisted that she was bound for the Olympics. And everyone, Madeline's coach included, knew that no such destiny awaited her. She had made sure of that by missing certain qualifying meets. But something had changed, and Madeline now took all criticism and teasing with a smile. She listened, worked and seemed to take real pleasure in competition.

"My God, Shockfire," Coach Livingstone had said when

she cut her freestyle time by several seconds and burst out of the pool with an uncharacteristic grin, "a person would think you were in love, the way you're flying through the water!"

I am, she thought, but she would admit no such thing out loud. She knew who she was swimming for and that was enough. Every time her body pushed through the water she felt Carmelle's hands fluttering across her skin; any time Coach Livingstone told her she needed to work on her strokes, she heard Carmelle's voice insisting that she needed to hold her wrists just so in order to hit certain notes on the piano.

"You're very cheerful these days," her mother observed. "Who's got you so keen to get to the pool?" Dianne became convinced that someone was wooing her daughter. She pressed for information, to no avail. She watched Madeline blossom and attributed it to the one thing that fuelled her own self-worth: the attentions of a male. But Madeline refused to say who it was that had managed to lift her usually saturnine mood. Whereas Madeline had previously begrudged Dianne's frequent absences from the house, she now smiled and told her mother to have a good time. Dianne wondered if her daughter was taking drugs; her cheerfulness seemed more and more suspect. When she called Coach Livingstone to inquire after Madeline's performance she was surprised to hear, "She's swimming better than ever, Mrs. Shockfire." It was the same with Madeline's teachers, who reported that Madeline's below-average marks were soaring. The only explanation was romance, but Dianne couldn't find a single piece of evidence.

Frustrated by the mysterious source of Madeline's unnerving glee, she turned to Carmelle. After all, it was

Carmelle who dropped Madeline off at the pool in the mornings and Carmelle who saw Madeline when Dianne wasn't around. "Does she talk on the phone a lot when I'm not here?" Dianne asked. Carmelle said, with all honesty, that she hadn't ever seen Madeline pick up the telephone. It was true. "Has she mentioned anyone special? Have you ever seen her talking to anyone at the pool when you pick her up?" No and no, according to Carmelle. If Madeline was the least sociable teenage girl in the universe, Carmelle knew it had everything to do with the demanding schedule Dianne had set for her daughter. But Carmelle, aware of her own key role in Madeline's bliss, didn't point that out. She simply reassured Dianne that she hadn't noticed any worrisome changes in Madeline's routine. She then suggested to Madeline that she might want to frown a little more often because her mother was suspicious and determined to find out what—or who— had cheered up Madeline so profoundly. Hearing the suggestion that she feign misery for her mother's benefit, Madeline threw back her head and laughed.

Dianne cornered Madeline in her room one evening. She sat on the bed and fixed Madeline with one of her you-will-not-escape-my-questions stares. "Honey," she said, patting the bedspread, "I want to talk to you about something." Madeline obeyed, if only because she knew that nothing her mother could think to ask her would require an actual lie. "Is there anything you'd like to tell me about, Madeline? Any sort of romantic dilemma?" Madeline shook her head. Dianne sighed. "Let me put it another way. Are you having intercourse?"

"Oh my God!" Madeline exclaimed, as if outraged at the idea.

Dianne took her hand. "You can tell me, sugar. There's no need to be ashamed. I won't be mad, I promise. Who is he?"

Madeline shook her mother's hand away. "All you ever think about is sex! Can't a person just be happy? Why does everything have to be about a man?"

"Of course," Dianne hastily apologized, "of course you can be happy without it having to do with sex. I just wondered, was all. You seem different these days, distant. I can't help thinking that sort of cheerfulness has something to do with love. Or narcotics." Dianne wet her lips and continued. "Don't shut me out of your life, Madeline, please. I know you feel all grown up now, but really, you're still my baby. I just worry that someone might hurt you terribly."

"No one's hurting me," Madeline said. "I'm fine, OK?"

"All right." Dianne fell silent, but it was clear that she wasn't satisfied with Madeline's reply. She flicked one of Madeline's curls and said, "You need a haircut. Why don't you come downstairs and let me give you a trim?"

"Aren't you going out tonight?" Madeline asked, suddenly fearful that her mother's plans had changed. She was counting on her mother's absence and so was Carmelle. It had been days since they'd done more than kiss, and Madeline couldn't wait for her mother to leave them alone.

"I can trim your hair before I go out," Dianne said. "I don't have to be on time—it's only Burt I'm seeing." She forced a yawn. "I may even cancel, I'm feeling so very tired all of a sudden."

Madeline reminded her mother of how hurt Mr. Oliver would be if she cancelled at the last minute, and Dianne narrowed her eyes for a second, then smiled. "You're right, that wouldn't be at all kind of me. If I'm going to break it off with him, I should at least do it in person, shouldn't I? That's the right way to do things."

"I guess," Madeline mumbled, now beside herself with worry. If her mother broke it off with Mr. Oliver, did that mean she'd be home all the time? Madeline consoled herself with the realization that her mother had broken it off with Mr. Oliver half a dozen times or more over the years. "I like Mr. Oliver," she said helplessly.

"I do too, honey. That's what makes the fact that outside the bedroom, he bores me to tears ... so hard to bear." Madeline cringed. She didn't want to know these sorts of things about her mother, but she remained silent. "When you do start having sex, Madeline," her mother said with a weary smile, "you'll see that people can lure you in with their sexual talents. Try and find someone whose mind impresses you as much as their body seems to."

I have, Madeline thought with a secretive smile. I have most definitely found exactly that. She decided to change the subject quickly and said, "I'd like to grow my hair out. Coach Livingstone says it doesn't make any difference to my time at all, whether or not I have short hair or long. He says that's a myth." She gave her mother a timid smile, thinking all the while about how Carmelle had said, the last time they were lying naked together, "You'd look even more beautiful with longer hair."

"You do as you please, Madeline." Her mother shrugged. "Seems to me that's what you always do anyway."

Madeline swallowed the unfair remark, but only because she knew she'd soon be tangled up in Carmelle's arms and legs, experiencing sensations she never got tired of, and making plans she knew would come true. She watched her mother go and tried not to let the unfairness of her words sink in too deeply. I'm in love, and nothing you can say or do will hurt me again.

"You did great," Madeline says to Cleo, leading her down the road and away from the ferry dock at Algiers.

"I forgot we were even on a boat." Unsteady on her feet, Cleo takes careful steps.

"Are you ever going to tell me why you're so frightened of boats?" Madeline asks gently.

"Topic change," Cleo whispers, giving Madeline a weak smile.

"I've changed my mind," Madeline says with a resolute nod. "I do want to get very drunk. Let's hit a store before we go to my place."

ON THE OTHER END of the line Dianne is accusatory. "I haven't heard from Madeline yet. You did give her my package, didn't you?"

Johnny sighs wearily into the mouthpiece of his telephone. "I gave it to her. She hasn't been home in a few days, that's all. She's been busy, playing the piano. Oh, and talking to a newspaper reporter."

Dianne laughs out of nervous suspicion. "About what?"

"About her swimming," says Johnny.

"What?" Dianne snorts. "That was a lifetime ago!"

Based on Madeline's imitations of her mother, Johnny can almost see Dianne stretched out on a chaise longue, wearing a smug expression, a tall cool drink in hand. "No, in fact the reporter is interested in her more recent swims," Johnny says with quiet pleasure. "The two she has taken in the Mississippi River in the past weeks." He waits, lighting a cigarette.

"Are you kidding me?" Dianne gasps. "Is she all right? Now what on earth is going on over there?"

Maybe if you'd asked that question a long time ago, Mrs. Shockfire, Madeline wouldn't be throwing herself into the river all the time, he thinks, but he doesn't say so. Because Johnny isn't entirely convinced that Madeline's swims have anything to do with her mother. He's almost willing to believe that the swims might be his fault, at least in part. "We're having a few problems," he admits. "Nothing serious, just a little ... quarrel."

"Well, I hope you get it sorted out! It doesn't sound like any little quarrel I ever heard of. I want to know more about these swims," Dianne insists.

"Me too," Johnny says. "And I'm sure that just as soon as Madeline has cooled off, she'll tell me. Until then, you have yourself a good day at the beach, all right?" He drops the phone smartly back onto the cradle and shakes his head. Tomorrow is Thanksgiving Day. He'll be spending it alone unless he can convince Madeline to drop her grudge and come home. He isn't sure he'll hear from her, though. Lena, whom he saw just this afternoon, has informed him that someone saw Madeline walking down Canal Street holding another woman's hand. Johnny had laughed it off, telling Lena that Madeline was the most heterosexual woman he'd ever met. "They were probably drunk and trying to hold each other up," he'd added with a trademark guffaw.

But now, reminded of the fact that Madeline did seem

intent on continuing her interview with Cleo without him present, Johnny feels troubled. Holding hands? C'mon, he cajoles himself, it's not like they were kissing or anything.

EVERYTHING'S FINE WHILE they're shopping. Cleo is shaky but triumphant, having conquered her fear of the ferry. For her part, Madeline is full of praise, all smiles. But almost as soon as they enter the studio, something shifts. Now Madeline seems cross, sorry that she invited Cleo in, or so Cleo imagines as she arranges and rearranges the food and liquor they purchased at a nearby store.

"Maybe I shouldn't have invited myself over." Cleo sets down the bottle she holds with shaking hands.

Madeline doesn't respond. She's moved across the room and is rather frantically pulling the lawn ornaments out from under the piano. Cleo watches, dumbfounded, as she observes Madeline's maniacal reassembly of the tables and chairs and statuettes in the cabaret formation they were in before. Cleo wonders what happened to Madeline's good mood. She realizes that ever since she met Madeline, she's been expecting to be expelled from her company. Not left, but sent away. Interesting, Cleo thinks, walking toward the windows because she doesn't know what else to do. When she glances over at Madeline she sees her sitting at the piano with her head bowed. Her reddish brown curls tumble around her face, and she's punching the tops of her legs with increasing force.

"Stop that," Cleo says, standing beside her now, one hand resting lightly on the piano's sleek surface, the other holding Madeline's hands still. Madeline doesn't look up right away, though she does stop pummelling herself. "What's the matter?" Cleo asks, moving closer.

Madeline gives a tiny shrug and looks up, her eyes blazing. "Nothing. It's nothing. Why don't you make us a drink?" She plays a few chords, repeats them and points her chin in the direction of the kitchenette as she plays them all again. A song rolls out under Madeline's fingers but Cleo doesn't recognize it. She only knows that Madeline looks happier now that she's playing the Steinway, her head thrown sideways in rapture as she pounds the keys. When Cleo comes toward her carrying two plastic cups full of brandy, Madeline gestures, again with her chin, to the table closest to her, where Snow White now sits alone. Cleo sits down and listens as she sips.

"How'd you get here, baby? How'd you come my way? Da da da all I know," sings Madeline in a pleasant, scratchy voice. She stops playing, picks up her drink and downs it in three quick gulps. "Whew!" She wipes her mouth. "What's your favourite song?" she asks, cracking her knuckles.

"Roxanne," Cleo says without hesitation. Madeline raises one eyebrow. "It's by the Police," she adds, in case Madeline isn't familiar with the band.

"I know that," Madeline snorts. "How old do you think I am, a hundred? I just don't know how to play that one, is all. Let me think." After a few attempts to capture the song on the keys, she shakes her head. "Nope, I can't figure that one out. I only know how to play the songs I've known for years or the ones I make up myself."

"I'd like to hear one of those," Cleo says. "Your favourite made-up song."

"Maybe later," Madeline replies. She moves away from

the piano and sits next to Snow White, loops her arm around the statue's shoulder. "Snow White and I would like a refill," she says. "Would you mind?"

"I'll get you another on one condition," Cleo says carefully, standing up.

"What's the condition?"

"That you'll tell me the real reason you jumped into the river," Cleo says. She hurries to the counter, grabs the brandy and marches back. She sits back down and pours them each a shot of B&B. Madeline sips but Cleo doesn't touch hers. There's a surprising anger in her voice when she asks, "Are you trying to kill yourself?" Madeline sets her glass down and stares at Cleo. "Just tell me if that's what you're doing, or trying to do."

"No," Madeline says, her brows knitted. "No, that's not why I swam the river." After a moment she picks up her glass and rolls it against her cheek. "Is that why you wanted to get to know me, because you think I'm trying to kill myself?"

"It was," Cleo says.

"Why?" Madeline asks, reaching out across the table, her palm upturned, her fingers uncurling. She wiggles her fingers and tells Cleo to take her hand. Cleo does, albeit reluctantly. "Why do you want to know if I was trying to kill myself?" Cleo looks up at Madeline, a thick tear slipping down her cheek. She shakes her head and tries to pull away but Madeline holds her wrist more tightly.

"I was just ... curious," Cleo says, flicking away the tear with her free hand. "I'm a poet, I'm supposed to be obsessed with death." She attempts a light laugh but it comes out more like a sob.

"I don't believe you," Madeline whispers, loosening her

grip. "Do you know how to swim, Cleo?" Cleo shakes her head. "Is that why you're afraid of the water, of boats?"

I'm not afraid of the water, Cleo thinks, just boats. She says so, realizing as she says it how ridiculous it must sound. Admits that she knows she sounds like a fool. She pulls her hand away from Madeline's. "I don't like boats, and I don't like anything risky." It's Cleo's turn to frown and Madeline's turn to want to erase it.

"Ahh," Madeline says, nodding. She refills their glasses. "Thus the avoidance of love and boats—in equal measure. I can't say I blame you there." She holds up her brandy to make yet another toast. "To fear!" She waits for Cleo to pick up her drink. "What was that quote you said the other day in the restaurant, the one about love and water?"

"'Thousands have lived without love, not one without water,'" Cleo recites.

Madeline touches her plastic cup to Cleo's. "Thousands of smart people have lived without love, but not one without brandy." Cleo laughs and dips her tongue into the liquor, and Madeline leans forward. "Cleo?"

"Uh-huh?" Cleo says into her cup. The look on Madeline's face is gravely serious, almost frightening. Cleo's giggle dissolves in her throat.

"Will you please tell me why you're afraid of boats?" Madeline asks. "Don't tell me to change the topic this time. I really do want to know. I feel like I need to know."

Eyes that green in the city of Florence, in New Orleans, anywhere. Cleo draws her knees up under her chin and hugs herself. "Why do you need to know?"

"Because I get the feeling you've never told anyone about it, not really. Maybe it would help to tell someone?"

"I think I'd better be going," Cleo announces.

"How will you get back?" Madeline asks, surprised, as Cleo rises from her chair.

Cleo shrugs. "I'll walk."

"Miss Savoy," Madeline says, fighting a smile, "I'm sure you have many talents, but I'm fairly certain that walking on water isn't among them." She laughs. "I told you, you can't walk over that bridge. There's no footpath for pedestrians. Why don't you stay and read me some of your poetry? I bet that'd be a lot less frightening than a ride on the ferry. And besides, we bought all that food. You can't leave until you help me eat it!" She has Cleo by the hand now. "I'll send you back in a cab after dinner, I promise."

"I'm not reading any poetry," Cleo warns.

"Well, all right, but if you were going to read your poetry, I was going to play you some of my songs. I thought we could have a little salon." She points at the lawn ornaments at the other tables. "There's nothing quite like a captive audience. And these little bastards can clap louder than anybody you ever heard, especially after a few cocktails."

Cleo laughs but as soon as she does, she thinks: Don't make me laugh, I don't want to fall in love with you. *Too late, Miss Cleo, much, much too late.* That particular moment came when Madeline sat organizing her salad vegetables into groups with no concern for what Cleo might think. That was the precise moment in which Cleo understood her immunity to love and desire had disappeared without her permission.

"Ladies and gentlemen, bunnies and elves, Miss White and your addled companions, may I introduce to you Miss Cleopatra Savoy," Madeline shouts from her seat, clapping wildly. The studio is black but for the few candles flickering in glass jars on the tables. Madeline's throat is raspy from singing and talking in between songs. Cleo has thus far been a happy member of the audience but not a participant, and she swallows as she stands up and makes her way toward the piano. Madeline settles in next to Snow White and waits.

"I don't have any poems for you tonight," Cleo begins, wetting her lips. Her knees tremble but her head feels warm and light from the brandy. "Instead I have a story," she continues, trying to work up the spit and courage she needs to keep on. She looks down at Madeline, whose face beams up at her from the "audience," and hesitates. Something in her goes a little cold and distant as she begins her story. Something in her needs to.

April 13, 1971
The Atlantic Ocean

They stood on the deck of the ocean liner, a mother and daughter bundled against the misty damp in matching rough coats of English wool. Twins of a sort, though the mother's coat had a grown-up collar trimmed with fur. Where the Atlantic waves collided with the boat side, a marvellous silver foam exploded. It mesmerized both the mother and wee daughter. The mother smiled and laughed for the first time since boarding the ship, but she gripped her daughter's hand a little too tightly. The little girl loved the way her mother's hair curled in the damp and the chime of her laugh, when it came. It was more and more rare, this bell-like laugh, and so the little girl was grateful that it came just for her. Also floating between them was the sweet swirl of Barclay's Dusting Powder that her mother wore and the sea-salted air, mixing with the biting iron aroma of the ship and its railings. In the daytime you could smell the wooden deck chairs with their blankets, the papery playing cards held stubbornly against the winds, but at night the colder smells won out.

The father of this family sat in the ship's piano lounge, brooding into a gin martini. His wife had barely spoken to him since they climbed out of his parents' family car. She was outwardly cheerful until they were alone in the cabin, where the façade quickly fell to pieces. In wanting what he wanted, he forgot to ask if his dream was hers, and here they were, again. Angry silence. He was banished from their cabin or did he storm out? He couldn't recall which it was, but in any case a separated peace was all that was available. He'd decided to sit in the lounge with its gaudy bowl-candles and dishes of nuts until the lounge, too, shut its doors against him.

A man banished, this father and husband watched as a svelte woman climbed onto a tiny stage next to a piano and its keen-eyed player. She smiled tenderly at her accompanist and began to sing. Her not-so-wonderful voice was countered by the entrancing swing of her hips, bright red curves blooming against the white piano. The man ordered another martini and continued to sulk. He hoped that his wife's black mood would lift once they docked in her old home town of Montreal. Who wouldn't want to go home again? It struck him as odd, her melancholia and stubborn home-loathing. He hadn't noticed these tendencies when he asked her to marry him. Where had the bright white side of her gone? She cursed him for this voyage, he knew. He also knew he couldn't win whatever battle she was silently waging.

No, he thought, I will sit right here and wait out the storm of her ungrateful temper. The singer wagged her fingers at the audience and began another song, this one torchy and delivered in surprisingly husky tones. Magnificent, he thought, watching the chanteuse with devout attention. Women weren't always as complicated and stubborn as his wife.

The moon was high and white over the water. The little girl pressed her lips to the ship's rail in a long and childish kiss. She wasn't scolded about germs and filth, and so continued to balance her entire weight on the muscle of her small mouth. Her mother watched her and saw her own romantic nature flickering in the small, elfin extension of herself. The little girl would probably stand as such for hours if uninterrupted. Oh, thought the mother, but interruptions will become more and more prevalent till she's swayed away from her dreams like all the rest of the human race. The mother's heart reeled back at the dark thought; she was so full of fears lately. . . . She tried to look at her daughter and see a gift, but there was no escaping what the child was: a constant reminder of things lost, a sweet but painful symbol of everything she had been talked out of. A human souvenir with no idea of what had passed and what was coming.

The mother heard the wide white smile of the moon say, *She'll be fine. She's more like her father.*

The little girl thought her mum was trying to make her laugh when her mum climbed up onto the railing and waved her arms at the moon. She swung both legs up over the balustrade and sat there, hanging on with one hand. The little girl watched and giggled nervously; her mum blew kisses at the moon and shouted nonsense Italian at the sea birds that darted by. The child worried a little—the rail was slippery with rain and sea spray. She was startled when her mother leapt away, falling with a dreamlike slowness to the foam below. But her mother didn't scream, and so the little girl was sure it was a trick, a good thing, like pence pulled from behind earlobes. Magic? The little girl waited and watched the waves, the mesmerizing silver. Pushed her tiny head through the railing to see better, not sure how long she should stay. She eventually decided to return to the cabin, where she knew her mum would be waiting with hot cocoa and a grin. They'd sip the warm chocolate, and her mum would tell her how she'd done the trick. The girl took tiny steps the whole way back along the deck to give her mum lots of time.

At 2:00 a.m. the father stumbled into the cabin to find his daughter seated on the trundle bed, wide awake and dressed in her red woollen coat and matching cap, her tiny mittens cast aside on the floor. The cabin lights were ablaze, his wife nowhere in sight. He loosened his tie with an angry yank and asked the whereabouts of the little girl's mother.

"She's in the sea," the little girl reported. She was no longer wholly convinced that her mum had played a joke on them. Her belly felt queer and tight.

"Cleo, I'm too tired for this!" snapped the father, pausing to measure his words more carefully as he repeated the question. "Where—is—Mum?"

The little girl studied her small hands in silence till her father swooped down upon her and shook her so violently that the trundle bed rattled. His breath smelled like sour cough medicine and tobacco, and she grimaced as he shouted into her face. He repeated his question and repeated it again, angry with his daughter, who didn't understand what she had done wrong. Her mum's joke was no longer funny but terrifying.

Once more she said, or rather whimpered, "She's in the sea!"

After telling her that if she dared to move from the trundle bed, her bottom would be tanned, the father ran from the cabin, leaving the door wide open. The little girl knew that something very bad was happening. Adults liked doors to be shut, and they shouted when things were scary. She lay down on the bed in her winter coat and fell asleep.

When she woke her father was sitting on the end of the bed with Cleo's coat in his lap. Seeing that she was awake, he squeezed her foot and frowned at her, his eyes red like a monster's, but sad, too.

"Is Mum still in the sea?" she asked, afraid to lift her head from the pillow.

"Sorry I shouted at you, luv," he said. He patted her foot and buried his face in the little red coat and sobbed, deep terrible sounds that frightened her. She didn't cry, though. Tears made her daddy mad. Other people's tears anyway, and so she watched her father as he shook and made queer animal noises. He didn't answer her question, just moved to the bigger bed and threw himself across it. She was confused as to the whyabouts of the whereabouts of her mum.

A bit of sunlight streamed in through the round window,

and the little girl knew it was daytime. The door was closed again and she struggled to open it without making any noise. Her dad had forgotten to lock it, a bit of luck, and she slipped out into the brightly lit corridor. With the same tiny steps as before, she crept down the soft blue carpet toward the door that led up to the deck. It was terribly cold by the railing, and a man standing with binoculars looked at her strangely, for she wore no coat and was awfully young to be wandering the deck alone. She peeked through the rails, looked down at the waves and the foam, and hoped to see her mum laughing and waving from the water. Mermaids did it, she reasoned, and her mum was as pretty as a mermaid. But she wasn't down there. Maybe she was hiding somewhere else?

Not a very nice joke, Mum, she thought, still hopeful, and the man with the binoculars came along and tapped her gently on the shoulder. He said she would catch her death of cold out here and asked her where her parents were. When she reported very matter-of-factly that her father was asleep and that her mum was in the sea, the man realized whose child she was. The breakfast room had buzzed with news of the horrible tale, and the man had been wakened in the early morning by a fierce knock on his door. A search of each and every cabin had been futile.

"Poor muffin," he said, scooping her up and carrying her back to her cabin. He handed her over to her very groggy father, who'd clearly fallen asleep, no doubt exhausted by his grief and shock. Her dad nodded at the man and then swiftly closed the door.

"Just like your mum, running off when it suits you!" he shouted at the little girl, who cowered by the door, wishing the man with the binoculars would come back.

A nanny was hired to keep an eye on the child till the ship docked in Montreal harbour. Her dad spent most of the voyage away from the cabin, grieving in the ship's piano lounge. She didn't remember the police, or the ship's captain giving her ice cream and asking her to explain about her mum being "in the sea." She saw their faces turn pale but didn't hear what they said after that. She wouldn't remember any of this until twenty-four years after the fact. In truth, she has always remembered this event in that part of the memory where the other broken-glass bits of life get stored. The nanny's explanation that her mother had gone to visit Jesus and the angels made no sense. The only angels this little girl had ever heard of lived in Italy, and she knew that the ship wasn't going there. They were going to a place called Canada. She'd hoped her mum would meet them there. No tears ever came. Nothing came but the feeling that she was waiting to grow up. And she did, although some part of her would never stop being four years old and bewildered.

"That's why I wanted to know ... why you did it and why you made me watch."

Madeline sits frozen, one hand clamped over her mouth. Cleo sways in place, seemingly unaware of her surroundings. She doesn't feel Madeline coming up behind, or Madeline's arms looping around her, drawing her toward the bed, easing her down on it. Nor does she feel Madeline's fingers unlacing her boots and pulling them off. Dimly, from somewhere far away, she hears someone whispering her name, feels the light touch of a sheet being drawn over her and tucked around her shoulders, the smooth cool of a pillow against her cheek when she turns to face a row of windows. She closes her eyes and feels the heat of a body easing itself up against her back, enveloping her. Feels lips brush against the back of her neck and something like hot raindrops spilling down on her skin. And Cleo sleeps: held, kissed and emptied at last of the one story she has been avoiding for a long, long time, the one she desperately wishes she had made up.

The trigger had been a splash of river water, though she'd managed to build another dam with unconscious speed. She'd added another level of bricks and another as the days passed, convinced the truth could never threaten to rush in again. Now it has rushed in, and it keeps on rushing through cracks made by vetiver and perfect fingers, the false foundation razed by the musical sound of easy laughter and the most penetrating gaze she has ever had the fearful pleasure of knowing. It's too much. She sleeps without dreaming of sinking ships for the first time in too many years.

Madeline lies awake. Distressed to discover that her heart hasn't been removed after all, she feels it hammering with a fervour that is simultaneously familiar and foreign.

"Not now," she says out loud, watching Cleo sleep. "I'm not good enough for this."

THANKSGIVING DAY IS ONE of the great all-American holidays. While highways all over the country fill with cars en route to familial tables, many bars in the French Quarter pull out all the stops, offering complimentary turkey dinners and easy companionship for those with nowhere else to go. Regulars and visitors alike come out in droves to gorge on deep-fried turkey and hot cornbread, potatoes, Creole corn-and-bread pudding, among other things. The festive aura in such benevolent barrooms helps to ease any loneliness their patrons might be feeling. While the shops close and the city takes on an even sleepier aspect than usual, the bars remain wide open. Today there is an almost springlike smell in the air as the sun peeps out and dazzles the sleepy buildings. By noon the bars will be full of hungry people looking forward to the good food laid out buffet-style on long tables. The All Saints is holding a barbecue, Charlie's is serving up more traditional fare, while over at Hank's the menu remains pretty much unchanged, for those who wish to pretend the holiday isn't really happening: stale popcorn and draft beer, all you can hold for six bucks.

Johnny has the day off and so takes his time waking up. Knowing that he could sleep in today, he went a little overboard at the All Saints last night. (Madeline would say: "When *don't* you go overboard, Giovanni?") At some earlier point during the night, he'd found himself in a grotty little boîte in the Ninth Ward. But like a homing pigeon Johnny had eventually returned to the All Saints, more out of habit than desire. In the Ninth Ward he hadn't known a soul, and had been able to drink in relative peace. The dramas that had unfolded around him at Fat Daddy's had nothing to do with him. When the resident bully did try to engage him in a discussion of the sad opera of his personal affairs, Johnny had simply bought the man a shot and excused himself. Tall and yet not very bulky, Johnny knows when to remove himself from unfamiliar territory.

The same sage instinct didn't seem to save him on his home turf. After a mostly peaceful hour in the All Saints Tavern Johnny hadn't been able to ignore the jibes and pointed questions aimed at him. What began as good-natured ribbing about Madeline's recent antics in the Mississippi eventually turned sour. One of Johnny's fellow patrons, addressing the entire congregation in the bar, suggested that they all watch the news to see what Madeline was up to these days. "Hey, Johnny," the buffoon had shouted, "maybe you oughta watch, too, seeing as it's the only chance you're going to have to see your wife naked from now on!" Johnny had hunched over a double shot of Jack Daniel's and done his best to ignore this, but when someone else added, "Yeah, and I hear she's turned queer!" and someone else shrieked, "Hey, Johnny V., what's it like to be married to a lezzzbian?" he'd snapped. With one swift, almost balletic movement, Johnny picked up a beer bottle, smashed it against the bar and held its jagged neck to the throat of his nearest tormentor. Being a pacifist at heart, Johnny didn't actually cut the man, but the gesture did silence the teasing. It also served to get Johnny eighty-sixed from the All Saints for what the bartender promised would be an "eternity."

And so this afternoon Johnny will not be partaking of the burnt offerings at the All Saints Thanksgiving barbecue. Which is fine, because he feels no great love for the place anyway, especially when he foggily reviews the events of last night. When Lena hears why Johnny has been banned, she'll feel guilty and sad. But because Johnny suspects that Lena started the rumour about Madeline and her new and mysterious female friend, he doesn't much care.

Johnny stretches his long frame and rolls onto his side, contemplating a little self-love to get the day off to a happier start. Contrary to what Madeline likes to believe, Johnny isn't undersexed, just easily distracted. And maybe if Madeline wasn't so determined to humiliate him on a regular basis—he's thinking of that incident at Shoney's.... He stops stroking himself and groans in despair. His erection wilts and he rolls onto his back, trying to gather evidence in his mind, proof that Madeline is still the straightest woman he has ever known. He thinks of the days of their early courtship, of the whirlwind nature of it and the ferocious, seemingly twenty-four-hour appetite she once had for sex. He thinks too of her mad determination to get married. What was that about? He reaches for his cigarettes on the night table, and in doing so sees his wedding ring gleaming yellow on his left hand. Is reminded of their wedding day. Coinciding with her twentieth birthday, it had been a happy day, or so Johnny had thought. But now that he remembers, it wasn't 100 per cent festive.

November 4, 1976
New Orleans, Louisiana

After a brief ceremony at City Hall, Madeline and Johnny had stopped for celebratory drinks at the Blacksmith on Bourbon, where several of Johnny's friends were waiting to meet Madeline for the first time. Madeline looked beautiful in a black silk dress, pearls and stockings, with her hair swept into a chignon. She'd dazzled Johnny's friends with her wit and undeniable good looks and seemed very much at ease surrounded by men. Her eyes glittered with each introduction; her sly and winning smile made more than one of Johnny's friends deeply envious of his luck.

As a relatively new arrival in the city, Madeline hadn't made many friends of her own. She had a part-time job at

Aunt Sally's in those days, and it wasn't until she met her pal Rodney that she showed any interest in socializing outside of Johnny's small circle of friends. At the time of their wedding Johnny was pretty much the centre of her universe, and she said she liked it that very few of his friends had wives or girlfriends.

After a few hours of cocktails and congratulations, Johnny and Madeline retreated to their then-new apartment at Decatur and Esplanade. Johnny opened a bottle of champagne, and Madeline carried their wedding cake from the refrigerator to the bed. Both had decided to tell their families about their marriage after the fact—Johnny because he didn't want to spend the money on the kind of wedding his large family would expect, and Madeline because she was no longer speaking to her mother for what she called "very good reasons resulting from very bad events." Of her father she said nothing, and for a time Johnny had assumed Mr. Shockfire was dead, since Madeline never mentioned him. It turned out he wasn't dead but missing in action after a rather messy divorce. Johnny had had to pry that morsel of information out of Madeline, who shrugged it off but was clearly grief-stricken in her quiet way.

After removing her clothes and hopping into bed with a flute of champagne, Madeline suddenly announced her wish to call her mother. Although this surprised Johnny somewhat, he handed her the telephone and began to strip down. He lay beside her, slurping champagne, and listened as she greeted her mother in a strained but pleasant tone. There was a long pause after Madeline informed her that she was a married woman. Johnny could hear the frenetic buzz of Madeline's mother's voice but couldn't make out what was being said. Madeline's expression darkened as she listened, and she held out her glass for a refill; Johnny quickly obliged her. Madeline gave her mother her address and telephone number. She then warned her against ever calling, which Johnny found odd. After a final "I'm sure you will," Madeline slammed down the phone and sipped her champagne, staring off into the distance.

Johnny reached out and stroked Madeline's bare stomach, hoping to remind her of the happiness of the occasion. When she glanced at him, he saw in her eyes a kind of smouldering anger that startled him, but then her expression changed and she gave him a sad smile instead.

"What is it, baby?" he cooed, snuggling up to her. "What's the matter?"

"Nothing," she muttered, draining her glass of champagne. "I was just thinking about a dead friend."

"On our wedding day?" Johnny cried, halting the attention he'd been paying to her nipples. He took her glass from her. "C'mere and tell Johnny all about it."

But Madeline did not want to tell Johnny anything about it, at least not in words. With a certain ferocity she straddled him and began rocking against him with her eyes closed and her head thrown forward. He interpreted the tears that slid down her cheeks as tears of joyful passion and abandoned himself to their first official romp as a married couple.

"Happy birthday, sugar," he panted as she collapsed against his chest. To his surprise, Madeline fell asleep first, thus setting a precedent for how it would always and forever after be.

She only mentioned the dead friend once more, after she'd been out drinking with her new friend Rodney, whom she met within a month of their wedding. Quite out of the blue, and as she tumbled drunkenly into bed beside Johnny, she informed him that the friend she'd mentioned wasn't really dead. "Dead to me," she slurred. When Johnny had tried to get her to talk about it, Madeline had become hysterical and shouted, "Never mention her again!" as if he'd been the one to bring it up. It was to be the beginning of Madeline's resolute practice of withholding information about her past. As long as Johnny refrained from asking questions, Madeline seemed happy.

Now these two things—Madeline's wedding-night conversation with her mother and her sudden reference to the "dead" friend—are troubling to Johnny these many years later. Until now, he hasn't given it much thought. "Never mention her again!" she'd screamed. Her. Is it true, what people have been saying? How could it be true when for years, many years, Madeline has willingly made love to Johnny? Nobody—not even Madeline—could fake love for nineteen years. Of this, he is certain.

This Thanksgiving Day Johnny doesn't feel like giving thanks to anyone. He's feeling pretty uncharitable toward most people, especially Cleo Savoy, whose claim that she wanted to interview his wife now rings as false as Madeline's early enthusiasm for marriage. It's much easier to blame Cleo for their problems than it is to blame Madeline or himself.

"She'll be back," he says to himself as he makes a cup of coffee. As soon as Cleo Savoy leaves town. And she did say she had to leave within a few days, unless of course that too was a lie.... Well, anyway, she'll have to leave at some point. It would be wonderful if Johnny could figure out some way to flush Madeline out of her love nest over on Algiers, but how? Start a fire? Johnny curses himself for having given Madeline a place to run to, and for having led Cleo Savoy right to her door. But surely the fun of her feminist retreat will wear thin sooner or later.

The phone rings and Johnny looks at it with narrowed eyes. What now? he wonders, listening to its insistent trill. Irritated, he grabs at the phone, if only to put an end to the noise.

"Yeah?" Johnny grunts, a cigarette clamped between his teeth, his Zippo raised to light it. The pleasant aroma of lighter fluid swirls up as he puffs.

"This is Booth Shockfire," says the male voice on the other end of the line, after a lengthy pause. "With whom am I speaking, please?"

Johnny's mouth hangs open and he's speechless. The lit cigarette tumbles into his lap, and he cries out, "Shit!" and flicks the burning ember off his bare leg. "Pardon me," he apologizes into the phone. "This is Johnny Valentucci, sir. Madeline's husband."

"Johnny, I wonder if you'd agree to join me for dinner this coming Saturday? I'll be in New Orleans as of late tomorrow evening. I do apologize for the short notice, but I spoke with Madeline's mother late last night. She seems to think I ought to pay a visit to Madeline as soon as possible. I gather that Madeline's not living with you at this time?" Johnny admits that this is so. "Well, I wonder if you and I might have a meal together? Would that be amenable to you?" Johnny scans Mr. Shockfire's weary voice for signs of . . . what? He doesn't know. All he hears is a formal, cautious politeness. No wonder he left Madeline's mother,

Johnny thinks as he sits in stunned silence. After a moment Mr. Shockfire says, "Are you there?"

"Saturday night would be fine," Johnny says, adding, "only Madeline isn't easy to reach just now. Should I try to see if she can come to dinner, too?"

"I'll see about a visit with Madeline after you and I have had a chance to talk. Dianne"—he says the name with subtle contempt—"tells me you two are having some marital difficulties. I'd like to talk to you about that, and some other things as well."

"Sure," Johnny wheezes, suddenly and irrationally picturing a large man carrying a shotgun. It's as if he's fourteen again and Susie Whatsername's daddy is heading down the basement stairs in Baton Rouge....

"How about the dining room at my hotel?" Booth suggests. "I'll be at the Royal Sonesta. I'll call you when I get into town."

"OK." Johnny nods but the dial tone buzzes in reply. Jesus, he thinks, rubbing his jaw, I've seen more of her parents than I've seen of her this past month.

His stomach growls and he decides to meander across the road to Charlie's for some much-needed holiday fare. Might as well do some laundry while I'm over there, he thinks sullenly, gathering up his dirty clothes and a few of Madeline's things, too. Although it isn't quite what he had in mind in terms of a Thanksgiving celebration, it will have to do. He feels sure that his upcoming meeting with Madeline's father will have a positive effect on things, and so he vows to get his—their—house in order in preparation. Better clean up *first,* he thinks, aware of the sedative effects of deep-fried turkey.

MADELINE SLIPS NOISELESSLY into the studio with a Styrofoam cup of coffee for Cleo and a root beer for herself. Cleo dozes on, her fists pulled tightly to her chest. Madeline slips off her shoes and watches the rise and fall of Cleo's body. She feels a little wave of guilt for having insisted that Cleo tell her about her fear of boats. Let her sleep, she thinks with tenderness. She sits down carefully on the bed and sets the coffee on the floor. Cleo's breath comes in steady puffs from her parted lips, and she doesn't stir, even when Madeline stretches out beside her.

Propped up against a pillow, Madeline stares at her left hand for several minutes, noting the absent ring, thinking about Carmelle. Why didn't I ever tell Johnny about all that? she wonders. It might've helped make it seem smaller. She takes a sip from her bottle of root beer and glances at Cleo to make sure she's still asleep; waits and listens to Cleo's lungs drawing and expelling breath in a peaceful rhythm; gazes down at her closed lids, fluttering with what Madeline imagines is a wonderful dream. "I wasn't trying to kill myself when I jumped into the river all those times," she whispers. "Maybe I thought I was. But no, after what you've told me, I know for sure that it wasn't death I was wishing for."

Sighing, she turns her back to Cleo. "Are you awake?" she whispers. Cleo says nothing.

June, 1976
St. Louis, Missouri

There was a whole month that went by without a single opportunity to play the piano, a row of weeks wherein

Dianne decided that she preferred time with her daughter. In fact, she seemed downright reluctant to leave the house for any reason, as if sensing the unspoken alliance between Carmelle and Madeline. She began to give Carmelle nights off, practically insisting that she go out. On one occasion she actually said, "Madeline has asked me if we could spend an evening together, just the two of us. You understand, I'm sure." Carmelle would slip away from the house, stay out late and, upon returning, find herself confronted by Madeline, who had been told by Dianne that it was Carmelle who felt she needed a life outside the Shockfire household. Let the games begin.

The worst of these evenings came when Dianne announced that she'd arranged a blind date for Carmelle. "I know a lovely young man," she'd said, "one of your people. Very polite, very well dressed. He works for a friend of a friend. I told him all about you, about how lonely you must be living with a divorcee and her daughter. He said he'd be delighted to take you dancing, so I told him to pick you up here, tonight, at seven." When Carmelle began to protest the arrangement, Dianne shook her head. "I was a young woman once, too. I know how it is. You're lonely! Of course you are. I don't expect you to be here forever, for goodness' sake. I know you'll decide to run away and get married one day soon, and what can Madeline and I do but wish you well? Hurry up and dress! You'll see that I have very good taste in men."

Hearing about this blind date, Madeline was furious. She interrogated Carmelle while she got ready, demanding to know why Carmelle didn't refuse to go. "I can't not go," Carmelle said. "Anyway, it's one date, Madeline. You know

I'm going to be thinking about you the whole time!" She gave Madeline a quick kiss and went back to applying her lipstick. Madeline stood watching Carmelle and watched again from an upstairs window when the young man arrived to collect her. She'd declined the opportunity to go downstairs and meet the infamous Willem. Her mother chose to see Madeline's refusal as one provoked by envy, not jealousy. It was obvious Madeline felt sorry for herself because she hadn't yet had any dates.

"Come down and watch television with me!" Dianne called from the bottom of the stairs. Madeline went, stomping and fuming. She sat next to her mother on the sofa in the living room but refused to speak. Instead she glared at the piano, wishing she could play it.

Dianne sighed, giving Madeline's leg a squeeze. "I can hardly believe you're a young woman already. It seems we have so little time left together, doesn't it, sugar? Honestly, I don't know where all those years went so fast!"

"They went into pools," Madeline said, struggling to maintain control of her voice. "They went into grapefruit diets and pools and getting up when it was still dark. Don't you remember, Mother? That's where all the time went."

Dianne gasped. "I know that, Madeline. I was there. Why are you so hostile? Don't you think I know how hard you've worked? I've been right here all this time!" She folded her arms across her chest and looked wounded. "Don't take your bad mood out on me, young lady. I will not have you snarling at me, do you hear me?"

"Yes, Mother," Madeline murmured robotically. "I think I'd better go to bed. I have practice first thing in the morning. Please excuse me." She stood up but didn't move away. Her eyes were on the piano she hadn't been able to play for a month. And now Carmelle was out on a date. She might go out on another date, and another, till she'd fallen in love with someone else, someone who wouldn't jeopardize her employment. Dianne watched Madeline with narrowed eyes.

"Go to bed, Madeline. You're very disciplined about your swimming, and that's wonderful, honey. I'm sure that will stand you in good stead no matter what you end up doing in life. I think the training's been good for you in that regard, don't you?"

"Yes, Mother," Madeline said, a trace of sarcasm leaking into her voice. She walked over to the Steinway, lifted the lid and tapped out "Mary Had a Little Lamb" on the keys with one finger.

"Where'd you learn to play that?" Dianne exclaimed.

"Ask Carmelle," Madeline replied, drifting out of the living room and up the stairs. If only she had known how dangerous those words would become. *Ask Carmelle.*

Cleo's eyes are still closed but her ears have been wide awake for quite some time. The whole time. She pretends to stir from a deep slumber and turns her head, blinking.

"How long have you been awake?" Madeline asks.

Cleo wants to lie but can't. "Awhile," she admits. She reaches up and caresses Madeline's cheek with her thumb. Madeline grabs her wrist and gently but firmly pushes her hand away. "I'm sorry," Cleo whispers, her face flushed with embarrassment. "I didn't mean to—"

"It's fine," Madeline assures her. "Let's go for a walk. I think we both need some air. I brought you a coffee, but it's probably cold by now. We'll get you another one."

Cleo sits up, her face turned away from Madeline. "I should go."

"But we haven't had our interview yet!"

"There's no interview," Cleo reminds her. "There's just me being a jackass and you being polite."

Madeline reaches out and turns Cleo's face toward hers. "I wasn't being polite. I was being a coward," she says, leaning in to kiss Cleo. Each time Madeline's tongue grazes Cleo's, Cleo feels as if she is falling from a cliff inside herself. Waves of fear wash in and out of Madeline but she chases them off. *I don't care, I just cannot keep worrying about what happens—or keep missing what doesn't.*

July, 1976
St. Louis, Missouri

Things were back to normal in the sense that Dianne went out and stayed out late, five nights out of seven. Sometimes she was with Mr. Oliver, other times she was out with "friends." Carmelle was worried. "I'm a lousy liar," she kept saying to Madeline. "You have to just tell her you don't care for swimming any more, that you've quit the team. She knows you're not going to the Olympics anyway. Why keep lying?" Madeline didn't know why she couldn't bring herself to tell her mother that she'd quit. Though the qualifying trials had come and gone without Madeline's participation, and though the actual Olympics were about to commence in Montreal, she still felt compelled to keep up the charade. What she didn't know was that her mother already knew she'd quit. Coach Livingstone had confirmed it. Whenever Madeline announced that she was off to the pool, her mother just smiled and said nothing, which in itself should have been cause for concern.

Most storms are preceded by a period of calm. And so it was with this one. During this seemingly tranquil spell, Carmelle did whatever she could to avoid being alone in a room with Mrs. Shockfire, who had taken to asking strange questions and making strange comments whenever Madeline wasn't around.

One afternoon Dianne stood in the living room and ran a finger along the Steinway. "You sure like to keep this piano polished, don't you, Carmelle? Pretty fond of music, I gather?"

Carmelle hadn't known what to say in reply beyond "Yes, ma'am."

"Madeline seems to be quite fond of music, too," Dianne had continued. "I didn't know she had an artistic side. But then, there's quite a bit I don't seem to know about my own daughter these days."

That same evening Dianne stood in the kitchen with a half-consumed bottle of B&B in her hands and murmured, "I seem to be drinking more than usual. That's strange. I suppose something's bothering me that I can't quite put my finger on. Does that ever happen to you, Carmelle—where you feel troubled but you don't know why?"

"Sometimes, I guess."

"It's just the worst feeling in the world, isn't it?" Dianne had asked in a conspiratorial voice.

"Yes, ma'am."

Without warning, Carmelle announced that things between them had to settle down. "Just for now," she promised when

Madeline began to cry. "I think she suspects something." Dianne's singsong voice came trilling up the stairs and Carmelle froze.

"Be good, ladies!" she called, slamming the front door on her way out.

"She's gone," Madeline hissed. "She'll be gone for hours! What's the matter with you all of a sudden?" When she tried to kiss her, Carmelle pushed Madeline away.

"Nothing," Carmelle insisted. "I'm going out, too."

"What?" Madeline cried. "Where to?"

Carmelle was cold. "Out, that's all. I'm going to see some friends. You oughta get some of those for yourself. Go on."

Madeline was stunned by this remark; it sounded a lot like something her mother would say. She stood staring wordlessly at the person whose sudden *froideur* was bewildering in light of her recent passion.

"I said GO ON!" Carmelle shouted. "I don't want to lose my damned job, do you hear me?" Seeing Madeline's face crumple, she softened a little. "Please, Madeline! If I lose my job we'll never get to be together. Come on." She put her arm around Madeline and led her down the hall to her room. "Trust me, we just have to cool it a little, only for a bit. I love you. That's why I'm so worried. Please, trust me now."

Left alone in the big old house on many subsequent nights, Madeline consoled herself by perfecting certain songs on the piano. Carmelle went out all the time now, as did her mother. Sometimes they even went out together. On those nights Madeline sneaked a glass of brandy, sometimes a glass of gin. If playing the piano seemed too depressing, she simply listened to records that reminded her of Carmelle. Have faith, she told herself. Those nights were the worst. It was as if her mother was determined to play Cupid and find Carmelle a man.

But was that it? She thought back to the recent weeks and felt a rush of nausea. Carmelle had pushed Madeline away and now spent a lot more time with her mother—willingly. No, she told herself, that's not it. She laughed out loud at the thought of her mother and Carmelle together, then felt sick all over again.

Three agonizing weeks had passed since Carmelle told her they had to be careful. Madeline waited up late, sitting at the piano in the dark with a large glass of liquor in hand. When she heard the front door opening she took a quick, deep gulp of the brandy, half expecting to hear her mother's voice along with Carmelle's. She'd planned to confront them somehow, or at least hear what they said when they thought she wasn't around. But no one spoke. The footfalls belonged to one person. Madeline listened and smiled as the footsteps approached the living room where she sat in the pitch blackness. She could tell by the erratic clatter of shoes that Carmelle was drunk.

"Yoo-hooo!" Carmelle called into the dark parlour. "Any prowlers in there?"

"Yoo-hooo, yourself." Madeline hit a sulky note on the piano. It hung in the air, sounding as lonely as she felt. Soon Carmelle was leaning against her. "You're drunk," Madeline said, pretending disgust.

Carmelle sat down beside her and threw her arms around Madeline's neck. "I miss you!" When her lips found Madeline's she moaned ever so slightly, and Madeline couldn't resist. All the hurt and anger she'd been storing up in the past few weeks melted as soon as Carmelle's mouth opened to hers.

"What happened to 'We have to be careful'?" Madeline grumbled as Carmelle tugged at the buttons on Madeline's blouse. Carmelle didn't answer and Madeline didn't really care, though she was aware that if her mother came home early....

"Take your top off," Carmelle insisted, tossing her own shirt to the floor. Madeline, surprised, laughed loudly. Carmelle said, "SHH! Be quiet!" then broke out laughing herself. Waiting for Madeline to disrobe, she clucked her tongue impatiently and tugged roughly at the front of Madeline's blouse. The buttons clattered to the floor.

"Let's play," Carmelle said, striking a chord on the piano. She waited for Madeline to join her on the keys.

"What if she—"

"There you go again," Carmelle complained, "being a damned chicken!" She grabbed Madeline's hand and pushed it down onto the keys. An unmusical sound resulted. "All right now! I wanna hear 'If I Didn't Care.' Slow and sweet and right away." Madeline began to play as Carmelle nuzzled her neck and sang sweetly into her ear, bit at Madeline's ear-lobes and giggled. "Ohhh, I missed you." Carmelle swung her legs over Madeline's lap.

The parlour wasn't dark any more. Madeline turned to see her mother standing in the doorway. Observing her daughter and Carmelle sitting in their brassieres at the piano, Dianne shook her head. "How interesting," she said, moving into the room. Carmelle unhooked her legs and stared at the carpet; Madeline sat frozen in place on the bench. When she did turn to look at her mother, the lump of fear in her throat made it hard to breathe normally. "Having fun?" Dianne asked with menacing sweetness. She kicked at their discarded blouses with the pointy toe of her shoe. She fixed her eyes on Madeline but spoke to Carmelle. "Please get your things together—Madeline and I will drive you to the bus station. I'm sure there's a bus to Memphis in the next few hours."

"What?" Madeline recovered her voice at last. "Mother, please! We were just being silly—"

"I know what you were being." Dianne kept her eyes on Carmelle. "Please pack quickly. As we've discussed, I don't think Madeline and I will be requiring any further assistance from you. I'd thought perhaps you might stay around for the summer, but now I don't think that'll be necessary. Or possible."

With her head held as high as she could manage, Carmelle retreated from the room without a word. When Madeline tried to go after her, Dianne blocked her way. "How dare you!" Madeline screamed. "Get out of my way!"

"Sit down, Madeline!" Dianne commanded, giving her a push with the heel of her hand. Madeline could hear Carmelle opening and closing drawers one floor above her head and wanted very badly to stop her. Instead she pulled on her buttonless blouse, sobbing as she held it closed. Through bleary eyes she glared past her mother, whose reassuring tone only enraged Madeline further. "I'm sure this all seems very unfair to you right now, honey, but trust me, that young woman isn't worth your tears. She's nothing but a lying, conniving, two-faced creature who has deceived us both."

"Describing yourself again, Mother?" The slap stunned Madeline. When she looked up she spat at her mother and tried to rise up from the piano bench. Dianne's eyes were blazing; she slapped Madeline a second time, harder.

Kneeling down, Dianne tried to take Madeline's face in her hands, but Madeline shook her off. Carmelle now stood in the doorway, a suitcase in her hands. Dianne straightened up and her voice quavered, "I've changed my mind. I think I'll take you right to Memphis myself." To Madeline she said, "We'll talk about all of this later, honey."

"Don't you 'honey' me, you bitch!" Madeline shrieked. "Don't you tell me what to do ever again!" She rushed toward Carmelle. "Come on, let's go!" Carmelle shook her head and wrapped her arms around herself. Madeline tugged at Carmelle's arm and pleaded, "Come on! Let's get out of here." She turned to her mother. "You can take us both to the bus station. I am not living here for another minute!"

"I'd like to go back to Memphis," Carmelle said, refusing to meet Madeline's gaze. She looked at the floor, her eyes brimming with shamed tears. "You stay here."

"NO!" Madeline cried. "Carmelle, please! I'm going to get my things—hold on one minute, all right? Just wait here!" She turned and glared at her mother. "I hate you, do you hear me? I HATE YOU."

Dianne shook her head and measured her words. "Now, Madeline. There's no need to blow this out of proportion. My decision to let Carmelle go has nothing to do with this silly little incident. Now please, calm down. You and I will talk about this later, when I get back. Get some sleep—you're drunk." Her mother's smile was forced but unyielding.

Madeline's face still stung where her mother had slapped her. She watched them go, her mother behind the wheel. Swore as she saw her mother touch Carmelle's shoulder and say something that made Carmelle *laugh*. They drove off like two people going on vacation. I hope you get into an accident, Madeline thought nastily, then burst into fresh tears. She ran upstairs to her mother's room and grabbed a small suitcase. Into it she threw a few dresses and several hundred dollars she knew her mother kept tucked into various pairs of shoes at the back of her closet. There she found a bottle of her father's cologne, left behind and yet never discarded, for some reason. Rocabar. She breathed in its scent and decided to take it with her, although she did not yet know where it was she planned to go. Waiting for the taxi to show up, she contemplated following Carmelle to Memphis, then remembered how willingly Carmelle had abandoned their plan to run away to New Orleans, the strangely convivial exchange in the car, their recent nights out. All of these things swirled inside Madeline like poison. And so, as she stood before the ticket seller at the bus station, she heard herself muttering a destination that was nowhere near Memphis. *I'll go without you, Carmelle. I will never, ever, think of either of you again.*

BOOTH SHOCKFIRE looks nothing like Johnny imagined. When Johnny tells the maître d' who he's looking for, the man escorts him to a table at the very back of the Sonesta dining room. The older gentleman who rises to greet Johnny is tall and tanned, with deep creases around his eyes and mouth. His hair is as white as his shirt, his suit a soft, expensive blue. Booth's handshake is firm, the grip of a man accustomed to making deals. Johnny sits down across from him, and Booth smiles with the same shy reluctance Johnny has seen in Madeline in awkward situations.

"It's good to meet you," Johnny says. He can't help feeling guilty. He knows that Madeline has been wondering for a long, long time where this man has been, and why he hasn't ever tried to contact her, even if she's never said so. Johnny wonders, too, observing Booth's elegant manners and soft-spoken confidence. But there's something bizarre about this whole thing—that it's Johnny sitting across from Madeline's father now, after all these years, instead of Madeline herself.

"So," Booth says, "what's all this about my daughter throwing herself into the Mississippi River?" He cuts to the chase, making no attempt to dance around the subject that concerns him most. Johnny admires this.

"Well," Johnny begins, "it could be about a lot of things. I won't pretend to know what they all are." Very carefully, and as politely as he can, Johnny explains that since he's known Madeline, she's been restless in the extreme, as if troubled by something. Booth listens, waving away the wine steward, then requesting double Scotches from a passing busboy. Johnny finishes his hypothesis with the suggestion that it's Madeline's relationship—or lack of one—with either of her parents that causes her to behave in what some would call an unusual fashion. "I think she must be a lot like her mother," Johnny says, "which is why she's been able to hold a grudge against her for so long. I don't even know what the grudge is really about, to be perfectly honest with you. I just know she seems to hate the woman who gave birth to her."

Booth shakes his head. Johnny raises an eyebrow in wonder. What does that head shaking mean? Booth doesn't say. He sighs and asks if Johnny knows why he and Dianne parted company. Johnny replies that he doesn't, that

Madeline has never mentioned any particular reason for her parents' divorce, only that it was messy.

"Messy it was," Booth agrees. "And a damned good thing it ended, too. I took my marriage very seriously, John. My wife, on the other hand, did not. But the saddest thing of all is what it did to Madeline. She was an unusual little girl, extremely sensitive. Pretty little thing, I'm sure you can imagine. I bet she's a beautiful woman, too...." Johnny nods. "Anyway, I'm guilty of something terrible here, and I want you to know that I know that. All I'll say for now is that if Madeline's able to hold a grudge with what must seem to you to be an extraordinary amount of stubbornness, it isn't her mother she takes after, but me. I know what it is to hate Dianne. I also know what it is to be proud beyond good sense." Booth studies his fingernails and frowns. Johnny can again see traces of Madeline in her father's expression, in his mannerisms.

"I'm sure she'd love to see you anyway," Johnny says.

"Well, I don't know about that, but I know I'd love to see her. It's not as if I didn't think about her all those years. I did. I've always wondered how she was and who she'd become. Which is why, and I'm sure you can imagine, I am deeply troubled to hear that my daughter is suicidal."

"She isn't," Johnny insists. "She's just... bored, I think."

"I hardly think boredom drives people to jump into the Mississippi River." Booth's tone is incredulous, verging on angry.

"No, I guess not," Johnny says, staring helplessly at his water glass. He lifts his dark eyes and stares at Booth. "The only thing I seem to know about Madeline these days is that I don't know a damned thing. I used to think I did—know her, that is—but now I see I have no idea. We got married kind of quick."

"Let's have a drink and something to eat, and you can tell me what you do know," Booth says, smiling in a friendlier way. "I'm dying to hear all about her."

"I'm SORRY," Madeline says at last, pulling away from Cleo. She sits up straight and runs her hands through her hair.

"I'm not."

"That won't happen again," Madeline promises, staring at the piano.

"Why not?" Cleo insists, touching Madeline's back. "I didn't forget you're married, if that's what you're worried about."

"But I did," Madeline says. "And that's what I'm worried about." Cleo rises up on her knees and kisses the back of Madeline's neck. "Please," Madeline whispers. "Let's go out somewhere. You can tell me one of your stories on the way."

At Madeline's insistence they make their way to the Shore-Do Café. The substitution of one oral art with another is as old as humankind itself. If it wasn't for food, Madeline thinks, who knows what people would get up to?

"Tell me about your love life," Madeline suggests, aware that she must seem to have a one-track mind. With a sly grin she elbows Cleo and adds, "And don't tell me that old saw about how you've never been in love. I want all the details."

"Sure." Cleo's heart sinks. It isn't a very glamorous story in comparison with the made-up tales of Italy. "Maybe when we're sitting down."

"That good, huh?" Madeline teases, linking arms with Cleo as they approach the restaurant.

The Shore-Do is jammed when they walk in, and the sudden noise of other humans is alarming. They take a seat on the upper level by the restrooms and try to acclimatize themselves as best they can. The jukebox is turned up loud, and the waitresses are hustling platters of fried food and frosty pitchers of draft beer, shouting and laughing all the while.

"A word of warning," says Madeline above the din, "don't have the roast beef dip. It's about as tasty as the heel of an old boot." Cleo nods, studies the menu without really taking it in. Although she's hungry in a remote sort of way, she can't imagine actually putting anything in her stomach.

"Can I get you ladies something to drink?" asks the waitress, this one a bleached-blond cherub with a thick Alabama accent.

"I don't suppose you have B&B here, do you?" Madeline looks up at the young waitress doubtfully. The woman shakes her head and says that they have JB, JD and CC but not B&B, whatever that is. Madeline smiles thinly. "A G&T would be fine. Cleo?"

"I'll have a coffee, please."

"Irish coffee?" the waitress suggests. Cleo nods without meaning to.

"OK, we're sitting now, let's hear it," Madeline says, grinning. "Just maybe leave out anything that'll make me too jealous, all right?"

"Why would you be jealous?" Cleo asks innocently.

"Because I'm a tiny bit jealous of everybody you've ever met." Madeline waves her hand. "Go on, I can take it." The waitress returns with their drinks. "Bless your speedy little self," Madeline says. The waitress glares, mistaking Madeline's genuine gratitude for sarcasm.

February, 1990
Toronto, Ontario

Cleo was engulfed in a spiritual winter made all the more unbearable by the bitterness of the weather itself. February deserves its reputation as the month of extreme blahs, especially in a city like Toronto, where grey concrete and leafless trees only serve to mirror—and thus increase—one's inner despair. At the age of twenty-two Cleo should have been out quaffing pitchers of beer at the Brunswick House or dancing moodily in one of the city's overheated nightclubs, but she wasn't. Instead she remained in her room at the Little Savoy, reading and rereading a tattered copy of Count Leo Tolstoy's famous essay, *What Is Art?*

Cleo wasn't the first aspiring writer in the history of literary effort to have had her dreams of glory temporarily squashed by Tolstoy's rigid philosophy of art and what it must offer to qualify as great. Thousands of fragile souls before her had been rendered creatively impotent by His Greatness's daunting output, as well as by his scathing assessments of modern artistic motives. Why bother? he seemed to ask, and though he mocked his own efforts in the process, it was difficult to imagine even picking up a pen after one was exposed to the Great Russian. She'd managed to remain optimistic while reading *Anna Karenina,* had decided with youthful arrogance that life was too short to tackle *War and*

Peace, but it was *What Is Art?* that sent her plummeting. Cleo tortured herself with the essay for much of that winter.

Add to this that Cleo, in an uncharacteristic fit of courage, also visited her first lesbian bar on the occasion of Valentine's Day, and you have a portrait of abject human misery. Why she chose to enter this particular social sphere on what has to be the most depressing day of any single person's life—gay, straight or undefined, as Cleo was—remains unclear. Suffice it to say that Cleo was a masochist of the highest order.

She stood in the bar on Parliament Street for a grand total of forty-five minutes, hoping against hope that the trick to enjoying oneself in such a place was comparable to the treatment for snake bites: eventual tolerance following the ingestion of adequate amounts of the offending poison. With this in mind she stood leaning against a beam beside the minuscule dance floor, but the more she looked around the bar, the more her despair increased. True, there did seem to be evidence of joy in the room. Women of all shapes and sizes swaggered by, and yet there was also something terribly alienating about it all. No one seemed to speak to anyone she didn't know, and when Cleo did make eye contact with a woman, she received a frosty, almost hostile glare in return. Cleo wasn't seasoned enough to realize that glaring is a lesbian mating ritual and so fled the smoky Sapphic cupboard, vowing never to return. She also surmised from her apparent aversion to the place that she was not, despite her numerous unspoken crushes on various women, a real lesbian. Where men were concerned she felt even less enthusiasm and so tried to make peace with the fact that she had no leanings at all in terms of sex. Those leanings she did have were not, she reasoned, strong enough to lead her to give such bars another try.

Between Tolstoy and her inability to find solace in lesbian society, Cleo was understandably ill-tempered when someone who seemed to expect the whole world to fall at her feet arrived at the Little Savoy. The young woman did not merely walk into the hotel but entered as only an actress can enter any room—or rooming house. She introduced herself as "Kiki Christopher, thespian" and then proceeded to fill out her hotel registration form as Irene Kaplitsky. When Cleo pointed out the duality of her identity, Kiki Christopher gave her an almost pitying smile. With a toss of her red mane she then explained that everybody knew actresses used stage names.

Kiki Christopher didn't endear herself to Cleo any further when she insisted that the room Cleo first showed her to was too dark. "I have SAD," she explained with another wave of her hand. She then proceeded to spell out the acronym with an impatient sigh. "Seasonal Affective Disorder? It's a serious condition among artists. I need light or I can't work." Cleo grudgingly showed her to the attic room, and, after Kiki had pronounced that the room had excellent karma, beat a hasty retreat.

Cleo should have guessed that the intensity of her dislike for Kiki Christopher was merely a presentiment of undying love. When Lyle announced that they had all been given tickets to see Ms. Christopher's Toronto debut in a play called *Boom Cow-Cow*, Cleo groaned. Kiki habitually referred to the production as "my show" and made no secret of her anxiety about its reception. Not wanting to seem entirely heartless, and curious against her will, Cleo agreed to accompany her father and Sadie for what was supposed to be "a night at the theatre."

The drafty garage-like building they filed into seemed as far from theatrical as anything could possibly be. They sat down on the folding chairs that were arranged around a high platform in the middle of the concrete floor. Sadie was overtly unimpressed and refused to take off her coat; Lyle expressed his discomfort with a series of bad jokes. Cleo felt a small shiver of excitement when the room went black and a larger frisson when the lights came up on a very naked female body with curves in all the right places. The body belonged to Kiki Christopher, whose face was obscured by the giant cow's-head mask she wore. Sadie snorted; Cleo was transfixed.

There was an eruption of bongo drums all around the room and Kiki began to dance—and then to smear a pot of what looked like strawberry jam down the front of her. Although she didn't speak for the entire duration of the play, it was obvious that Kiki was a genius of a performer. By the time the room went black again, Cleo was in love. She didn't care that Kiki's talents had been sacrificed to the over-wrought agenda of the vegetarian playwright who had penned *Boom Cow-Cow*. And she had most definitely for-gotten all about Tolstoy's rabid dismissals of all such experi-ments. Beguiled on all levels, Cleo went back to the hotel and, that very night, began to write a play.

To Cleo's delight and Sadie's absolute dismay, *Boom Cow-Cow* was a great success on the Toronto independent theatre scene. While Kiki went off to reprise her role as "Bovina" each night, Cleo worked furiously on her play. She then summoned the courage to attend a second perfor-mance, after which she lingered by the door of the theatre.

When Kiki emerged she seemed genuinely happy to see her and promptly insisted that they go for a drink. To Cleo's disappointment Kiki invited several of her castmates along. Cleo had hoped to discuss her fledgling play alone with Kiki but then decided that the Fates had decreed that it wasn't the time. Instead Cleo trailed along after the small crew of actors and sat with them in the glorious main room of the Silver Rail Tavern, hanging on their every mean-spirited word. As they gossiped and kvetched about this and that aspect of the night's performance, Cleo tried not to stare at Kiki. One by one the actors departed, leaving only Kiki and Cleo in the cozy back booth.

"OK," Kiki said, leaning forward and taking Cleo's hand. "Now tell me what you really think." She tossed her red curly hair, still damp with sweat from the exertions required of the leading cow-lady. Her pale eyebrows were stern with anticipation above her immense brown eyes.

"About what?" Cleo stammered, trying not to notice Kiki's ardent grip as it travelled up her arm.

"About me!" Kiki cried, letting out a yelp of laughter that turned heads. "You're so sweet, Cleo," she cooed. "I know you hated me when you met me, but I hope you don't any more. It would really break my heart." She gulped at her rum and Coke. "I think you're fantastic, I really do." She narrowed her eyes like a cat. "So tell me, what do you do in that room of yours?"

"I write," Cleo peeped, relieved when Kiki let go of her arm at last.

"I KNEW IT!" Kiki widened her eyes and gave Cleo a slow, sweet smile. "Would you ever write something for me?"

"Sure," Cleo croaked, sweat springing from her palms.

"Let's go." Kiki drained her glass. "Let's walk home. That way you can tell me what you think about the scene where I get slaughtered. My director says it's too under-stated, and my producer says it's over the top. I want to know what the common person thinks of it."

When they reached the Little Savoy, Cleo had managed to squeeze out what she thought was a fair assessment of the scene in question, and Kiki expressed her gratitude by seizing Cleo by the shoulders and kissing her on both cheeks. Not exactly a French kiss, but rather a kiss in the tradition of the French. It was a kiss nevertheless. "Come to the closing night party!" Kiki enthused as she released Cleo and flew up the stairs to her room.

"That's pretty much it," Cleo says, aware that the Shore-Do is winding down for the night. Even the jukebox sounds weary.

Madeline rolls her eyes. "Oh, please! I know that isn't where it ends. What about the consummation? What about the play you wrote for her?"

Cleo shrugs and examines their tab. "There was no 'con-summation.' I showed her the play and she told me I was 'cute' and that was that. She moved out of the hotel and in with her director. End of story."

"No kiss?" Madeline prods. Cleo shakes her head, winc-ing as she remembers what really happened. There had been a kiss, but only after a brave advance on Cleo's part. And though it had been lovely, something less than lovely had followed it.

"Surely there were others." Madeline is determined now.

"Uhmm, one." Cleo waves her hands impatiently. "I don't think it counts."

"Everything counts, in my opinion. Everything informs. Come on, let's hear it."

But Cleo's mind is still stuck on the true humiliation of her obsession with Kiki Christopher. The other "one" was a ninth-grade classmate named Leah, who dazzled Cleo with her looks and tortured her with graphic tales of her various sexual exploits with boys. They'd spent a great deal of time lying on the floor of Cleo's bedroom, listening to Lionel Richie records with their legs entwined. Hardly a romance, though Leah did introduce Cleo to the intoxicating world of wanting what she couldn't have and having what she didn't want. Namely, the undesired attention of Leah's gangly older brother, Borden, the first person who ever called her a lesbian—to her face. She hadn't thought much of the word at the time, and had merely seen it as Borden's standard put-down for any girl who refused his charms, such as they were.

"Cleo?"

"Yes?" She looks up.

"Do you want to take the ferry back or stay over?" Madeline is asking. "You might make the last ferry if you hurry, but you're more than welcome to stay."

"I guess I'd better get the ferry," Cleo says, distracted. Her memory of Kiki Christopher has chastened her somewhat. Who could blame her when what happened was that Kiki, home early from a performance in which she sprained her ankle, caught Cleo rolling around half-naked in her bed? Cleo hadn't meant for Kiki to catch her. She had in fact been visiting Kiki's room since seeing that first performance of *Boom Cow-Cow*. Under the pretence of cleaning the room, and more important, under the influence of unrequited love, Cleo hadn't been able to keep herself from touching and smelling Kiki's fascinating array of toiletries and clothes. She hadn't meant for the incident in the bed to happen, and she certainly hadn't expected Kiki to come home during what were usually her on-stage hours. Who wouldn't be scarred after being caught in flagrante delicto in the bed of their beloved? That Kiki then took her indignation out on the first draft of Cleo's play (which Cleo had bashfully given her to read the morning after their seemingly magical kiss in the kitchen of the Little Savoy) was more damaging than any decree from Tolstoy himself. Kiki's professional opinion of the play—"Shakespeare meets a lobotomized Jackie Collins"—hurt like hell. This denunciation, combined with Kiki's sudden amnesia regarding the fact that she had willingly kissed Cleo back mere nights before (and had even seemed to enjoy it) resulted in a kind of two-tiered tirade against lesbians and literature that in effect killed—or at least seriously maimed—two birds in Cleo's soul with one well-aimed stone.

Madeline loudly announces that she needs to use the restroom. Cleo, roused from her fiesta of shame at last, offers to settle up with the waitress. While she's waiting for Madeline to return, Cleo hears the ferry blast its horn and her heart begins to thump. What is taking Madeline so long? The ferry horn sounds again. Cleo is tempted to go to the restroom to see what's keeping Madeline when she emerges at last, swinging her purse and wearing fresh lipstick.

"Oh no, did you miss it?" she asks, feigning remorse.

"I think so." Cleo nods.

"That's too bad." Madeline fights a grin, tries to sound forlorn. "I guess you're stranded, then."

BOOTH LEANS BACK in his chair and dabs his lips with a linen napkin. Johnny lights a cigarette and smokes it self-consciously. A pall of silence has fallen over the table between courses, and both men are at a loss for how to fill it. Having heard a great deal about his daughter's adult life, Booth wishes he could provide Johnny with some kind of explanation for how she's come to be the way she is. His son-in-law sits smoking as if waiting for illumination.

"I've never been much of a joiner myself," Booth says suddenly. Without meaning to, Johnny raises a bushy eyebrow. "By that I mean I've never been one for socializing and noisy parties and such. Now Dianne, she's the opposite. That woman was never happy unless she was out with a bunch of people. I wonder who Madeline takes after in that regard?" Booth takes a quick sip of water and resumes talking before Johnny can answer. "Madeline was always such a delicate child. You had to be careful how you spoke to her or she'd bawl for hours. Dianne isn't known for her gentleness, as you may have gathered. I'm sure that the strain of raising Madeline on her own didn't exactly help to mellow her. For that I feel bad. But there has to be more to it than blaming childhood events and who Madeline does and doesn't take after, hasn't there? I mean, sometimes people are simply born with a lot of energy. We get so busy trying to decide what's wrong with them when, really, they're spirited, maybe a little moody." Caught up in his own theory, Booth gulps at his tumbler of Scotch. "I was watching a television program the other evening and they had kids on there—tiny little kids—all doped up on this and that pill. And I sat back and thought, What happened to kids being kids, being wild? I'm no model parent, I know that.

Anything I did wrong where Madeline is concerned, well, it's way too late. But I have to say that I simply do not understand this cult of mental illness. Why do we want to slap a label on anyone who shows a little spunk now and then? When you tell me about my daughter and the things she does and the strange ways she behaves, and you assure me that she isn't suicidal, I can't help feeling awfully damned excited to meet her. Do you think there's something wrong with her, John, or is she just *spirited?*"

Johnny sits dumbfounded. He doesn't know what to say to this man who can talk in plain English and make so much sense. He suddenly feels ashamed of himself for thinking that Madeline might be crazy. No, he can't deny that life with her hasn't exactly been a walk in the park, and no, Madeline's father wasn't there for her. She never benefited from all his apparent wisdom. But blaming Dianne doesn't quite cut it, either. In some ways this dinner with Madeline's father has been a revelation; in other ways, Johnny feels more confused than ever. He remains silent and lights another cigarette, this time without a trace of self-consciousness.

"What first drew you to my daughter?" Booth asks. "I mean, way back, how long has it been?" Johnny tells him: nineteen years. "Nineteen! Now I really do feel like an old man.... Well, tell me, what was it that first made you think, There's the woman I want to marry?"

"To be honest, I don't remember ever thinking that, Mr. Shockfire. Madeline was the one who wanted to get married. But I do remember liking the way she looked and the way she carried herself around." Johnny pauses and then explains that he met Madeline aboard the *Natchez* riverboat. He pauses again before admitting that Madeline was about to hop overboard when he intervened.

"You see!" Booth says, slapping his palm with the back of his other hand. "That's the trouble! You wanted to save her. I did the exact same thing with Madeline's mother. I pulled her out of swamp country and took her to civilization, thinking I loved her. How a thing starts tends to determine where it will go, don't you think?" Booth looks mildly triumphant.

Johnny butts out his cigarette. "You may be right. But I'm not sure I've ever given Madeline anything much beyond a hand down from the railing of a riverboat. In fact, I'm pretty much the same guy I was when we met. My deep-down feeling is that she's bored and that being with someone like me doesn't help. I like a simple life. Maybe Madeline's just too smart for me."

"Now, John, don't be too hard on yourself. People get a little too comfortable with each other over time, take each other for granted. That's natural. You seem like an intelligent man, a good, solid type of person."

Johnny shakes his head. "No, I mean I don't think I ever inspired Madeline, even early on. We were happy, I thought, but then we sort of cancelled each other out at some point. And I do think there are things bothering Madeline. For example: your... Dianne came by on her way to Florida recently. She dropped off some kind of package and said I should give it to Madeline only when she was calm. She said something about a friend of Madeline's passing on. I didn't get a chance to give Madeline the parcel myself; she came by the apartment and took it. The next thing I knew—well, maybe a few days later—she'd been arrested for swimming the river again."

Booth nods. "Dianne did mention something about that." He clears his throat and shifts uneasily in his chair.

"What'd she say?" Johnny asks.

"She said the ... uh ... friend in question, the one who passed on, was apparently their—Dianne's—maid. Dianne said she hired her because she couldn't manage on her own." Booth makes a face and takes a swig of his drink. "Anyway, Dianne had to fire her, she says, because the girl was a bad influence on Madeline." Booth runs his hand over his face and covers his mouth to hide a nervous smile. "I gather Madeline and this girl had some kind of a romance going on. Dianne says she now thinks that might be why Madeline tore out of her life without a word. Madeline was very attached to Carmelle, and she wasn't very happy when Dianne sent her away. I gather Dianne had her own rapport with the girl. Dianne likes attention, always has, and she doesn't mind who it comes from." He drains his glass of Scotch. "I guess that's why Madeline ran away and came here. She's never told you about this?"

Johnny shakes his head, stunned. "She just said she'd always wanted to live here. But could that really be the only reason Madeline refuses to speak to her mother? I mean, that was a long time ago. Do you believe Dianne?" He chews his moustache and waits.

"To be honest, I'm not sure what to believe," Booth says with a distant smile. "Dianne has been known to bend the truth whenever it suits her...." He frowns, lost in his own bitter recollections. Noticing Johnny's worried expression, he quickly tries to reassure him. "I wouldn't worry about it, John. It's well in the past. If Madeline's been acting strangely more recently, well, this woman's passing on might be part of it, but I doubt it's the whole trouble. It sounds to me like it got started well before that."

All Johnny can think is, Did you hear Johnny V.'s wife left him for a woman?

Somewhere between the studio door and the bed, the crackle in the air had returned. At first both Madeline and Cleo tried to ignore it, but as it increased, their ability to play dumb disappeared. As grown-ups often will when confronted by their own intense adult desires, they metamorphosed into eight-year-olds and began chasing each other around the room. Cleo, travelling at a dangerous velocity as she rounded the piano with Madeline at her heels, slipped and fell. She was still laughing as she hit the floor, but Madeline was alarmed to see blood pouring from Cleo's nose a few seconds later. She collected a cool cloth and knelt to wipe Cleo's face clean, then instructed her to lie back with her head in Madeline's lap. When the blood had ceased to flow, she bent over and kissed Cleo on the mouth, upside down, a gesture that re-ignited every iota of their previously repressed ardour.

While sex on hardwood floors is wildly overrated, sex that migrates from floor to bed is pure choreography if properly handled. Although new to each other's body, Madeline and Cleo demonstrated an unparalleled first-time finesse, or believed they did, which is all that matters to any two lovers. Cleo's relative inexperience was swiftly eradicated by her enthusiasm; Madeline's fear of the consequences of such pleasure floated out the window soon after her bare stomach grazed Cleo's. Without saying an intelligible word they seemed able to read each other's desires, making love with the fury of adults who suddenly possessed the trusting instincts of children. The sense of erotic possibility between them only increased with the passing hours; the voracious reprises and variations seemed endless, perhaps because they sensed that it would all, in fact, end—whether they wanted it to or not.

Now the room is silent again but for the sound of their breathing, of cars passing below the windows and the word-less return of bodies to themselves. It's very late, or very early, depending on your personal perception of darkness.

"We should eat something." Madeline flops onto her stomach, resting her chin on her fists. "I don't feel like eating anything we bought, do you?"

"Not really," Cleo admits. Her fingers slip unknowingly over a dark mole on Madeline's shoulder, the only such mark on her body, though it's too dark to see that and memorize it.

"I wish I was free to—" Madeline says.

"Shhh," Cleo answers, wishing Madeline wouldn't talk. What happened to 'I have all the time in the world, I answer to no one'? Reality, that's what—that dull force hovering just outside the door.

"What do you want to eat?" Madeline rolls onto her side and runs her finger down Cleo's sternum to her belly button. "Maybe we don't have to eat," she says, kissing Cleo on the throat, feeling something leap up again between them. "Maybe it'd be better if we just stayed here. I promise to feed you later. I won't let you starve." Madeline pulls Cleo on top, wraps her arms and legs around her.

"Tell me what it was like, jumping into the Mississippi,"

Cleo murmurs, tasting Madeline's cologne as she nibbles her collarbone. "Tell me how it felt being in there."

"Well," Madeline says, "first it was kind of like this...." She pokes her tongue into Cleo's ear, one deft stroke, her hands moving elsewhere. "Your body is real, real tense at first, you know, with fear." When Cleo moans her understanding of the concept, Madeline smiles to herself. "But then you're not scared, you just want to keep going. And so you do just keep going, sort of like this...."

THERE'S A DIFFERENCE BETWEEN being spirited and being haunted, and it's a difference that keeps Johnny pacing around the apartment for much of the night. Unable to sleep, he alphabetizes their entire record collection, then their books. They've been meaning to do this for years, and tonight seems as good a time as any. While he indulges his irrational pursuit of order, he fumes. How is it fair to be with someone for close to twenty years and never tell them who you really are? He touches the spines of Madeline's books and opens one, hoping to stumble across some clue to who she is. Or was. The tattered copy of *To Kill a Mockingbird*— her favourite book of all time—yields nothing in the way of information. Why would it? he thinks, reshelving it angrily, stomping toward the bedroom.

There's a difference between privacy and outright deception, too. Johnny doesn't rest until he's been through every dresser drawer, till he's pillaged every pocket, purse and pair of shoes. The complete booty of his exhaustive search is two ticket stubs from a matinee showing of *Thelma & Louise* at an uptown theatre. He remembers there was a flood in the city that day, that Madeline called him at the restaurant to make sure he was all right. She and Rodney were trapped at the Camellia Grill, but she'd be home as soon as she could manage it. He believed—and still does—that she was with Rodney whenever she said she was. Can you be jealous of a dead man's confidence, resentful of the things he takes to his grave? Although he wasn't jealous of Madeline's friend before, Johnny now wonders how well Rodney knew her, if she told him things she never shared with her own husband. Or maybe it was true, what Booth said, that it was long in the past. He suddenly wishes Madeline were one of those women who keeps everything—every corsage, postcard and threatening memento of her past—out in full view. His first girlfriend was like that and it had driven him nuts, the way she paraded her past right under his nose. Why, she had gone so far as to frame old love letters. But he sees now that Madeline is the worst, most dangerous kind of sentimental-ist: the kind who keeps her souvenirs (and scars) where no one can see them.

"How can you not have any goddamned mementos?" he shouts at the photo of Madeline on the bedside table. She gazes back from the photograph, wrapped in a black shawl, a big devious smile on her lips. Or maybe just a regular smile, he thinks.

"TELL ME AGAIN WHY you swam it," Cleo says.

"Because I could," Madeline whispers. "Because it seemed like a good idea at the time. Times." She smiles into Cleo's hair.

"Maybe that's what my mother was thinking," Cleo

334

says, resting her ear on Madeline's breast, listening to the steady thud of her heart. "Maybe that's why she killed herself—because she knew she could. It's always an option."

"That doesn't make it right," Madeline says, gripping Cleo more tightly.

"Actually," Cleo whispers, "it does. I might never forgive her for it, but it was definitely her right. It's anybody's right." She sighs. "I suppose I ought to try to be more forgiving."

"Forgiveness is an overrated virtue," Madeline says, thinking of her own mother, and of Carmelle, whose only crime, Madeline sees now, was that she was young and naive, not to mention scared. Look at me, she thinks, I'm old and selfish and an infidel to boot—proof that the rotten apple never falls far from the tree.

"Do you think you'll ever forgive Carmelle?" Cleo asks, reading Madeline's thoughts.

"Well"—Madeline thinks for a moment—"I don't know. Maybe I already have. If I haven't, I suppose it'll be easier to forgive her now that she's 'no longer with us,' as the saying goes."

Cleo pulls back from Madeline. "She died? Why didn't you tell me that? When did she—?"

"Not long ago, I guess. I got a letter from—of all people—my mother. It arrived very recently, in fact. *Very* recently."

"You must be shattered." Cleo squeezes Madeline's hand.

"Strangely not," Madeline says with a sigh. "It's the most unusual feeling in the world. I feel sad, and a little hollow, but not shattered exactly. I lost her well before I lost her, if that makes any sense. And anyway, it was an adolescent romance, a kind of dream I ought to have waked from long ago."

"Did you ever write to her, let her know how much she hurt you?" Cleo wants to know. "Did she ever contact you?"

"Oh, I wrote to her. In my head, a hundred times a day, early on. And then—I just stopped. Put it away, so to speak. And no, she never tried to find me. I seem to have that effect on people." Madeline thinks of her father, tugs the sheet up under her chin. "But even when I was sure I wasn't thinking about her any more, I blamed her for the way I felt. It was her fault I was lonely, her fault I couldn't trust anybody, her fault I was lazy when it came to loving Johnny—all those things. I didn't like what she'd stirred up in me. I wanted it to go away. For a time, it did."

"And now?"

"Now? Now I just blame my mother for my unhappiness." Madeline laughs. "And Johnny, and the corner grocer, and anyone else within firing range." She sighs deeply, chasing off an urge to cry.

"Yourself," Cleo suggests, touching Madeline's face.

Madeline scoffs. "Oh, no, never myself. I'm just a sore loser, is all."

"Uh-huh," Cleo says, "and I've never been in love."

Madeline laughs. "You're good." She kisses Cleo. "I know you're going to have to get on a bus and go home to Canada, and that I'm going to have to be the one to put you on that bus."

"Why?" Cleo demands, stiffening slightly. Why can't we stay in this room forever, making love and talking, telling each other about every minute of our lives that we can recall and making up the rest? "Why would I have to leave?" Cleo asks, an angry sorrow building up inside her.

"Because you can," Madeline murmurs pulling Cleo to

her, "and because you'll need to. There's more to life than New Or-leenz. You'll see, you'll get bored."

"No, I won't," Cleo insists.

"Tell me what you miss about Toronto."

Cleo sits up. "There's nothing I miss. Why are you bringing up buses and goodbyes all of a sudden?" She peers at the floor, searching for her clothes.

"Shhh," Madeline whispers, pulling Cleo back into her arms. "Let's not talk. You don't have to leave right this minute, or even tomorrow. Hell, I hope you'll stay here till Mardi Gras 2020. But let's not worry about it tonight. This morning. Aren't you sleepy yet?"

Cleo grins in the dark. "Almost."

JOHNNY'S MIND IS STILL ON Booth Shockfire as he makes his way to work. In addition to tearing the house apart looking for clues, he's been up half the night thinking about the things Madeline's father said, and all the things he'd asked that Johnny couldn't answer. Booth was shocked when Johnny told him that Madeline had jumped into the Mississippi on her tenth birthday. Johnny was equally sur-prised that Dianne hadn't told her husband about it. "I knew she was on a swim team," Booth had said, "but only because Dianne wanted more money for a private coach. She told me that much." Something about talking to Booth last night makes Johnny feel better—and worse. He tries to focus on the fact that Booth is on his way to see Madeline in Algiers this very afternoon. Although it'll be the last thing she'd ever expect, Johnny feels sure that it's happening for a good reason.

What he doesn't want to think about right now is Cleo

Savoy. He feels certain that as soon as Madeline has seen her father, she'll call Johnny wanting to talk, and that she'll decide to come home. But what if she isn't at her studio? Johnny worries. What if she's somewhere else—hiding out in Cleo's hotel room, for example? Johnny backtracks and hurries to the Pommes Royales.

"I don't have a clue where she is," Mrs. Ryan says tartly. "This is a hotel, not a jail."

"I realize that," Johnny says as politely as he can. "It's just that I'm trying to find my wife, and Miss Savoy was supposed to be interviewing her for the newspaper she writes for up in Canada. I thought they might be here."

"She writes for a newspaper?" Mrs. Ryan is taken aback. "She never mentioned that. Huh. I'm not sure how I feel about that—I never let reviewers in here if I can help it. Nothing like a mention in a newspaper article to ruin—well, everything." Mrs. Ryan looks worried, so Johnny tries to be patient. "She told me that she's a poet. She never did show me any of her work. Huh, huh, huh. Maybe she isn't really a poet. Or maybe she's both, that's quite possible...." Mrs. Ryan drifts off into a world of her own and Johnny has to work to reel her back.

"So they aren't here?" Johnny repeats. "No chance Cleo could have slipped in on her own? Maybe they came in late?"

Mrs. Ryan frowns. "I might not know where my guests go when they leave, Mr. Valentucci, but I do know when they're in the building and when they have guests. That's my job. As for the whereabouts of your wife, I have no idea. I guess that's your job, so to speak. Perhaps if you run into Miss Savoy you can tell her to give me a call. She has a message that I believe is from her mother."

"Sure, I'll tell her," Johnny says, "if I see her." As he hurries out of the hotel Johnny feels both hopeful and discouraged. Madeline must be at her studio, which is good. Her father will be able to see her at last. But it's also obvious that Cleo is still with Madeline, and that isn't so good, for reasons Johnny can't quite—or doesn't wish to—put his finger on. He'd like to sit down with Madeline and conduct a little interview of his own, but until Cleo leaves this seems impossible. Madeline is strangely—or not so strangely—taken with the girl. Or taken in by her; she's obviously a liar. Yes, Johnny would like to interview his own wife. The questions he is busy formulating are quite simple: Who are you, Madeline? What do you want? And, Is there room for me in there somewhere? He has one other question, too: What the hell was in that letter, that "envoi" as Dianne called it?

When Carlo shouts, "Hey! You're late! What is this, a drop-in centre to you?" the minute Johnny walks into Papa Leone's, he can feel everything in his universe slowly turning back to what passes for normal.

MADELINE SCAMPERS TO THE DOOR, clutching a bedsheet to her body. Cleo is half awake on the bed, confused by the pounding on the studio door. It's well past noon now; the sky is bright outside the windows. Until somebody started hammering on the door, Cleo and Madeline were enjoying their peaceful slumber, sleeping belly to back and feeling rather cozy despite the chill in the room. As Madeline listens at the door, she feels pretty sure she knows who's waiting on the other side. She's also pretty sure she doesn't want to open the door just now. But Cleo is already hurrying into her clothes, making hand gestures at Madeline to wait two minutes. She makes the bed without the sheet and sits, giving Madeline the OK signal.

"Who is it?" Madeline calls out, her voice hoarse and thus betraying her participation in last night's marathon of passion. When the person on the other side of the door doesn't respond, she swears and releases the three locks. She flings the door wide, fully expecting to see Johnny. Instead it's one of her downstairs neighbours, a shaggy-headed boy with bright blue-red eyes and a bashful look on his pale face.

"Sorry to bother you," he says dreamily, "but there's some guy downstairs who says he needs to see you. He's been pounding on the door for, like, ten minutes. You want me to let him in, or what?" The boy touches his chin and then his hair, as if to make sure he really exists.

Madeline glances at Cleo, sitting bolt upright on the bed. "It's all right, I'll come down," Madeline says, trying to hide her irritation. She thanks the boy and closes the door, slips on a pair of pumps, knots the sheet around herself and grumbles at Cleo, "Himself, come to try and drag me home by the hair, no doubt." As Madeline makes her way down the staircase she realizes she must look like what she is: someone who's been rolling around in bed all night. The hair at the back of her head is frizzed and knotted; she has the fuzzy-eyed look of a true passion flower. She's still angry with Johnny for a number of reasons, not the least of which is the fact that he keeps popping up at her door, acting as if he wants to catch her doing something wrong. Well, fine, she thinks, passing through the foyer, let him see that at last I have done something wrong. People do. Just as doing the right thing often feels so awful, sometimes doing the wrong thing can feel awfully damned good, especially if done more than once.

She puts her hand on the handle of the downstairs door and prepares herself for Johnny's outrage. Let him see me the way I really am, she thinks, flinging the door wide.

Madeline blinks. The man standing at the bottom of the steps blinks back at her.

"Madeline?" he asks, his uncertainty giving way to surprise.

"Daddy?" She feels her knees beginning to buckle, grabs on to the nearby railing and blinks again.

"I know I should have called," Booth apologizes, "but Johnny said you don't have a phone here." He indicates the building and tries to smile. "How ... how are you, honey?"

"Fine," she whispers, still not wholly convinced that the man who stands before her isn't an impostor, some sort of eerie likeness of her father.

"Can I ... may I come up for a bit?" He surveys her strange costume.

"Umm, sure," she says, holding the door open so that her father can pass by. "Of course." He still wears Rocabar; she's both sad and pleased to note this. She turns and tells him, "I have company this morning." Madeline feels like a zombie as she makes her way up the staircase ahead of her father. This can't be happening, she thinks, pushing the door to her studio open. Cleo will not believe this. But Cleo isn't in the studio, or if she is, has decided to hide.

"Hello?" Madeline calls, tapping on the bathroom door. She looks around the room and frowns. "I guess she stepped out," Madeline says to her father, grateful but also confused. How did she—? Madeline turns to look at her father, who waits patiently by the door. How white his hair is, Madeline thinks, how nervous he seems. "So, what brings you here to New Orleans?" she asks with ridiculous flippancy, as if they've had the pleasure of inane conversation all these years. Where did Cleo go? she wonders, offering her father a chair. Then she sees Cleo's notebook on top of the piano.

Booth sits down beside the statue of a dwarf, trying to hide his dismay as he looks at the assortment of lawn ornaments seated at other tables. "I spoke with your mother a couple of days ago," he says.

"Miracles do happen!"

Booth smiles at her sarcasm. "Yes, well." He blushes. "I thought we might go for lunch at Galatoire's."

"Why now?" Madeline shrugs airily. Then she feels worried. "Are you sick?"

Booth shakes his head. "No, I'm not sick. I just want to see you, that's all. Your mother's pretty worried about you, too."

Madeline laughs. "Another miracle! What *is* going on in the world these days?" She looks down at what she's wearing and suddenly feels embarrassed. "Would you mind if I change before you tell me why you're here?"

"Go right ahead," he replies. "Is that the Steinway we had at home?" He moves toward the piano.

"One and the same!" Madeline calls from the bathroom door. Inside the bathroom she sits down on the toilet and begins to cry. She can't sort her tears of joy from her tears of rage. There are some fearful tears in the mix, too, because she's afraid that Cleo has left for good. Damn that back staircase, she thinks, washing her face. Be all right, she thinks, not sure who she's addressing. Be all right.

"YOUR MOTHER CALLED," Mrs. Ryan says as soon as Cleo walks into the small lobby of the Pommes Royales.

"I don't have a mother," Cleo announces matter-of-factly, caught off guard. "It must have been my stepmother," she says with a little more warmth.

"Oh, yes, she did say that. Forgive me!" Mrs. Ryan blusters. "You look tired," she observes. "Are you all right, honey?"

"Fine, thanks. How was your Thanksgiving?"

Mrs. Ryan shrugs. "Good. Quiet. I took a few of the guests over to one of the larger hotels for dinner. I gather the Japanese don't eat a lot of turkey—they seemed pretty excited by the whole production. How about you, did you have a nice holiday?"

"Yes. I spent it in Algiers with my friend."

"Mr. Valentucci's wife?" Cleo nods. "He was by this morning looking for her. He thought she might be here, for some reason." Mrs. Ryan purses her lips and looks hesitant, then dives in. "He mentioned that you write for a newspaper, Cleo. Is that true?"

"No," Cleo says, "it isn't. It's sort of a long story. If you don't mind I'd like to call my stepmother back."

"Of course, of course!" Mrs. Ryan's relief is immediately apparent. "I hope everything's all right at home."

"Thank you, I'm sure it can't be anything too serious." Cleo heads through the corridor to the courtyard. Nothing ever is, she thinks bitterly.

"Hi!" Sadie's voice is bright. "Are you all right? I've been calling you for two days!"

"I'm fine," Cleo mutters. The lie is only partial—parts of her are more than fine, others less than. "What's wrong?"

Sadie lowers her voice. "Oh, nothing really. When are you planning to come back? *Are* you planning to come back?"

"I don't know. I'm getting kind of low on money, but I don't want to come home just yet. I'm not even sure Toronto *is* home any more. Is he furious?"

"Not at all. Not now, anyway." Whispering, Sadie says, "He wants to talk to you about some things."

"Why now?" Cleo's voice is dull with disbelief. People don't change, she reminds herself. Not really.

"Do you think you'll be home in time for Christmas?" Sadie asks, ignoring Cleo's question.

"I really don't know," Cleo says, impatient. "So there's nothing wrong?"

"No, nothing's wrong. Sorry if I scared you. I know you gave me the number in case of an emergency, but ... are you OK? How is it down there?"

Cleo grins to herself. "I'm great." I'm having a wild love affair with a married woman. It's wonderful. All we do is drink brandy and talk and ... "It's incredible here. Everything you'd imagine, and more."

"Good," Sadie squeaks. "Well, have a good time. Can you give me a ring when—if—you're coming back? I know your father really wants to talk to you."

"Sure," Cleo says, abruptly hanging up the phone. Americans never say goodbye, she thinks. I don't need you to tell me anything now; I've figured it all out for myself. Not because I wanted to, but because I had to. I rode the ferry by myself, too. I rode it without the slightest bit of fear! Cleo won't be rushing out to book passage on a cruise anytime soon, but sometimes the small triumphs in our lives are worth noting.

She'd listened at the top of the studio stairs when Madeline went down to see who was calling on her. As soon as Cleo heard Madeline say, "Daddy?" she knew she had to disappear. She'd crept down the hall, intending to hide, and found the back staircase. Hearing Madeline and her father coming up the main staircase, she flew down the back one without knowing where it led. The room she found herself in was dark; there were bodies moving in the shadows, the orange tips of cigarettes glowing in the dark. "Hi," she said, trying to sound casual. "Just ... trying to find the door." Someone moved toward her and she tensed. "It's over there," a sleepy male voice said. Someone else opened the door in question and she tumbled out onto the street. She contemplated waiting for Madeline in the Larkin Parkette but decided against it. The sudden arrival of Madeline's father was obviously a surprise. Cleo had slunk away from Madeline's building, happy for Madeline but desperate to get back to the French Quarter, to the safety of her room.

And now my own father wants to have a big heart-to-heart. This is what we call synchronicity. Serendipity is something else, or must be. Cleo rummages in her duffel bag and retrieves her dictionary. In the process she uncovers the *National Geographic* magazine and smiles, pulling it out, too. Sometimes a lie is just as pretty as the truth, she thinks, quoting Madeline in her mind. She carries both the dictionary and the magazine to the bed and sits down.

"'Synchronicity,'" Cleo reads aloud, "'noun. 1. existing or occurring at the same time.'" She ponders this silently, then says to the Degas print above the armoire, "Basically it's just like serendipity, only without the suggestion of happiness." She reclines on the bed and stares at the *National Geographic,* reaches out and rests her palm on it and closes her eyes. I should go home, she thinks, but I'm almost afraid to hear the real story. My version might be better. In fact, I know it is. Madeline was right: sometimes a lie is just as pretty as the truth, if not more so. The truth hurts, as the truism goes. But so does love, as the songs keep saying, and still we chase after it.

It isn't until MADELINE is seated across from her father at Bill's Bar (she refused to go to the French Quarter, insisting Galatoire's was overrated) that she realizes just how angry and sad she's been all these years. About a whole lot of things. When the rage inside her threatens to bubble up and over, she's shocked and almost ashamed. As an adult, Booth had the power to leave a bad situation. As a child, Madeline did not have the same freedom. What Madeline is most angry about and only realizes now, sitting in the middle of the pleasant chaos of the bar, is the lesson she learned too early in life: people leave. They say they love you more than anything—and then they leave without another word.

"Why didn't you leave when I was a baby?" she wants to know. "I wish you had. Surely you knew you'd married the wrong woman about five minutes after the wedding?" But the truth is, Madeline is grateful for the years she *did* have with her father. *Who knows what I'd be like today if he'd left any sooner.* Before Booth can respond, Madeline continues, "Never mind, I know why you stayed. You thought you had to. You thought, Maybe I'll learn to love her. Well, Daddy, I applaud you for not wasting too much of your life with my mother, I really do. Life is too short to spend with the wrong person." She leans back in her chair and regards him with cool anger, then leans forward, her voice betraying her emotions. "What I can't forgive is that you never once, not once, bothered to come and see me. Or call. Or write."

"I don't expect you to ever forgive me, Madeline. It's true your mother made it almost impossible for me to think of being anywhere near her, which is why I left and never returned to Missouri. I tried to set aside my anger, but I couldn't seem to. I just could not forget the image of her—doing what she was doing." He begins to choke up. "And time slipped by, and it became harder, not easier. Oh, I sent the money, sure. But money was all I sent. I didn't even try to reach my little girl, and then, well, it seemed to me to be too late. I did nothing to make sure you knew how much I loved you. Nothing! And I can only imagine what that did to you, how it made you feel. I'll never be able to forgive myself for not calling and not writing, for never making the least bit of effort to let you know I was still there." His eyes glitter with tears, and Madeline looks away, biting her lips to prevent her own sobs from coming.

"Have you remarried?" Booth nods. "Do you have— never mind." Under the table Madeline pinches herself, hard.

"I don't have any children, if that's what you mean."

"It doesn't matter," Madeline says, and shrugs, slowly pulling her invisible armour back on. "It was fine without you. We managed fine."

"I know you did," Booth says. "But it does matter. I was a selfish ass. But about this feud with your mother," he begins, and Madeline rolls her eyes, looks around impatiently for the bartender. Her father treads more carefully. I know she's a difficult woman. I know she can be downright mean at times. But she did love you, does still. I'm sure she only ever wanted what she felt was best for you. And, honey, not speaking to your mother, well, that's a very dangerous path for anyone to decide to travel. It's probably not healthy to distance yourself from the person who—"

"Nice of you to come down and tell me what is and isn't healthy, Daddy. I didn't realize you were an expert on familial bonds!" Booth blushes, falls silent. Madeline's face is red with fury. She laughs suddenly and haughtily. "She's selfish, and so are you. My turn now." A tear slides down and Madeline lets it. "I suppose it was her idea that you come down here?"

He nods sheepishly. "But I wanted to. I've wanted to see you for a very long time. And that's how I know that staying mad, not listening to reason, can be so dangerous." He reaches across the table and touches her hand. "I am sorry, sugar. There's no good reason for what I did. But don't be like me, that's all I'm saying. All that happens is you miss out on everything."

Madeline is vehement. "I don't miss her." She swats angrily at her most recent teardrop. "I may have missed you from time to time, I suppose." She smiles ever so faintly, still amazed to find herself sitting across from her father.

"I promise you'll be sick of me by this time next year, honey. I don't plan to ever fall out of touch with you again. If that's what you want."

Madeline can't speak. Her mind drifts to Cleo, to Johnny, then back to her father. Booth's voice as gentle but stern. "And what's this business about leaving Johnny? From what I can see, he loves you an awful lot.... I'm sure whatever he's done, or hasn't, is forgivable, isn't it?"

"Please," Madeline says, scowling, "one olive branch at a time. I don't have a whole treeful! Are you working for the United Nations now?"

Booth grins. "You do have her sense of humour, like it or not. For all her flaws, your mother always had a smart comeback. I bet it's just one of the things Johnny loves about you."

Madeline makes a face, dismissing the remark. "Do you still live in Ohio?"

"Yup, still in good old Cleveland. It's not nearly as exciting as New Orleans. I gather you've got quite a life here."

"Not much of one, no." Madeline sighs. "Not right now. It's showing definite signs of improvement, though."

"You can come up and see me anytime you like," Booth says, rising up from the table. He reaches out to embrace her. For a moment she looks as if she'll refuse his arms, but then she moves toward him. "Thank you for seeing me, sugar," he murmurs.

"You didn't give me much choice." She hugs him back, stiffly at first and then with less restraint. "I'll need a more detailed explanation of where you've been." She scowls into his jacket. "Not right now, but maybe another time." He nods, swatting at his own tears now. Stepping out of the embrace, she folds her arms across her chest. "I'll need to hear it all."

Outside Madeline's studio, Booth hugs her again. "Get a telephone, would you?" he grunts before he releases her. He fishes in his inside jacket pocket and pulls out a business card. Before handing it to her, he takes out a fountain pen, crosses out his name and writes, in barely legible script, *Daddy.*

"Come see me," he tells her, waving goodbye.

She watches her father move down the road, noting the slowness of his gait and the cautious air with which he now does all things. They have both missed certain transitions. God only knows what he thinks of what *I've* become, she sighs. She feels slightly overwhelmed by what lies ahead and yet doesn't really know what that involves. Cleo, Johnny— it's all pretty daunting. And then there's her mother, whom she's promised her father she'll call. But promises, like rules, were made to be broken.

First things first, Madeline, she tells herself as she heads back upstairs to the studio. Again its echoing emptiness strikes her as simultaneously hopeful and sad, full of possibility and yet full of ghosts, too. She isn't sure which ghost to tackle first, and so sits down at the piano. Cleo's notebook is there, with the handwritten sign on top that reads, simply, INSURANCE. She smiles as she picks it up and carries it to the place where she hides things, down between the bed and the windows. "This is where I put the things I don't intend to look at," she says to the empty room, then bends down to retrieve the parcel.

The only surprising thing about the record albums from Carmelle is that she thought to set them aside for Madeline in the first place. There's no note, but the albums speak for themselves: Nina Simone, The Ink Spots, Joan Armatrading, Claudine Longet, Bach's Italian Concerto. Here are all the nights when I felt most myself, Madeline thinks with a sad smile, shuffling through the records. You taught me to dance, to play piano, to laugh and rebel. Maybe it wasn't you I missed, but what you gave me.

"Fuck you," Madeline whispers to the Nina Simone record, smiling through tears. "And thank you—from the bottom of my deluded little heart."

There's a part of the story that died with Carmelle. One might call it the whole truth—if there is such a thing.

July 2, 1976
St. Louis, Missouri

"I'm so glad you're here," Dianne said sweetly, moving toward Carmelle. "Let's have a drink together, shall we? Madeline won't be home for hours." She poured two generous shots of brandy and motioned for Carmelle to join her in the living room. Carmelle followed with trepidation, swallowing hard.

In the living room Dianne began shuffling through some record albums, clucking her tongue. "Are these yours?" she asked, a coy smile twisting her lips.

"Yes, ma'am."

"But when do you play them? I've never heard any of this music!" She held up a Nina Simone record and moved toward the sofa, repeating, "When do you play these records, Carmelle?"

"When you're out, ma'am."

"I see. And does Madeline also enjoy Nina Simone?"

"I don't know."

Dianne took a long swallow of her drink and put the record on the turntable. She turned the volume up high and bobbed her head in time with "See Line Woman." "Come dance with me, Carmelle," she said, gesturing with her arms. Carmelle's distress showed on her face, but Dianne insisted and Carmelle moved into her embrace. "I do so love to dance," Dianne murmured, "don't you?"

"Yes, ma'am."

"Does Madeline know how to dance like this?"

"She's never said so."

"'She's never said so'?" Dianne threw her head back and laughed. "Oh, Carmelle, do you think I don't know what goes on in my own house when I'm not here? Do you think I think my brandy drinks itself up in the night?"

Carmelle was speechless. Amused, Dianne pulled away, turned off the music and picked up her glass.

"Don't look so worried, Carmelle! I trust you completely. I know you'd never do anything to harm Madeline."

"No, ma'am, never."

Carmelle stared at her shoes and Dianne sat down next to her. She rested one hand on Carmelle's knee, put her other arm around the girl's shoulder and gave her a meaningful, coquettish look. "I don't feel I know you very well at all, even after a year's time. I'd like to, very much. Tell me something exciting about yourself—something I don't already know." She then moved in as if to kiss Carmelle, who untangled herself and leapt from the sofa.

"I have to go check something in the oven, excuse me!" Carmelle gasped, rushing from the room.

Dianne sat on the sofa. She frowned and emptied her glass. *Ask Carmelle.*

She'd been watching the two of them for over a month. Whenever Carmelle came into a room Madeline's posture changed; it reminded Dianne of a plant hunting for a sunbeam. Or she did the opposite, displaying an exaggerated indifference to Carmelle that was far more suspicious than any overt affection. Dianne's anger about the deception was slow to build, but its target was undeniable. It was clear that Carmelle Sanchez-King, entrusted to care for Madeline in Dianne's absence, had corrupted the girl to the point where she'd lost interest in swimming, and in any other aspects of her future. The truly unforgivable outcome of Carmelle's nefarious influence wasn't that she'd obviously introduced Madeline to alcohol. Girls would be girls, after all. It wasn't even the possibility of a romance between her daughter and the maid that most enraged Dianne, although that, too, was vaguely unsettling in its way. Surely that aspect of their alliance had been fleeting, an experiment or practice run, so to speak. No, the most infuriating thing was that Carmelle had managed to come between mother and daughter. In Dianne's mind, she and Madeline had been through so much together, and yet now, because of her friendship with the maid, Madeline barely spoke to her. Those words she did utter were almost always belligerent and cold-hearted, a sure sign of Carmelle's poisonous influence. She might've chosen to just come right out and ask Madeline if she imagined she was in love with Carmelle, but that wasn't Dianne's style. She had other ideas, ways of making sure Carmelle was too busy to continue filling Madeline's mind with foolish notions. If that didn't work, she reasoned, well, she'd simply fire her.

What you don't know can't hurt you, as the cliché goes. But the passage of time has given Madeline this: she's well aware that there was more to the whole situation than a random act of vindictiveness on the part of her mother. But somehow, today, the rest of the story no longer matters. She walks up the levee and down to the river, contemplating another swim. *Because I can.* Be brave, she thinks, heading back to the studio, where she promptly sits down at the piano and plays every song that Carmelle ever taught her, straight through and without looking at the lawn ornaments. Where one door slams shut, another opens.

CLEO STARES AT THE FOLD-OUT MAP of the United States she purchased this afternoon. She's circled all the cities and states that begin with the word *New* and is now trying to connect them with a red pen. It's her plan to ride the bus to all of these places and to read as many books as she can in transit. Love, sweet as it has been, has definitely interfered with her intellectual aspirations; she hasn't read anything more complicated than a menu in days. She's determined not to miss Madeline to the point of distraction, is bent on becoming the most well-read celibate in the world. Absorbed in her work on the map, Cleo doesn't see Mrs. Ryan enter the courtyard.

"Moving on?" Cleo jumps before she turns and nods. "Careful how fast you leave New Orleans, heart," Mrs. Ryan says, smiling. "It'll haunt you forever if you leave too quick." She sets a silver-plated coffee pot on the table between them and brushes away some dried leaves that have blown down from the flower boxes on the upper balcony. "Mind you, it'll haunt you either way, so I guess it doesn't really matter how you leave."

"I'm only thinking about it," Cleo explains, gratefully accepting the cup of coffee Mrs. Ryan hands her. "No definite plans yet." She glances at the map with all of its circles—New Hampshire, New York, Newport, New Mexico, and other smaller places—and feels a bit foolish. Mrs. Ryan is looking at it, too.

"I admire anyone who travels," Mrs. Ryan says. "I've always found it so ironic that one of the best ways to get stuck in a place is to end up running a hotel." She gives Cleo an impish smile over the rim of her coffee cup. "Maybe I'll write about *that* one day!" She gazes off into the middle distance and heaves an artful sigh. "Even if it has already been done. Well, what hasn't been done before? The world is too old to allow for much innovation. Or maybe I am!" She taps Cleo's map. "I see you don't share my view. That's what's so good about being young—you still have the energy to be optimistic, to take risks. Try and hang on to that if you can, darlin'."

"How's your novel coming?" Cleo asks, no longer feigning interest, perhaps because she can feel poems burning through the fog in her own mind.

Mrs. Ryan clucks her tongue. "Not too well. I keep getting stuck at the part where they make love. It's been so long—I can't seem to remember how all that works!" She laughs and Cleo laughs with her. With sudden sobriety, Mrs. Ryan says, "I do miss sex." She says it without any self-consciousness whatsoever. She states it like a fact tinged with a tiny note of sadness, but no self-pity.

Cleo feels more curious than embarrassed. She waits,

sipping her coffee, wondering what to say in response. Not knowing the story behind the *Mrs.* part of Mrs. Ryan's name, Cleo doesn't want to say the wrong thing. "Do you have children?" Cleo measures her words carefully.

"Lord, no. Never wanted any. I guess I never wanted to have that kind of power over another human being. I suppose that's why I treat my guests—some of them anyway—like they're my own children." She gives Cleo a little pat on the arm. "I hope I haven't been too intrusive, Miss Cleo. When I'm fond of someone I have a hard time hiding it. To be honest, I've been worried about you. Don't get me wrong, I know it's silly. You're not a child. I just mean, I hardly know you—but I liked you right away. And this is, like it or not, a crazy city. It's easy to forget that, sitting out here in this little oasis or strolling through the oaks in City Park. But there's another side to this elegant old madhouse, as I'm sure you've seen."

"I've been aware of it, though I guess I've been pretty lucky."

Mrs. Ryan looks around frantically. "Knock wood! You have to knock on wood right away after saying that!" She gestures to Cleo to go to the flower box nearest her. Cleo obliges, amused by the superstition. "You might think it's foolish," Mrs. Ryan says without smiling, "but I do believe in spirits. This city is full of 'em. That's why we do all kinds of little things to make sure the ghosts don't take over."

Cleo smiles and thinks, What would happen if they did take over? She's thinking of her mother, of all the stories she has invented and told herself to ease the pain of her loss. They're all ghost stories, really, she concludes. I should write them down.

"That damned phone!" Mrs. Ryan cries out. "I just hate the way real life intrudes on an otherwise pleasant afternoon!" She excuses herself and hurries out of the courtyard. Cleo folds up her map and retreats to her room, wishing she hadn't left her notebook behind at Madeline's. She can't possibly leave the city without it, or without saying a proper goodbye.

IT ISN'T GOING QUITE the way she imagined. For one thing, Johnny seems genuinely happy to see her. Her certainty begins to crumble. After all, there's nothing wrong with him. To be fair, he's put up with an awful lot from Madeline over the course of nineteen years. *Maybe I'm being rash.* Johnny tosses his apron on the bar at Papa Leone's and escorts her outside so they can talk in private.

"Your dad's great," Johnny says, lighting a cigarette. "How'd it go? Was it hard?"

Don't be nice, Madeline thinks. Don't be so goddamned affable and sweet when I'm about to hurt you.

"It was wonderful and awful all at once," she replies, peering down North Rampart as if seeing it for the first time. She's never really noticed how the autumn light makes things look more crisp, how the buildings can look so run-down and yet so stubbornly elegant at the very same time. In the unrelenting humidity of summer, the same buildings look more fawn coloured and romantic, as if they might drop to the knees of their foundations in sleepy prayer.

"You gonna go up and see him?" Johnny presses.

"Eventually." She squints up at him and feels a flash of self-hatred like a lightning bolt running through her. How much easier it'd be if I could hate you, she thinks helplessly. How much simpler if there was some kind of explosion, some dramatic event we could point to and blame for all our troubles. Is that what I've been trying to do? she wonders, contemplating her swims. "Johnny," she begins. He watches her with an open, fearless expression that makes what she has to tell him all the more difficult. Say what you have to say, she urges herself, but nothing that's in her mind makes its way to her throat.

"Here's the thing, Madeline," he says, tossing away his cigarette. "I think you need to give your head a shake. We've been together for nineteen years. Tell me this: how are you ever going to beat that?" Slapping the side of the restaurant with his palm, his voice gains volume. "As far as I can see, darlin', this is your mess. You made it, not me. I was happy." He then slaps his forehead in self-mockery. "'Guess what, Johnny? Your wife's a dyke! How about that? And guess what, Johnny? You're the last one to find out! Ha ha!'" He laughs with a hysteria she's never seen before.

Madeline shakes her head. "I'm nothing in particular, Johnny."

He thrusts his face close to hers. "How convenient for you! Does Cleo know that, or are you hoping to keep her in the dark, too, till you make up your mind?"

"I don't want to keep anyone in the dark, John. Least of all myself. You're being unfair. You don't know a thing about my friendship with Cleo." She folds her arms across her chest, defiant.

"Well, I know it's not just a friendship." He moves his face right into hers, leaning down so that his moustache is mere inches from the end of her nose. His tone is half pleading and half stern. "Here's what's going to happen. You're going to get this out of your system and say goodbye to Cleo. I'm going to pick you up in two days, three if that's better for you. I'm a pretty generous guy, as you may or may not recall." He continues on quickly before she can interrupt. "I'll get a week off and borrow Carlo's car. We're going to drive to Florida and see your mother, get that shit sorted out once and for all." Straightening a little, he puts his hands on her shoulders. "I want to be with you when you see her. We both need a holiday anyway. We can stop and stay at that little place on the beach in Biloxi on the way down, talk about a few things." He grins and continues, "I think we need to get to know each other again, don't you?" When she doesn't answer, his expression darkens. "I wouldn't mind a little honesty for a change. I think you owe me that much, Madeline. And guess what? Just this once you're gonna do what I tell you."

Madeline gives a little gasp and backs away from him. "I don't think that's necessarily how it's going to be, John. That doesn't seem particularly fair to either of us. Or to Cleo, for that matter."

"Oh, yes, I forgot—I'm supposed to be considering the feelings of the poor girl who's wrecking my marriage!" Madeline says nothing. "Well, fuck it, that's what's happening. I'll see you in three days."

"OK," she croaks.

Johnny clears his throat and stares out at the street. Finally he says, "I know I can't give you all of what you seem to need, Madeline. But I know I can offer you some of it, just like you give me things nobody else can. If you decide you don't want to be with me after the trip, I promise not to hold you back. But I am not letting go without a fight, no way."

"You're a good man, Johnny."

He guffaws. "That's right. A good *man*. Not exactly what you're looking for, I gather."

"Johnny, please, don't. I don't know what I'm looking for," Madeline says.

"But it isn't me," he says. "Was it ever?"

"It was."

"Well. Ouch. The truth hurts." His eyes are wet but he smiles on. A lilt of hope lifts his deep voice an octave. "So you'll agree to a trip? Another try?"

"Of course," she says.

Johnny leans and kisses her lightly on the cheek. "Good! See you soon." He disappears back into Papa Leone's.

For a moment Madeline can't seem to walk away from the restaurant. She wants to see Cleo more than anything right now, but there's something disturbing about the idea that she'd be doing so with Johnny's permission. And a time limit. Confusion overwhelms her. Maybe I should call Cleo and tell her I can't see her at all, she thinks. That might be the kindest thing to do. Maybe Johnny's right, maybe I should go home and try a little harder to make things work. She wishes she could believe that old saw about how things always work out the way they're meant to. As she walks away from the restaurant she knows she has to make a decision, and that no matter what she decides, someone is going to get hurt.

"Strength, flexibility, endurance," she chants to herself. Maybe all those hours in the pool were good for something, after all. She continues shouting the three principles all the way back to the Quarter to the amusement of the various people she passes. Seeing their smirking faces, she shouts louder. I don't care what you people think, she smiles to herself, because for once in my life I care what *I* think. And I think what I'm going to do is beg Cleo to stay in the city for at least another three days.

CLEO'S BAGS ARE PACKED. Although she doesn't know exactly when she'll leave or where she's headed, she's determined to board a bus heading somewhere as early as tomorrow. With luck she'll see Madeline one more time. She realizes now that too many sudden exits could make for a very messy life story. Exciting perhaps, but messy. Cleo the poet wants to keep things as neat and contained as verses.

Stepping out of the shower, she hears a knock on her hotel room door. Mrs. Ryan? she wonders, tugging on a pair of jeans over wet legs. Or, she thinks with mounting alarm, could it be Johnny? She wriggles into a clean T-shirt and moves toward the door. "Hello?"

"Rapunzel, Rapunzel, let down your hay-uh," Madeline calls from beyond the door.

"Hi!" Cleo says, her stomach giving a reflexive little flip when she opens the door to Madeline. "I was just about to come over and see you. How was your visit with your dad?"

"Good. Listen—" Madeline lowers her voice "—I was thinking, why don't you pack up your bags and come stay with me? There's no use spending money on a hotel when you don't have to."

"Well." Cleo blocks Madeline's view of her duffel bag with her body. "I mean, you're right, that would make sense. But I was sort of thinking of leaving. Town."

"Oh, well, I know. I mean, I knew that you would, but I'm hoping I can convince you not to, at least for a couple of days. Three, actually. Things with Johnny ... well, they're ... complicated. I just don't know what to do about all of that. But right now ..." Her words come in a manic flurry and trail off when she sees Cleo's expression. "When were you planning to head home?"

Johnny. Complicated. A series of alarms go off in Cleo's heart and she feels a sudden desire to climb onto a bus, alone and right away. And why does Madeline assume she's going home? She might be heading somewhere else after this. She says so as flippantly as she can manage. The words *New Mexico* ring hollow.

"Oh, I didn't realize." Madeline frowns. "I just assumed ... I was thinking maybe we'd have some time together. Here's the situation: I've promised Johnny that I'll go with him to Florida in three days, to see my mother. I can't not go, but I can't not see you, either. Can you understand?"

Cleo ponders this. "I don't know."

"Why don't you think about it for a few minutes?" Madeline suggests. "I'll wait out here. No rush. I'll just sit and talk to the geraniums while you decide." Cleo nods and closes the door and stares at her duffel bag. She picks it up and tucks her dictionary and the *National Geographic* magazine under her arm. She touches the armoire and grins, then goes out to meet Madeline in the courtyard.

"That was fast!" Madeline exclaims, looking pleased. "Are you sure you gave it enough thought? Do you have all your things?"

"I gave it no thought whatsoever," Cleo says. "Let's go before one of us develops a practical streak." But just as she reaches the foyer, something occurs to her. "So ... what about Johnny?" she asks.

"Tsk, tsk." Madeline wags her finger. "No practical thoughts, remember?" She sees concern in Cleo's eyes and relents. "I don't know. All I know is that I need to be with you for the next three days, if you'll let me."

"Sure, but—" Cleo stammers. Madeline pushes past her to the front desk, where Mrs. Ryan is waiting.

Cleo dreads the idea of telling Mrs. Ryan she's leaving so abruptly, but Mrs. Ryan only smiles. "I'll sure miss you, Cleopatra," she says. "You come back again, doll. Remember what I said about being haunted!" Cleo looks at Madeline and then back at Mrs. Ryan, who leans over the desk, presenting her powdery cheek for a kiss. It seems Madeline has already informed Mrs. Ryan that Cleo is checking out. But Cleo can't be too angry with Madeline because she *was* already packed in anticipation of some kind of departure. They move out into the street, Madeline calling "Take care!" and "Thank you!" to Mrs. Ryan, who waves madly from the front walkway of the Pommes Royales Maisonnettes.

"What'd she mean about being haunted?" Madeline wants to know when they begin walking down Royal Street, below the balconies Cleo will definitely miss.

"She said if you leave New Orleans it haunts you forever," Cleo says, and grins, hoisting her duffel bag onto her shoulder. "Whether you leave it fast or slow," she adds.

Madeline loops her arm around Cleo's waist and says, with great self-satisfaction, "Precisely why I think you should leave very, very slowly. I have a fairly detailed list of places and things I want to show you, some absolute musts for the first-time visitor. I'm afraid I haven't been a very good tour guide."

Cleo insists that Madeline has been an excellent guide and they both blush. She quickly changes the subject to keep herself from spiralling into a dark mood. They amble along, slowed down by the weight of Cleo's cumbersome duffel bag. Madeline takes the dictionary and magazine and holds them carefully in the crook of her arm, treating them like the sacred objects they are.

"So, how do you feel about seeing your mother?"

"Topic change," Madeline retorts, then changes her mind. "Fine. I promised my father I'd see her. Apparently she's heard all about my swims in the Mississippi and thinks I've lost my mind." Madeline cackles. "Little does she know, I lost it years ago."

"My father wants to talk to me, too," Cleo announces. "My stepmother called to tell me."

Madeline stops and looks at Cleo with wide eyes. "That's wonderful! I'm sure he's sorry for not talking to you sooner." Somewhere in the midst of all their brandies and horizontal conversations, Cleo told Madeline about her father's stubborn silence. All Madeline had managed to say was "Seems both our fathers need to go to talking school."

"I don't know," Cleo says, walking on. "I think I like my version of the truth better. And anyway, nothing he says can turn back time. It's not like it'll make any real difference."

"Beware hubris," Madeline advises, thinking of her own stubborn pride where *her* mother is concerned. She watches as Cleo marches toward the ferry without any hesitation.

"Tell me a story," Cleo says when they're seated. A light rain begins to pat against the windows of the boat.

"Close your eyes," Madeline insists. Cleo obeys with exaggerated formality. "Once upon a time there was a flood in Italy that happened just for me." Cleo smiles but keeps her eyes closed. Madeline says nothing more. Instead she leans and kisses Cleo, who starts and then kisses her back. "I like your story, Cleo," Madeline murmurs. "And I'd be honoured to be in it in whatever way I'm meant to."

THINGS THAT WILL BE forever altered: used bookstores wherein every volume becomes fascinating and necessary; candy bars (known hereafter as appetite suppressants or unapologetic meal replacements: "Dinner? Who has time?"); the tourist attractions and the unsung streets that have nothing to offer but quiet. The cough-syrup-and-gumbo smell of the Quarter, the smell of rain as it hits the Mississippi River, the safety of moonlight and the discouraging rush of sunrise, eroding time. The colour green as in eyes; the colour blue for the same reason. The smell of Rocabar and Pears soap and take-out coffee, signalling the start of a new day. Lawn ornaments, never to be spied again without specific recollections and a certain sorrow. Ferries. Heavy rain. The sick thrill of making someone cry for all the right reasons. The sight of someone reading poetry in a pair of high heels and nothing else, laughing between line breaks. Root beer, toast, pianos and notebooks. Shoes in hasty, kicked-off piles, the look of T-shirts and camisoles together on hardwood floors.

Things that would seem like promises in any other situation: a visit to Hansen's Sno-Bliz in the middle of the sauna that is New Orleans in July. A trip into the bayou and another across the lake. The New Orleans Jazz and Heritage Festival—"Honey, do *not* come for Mardi Gras!" A drive to

Bay St. Louis, where time stands still and crawfish are sold in bulging ten-pound bags along the highway to and from. The feel of hurricane winds without the consequence of flooding. A Toronto blizzard that must be experienced to be believed, best enjoyed while ice-skating in Nathan Phillips Square. Niagara Falls, because they exist to be seen.

"So, what do you want to see today, Miss Tourist?" Madeline leans over to kiss Cleo awake. It's barely even light outside the windows, and Cleo shuts her eyes, groaning. This is their third and final day together; Johnny is coming to pick up Madeline tonight and take her to Florida. Consequently, Cleo would prefer to remain asleep and pretend it's all a dream that happens to have featured a great deal of walking and talking, among other things.

"What time is it?"

"Early. Disgustingly so. How about a coffee at Café Du Monde, followed by a leisurely ride on the St. Charles Avenue streetcar?"

"How about another three hours in bed?" Cleo begs, pulling a pillow over her face.

"NO." Madeline tears the covers back and wolf-whistles, then tries to wrest the pillow away from Cleo's face. She tickles her until Cleo screams for mercy and the pillow falls to the floor. Face to face, they stop laughing.

"I still can't believe you swam the Mississippi *four* times," Cleo whispers. "I dreamt about it all night. You could have died."

"But I didn't. Wasn't meant to. And anyway, swimming it is no more frightening than trying to spell it."

"I find that pretty hard to believe." Cleo props herself up on one elbow and gazes at Madeline. We're beautiful, Cleo decides, touching Madeline's cheek.

"It's true! There are shorter words that are *much* more frightening."

"For example?"

"For example: love."

"Hmmm, I think I know that one, but I'm not sure. Spell it for me?"

"M-i-s-s"—Madeline kisses Cleo's throat—"i"—her breasts—"s-s-i"—her ear "p-p"—her lips—"i." She moves her lips back to Cleo's ear, to the hard bone just behind it where her skin smells so sweet. "I don't think I can do this." Madeline presses her cheek to Cleo's shoulder in defeat.

"Do what?" Cleo asks, frightened.

"This. This day. I wish I was able to be with you the way I feel I could."

"Shhh," Cleo says. "Maybe this is how it's supposed to be. Maybe we should concentrate on having fun while we can and try not to think about the rest." She flicks away a tear before Madeline can see it. "And maybe we should say goodbye in the French Quarter. It might be easier. You could meet Johnny over there instead, and then I could go right to the bus station." *Because the only sight I feel like seeing is you.* As they kiss again each has to fight back tears, and neither of them wants to be the one to stop it.

Madeline pulls back first, but only because she's afraid that if they don't stop soon they never will, or at least not till Johnny is pounding on the door. "You're sure you know how to spell Mississippi? You won't forget?"

"Never."

"Good, because, you know, there's gonna be a test someday."

"I look forward to it." Cleo gets up from the bed and gathers her belongings as quickly as she can. They shower and dress with stoic swiftness. Madeline protests when Cleo picks up her duffel bag, notebook, *National Geographic* and dictionary. "Leave them here, why don't you? We can come back and get all that later."

"I'd rather not."

"All right," Madeline says. "Oh! Just a minute—there's something I need to grab. Would you mind waiting in the hall? I won't be long."

Cleo complies, too sad to be curious.

When Madeline joins here in the hallway, she's carrying a plastic bag. "All set," she says, heading down the staircase.

Without discussing their plans, they walk from the ferry dock to Café Du Monde. Madeline surprises Cleo by ordering a coffee. "All the best people drink coffee," she explains with a wink.

"Let's have it to go," Cleo suggests. "I know somewhere better where we can drink it in peace."

"Lead the way." Madeline bows, knowing exactly where they're headed. It's still very early in the day. They have plenty of time for streetcar rides and the other remaining sights on Madeline's itinerary. It takes a long time to reach their desired destination; Cleo's luggage slows them down. Madeline suggests that they ought to climb right onto the wharf itself for the sake of posterity, but Cleo shakes her head.

"This is close enough," she says. "From now on we'll both have to be law-abiding citizens, follow the rules." She sits down with her back against the fence that blocks access to the Governor Nicholls Street Wharf.

"How dull." Madeline pouts, sipping her coffee, the fingers of her other hand tightly wound around Cleo's wrist. "Are you excited to talk to your father?"

Cleo gives a little shrug, her eyes on the Mississippi. Finally she turns to Madeline. "Don't ever swim that river again, all right? I don't want to read about you in the newspaper. At least, not because of that."

Madeline's surprise is genuine. "Why would I?" She bites her lip and takes in Cleo's face feature by feature, committing every curve and freckle to memory. Gazing into her eyes for what she fears may be the last time, Madeline braves a smile. "I'll only be gone for a week. Might you be here when I get back, Miss Savoy?" Cleo says nothing in reply and Madeline laughs. "Of course you won't, what am I saying?" She takes both of Cleo's hands in hers. "I'm gonna go now. I don't know about you, but I can't stand this. I'm not up for a farewell tour. Here," she says, thrusting the plastic bag at Cleo. "For you."

"What is it?" Cleo asks, peering into the bag at a withered and muddy high-heeled shoe.

"I was wearing that the night you saw me in the river. Nobody but you can appreciate its value."

"Thank you."

"You are so welcome."

Cleo swallows, hard. "I hope it goes all right with your mother, and with Johnny."

"Will you do me one small favour when you get back to Canada?" Cleo nods. "Buy a mirror so you can see what all the fuss is about."

"No swimming," Cleo warns her again.

"Send me poems," Madeline says, turning away. "*Lots* of poems." Cleo faces the fence and the wharf beyond it so she won't see Madeline go. When she's certain that Madeline has disappeared over the streetcar tracks and up Governor Nicholls Street, she turns back to the water.

How different everything looks, how charged and changed. The name of the river is no longer the stuff of spelling bees. She watches the water, letting her lungs drink up the cool, muddy air. Lifts her eyes to take in the shoreline of Algiers Point and fights the urge to leave her duffel bag and run for the ferry. And she knows she'll leave the city tonight, feeling haunted, just as Mrs. Ryan promised.

Miss Savoy,

You've left a smudge of chocolate in my copy of Walker Percy's Moviegoer, *which you so kindly gave to me (and read aloud from) just yesterday. I believe the offending chocolate came from a Clark Bar but I can't be sure. There's a strand of your hair on one of my sweaters. The glass you drank from is sitting on the counter—I drank from it about ten minutes ago. We've been apart now for approximately two hours. It's a good thing I'm living in a room without clocks, though as a former swimmer and sometime musician I have an all-too-accurate feel for time. Snow White says hello, as do the other inhabitants of this now very empty room. Guess which dwarf I am? Stupid, for letting you go. I could probably still find you and beg you to stay, but I'm trying to be kind. Or maybe you did what all brave poet-ladies*

*do, and jumped on the next available bus to that place
they call Anywhere Else, also known as Far from Me.*

Dear Cleo,
*I've been reduced to inhaling the sheets and pillows, to
all manner of shameless acts including (but not limited to) writing very bad lyrics to very bad songs. If for
no other reason than the salvation of the future of
American music, I urge you to return to New Orleans
at your earliest convenience.*

C,
*Tell me we didn't make this whole thing up.... Tell me
I haven't become a story you'll tell to ... well, that's not
fair of me to ask. (God bless the man who invented the
wastepaper basket—though I suspect it was a woman.)*

WEARY FROM THE LONG RIDE north and reluc-
tant to return to the Little Savoy, Cleo considers checking
into a hotel near the bus station in Toronto. It seems like a
grand idea until she examines her wallet and finds that she
has exactly twenty-five U.S. dollars to her name. She experi-
ences her first taste of culture shock as she endeavours to get
change for the pay phone and is curtly informed that she'll
have to purchase something in order for the clerk to make
change. Apparently the concept of Southern hospitality hasn't
migrated along with her. She decides to head for the Little
Savoy without calling ahead.

Though she's been gone just over a month, everything inside her feels changed, unsettled. When she walks

through the door she feels like a stranger in what used to be her home, but there's nowhere else to go just now. The hotel smells the same, still has the same curious mixed aroma of wood polish, roast beef and stale cigarette smoke. She sets down her duffel bag in the front foyer and calls out, "Hello? Any vacancies?" Upstairs a TV set roars out canned laughter; on the main floor, all is quiet. A fire crackles in the living-room fireplace and she moves toward it, her hands numb from the biting wind she'd hoped never to endure again. Where is everyone? she thinks, looking around, listening. A half-drunk cup of coffee sits on the mantel; she touches it and notes that it's still warm. Someone must be home, she decides, moving toward the kitchen.

She hears Sadie's voice first, the familiar trill of it a welcome sound. "I'm not sure she'd be thrilled about a surprise visit. And anyway, flights are terribly expensive at this time of year." A fork scrapes against a plate, someone turns on the kitchen faucet. Cleo stands outside the door for a moment longer.

Long enough to hear her father say, "I just don't think it's Christmas without her. What good will it do her to sit down there by herself at Christmas? What will that prove? There's independence and then there's pig-headed—"

"Hello," Cleo says, poking her head through the doorway. "I wondered if you have any rooms for rent?"

"Good Christ!" Lyle exclaims, his fork halfway to his mouth. A shard of pie tumbles from his lips to the tabletop. Sadie stands gawking at the sink, a half-rinsed cup in hand. Recovering, Lyle stands up and offers her a feeble smile. "Hello, Clee. We were just talking about you! Hungry?"

"Tired, mostly." Lyle motions for her to sit down at the table and hurries to put the kettle on to boil. He gives Sadie a look that says, She's home! as he scoops some potatoes and meat onto a plate and places it in front of Cleo.

"How was it?" he asks gruffly. "You might have sent a postcard, at least."

"Lyle!" Sadie barks.

"Right, sorry," he apologizes. "I'm glad you made it back all right. Can't wait to hear all about it." He glances at Sadie, who raises her eyebrows meaningfully. "I suppose we have quite a bit to chat about, hey?" He looks uncomfortable, lost in his own house.

"Well, I'm off," Sadie announces with an exaggerated yawn. "Don't sit up all night, you two." She leans and kisses Cleo on the cheek. "Welcome back, sweets."

Left alone in the kitchen, Lyle and Cleo fall silent. He waits for her to finish her meal, pours them each a cup of tea and motions for Cleo to follow him to the tiny office at the end of the downstairs hall.

Cleo watches as her father rummages about in the closet, gives him a questioning look as he emerges holding a pale yellow toiletry case. "What's that?" she asks, a cold feeling churning in her stomach.

"It was hers," he says, setting it down on the desk in front of Cleo. "Open it." He watches as Cleo undoes the latches with trembling fingers, raises the lid and peers inside. "She left it behind," he says, struggling to find the right words. "I've been waiting for a time when I could show it to you, tell you about her. Sadie says I waited far too long." Cleo retrieves a pocket notebook from the sateen interior of the case, stares at it, then looks up at her father. "Have a look," he says nervously, gesturing with his hand. Inside the notebook are pages covered in her mother's girlish handwriting. Cleo turns the pages quickly, unable to focus on the words. She sets the book aside and continues examining the contents of the case. Talcum, a handkerchief, three unsharpened pencils, a tattered copy of Boccaccio's *Decameron* in English.

"So?" Cleo shrugs, avoiding her father's eyes. She picks up the notebook again and flips through it, stopping at a list. "Books Cleo Should Read," it says. Below it are the titles of several books, all of which Cleo had read by the age of six, all of which had been given to her by Sadie. Her eyes burn and she squeezes them shut. She feels a strange mixture of everything and nothing all at once. When she opens her eyes and stares up at her father, her jaw is clenched. "Why'd she bother? I'd rather have had a mother than a list of bloody books!"

"I know." Lyle kneels down beside her, takes her hand. "I didn't realize how much there was to say till you'd gone."

Cleo turns to him, her eyes wide. "It's too late, Dad! Don't you understand? It's too goddamned late!" She throws the notebook to the floor and swears under her breath, chants every expletive she knows and invents some new ones in the process. Lyle wraps his arms around her and squeezes her tight, saying nothing. Twenty-eight years of tears begin to pour out of her, and then she falls silent, her limbs loose and exhausted. She rises up and grabs for a box of tissues on the desk. Stares into the little suitcase, as if expecting it to tell her something profound. "I'd forgotten," she says finally, her back to Lyle. She takes a deep breath and expels it in slow, jagged puffs. "And then I remembered. Sort of."

"I'm sorry," Lyle says.

"Me too." She turns around and looks down at her father, still kneeling beside the chair. "It must have been something. The flood, I mean."

"It was. Want to hear about it?" He looks tired but willing.

Cleo shakes her head. "Not tonight, no." She picks up the little notebook and places it back inside the suitcase, then shuts the lid. "Why'd you keep this?" she asks, cradling the case in her arms. Her father bites his lip, gives a helpless little shrug and says nothing. "It's all right," Cleo ventures, "I think I know why."

"Do you?" He tucks his hands under his thighs and sits on them, and Cleo laughs out loud. "What?"

"I do that, too," she says, pointing at his hands. "Chip off the old nervous block."

"In some ways," he admits. "In other ways, not, thank God. Most of your good qualities come from her, I don't mind saying."

"But not all of them." Cleo frowns, leaning to kiss his cheek. "You'll have to tell me all about that flood sometime, and about England. But I'll warn you, I've come up with a *pretty* exciting version of my own."

"No doubt," Lyle chuckles as he follows her out of the office and down the hallway. Cleo heads for the living room. "Aren't you going to bed?"

She sets the suitcase down on the coffee table and moves to stoke the fire. "Soon. I'm still on New Orleans time, you know. Not used to going to sleep before three a.m."

"I guess," Lyle mutters, well aware of the fact that New Orleans is only an hour behind Toronto. "I wouldn't mind hearing about *that* sometime. Father's version, of course."

"Soon," she mumbles, busy with the latches on the toiletry case, her eyes on the fire. Realizing he's still standing in the doorway, she adds, "See you in the morning, Dad."

"Yes, see you."

"Dad?" she calls up the staircase a few seconds later. He pauses on the landing and looks down. "Do you have any photographs?" He nods, blows her a kiss and hurries up the stairs.

THOUGH SHE COULDN'T MAKE herself go with Johnny when he arrived to take her to Florida, and though the next communication she had from him came via a lawyer who specialized in "dissolving unions," Madeline did manage to have a telephone installed in the studio. Just in case. Like the piano, it's shiny and black, though the Steinway gets more action.

She stares at the silent telephone often, tells the lawn ornaments, "That's my whole trouble: I'm rotary dial in a touch-tone world!" There are a number of people she might call: her mother, a lawyer, her father. *Cleo.* She hasn't been able to bring herself to answer Cleo's numerous letters with anything but music, creating her own daily version of Mendelssohn's *Songs Without Words.*

I feel this, she plays, I think about this, and this, and that—a hundred times a day. In between, I wait tables at the Shore-Do (who knew?) and shop for clothes. Every time I miss you I buy a new pair of shoes. Imelda Marcos has nothing on me.

There'll be other songs, too: I'm about to become a divorcee; I told my mother she can come to New Orleans—for a maximum of twenty-four hours; I saw Johnny walking with Lena in the French Quarter the other day and I was *happy for him*. I feel sorry for myself, then incredibly blessed. I have known great love and may again; I can breathe in and out with nobody watching for the first time in my life.

"Have you ever heard of Marilyn Bell?" Cleo writes. "She's a Canadian who swam across Lake Ontario, the English Channel, the Strait of Juan de Fuca. Am sitting here (freezing to death) as I write this, facing the aforementioned Great Lake. You should come see it for yourself one day. Toronto: very near Cleveland. See atlas."

I will come, Madeline plays, I will come see you as soon as I can. This is good silence, Cleo. We must both believe that such a thing exists, that it might not last forever. You are here, right next to the Mississippi River on the map of my life: all strength, wild curves and magic. But I'm not ready for you yet—and I don't think you're really ready for me.

CLEO SITS WITH HER FATHER at the kitchen table, a small box of photographs spilled out on the Formica. She waits for her father to present each one, a cup of coffee growing cold at her elbow. She misses the coffee in New Orleans (among other things) and wonders if Madeline would be kind enough to send her a can of Café Du Monde's famous chicory roast, just to tide her over till she's able to get down there herself. Her return to the Little Savoy has been exhausting. It's as if her father, silent for so long, now wants to make up for lost time. How can she tell him that a sudden rush of information is almost as devastating as having had none all those years?

"These are her parents, your grandparents. They live in Montreal. Would you like to meet them? They've asked after you." Lyle holds out a snapshot of a very tense-looking man and a pretty, much younger woman. She's plump and cheerful; he's rail-thin and stern.

"Do they know about Mum?"

"Yes, of course. I had to tell them."

"But not me?"

Lyle says nothing, then, "I couldn't. I didn't want to believe it myself for a very long time. And then I didn't know what to say, how to put it."

"How about, 'Your mother killed herself'? Didn't you worry that I might remember, or do something similar myself one day?"

"She was ill. You're not." Lyle shuffles through the photos in his hand, pulls one out and holds it out to Cleo. "Here, this one was taken in Florence. I'm afraid I'm not much of a photographer, never have been." He watches as Cleo studies the photograph, waits for her to say, Not much of a father, either. She doesn't.

The woman in the fuzzy snapshot seems as much a stranger as the woman pictured in the *National Geographic* article about the flood. "Did you love her?" Cleo asks.

"Not enough."

Cleo looks up and stares at her father, says, "Sometimes things just happen and no one knows why." She looks at the photo again, sees the smiling blond, blue-eyed young woman in her overalls and yet can't quite reconcile it with the other picture in her head. Both are blurry, if for different reasons. "Sometimes I hate her; other times it seems like she never existed in the first place. What was she like?"

"Well, she loved to read, just as you do. I didn't realize it at first—maybe because I didn't want to—but she was a very serious person, very intimidating in her own way. She kept her thoughts to herself, but she had a lovely—"

Cleo holds up her hand. "Never mind. I don't think I want to hear about this right now." She throws the picture down onto the kitchen table. "I've wanted nothing more for most of my life, and now it's the last thing I want to hear, I don't know why." *Sometimes a lie is just as pretty as the truth.* "Why don't you tell me about *your* life?"

"Me?" Lyle asks, embarrassed.

"You." Cleo gets up to make a fresh pot of tea for her father, coffee for herself. "I'm thinking of becoming a journalist. Consider this a practice run for my future career."

CLEO AND SADIE ARE PROWLING around St. Lawrence Market shopping for food when the topic of Cleo's future plans arises.

Cleo says that her plans are school and more travel, not necessarily in that order.

"I wonder where you'll go off to next? Back to New Orleans, perhaps?"

"I guess we'll have to ask Madame Goodluck what she thinks," Cleo says, grinning mysteriously.

"Oh! What a memory! I'd forgotten all about that." Sadie blushes with pleasure.

"I never did," Cleo says. "I'm not sure what I would have done without her magical presence all those years. I wasn't very nice to her a lot of the time."

"You'd have managed." Sadie pretends to assess the quality of a handful of snow peas.

"Maybe," Cleo replies, "but I'm glad I didn't have to."

"Are we ever going to hear about your trip down south?" Sadie asks, her gaze still averted.

"Maybe after a whole lot of bourbon." Cleo smiles, watching Sadie, who continues flicking the snow peas with false intensity. "I met someone down there," she admits. "But you can't tell my dad. Not yet. He only just discovered I'm not a child any more. Anyway, I'll probably never see her again." Cleo gives what she hopes is an indifferent shrug.

"I say we pick up some bourbon," Sadie suggests. "Sooner rather than later. I'm not very good at being the Vessel of All Truth." She cracks a smile. "I'm getting old and can't be trusted to keep my thoughts to myself for much longer."

Epilogue

ON NOVEMBER 4, 1996, the *angeli del fango*—the mud angels—gathered in Florence, Italy, for a reunion commemorating the thirtieth anniversary of the flood of '66. Among the participants who made the journey from countries all over the world was Cleo Savoy, the only child of one such angel.

Lyle's formal invitation to the reunion was sent to his parents' address in England. By the time it was forwarded to the Little Savoy, Cleo was taking summer courses at the University of Toronto, where she happened to see a memo about the anniversary pinned to a bulletin board. She tore the notice from the board and raced back to the Little Savoy to show her father.

"I can't go anywhere," he replied in his typically gruff manner. "I've a business to run." The Little Savoy was by then enjoying a renaissance as one of the city's more successful bed-and-breakfast hotels, a transformation aided by Cleo's helpful suggestions—most of them based on her fond memories of the Pommes Royales Maisonnettes.

"You could go," he said, producing the official invitation. Cleo was about to chew him out for keeping yet another secret, when he tossed a plane ticket on the table. "Early Christmas present."

By the time Cleo boarded the plane to Florence on November first, she still hadn't heard from Madeline. Cleo's dream of seeing her again hadn't wobbled, but Madeline's silence suggested that a reunion was no longer desirable. Something had obviously changed.

Wandering through the photo exhibits, dining late into the night and chatting with some of the former student flood-workers over breakfasts of hard rolls and the second-best coffee Cleo had ever tasted, she found the whole situation surreal. It was strange to meet men and women who had known her mother as a student, and stranger still to discover that her mother had indeed had an American friend. Though the woman's name wasn't Gwendolyn, she bore a striking resemblance to the woman Cleo had conjured up. In this sense the pilgrimage to the city her mother had loved above all others was as inspiring as it was sad. Just to be there, seeing with her own eyes what her mother had once seen, was incredible. It was also rather lonely.

Cleo joined a walking tour of the sections of Florence most ravaged by the flood. On the walls of certain buildings and landmarks, plaques explained the startling levels to which the water had risen thirty years before. As the group proceeded toward the Ponte Vecchio, Cleo tried hard to pay attention to the tour guide's running commentary. The bridge was plugged with souvenir vendors whose carts overflowed with plastic copies of Michelangelo's *David*. Cleo paused to buy one in remembrance of the lawn ornaments in Madeline's studio. She then purposely lagged behind the rest of the group, gazing over the bridge at the Arno. In New Orleans Cleo had thought about her mother constantly; in Florence she found her thoughts drifting to

Madeline. The river reminded; everything did. *Happy Birthday, Madeline.*

As she stared down at the water Cleo began to compose a poem—first in English and then in Italian (which she'd been studying at university along with literature of the American South). As Mrs. Ryan had sagely pointed out, most things had been said before. But where love and grief were concerned, it seemed there was no end to the different ways a person could explore the universal incantation: *I miss you.*

Standing on a bridge over water
that looks so good, so green
This was her question, and it is mine
To jump into the rivermouth,
Or jump into the mouth of Love...

Soffermandosi su di un ponte sopra l'acqua
Che è così bella e così verde
La sua demanda era, ed è la mia,
Gettarsi nella voragine acquosa,
O gettarsi nella voragine d'amore...

Lost in her cautious translation, Cleo didn't hear anyone coming up behind her. No familiar scent wafted toward her as she murmured the lines of her poem aloud, nor did she hear the click of high, high heels on the ancient stones of the Ponte Vecchio. And yet Madeline was with her, as she always would be, a phantom both imagined and real.

That *phantom* was real enough to write the postcard that awaited Cleo in Toronto. "Thousands have lived without love, but not one without water," it read. "I'd rather not live without love—how about you?"

Acknowledgments

WITHOUT THE LOVE, FAITH and humour of Suzanne Brandreth, this book might never have become a book. From start to finish, and for her many roles, I am beyond grateful.

Tina Jones was the first to insist. Timothy Findley and William Whitehead gave me the gifts of space, time and enduring friendship. Catherine Hunter's hilarious emails saved my sanity. Kenneth Grey is the best big brother ever. Warm thanks to Suzy Richter, Camilla Gibb, Tracy Ryan, Alison Weir, Frans Donker and the gang at Book City. Steve Walters and Tribe Pazzo make Stratford a heaven on earth. Sabrina Grdevich is to blame for my love of things Italian. Many thanks to my family (Carol, Howard, Martin, Janice, et al.) for their blind faith, and to Laurie, Tony, Gay and Gordon for additional support. Oliver Salzmann, Barbara Pulling, Ziggy Lorenc, Katherine Govier and Helen Wakefield contributed in important ways, as did many others.

Many thanks to my talented editor, Diane Martin, and publisher Louise Dennys, copy-editing whiz Noelle Zitzer, designer Scott Richardson, the very worldly Samantha Haywood and the entire team at Knopf/Random House for their hard work. Dean Cooke, Madame Bix and David Johnston are my fabulous representatives. To the independent booksellers and literary magazines who've supported my work, and to Colleen Perrin, who published me first: thank you.

Four very kind strangers assisted me during the research for this fictional story set in very real places: Mara Miniati of the Istituto della Scienza in Florence, Italy; former Mud Angel Catherine Williams of Bradenton, Florida; Betty-Carol Sellen of the Bywater Bed and Breakfast, and Joanne Sealy of Faulkner Books, both of magical, incomparable New Orleans. I am likewise indebted to the publishers of *National Geographic* magazine for photographic inspiration.

The Muses must always be thanked: Glenn Gould for his interpretation of Bach's Italian Concerto; W. H. Auden for his poem "First Things First"; and Susan Sarandon, whose photograph provided an inspiring view as I worked.

I am deeply grateful to the Ontario Arts Council and Canada Council for the financial assistance that made focus possible.

Last, but never least, my love and thanks to Kelly, who gave me big love, understanding and invaluable editorial insights as she read and re-read with immense good humour.

Marnie Woodrow is the author of two acclaimed collections of short fiction, *In the Spice House* and *Why We Close Our Eyes When We Kiss*—both praised for their richness of detail, authenticity and passion. Marnie Woodrow lives in Toronto.